AGAINST ALL ODDS

"This should not be happening," Robert said.

"What?" Joana gazed up into his eyes, her hands spread across the broad expanse of his chest. "What should not be happening?"

"This," he said, and he kissed her forehead, her temples, her eyes, and her cheeks. And he looked deeply into her eyes as his mouth hovered close to hers.

"But it is," she said.

"But it is." He closed the gap between their mouths, and she moved her hands up to his shoulders and about his neck. One hand played with his close-cropped hair, as she arched her body into his . . .

and she could not stop what was happening . . . did not want to stop it . . . wanted it to happen now with all her body and soul. . . .

BEYOND THE SUNRISE

by

Mary Balogh

AN ONYX BOOK

ONYX
Published by the Penguin Group
Penguin Books USA Inc., 375 Hudson Street,
New York, New York 10014, U.S.A.
Penguin Books Ltd, 27 Wrights Lane,
London W8 5TZ, England
Penguin Books Australia Ltd, Ringwood,
Victoria, Australia
Penguin Books Canada Ltd, 10 Alcorn Avenue,
Toronto, Ontario, Canada M4V 3B2
Penguin Books (N.Z.) Ltd, 182–190 Wairau Road,
Auckland 10, New Zealand

Penguin Books Ltd, Registered Offices:
Harmondsworth, Middlesex, England

First published by Onyx,
an imprint of New American Library,
a division of Penguin Books USA Inc.

First Printing, November, 1992
10 9 8 7 6 5 4 3 2 1

Copyright © Mary Balogh, 1992
All rights reserved

 REGISTERED TRADEMARK—MARCA REGISTRADA

Printed in the United States of America

ENGLAND,
1799

1

THE entertainment in progress at Haddington Hall in Sussex, country seat of the Marquess of Quesnay, could not exactly be dignified by the name of ball, though there was dancing, and the sounds of music and gaiety were wafting from the open windows of the main drawing room. It was a country entertainment and the numbers not large, there being only two guests staying at the house at that particular time to swell the ranks of the local gentry.

It was not a ball, but the boy sitting out of sight of the house on the seat surrounding the great marble fountain below the terrace wished that he was inside and a part of it all. He wished that reality could be suspended and that he could be there dancing with *her*, the dark-haired, dark-eyed young daughter of his father's guest. Or at least looking at her and perhaps talking with her. Perhaps fetching her a glass of lemonade. He wished . . . oh, he wished for the moon, as he always did. A dreamer—that was what his mother had often called him.

But there were two insurmountable reasons for his exclusion from the assembly: he was only seventeen years old, and he was the marquess's *illegitimate* son. That last fact had had particular meaning to him only during the past year and a half, since the sudden death of his mother. Through his childhood and much of his boyhood, it had seemed a normal way of life to have a father who visited him and his mother frequently but did not live with them, and a father who had a wife in the big house though no other children but him.

It was only in the year and a half since his mother's death that the reality of his situation had become fully apparent to him. He had been a fifteen-year-old boy

9

without a home and with a father who had financed his mother's home but had never been a permanent part of it. His father had taken him to live in the big house. But he had felt all the awkwardness of his situation since moving there. He was not a member of the family—his father's wife, the marchioness, hated him and ignored his presence whenever she was forced to be in it. But he was not one of the servants either, of course.

It was only in the past year and a half that his father had begun to talk about his future and that the boy had realized that his illegitimacy made of that future a tricky business. The marquess would buy him a commission in the army when he was eighteen, he had decided, but it would have to be with a line regiment and not with the cavalry—certainly not with the Guards. That would never do when the ranks of the Guards were filled with the sons of the nobility and upper gentry. The legitimate sons, that was.

He was his father's only son, but illegitimate.

"You are not at the ball?" a soft little voice asked him suddenly, and he looked up to see the very reason why he had so wished to be in the drawing room—Jeanne Morisette, daughter of the Comte de Levisse, a royalist émigré who had fled from France during the Reign of Terror and lived in England ever since.

He felt his heart thump. He had never been close to her before, had never exchanged a word with her. He shrugged. "I don't want to be," he said. "It is not a ball anyway."

She sat down beside him, slender in a light-colored flimsy gown—he could not see the exact color in the darkness—her hair in myriad ringlets about her head, her eyes large and luminous in the moonlight. "But I wish I could be there even so," she said. "I thought I might be allowed to attend since it is just a country entertainment. But Papa said no. He said that fifteen is too young to be dancing with gentlemen. It is tiresome being young, is it not?"

Ah. So she had not been with the company after all. He had tortured himself for nothing. He shrugged again. "I am not so young," he said. "I am seventeen."

She sighed. "When I am seventeen," she said, "I shall

dance every night and go to the theater and on picnics.
I shall do just whatever I please when I am grown up."

Her face was bright and eager and she was prettier
than any other girl he had seen. He had taken every
opportunity during the past week to catch glimpses of
her. She was like a bright little jewel, quite beyond his
reach, of course, but lovely to look at and to dream of.

"Papa is going to take me back to France as soon as
it is safe to go," she said with a sigh. "Everything seems
to be settling down under the leadership of Napoleon
Bonaparte. If it continues so, perhaps we will be able to
return, Papa says. He says there is no point in continuing
to dream of the return of a king."

"So you may do your dancing in Paris," he said.

"Yes." Her eyes were dreamy. "But I would just as
soon stay in London. I know England better than I know
France. I even speak English better than I speak French.
I would prefer to belong here."

But there was a trace of a French accent in her voice.
It was one more attractive feature about her. He liked
to listen to her talk.

"You are the marquess's son, are you not?" she asked
him. "But you do not have his name?"

"I have my mother's name," he said. "She died the
winter before last."

"Ah," she said, "that is sad. My mother is dead too,
but I do not remember her. I have always been with
Papa for as long as I recall. What is your name?"

"Robert," he said.

"Robert." She gave his name its French intonation and
then smiled and said it again with its English pronuncia-
tion. "Robert, dance with me. Do you dance?"

"My mother taught me," he said. "Out here? How can
we dance out here?"

"Easily," she said, jumping lightly to her feet and
stretching out a slim hand to him. "The music is quite
loud enough."

"But you will hurt your feet on the stones," he said,
looking down at her thin silk slippers as she led the way
up onto the terrace.

She laughed. "I think, Robert, that you are looking
for excuses," she said. "I think that your mother did not

teach you at all, or that if she did, you were unteachable.
I think perhaps you have two left feet." She laughed
again.

"That is not so," he said indignantly. "If you wish to
dance, then dance we will."

"That is a very grudging acceptance," she said. "You
are supposed to be thrilled to dance with me. You are
supposed to make me feel that there is nothing you wish
for more in life than to dance with me. But no matter.
Let us dance."

He knew very little about women's teasing. It was true
that Mollie Lumsden, one of his father's undermaids, frequently put herself in his way and showed herself to him
in provocative poses, most frequently bent over his bed
as she made it up in the mornings. It was true too that
on the one occasion when he had tried to steal a kiss she
had whisked herself off with a toss of the head and an
assurance that her favors did not come free. But there
was a world of difference between the buxom Mollie and
Jeanne Morisette.

They danced a minuet, the moon bathing the cobbles
of the terrace in a mellow light, both of them silent and
concentrating on the distant music and their steps—although his attention was not entirely on just those two
things either. His eyes were on the slender moonlit form
of the girl with whom he danced. Her hand in his was
warm and slim and soft. He thought that life might never
have a finer moment to offer him.

"You are very tall," she said as the music drew to an
end.

He was close to six feet in height. Unfortunately his
growing had all been done upward. To say that he was
thin would be to understate the case. He hated to look at
himself in a looking glass. He longed to be a handsome,
muscular man and wondered if he ever would be anything more than gangly and ugly.

"And you have lovely blond hair," she said. "I have
noticed you all week and wished that I had hair that
waved like yours." She laughed lightly. "I am glad you
do not wear it short. It would be such a waste."

He was dazzled. He was still holding her soft little
hand in his.

"I am supposed to be in my room," she said. "Papa would have forty fits if he knew I was out here."

"You are quite safe," he said. "I shall see that no harm comes to you."

She looked up at him from beneath her lashes, an imp of mischief in her eyes. "You may kiss me if you wish," she said.

His eyes widened. What Mollie had denied, Jeanne Morisette would grant? But how could he kiss her? He knew nothing about kissing.

"Of course," she said, "if you do not wish to, I shall return to the house. Perhaps you are afraid."

He was. Mortally afraid. "Of course I am not afraid," he said scornfully. And he set his hands at her waist—they almost met about it—and lowered his head and kissed her. He kissed her as he had always kissed his mother on the cheek—though he kissed Jeanne on the lips—briefly and with a smacking sound.

She was all softness and subtle fragrance. And her hands were on his shoulders, her thumbs against the skin of his neck. Her dark eyes looked inquiringly into his. He swallowed and knew that his bobbing Adam's apple would reveal his nervousness.

"And of course I wish to," he said, and he lowered his head and laid his lips against hers again, keeping them there for a few self-indulgent moments and noting with shock the unfamiliar effects of the embrace on his body—the breathlessness, the rush of heat, the tightening in his groin. He lifted his head.

"Oh, Robert," she said with a sigh, "you can have no idea how tiresome it is to be fifteen. Or can you? Do you remember what it was like? Though it is entirely different for a boy, of course. I am still expected to be-have like a child, when I am not a child. I must be quiet and prim, and welcome the company of your father and mother—no, the marchioness is not your mother, is she?—and of my own papa. And I am to be denied the company of the young people who are at present dancing and enjoying themselves in the drawing room. How will I endure it here for another whole week?"

He wished he could pluck some stars from the sky and lay them at her feet. He wished that the music would

continue for a week so that he could dance with her and
kiss her and help see her to the end of the boredom of
an unwelcome visit to the country.

"I will be here too," he said with a shrug.

She looked up at him eagerly—the top of her head
reached barely to his shoulder. "Yes," she said. "I shall
steal away and spend time with you, Robert. It will be
fun and my maid is very easy to escape. She is lazy,
but I never complain to Papa because sometimes it is an
advantage to have a lazy maid." She laughed her light
infectious laugh. "You are very handsome. Will you take
me to the ruins tomorrow? We went there two days ago,
but the marchioness would not let me explore them lest
I hurt myself. All I could do was look and listen to your
father tell the history of the old castle."

"I will take you," he said. But he noted the fact that
she had spoken of *stealing* away to be with him. And of
course she was right. It was not at all the thing for the
two of them even to have met. They certainly should
never have talked or danced. Or kissed. There would be
all hell to pay if he were caught taking her to the ruins.
He should explain that to her more clearly. But he was
seventeen years old, and the realities of life were new to
him. He still thought it possible to fight against them, or
at least to ignore them.

"Will you?" she asked eagerly, clasping her hands to
her slender, budding bosom. "After luncheon? I shall go
to my room for a rest, as the marchioness is always urging me to do. Where shall I meet you?"

"The other side of the stables," he said, pointing. "It
is almost a mile to the ruins. Will you be able to walk
that far?"

"Of course I can walk there," she said scornfully.
"And climb. I want to climb up the tower."

"It is dangerous," he said. "Some of the stairs have
crumbled away."

"But you have climbed it, have you not?" she said.

"Of course."

"Then I shall climb it too," she said. "Is there a good
view from the top?"

"You can see to the village and beyond," he said.

The music was playing a quadrille in the drawing room.

"Tomorrow," she said. "After luncheon. At last there will be a day to look forward to. Good night, Robert."

She held out one slim hand to him. He took it and realized in some confusion that she meant him to kiss it. He raised it to his lips and felt foolish and flattered and wonderful.

"Good night, Miss Morisette," he said.

She laughed up at him. "You are a courtier after all," she said. "You have just made me feel at least eighteen years old. It is Jeanne, Robert. Jeanne the French way and Robert the English way."

"Good night, Jeanne," he said, and he was glad of the darkness, which hid his blushes.

She turned and tripped lightly over the cobbles of the terrace and around to the side of the house. She had, he realized, come out through the servants' entrance and was returning the same way. He wondered if she had come out merely for the fresh air or if she had seen him from an upstairs window. The window of her bedchamber overlooked the terrace and the fountain.

He liked to believe that it was his presence out there that had drawn her. She had called him tall. She had not commented on his thinness, only on his height. And she had called the blondness of his hair lovely and had approved of the fact that he liked to wear it overlong. She had called him handsome—*very* handsome. And she had asked him to kiss her. She had asked him to take her to the ruins the next day. She had said that at last there would be a day to look forward to.

He was no longer merely attracted to her slim dark beauty, he realized, the sounds of music and gaiety from the drawing room forgotten. He was deeply, irrevocably in love with Jeanne Morisette.

She had caught sight of him several times since her arrival at Haddington Hall, though she had not been formally introduced to him, of course. Her father had explained to her that he was the bastard son of the marquess and that really it was not at all respectable for him to be living at the house. It must be very distressing for the marchioness, her papa had said, especially since the poor woman was apparently barren and had been unable to present the marquess with any legitimate heirs or even any daughters.

Jeanne did not care about the fact that he should not be there at the house. She was glad that he was, and only sorry that it was not possible to be openly friendly with him. She had not met many boys or young men during her life, having had a sheltered upbringing with her father and having been sent to a school where she and her fellow pupils were kept strictly from the wicked male world beyond their walls.

In her boredom and loneliness at Haddington Hall, she had watched him covertly whenever she had had a chance, most notably from the window of her bedchamber. And she had quite fallen in love with his lean and boyish figure and his longish blond hair.

On the night of the ball—though both her father and the marchioness had tried to console her by assuring her that it was not really a ball—she had stood moodily at the window of her room and seen him, at first on the terrace and then disappearing to the far side of the fountain and not reappearing. He must be sitting on the seat there. She had already dismissed her maid for the night. Her breath had come fast and excitement had bubbled in her as she felt the temptation to slip downstairs and outdoors unseen to talk with him.

She had given in to temptation.

She had been dazzled. She had not realized quite how tall he was or how handsome his face with its aquiline nose and firm jaw and very direct eyes. He was seventeen years old, a young man, not the boy she had at first taken him for.

He was the first man she had danced with apart from her dancing master at school, and he was the first man to kiss her, not just that first time in the way her father might have kissed her, but the second time, when his lips had lingered on hers and she had felt delightfully wicked right down to her toes.

She was in love with him before she had finished running lightly upstairs to her room and before she had closed her door behind her and leaned back against it, her eyes closed, and tried to remember just exactly how his mouth had felt. And then she opened her eyes and raced to the window and drew back again half behind the heavy velvet curtains so that she could watch him wander up and down the terrace without herself being seen. But she need not have worried—he did not look up.

She was in love with him—with a tall and slender blond god who was all of seventeen years old. And who had the added attraction of being forbidden fruit.

They had four days together—four afternoons when she was dutifully resting in her room as far as her father and the marquess and marchioness knew. They went to the ruined castle on the first day and he climbed the winding stone stairs of the tower ahead of her, turning frequently to point out to her a chipped or crumbled stair where she would have to set her feet carefully. She was more frightened than she would admit and almost squealed with terror when they came out into daylight at the top and she discovered that the parapet had quite fallen away so that there was nothing to protect them from the seemingly endless drop to the grass and ruins below. But she merely shook out her hair—she had disdained to wear a bonnet—and looked boldly about her.

"It is magnificent," she said, stretching out her arms to the sides. "How wonderful it must have been, Robert, to be the lady of such a castle and to have watched from the battlements for her knight to come riding home."

"After an absence of seven years or more, doubtless," he said.

She laughed. "What an unromantic thing to say," she said. "Anyway, I would not have let him go alone. I would have ridden with him and shared all the discomforts and dangers of the military life with him."

"You would not have been able to do it," he said. "You are a woman."

"Because it would not have been allowed?" she said. "Or because I would not be able to stand the hardships? I would too. I would not care about having to sleep on the hard ground and all that. And as to not being allowed, I should cut off my hair and ride out as my knight's squire. No one would even know that I was a woman. I would not complain, you see."

He laughed and she discovered that white teeth and

merry blue eyes made him even more handsome in the daylight than he had been in the moonlight the evening before.

She invited him to kiss her again when they reached the bottom. Indeed, she had found coming down to be a far greater ordeal than going up had been. She was glad of an excuse to lean back against a solid wall and to rest her arms along his reassuringly sturdy shoulders. He felt strong despite his leanness.

His arms slid about her waist as his lips rested against hers and her arms wrapped themselves about his neck. She tried pouting her lips against his and felt their pressure increase. She was being kissed by a man, she told herself, by a tall and handsome young man. And she was in love with him. It felt wonderful to be in love.

"I will have to go back," she said, "or they will be sending up to my room to see why I am sleeping so long."

"Yes," he said making no attempt to delay her. "I will take you back as far as the stables."

For the three afternoons following, they walked— across fields, among the woods, beside the lake a mile distant from the house in the opposite direction from the old castle. The weather was their friend. The sun shone each day from a blue sky, and if there were any clouds, they were small and white and fluffy and merely brought brief moments of welcome shade. They walked with fingers entwined and they talked to each other, sharing thoughts and dreams they had confided to no one before.

His father wanted to buy him a commission in the army when he was eighteen, he told her. But it was not a life he looked forward to. For as long as he had lived with his mother he had assumed that he would always live quietly in the country. It was the kind of life he loved. But he must do something. He realized that. He could not continue to live at Haddington Hall indefinitely, and he was not, of course, his father's heir.

"But I have no wish to be an officer," he told her. "I don't think I could stomach killing anyone."

She told him that her mother had been English, that her grandparents, the Viscount and Viscountess Kingsley, still lived in Yorkshire. But her papa had allowed her to visit them only twice in all the years they had been in England. Her father wanted her to be French and to live in France. But she wanted to be English and to live in England, she told Robert with a sigh. She wished she did not belong to two countries. It made life complicated.

She told him again of her dream of being old enough to attend balls and theater parties, of meeting and mingling with other young people. Except that the dream did not seem quite so important during those days. She was living a dream more wonderful than any she had ever imagined.

They lay side by side on a shaded bank of the lake during the fourth afternoon, their arms about each other, kissing, smiling at each other, gazing into each other's eyes. He touched her small breasts lightly and she felt her cheeks flaming, though she did not withdraw her eyes from his or make any protest. His hand felt good there, and right. And then he rested his hand against her waist. It felt warm through the cotton of her dress.

"Robert," she said, "I love you."

And she loved the way he had of smiling with his eyes before the smile touched his lips.

"Do you love me?" she asked him. "Tell me that you do."

"I love you," he said.

"I am going to marry you," she said. "Papa will not like it, I know, but if he will not give his consent, I will elope with you."

He smiled slowly again. "It can never be, Jeanne. You know that," he said gently. "Let's not spoil these few days by dreaming of the impossible. Let's enjoy them."

"It can be," she said, wrapping her arm about his lean waist and moving closer against him. "Oh, not yet, of course. I am too young. But when I am seventeen or eighteen and have not changed my mind, Papa will see that I can be happy with no one but you and he will give his consent. And if he does not, then I shall follow the drum with you. I shall ride to war with my knight."

"Jeanne," he said, kissing her mouth and her eyes one by one. "Jeanne."

"Say you will marry me," she said. "Say you want to. You do want to marry me, Robert?"

"I will love you all my life and even beyond that," he said. "You will always be my only love."

"But that is not what I asked you," she said.

"Sh." He kissed her again. "We must go back home. We have been away longer than usual. I don't want you to be missed."

"Tomorrow," she said, smiling at him as he got to his feet and reached down a hand to help her up. "Tomorrow I shall get you to admit it, Robert. I always get what I want, you know."

"Always?" he said.

"Always." She brushed the grass from her dress and peeped up at him from beneath her eyelashes. He looked adorably handsome with his hair disheveled from the ground.

"I shall come for you on a white charger on your eighteenth birthday, then," he said, "and we will ride off into the sunset—no, the sunrise; the sunrise would be better—and marry and have a dozen children and live happily ever after. Are you satisfied now?"

She stood on tiptoe, kissed his cheek, and smiled dazzlingly at him. "Utterly," she said. "I have heard what I want to hear. I told you that I always get what I want, you see." She laughed merrily. She thought that she had never been so happy in her life, though she knew it was a happiness for the present only. She knew as well as he that they would never marry, that after that particular week was past they would probably never meet again.

But she would always love him, she believed with all the passion of her fifteen years. He was her first love and he would be her last. She would never love another man as she loved Robert.

2

JEANNE'S happiness lasted for an even shorter time than she had expected. She had hoped for three more days. Three more brief days out of eternity. But she was granted only half an hour longer. Her father was waiting for her in her bedchamber when she returned.

"Jeanne? Where have you been?" he asked her in the French he always spoke when they were alone.

She switched to his language. "Out walking," she said, smiling at him. "It is such a beautiful afternoon."

"Alone?" he asked.

Her smile broadened. "Madge does not like walking," she said. "I did not insist that she accompany me."

"Three would have been a crowd," he said, not returning her smile.

She looked at him warily.

"He is a bastard, Jeanne," her father said sternly. "He should not even be housed beneath the same roof as decent people. I would have thought twice about accepting the marquess's invitation here had I known that you would be subjected to such an indignity. I believe he keeps the boy here only to taunt his wife with her barrenness. You have been meeting him every afternoon while you have been 'resting'?"

"Yes," she admitted defiantly. "He is fun to be with, Papa, and there are no other young people here for me. You would not allow me to attend the assembly although I am fifteen years old."

"Has he touched you?" the count asked, his voice cold and tight.

Jeanne could feel the color drain from her cheeks as she remembered the kisses she had shared with Robert on several occasions and his touching her breasts that afternoon.

"Has he touched you?" her father repeated harshly.

"He has kissed me," she admitted.

"Kissed you? Is that all? Tell me!" The count took her none too gently by one arm.

"Yes," she said, feeling guilty about the lie. "That is all." How could she tell her father that Robert had touched her where no one had touched her since she had begun to blossom into a woman?

He shook her roughly by the one arm. "Fool!" he said. "Madge must go, I see. I must find someone else to look to your virtue, since you cannot seem to look to it yourself. Do you not realize how he must be gloating, girl? Do you not realize how he must be laughing with the servants at his conquest of you?"

She shook her head. "No, Papa," she said. "He loves me. He is not like that."

"And I suppose you love him too and have told him so," he said.

"Yes." Her chin rose stubbornly. "And I have told him that I will marry him when I am eighteen."

Her father laughed harshly. "Then I will have to be in my grave first," he said. "You will not be marrying anyone's bastard, Jeanne. Or anyone English if I can help it. And if you must know the truth, then I will tell you that I learned of your movements for the past afternoons from a stablehand to whom the bastard has been boasting of his conquests and of his plans to completely ruin you before you leave here."

"No," she said. "You are making that up, Papa. That is not true. Robert would not do that."

"You call me a liar, then?" he said coldly. "He would take your honor and then laugh in the face of the French bitch who thought herself so much better than he—his very words, Jeanne, spoken to the stablehand and doubtless to all the other servants too. His very words—the French bitch."

"No." She shook her head.

"Who first mentioned marriage?" he asked. "Which one of you?"

"I did," she said. "I wanted him to know that I was willing to marry him no matter what."

"And he agreed?" her father asked.

"Yes," she said. "Eventually."

"Ah," he said. "Eventually. And did he tell you he loved you before you told him?"

"No," she said, "but he said it immediately after me."

"Jeanne," he said harshly, "you are a green girl. Love and marriage have no part in the plans of such a man. Only revenge on those more respectable then he. You are 'the French bitch' to him. Do you think I will ever forget or forgive those words? I would thrash him within an inch of his life if I were not a guest in his father's house. As it is, I will have a word with the marquess. Respectable people are not safe around such a boy."

"No," she said. "Please, Papa, say nothing. I would not wish to get him into trouble."

"You will stay in this room," he said. "I shall say you are indisposed. You are not to leave under any circumstances without my permission. Do you understand me?"

"Yes, Papa," she said.

But she would not believe any of those things he had said, she thought after he had left. He had said them to turn her against Robert, whom he would of course consider ineligible. She would believe none of it. Robert loved her. Robert wished to marry her even if he had realized all along, as she had, that they would never be able to marry. She would not believe her father.

But in the silence of her room during the ensuing hours she could not help remembering that he had not said that he loved her until she had said the words first and begged him to say them too, and that he had avoided several times telling her the fact that he wished to marry her. She remembered the fact that his kisses had become more prolonged and more ardent each day and that he had touched her breasts that afternoon.

How much farther had he planned to go in the three remaining days before she and her father were to leave Haddington Hall? If he *had* planned ahead, of course. Or had all his words and actions been spontaneous, as she had believed all along? But she recalled his saying that they should not think of impossibilities but enjoy the days that remained to them. Enjoy? How?

And those words stuck in her mind, the words by which he had reputedly described her to a stablehand. *The French bitch.* Was it possible? But would Papa have made up such words? Or would the stablehand have made them up and repeated them to her father if they were not true?

Doubt and anguish and youth gnawed at her through the endless remainder of the day and the sleepless night that followed. Mostly it was youth. She was fifteen years old, she reminded herself. She knew nothing about men, except for the fact that the teachers at her school had always emphasized their wickedness and their eagerness to prey upon a young lady's innocence. Papa, on the other hand, had lived in several different countries and had been a diplomat for years before fleeing to England during the Terror. Papa knew far more about life than she. And he loved her. He had always told her that, and she had no reason to doubt him.

She had been made a fool of—because she was fifteen and eager to be a woman and to be loved and appreciated.

Robert was seventeen, a man already. How he must have been laughing at her. How he must have been enjoying the free favors she had been handing him. How he must have been looking forward to the remaining three days, when distress over their impending parting would have made her a great deal freer with her favors. Oh, yes, he would have enjoyed those days.

And how she hated him!

Perhaps she *was* only fifteen, she thought finally. But she had done a deal of growing up within a few hours. She would never fall in love again. She would never allow any man to have any power whatsoever over her again. She would learn how to have that power herself, and how to wield it too. If there were any more fools to be made, it would be the men in her life who would be at the receiving end.

Robert loved the early morning. Most days, unless it was raining too hard, he rode for miles, enjoying the sense of freedom and solitude. He did not like being at the house, where there was always the chance that he would come face-to-face with his father's wife. Even his father's company made him uncomfortable now that they no longer met in the familiar surroundings of his mother's cottage just beyond the boundaries of Haddington. His father no longer seemed like the same cheerful and indulgent papa who had used to bring him presents and play with him and sit sometimes talking with him while Mama sat on his lap.

Robert was returning from his morning ride the day after he had kissed Jeanne at the lake and promised to ride off with her on a white charger on her eighteenth birthday. He smiled at the memory, though the smile was somewhat rueful. There were only three afternoons left and then he would see her no more. He would love her all his life, but he would never see her again once she left Haddington. Her father was talking about returning to France when they could, she had said. And even if that were not so, there was no possibility of a future for them. None whatsoever.

Once again the reality of his situation as an illegitimate son stabbed home. And yet he was growing to manhood. Reality had to be faced and accepted. There was no point in raging against it.

There was a carriage drawn up on the terrace before the house, he saw as he neared the stables. The Comte de Levisse's carriage. He frowned as he swung down from the saddle and hailed a passing groom.

"The count is going somewhere?" he asked.

"Leaving," the groom said. "Grumbling, his coachman was about it, Master Robert. Likes the tavern at the village here, he does. But the orders were given last night."

Leaving! The bottom felt rather as if it had fallen out of Robert's stomach as he handed the reins of his horse absently to the groom—he usually looked after his own mount—and strode in the direction of the terrace.

But he halted at the corner of the house. Both his father and the marchioness were outside bidding farewell to the count and Jeanne. The latter was dressed in a dark green traveling dress and bonnet and looked slender and very young in company with the three adults. And very beautiful. He knew now that her dark hair was more brown than black, that her dark eyes were gray, not brown. He knew a great deal more about her than he had known the night of the ball.

Jeanne!

But though he stood quite still and was some distance away, she saw him as she turned toward the open door of the carriage. She hesitated for a moment and then hurried toward him. Her father stretched out a hand toward her but then dropped it to his side and watched.

Robert said nothing. Why ask her if she was leaving? Obviously she was leaving. He looked at her in anguish. Even a private good-bye was to be denied them.

"Robert." She smiled brightly. "How glad I am that I have seen you before I leave. I wish to say good-bye."

He swallowed. Unlike her, he did not have his back to the three watching adults and the servants. He felt very exposed to public view.

"I want to thank you for four lovely afternoons and for the dance on the terrace," she said, her voice light and teasing. She was looking up at him from beneath her lashes.

"I need no thanks," he said. He found it difficult to get the words beyond his teeth. "Jeanne." He whispered her name.

"Oh, but you do." She smiled dazzlingly. "The days would have been so very dull if I could not have amused myself with you."

She was out of earshot of the people on the terrace and she had her back to them. She did not need to act a part.

"Jeanne," he said again.

"Why are you looking so sad?" she asked. "We are leaving early, is that it? But I asked Papa to take me back to London because life is so dull here. Oh, Robert, you are not feeling sad, are you? You did not take those kisses seriously, and all that foolish talk about love and marriage?"

He looked at her and swallowed again.

"Oh, poor Robert." Her eyes fell to his Adam's apple, and he felt overtall and gangly again. She laughed merrily. "You did, did you not? How foolish and rustic of you. You did not think I would seriously fall in love and consider marriage with a bastard, did you? *Did* you, Robert?"

He merely looked at her as her eyes swept up to meet his again.

"Oh, poor Robert," she said again, and her laugh tinkled about him like broken glass. "How droll. The bastard and the daughter of a French count. It would make a wonderful farce, don't you think? Papa is waiting. Goodbye." She held out a gloved hand to him.

He ignored it. He did not even see it. He did not see her even though he looked directly into her eyes. He felt only the blinding hurt of a reality that he had thought he was growing accustomed to.

She shrugged and turned from him. And two minutes later her father's carriage was bearing her away from Haddington Hall. Robert had not moved. He had not noticed the approach of one of his father's servants.

"His lordship would have you wait upon him in the library immediately, Master Robert," the servant said.

Robert looked at the man and made no reply. But he began to move along the now-deserted terrace.

"And so you see why they decided to cut their visit short by three days," the marquess was saying to his son. He was reclining in a deep leather chair behind the oak desk in the library, his elbows on the arms, his fingers steepled beneath his chin. His son was standing before the desk. "It is an embarrassment to me and a disappointment to her ladyship."

Robert said nothing. He looked steadily back.

"She is a pretty and alluring little thing," the marquess said with a laugh. "I can hardly blame you for having an eye to her, boy. And she must be a hot little piece to go off secretly with you as she did for several afternoons. French, you know. They are usually hot to handle. But she is not for the likes of you, Robert."

No, obviously not. He had not needed to be told that.

"You are seventeen," the marquess said with a chuckle. "Ready for a woman, are you, boy? It would be strange if you were not. You haven't had one yet? No rolls in the hay with a willing wench? I have been neglecting your education, it seems. Name the wench you want and I shall buy her for you. But there are limits, Robert." He laughed heartily. "You cannot aspire to a respectable woman, you know: Not above a certain class, anyway. You are my bastard, after all. That must not be forgotten, lad, despite who I am."

No, he would not forget it.

"Your mother was my mistress, not my wife," the marquess said. "You understand the difference, boy?"

"Yes." It was one of the few words he had spoken during the interview.

"I loved her," the marquess said, his joviality deserting him for a moment. "She was a good woman, boy, and don't you forget it even is she was a fallen woman."

She was his mother. He had loved her too. And he had never doubted her goodness. Or thought about the fact that she was not respectable.

"But I had to marry within my own class," the marquess said with a shrug. "And so you were born a bastard. My only child. Fate can deal strange tricks, eh? Now, what woman do you fancy?"

"I don't," Robert said. "I don't want a woman."

His father threw back his head and laughed. "Then you must be no son of mine," he said. "Did your mother play me false after all? Come now, lad, you are not going to be moping over a little bit of French skirt, are you?"

"No," Robert said.

"Well." His father shrugged. "When you are hot for a wench, boy, come and tell me. Though you are a handsome enough lad, or will be when you have a little meat on your bones. Perhaps you can entice your own wenches into the hay. You are a restless boy, aren't you? Out riding or walking at all hours of the day."

"I like the outdoors," Robert said.

"Perhaps you need more to occupy you," the marquess said. "Perhaps I should purchase that commission for you before your eighteenth birthday. What do you say? Her ladyship would be glad enough to be rid of you." He chuckled again. "The sight of you is a constant reproach to her. And no one would be able to say that I had not done handsomely by my bastard, would they now?"

"No, sir."

"I have never shirked responsibility for you anyway, lad," his father said heartily. "Even though you look as unlike me as you could. It is a good thing that your mother had your blond and wavy hair and blue eyes, is it not? But I never denied you, Robert, and I'll not do it now. You can boast to all your regiment that the Marquess of Quesnay is your father. I'll not try to impose silence on you."

Robert said nothing.

"Run along, then," the marquess said. "You had better stay in your room for, ah, the rest of today and the next three days. I promised her ladyship that I would punish you harshly for your presumption in lifting your eyes to a lady. Wives must be humored, Robert. It seems a small matter to me, though you must learn for your own good to keep to your station in your wenching. I suppose I had better impose bread and water as well. Yes, that will please her ladyship. I shall tell her that I thrashed you too. She won't know the truth since she is unlikely to go to your room to check the evidence for herself." He laughed heartily. "Away you go, then. I shall do something about that commission as soon as possible."

"Yes, sir," Robert said, and turned away.

That same night Robert packed a few belongings—no more than he could carry in a small bundle—and left both his room and his home to seek his own way in the world.

Two days later, in a town not twenty miles distant from Haddington Hall, he listened to the persuasions of a recruiting sergeant and enlisted as a private soldier in the Ninety-fifth Rifles infantry regiment.

Three months passed before his father discovered him. It was less than a week before new recruits to the regiment, Private Robert Blake among them, were to embark for service in India.

Robert refused the marquess's urgings that he be allowed to buy a commission for his son. He took leave of his father with a stony face and no visible emotion at all.

If he was a nobody, he had decided—and clearly he

was—then he would prefer to enter adult life with no label at all. Not son of the Marquess of Quesnay. Not bastard. He was Private Robert Blake of the Ninety-fifth. That was all. He would make his own way in the world—if there was a way to be made—by his own efforts or not at all.

And he would know his place in the world for the rest of his life. His place was at the bottom—in the line of an infantry regiment as a private soldier.

From now on, he decided, he needed no one—man or woman. Only himself. He would make a success or a failure of life alone, without help and without emotional ties.

He would never love again, he decided. Love had died with his mother and innocence.

PORTUGAL
AND SPAIN,
1810

3

NO one standing invisible in the ballroom at the Lisbon home of the Count of Angeja would have guessed that there was a war in progress. No one would have known that the British troops sent to Portugal under the command of Sir Arthur Wellesley to defend that country from occupation by the forces of Napoleon Bonaparte and to help free Spain of their domination had been pushed back in ignominious retreat the previous summer despite their magnificent victory over the French at Talavera on the road to Madrid.

No one would have guessed that it was generally believed in both Portugal and England that once the summer campaign of 1810 began and the French armies then poised beyond the border with Spain finally made the expected advance, the Viscount Wellington's army—Sir Arthur had acquired his new title as a reward for Talavera—would be pushed into the sea, leaving Lisbon to the mercy of the enemy.

No one would have guessed it despite the fact that the silken and gaily colored gowns of the ladies were quite overshadowed by the splendor of the gorgeous military uniforms of the majority of the gentlemen. For one thing, most of the divisions of the English and Portuguese armies were not stationed at Lisbon or anywhere near it. They were in the hills of central Portugal, awaiting the expected attack along the northern road to Lisbon, past the Spanish fort of Ciudad Rodrigo and the Portuguese fort of Almeida. Only a relatively small detachment had been posted closer to Lisbon on the chance that the French would choose the southern road past the more formidable Spanish fort of Badajoz and the Portuguese Elvas.

For another thing, the general mood of the dancers
and revelers, gentlemen and ladies alike, was gay and
carefree. War and the possibility of disaster seemed the
farthest topics from anyone's mind. Perhaps many of the
gentlemen were rejoicing in the fact that they were alive
at all. Although some of the officers—and all the military
gentlemen who had received invitations to the ball were
officers—were in Lisbon on legitimate business, many of
them were convalescents from the military hospitals
there. Some were quite content to remain convalescent
for as long as they could. Others chafed to be back with
their regiments, back in the world where their duty lay.

Such a man was the one who stood in a shadowed
corner of the ballroom, a glass of wine in his hand, a
look on his face that might have seemed morose to an
uninformed observer but was in fact merely uncomfortable. He hated such entertainments and had been dragged
protesting to this one by laughing comrades who had refused to take no for an answer. He felt utterly out of his
depth, out of his milieu. Though the ballroom was
crowded beyond comfort and though his corner was relatively secluded, he felt conspicuous. He looked determinedly and defiantly about him from time to time as if
to confront those who were staring at him, only to find
that no one was.

It was the men at whom he glared. Had he looked at
the ladies, he might have found that several were in fact
giving him covert glances even if good breeding forbade
them from staring. He was the sort of man at whom
women often looked twice, though it would be difficult
perhaps to explain why it was so.

His uniform was without a doubt the least gorgeous at
the ball. It had none of the bright facings and gold and
silver lace that abounded on the uniforms about him. It
did not even have the advantage of being scarlet. It was
dark green and unadorned. Although clean and carefully
brushed, it had seen better days. Most men would not
deign to be buried in it, Major John Campion had told
him earlier with a hearty laugh and a friendly slap on the
back.

"But we all know that wild horses would not separate
you from it, Bob," he had added. "You riflemen are all

the same, so bloody proud of your regiment that you would even prefer to look veritable dowds rather than transfer to another."

It was the man inside the green coat, it seemed, then, who was the attraction. He was tall, broad-shouldered, muscular, not an once of spare fat on his body. And yet he was not an obviously handsome man. His blond wavy hair, perhaps his best feature, was close-cropped. His face was hard and looked as if it rarely smiled, the jaw-line pronounced and stubborn. His aquiline nose had been broken at some time in his life and was no longer quite straight. An old battle scar began in the middle of one cheek, climbed over the bridge of the nose, and ended just where the other cheek started. His face was weathered brown, his blue eyes looking startlingly pale in contrast.

He was not a handsome man, perhaps. He was something better than that, the woman with whom he was whiling away the tedious months in Lisbon had told him several weeks before, propped on one elbow on the bed beside him while she traced the line of his jaw with one long-nailed finger. He was quite irresistibly attractive.

Captain Robert Blake had laughed shortly and reached up with one powerful arm to draw her head down to his.

"If it is more of this you want, Beatriz," he had said to her in her own language, "you have only to ask. The flattery is unnecessary."

The dancing had ended and the captain stepped back farther into the shadows. But he was not left to his own thoughts. Three of the officers from the hospital who had insisted that he attend this and several other entertainments over the past few weeks, when he was no longer bedridden with his wounds, were bearing down upon him, Lieutenant João Freire of the Portuguese skirmishers—the cacadores—with a curly-haired young lady on his arm.

"Bob," he said, "why are you not dancing? Never tell me that you cannot."

Captain Blake shrugged.

"Sophia wishes to dance with you," the lieutenant said. "Don't you, my love?"

He grinned down at the girl, who looked blankly at him and at Captain Blake.

"It would help if you talked Portuguese to the poor girl," Major Campion said. "I suppose she speaks not a word of English, João?"

The lieutenant continued to grin at her. "She is hot for me," he said, still in heavily accented English. "Now, if I could just separate her from her chaperone and her mother and father, perhaps . . ." He raised the girl's hand to his lips. "You want to dance with her, Bob? I daresay I will not be permitted the next."

"No," the captain said shortly.

"Bob, Bob," Captain Lord Ravenhill said with a sigh, reaching up with a finger and thumb to smooth the outer edges of his mustache, "what are we to do with you? You have none of the social graces."

"And have never craved any of them," Captain Blake said, nettled despite the fact that he knew his friends' teasing to be good-natured.

"If you could dance as well as you fight," the major said, "the rest of us might take ourselves back to our beds while the ladies flocked to you, Bob. From private to captain in how many years?"

"A little over ten," the captain said, shifting uncomfortably on his feet. He did not particularly enjoy being reminded that he had taken the almost insurmountable step up from the ranks to a commission without the aid of either influence or purchase. It was easier, he had found since being promoted from sergeant to ensign in India, to do the deed of exceptional bravery that had made possible the promotion than to live with the fact that his place was now with officers rather than the enlisted men. Socially he did not belong. "I was fortunate. I happened to be in the right place at the right time."

Lord Ravenhill slapped him on the back and bellowed with laughter. "You have been in more right places at more right times than anyone else in the army, if I have heard the facts correctly," he said. "Come out of the corner, Bob. There are doubtless people here who would be fascinated to converse with a genuine hero. Let me introduce you to some of them."

"I am going home," Captain Blake said.

"Home being the hospital or the arms of the delectable Beatriz?" Lord Ravenhill asked. "No, really, Bob, it won't do, old chap. The marquesa is supposed to be coming tonight. She has been in Lisbon for a few days already. If you think your Beatriz lovely, you must stay and gaze upon true beauty."

"The marquesa?" Captain Blake frowned. "Who in hell is she?"

"In heaven, my boy, in heaven," Lord Ravenhill said, kissing two fingers. "The Marquesa das Minas, the toast of Lisbon. The streets are strewn with her slain admirers—slain by one glance from her dark eyes, that is. And you ask 'Who in hell is she?' Stay and you will see for yourself."

"I am leaving," the captain said firmly. "I agreed to an hour and have been here an hour and ten minutes." He downed the wine that remained in his glass.

"Too late, Bob," the major said with a laugh. "That extra buzz and excitement at the door is the signal that she has arrived. One glance will root you to the spot for another hour and ten minutes at the very least, take my word on it."

"And how," Lieutenant Freire said in English, smiling pleasantly down at the girl on his arm, "am I to divest myself of this encumbrance so that I may fall at the feet of the marquesa and pay my homage?"

"You return her to her chaperone and sigh over the fact that propriety does not permit you to dance the next set with her," the major said.

"Ah," the lieutenant said, "of course. Come, my dear," he said to the girl in Portuguese, "I shall return you to your chaperone. It would not do, alas, for me to sully the reputation of so delicate a flower by keeping you with me one moment longer. But the memory of this half-hour will sustain me through a lonely night."

Lord Ravenhill snorted. "It would serve him right if the girl were a secret student of languages," he said. "I suppose he was taking his leave with protestations of undying love for the girl. Was he, Bob?"

"Something like that," the captain said.

But his attention had been distracted. Ravenhill had not exaggerated—not much, anyway. It was as if the

crowds had parted and the Queen of Portugal—or of
England—had entered the room. Not that all the noise
or activity had ceased. Conversations continued and gentlemen were choosing their partners for the next set of
dances. But somehow the focus of general attention had
suddenly centered on the new arrival.

She was dressed rather simply in a white gown. And
her hair, dark and glossy, and yet a shade lighter than
that of most Portuguese women, was not elaborately
dressed. It was combed back smoothly from her face and
her ears and dressed in curls at the back of her head.
Her gloves and fan and slippers were all white. It was
difficult at first glance to understand why her presence
commanded such attention. But there were several reasons, he realized as he continued to gaze at her across
almost the entire length of the large ballroom.

She was dressed all in white. Amid the rich and glorious colors of the gentlemen's uniforms and the lesser
brightness of the ladies' gowns, she was as startlingly noticeable as the first snowdrop of spring. And the contrast
of her dark hair and the creaminess of her skin—there
was plenty of it visible about her shoulders and bosom—
made the whiteness of her clothing all the more dazzling.

He could not tell if her face was beautiful. She was
too far away. But she had an exquisite figure, slim but
curved lavishly in all the right places. It was the sort of
figure that could make a man's loins ache without even
a glance at the face above it.

But it was not just her appearance or her figure that
accounted for the disproportionate amount of male attention she was attracting. There were other women in the
room who were perhaps almost as beautiful—almost if
not quite. Captain Blake watched her through narrowed
eyes. There was a presence about her, a sense of pride
in the lifted chin and the curve of her spine, an expecta-
tion of homage.

And homage was what she was getting. There were
copious amounts of scarlet regimentals and gold lace
about her, their owners dancing attendance on her, taking her shawl, fetching her a glass of wine or champagne,
taking her hand, kissing it, being tapped on the arm with
her white fan.

"One would willingly spend eternity in hell in exchange for one night—just one night, eh?" Lord Ravenhill said, reminding Captain Blake that he had been staring at the woman and that he had not taken himself off home after all.

"I daresay the body between the sheets and in the darkness would give no more pleasure than that of a willing whore," he said, watching the woman smile as both she and the small court who had gathered about her ignored the fact that the dancing was beginning again.

Both the major and Lord Ravenhill laughed. "I don't think you believe that any more than we do, Bob," Major Campion said. "Just the thought of my hand in the small of that little back is enough to send me in search of a pail of cold water. Has anyone seen one anywhere?"

The marquesa was looking about her while her court danced attendance on her. Captain Blake felt an unreasonable resentment growing in him. She was everything that was exquisite and expensive—and beyond his reach. Not that he ever hankered a great deal after what he could not have. He could have had more had he wanted. He could have started his military career in the ranks of the officers instead of having to claw his way upward the hard and almost impossible way. He might have been a major or a lieutenant colonel by now. And he might have been known as the son of the Marquess of Quesnay. The illegitimate son, it was true, but still the son. The only son.

He had never regretted what he had done. And having tasted the life of a soldier and found that after all it suited him admirably, he had no wish for the soft life of an aristocrat. He did not crave money, which was just as well, since the English government was notoriously slow in sending the wherewithal to pay its soldiers. It did not bother him that he could not afford the fancy dress uniforms that he saw about him in the ballroom. It did not even bother him that he could not renew the rather shabby plain one that he was wearing.

He was satisfied with his station in life and with the incidentals of that life. Except sometimes. Oh, just sometimes when he saw something beyond his grasp—

something like the Marquesa das Minas—then he felt the stirrings of envy and jealousy and even hatred. He hated the woman as her glance swept over him from across the room and back again as if she had noticed for the merest moment the strange abnormality of his shabby appearance.

He hated her because she was beautiful and privileged and expensive. Because she was the Marquesa das Minas, a grand title for such a small lady. And because he wanted her.

He turned abruptly to the major, who unlike Lord Ravenhill had not gone wandering off to choose himself another dancing partner.

"I am leaving, sir," he said. "I have put in my hour and more."

The major chuckled. "And will be at the surgeon again tomorrow, doubtless," he said, "threatening him with torture and death and worse if he will not send you back to your regiment. When will you ever learn to relax, Bob, and enjoy the moment?"

"I will enjoy the moment when I see my sergeant's ugly face and listen to the profane greetings of the men of my company," Captain Blake said. "I miss them. Good night."

The major shook his head and laughed again. "Just be sure to thank him before you leave," he said. "The surgeon, I mean. You were within a whisker of death for a long time."

"So I was told," the captain said. "I seem to remember the old sawbones telling me it was a shame a chest and shoulder could not be amputated. If only the ball had lodged in my arm instead of above my heart, he said, he could have had it off in a twinkling and all the inflammation and the rest of it would have been avoided. I believe I was still too weak at the time to spit in his eye." He turned to skirt the edge of the ballroom with purposeful strides. He did not glance at the marquesa or the officers surrounding her as he drew closer.

But one of the latter—Major Hanbridge, an engineering officer with whom the captain had had some dealings, stepped away from the group as he would have passed behind it and set a lace-covered hand on his arm.

"Not sneaking out, are you, Bob?" he asked. "A foolish question, of course. Certainly you are sneaking out. The only wonder is that you came at all. Were you dragged by the heels?" He grinned.

"I was invited, sir," Captain Blake said. "But I have another commitment."

Major Hanbridge raised his eyebrows. "A pretty one, I have no doubt," he said. "The marquesa wishes to be presented to you."

"To me?" the captain said foolishly. "I think there must be some mistake."

But the officers around the marquesa had stepped to one side and she had turned to look at him.

"She is tired of meeting only gentlemen pretending to be soldiers," Major Hanbridge said with another grin. "She wishes to meet the real thing. Captain Robert Blake, Joana. A bona fide hero, I do assure you. The scar is real, as are the others you cannot see—all of them courtesy of various French soldiers. Bob, may I present Joana da Fonte, the Marquesa das Minas?"

He felt like a gauche boy and wished more than anything that he had stayed in his safe corner. He inclined his head curtly and then realized that he should have made a more courtly bow, though with so many interested spectators he would doubtless have made an utter idiot of himself. He took the gloved hand she offered and shook it once and then was thankful that he was past the age of blushing. Obviously he should have raised the hand to his lips.

"Ma'am?" he said, looking into her face for the first time. It was as lovely and as flawless as the rest of her person. Her eyes were large and dark—but gray, not brown, as he had expected—and thick-lashed.

"Captain Blake." Her voice was low and sweet. "You were wounded at Talavera?" Her English was flawless and only slightly accented.

"No, ma'am" he said. "My regiment arrived there one day too late, after a forced march. I am afraid I was no hero of that battle. I was wounded in a rearguard action during the retreat that followed it."

"Ah," she said.

"He makes it sound quite ignoble, does he not?"

Major Hanbridge said. "Shot in the back as he was running away? He just happened at the time to be holding back a surprise attack across a bridge almost single-handedly until his bellowings—and mighty profane ones at that, from all accounts—brought the whole of his company and others running. Several battalions might have been cut to pieces if he had run in fright as any normal mortal would have done."

"Ah," she said, "you are a genuine hero after all, then, Captain.'

How could one reply to such a comment? He shifted his weight from one foot to the other.

"You were leaving," she said. "Do not let me detain you. I have invited some friends to a reception at my home two evenings from now. You will attend?"

"Thank you, ma'am," he said, "but I am hoping to be allowed to return to the front within the week. I am well-recovered from my wounds."

"I am happy to hear it," she said. "But you will not be leaving within two days, surely? I shall expect you."

He bowed a little more deeply than he had done initially, and she turned away to make some comment to a colonel of dragoons who had hovered at her elbow since her arrival. He was dismissed, Captain Blake assumed. He left the ballroom and the house without further delay.

He had watched her from across the room for surely fifteen minutes, he thought. Of course, the distance had been great and the crowds milling. But even when he had been close to her he had looked into her face and not immediately recognized her. She was so very changed—a mature and assured woman. He had recognized her only gradually—something in her gestures and facial expressions, perhaps.

She had not recognized him. She had talked to him as to a stranger—a stranger who she assumed had come to pay homage to her beauty. A stranger whom she had invited to an entertainment he had no intention of attending, under the assumption that he would be only too eager to join her court of devoted admirers.

Joana da Fonte, Major Hanbridge had called her. Jeanne Morisette when he had known her.

Jesus, he thought as he strode uphill to a less-aristocratic part of Lisbon, where Beatriz awaited him. Sweet Jesus, she was French!

Joana da Fonte, the Marquesa das Minas, tapped Colonel Lord Wyman on the arm with her fan.

"Another glass of champagne, if you please, Duncan," she said. She turned to another of her admirers as the colonel hurried away to do her bidding. "You may dance the next set with me, Michael."

There was a chorus of protests from a half a dozen male voices.

"Unfair, Joana," one young man said. "I made a point of being at the door in order to be the first to ask you."

"You must wait your turn, William," she said. "Michael had the forethought to call upon me this afternoon."

The protests receded to grumbles and reproachful glances at the wily lieutenant who had given himself an unfair advantage in a manner they all wished they had thought of.

He would come, Joana thought. He had appeared unexpectedly reluctant, it was true, and she would wager on it that at that particular moment he was convinced that he would not come. But he would. She knew enough about men to have recognized that particular look in his eyes.

He was not at all as she had expected, although she had been warned that he was a soldier rather than an officer—sometimes there was quite a distinction between the two terms, she knew. But even so she had expected a gentleman soldier, not a tough-looking man with a hard war- and weather-beaten face and very direct blue—startingly blue—eyes. He had seemed totally unconcerned by the near-shabbiness of his green jacket.

And yet, she thought, tapping one foot in time to the music and allowing her mind to wander—as it frequently did—away from the shallow and somewhat foolish conversation flowing about her, gentlemen and soldiers aside, Captain Robert Blake had looked all man.

She had not met many men in her life, she thought, although she was surrounded now, as she usually was when she was out in society, by males. Of course, there were Duarte and his band, but they were a different matter.

She had had the feeling on her first close look at Captain Robert Blake that she had met him before. It would not have been surprising. She had met a large number of British officers before. But she would not have forgotten such a man, she thought. She would not have forgotten either the shabbiness of his appearance or the toughness of his face and figure. Or the battered attractiveness of his face. No, she had not met him before.

She wafted a careless hand toward the colonel as he returned with her champagne. "You may hold it for me, if you please, Duncan," she said, "while I dance with Michael."

"What?" he said. "Young Bristow has solicited your hand when I was not here to argue, Joana? I shall call him out at dawn tomorrow."

"Duelists are forever banished from my presence," she said carelessly, laying one gloved hand lightly along the lieutenant's scarlet sleeve. "Have a care, do, Duncan."

"It will be my pleasure and my privilege to hold your glass until you return," Colonel Lord Wyman said, bowing elegantly without spilling a drop of the liquid.

He had moved up from the ranks, she had learned since arriving in Lisbon. She had not been told that before. He must indeed be a brave man. Not many enlisted men ever became officers. It was fortunate that she had met him so easily without having to make any overt move to do so. She had been looking for green jackets for three days. There were not many in Lisbon, most of the riflemen being stationed with the rest of the Light Division on the Coa River close to the border between Spain and central Portugal, protecting the army from sudden attack and preventing the French from obtaining any information about what was happening in Portugal.

It was fortunate that he had been at the ball. Her attention had been drawn first to the green jacket and then to the man inside it. He had looked an unlikely candidate at first. But perhaps not. A man with a facility with languages was not necessarily a thin, ascetic-looking scholar—certainly not if he was a captain with the famed Ninety-fifth Rifles. And this man, she knew, had done reconnaissance work before. He must be a man of some daring.

Yes, she had thought, he could quite possibly be her man. And discreet inquiries had drawn the information she had hoped for from Jack Hanbridge.

He would come, she thought again, smiling at Michael Bristow as they began to dance. She remembered the rough awkwardness of his manners, the faint hostility in his voice, the overwhelming masculinity of his person.

And she remembered his eyes—his blue eyes—and the look of awareness in them. An unwilling awareness, she was sure. He had not looked at her with open appreciation. He had made no attempt to flirt with her, and never would, she suspected. But the awareness had been there nonetheless. And she had been more intrigued by it than she had been by all the flattery and adulation of his more elegant peers.

Yes, he would come.

4

JOANA da Fonte, the Marquesa das Minas, had no particular business in Lisbon apart from the opportunity being there gave her to become acquainted with Captain Robert Blake more at her leisure than would have been the case if she had stayed at Viseu until he came. And when she had suggested her plan to Arthur Wellesley, Viscount Wellington, he had thought it a good idea.

"You will of course meet him here eventually, Joana," he had said when she had talked with him in Viseu. "I shall see to that. But it will be important that you get to know him fairly well."

"But getting to know him here would take time, Arthur," she had said. "And time is a commodity of which there is not an abundance?"

She had phrased her words as a question. But she might as well have saved her breath, she had thought philosophically. Viscount Wellington was always flatteringly attentive and gallant to ladies, as he was apparently not to the men under his command, but he kept his own counsel more than any other man she had known. He might of necessity have to divulge secret information to the numerous spies and reconnaissance officers who were essential to the success of his campaigns in Portugal and Spain, but he would not divulge one iota of one secret if he did not have to do so or before he had to do so.

So although Joana knew that soon she was going to be working with Captain Blake, without his knowing it, in Salamanca, Spain—behind enemy lines—at the present headquarters of the French army—she had no idea what exactly her task was to be, or his either. It was most annoying—and intriguing.

"You see, Joana," Viscount Wellington had said, smiling at her apologetically, "perhaps after all Captain Blake will prove unsuitable or unwilling for the task I have in mind for him. Or perhaps his wounds have not healed well enough yet, though he has spent a whole winter and spring in the hospital at Lisbon. And perhaps you will change your mind about going back into the danger of Salamanca."

She had opened her mouth to protest, but he had held up a staying hand.

"Let me put that a different way," he had said with another smile. "Perhaps this time I will succeed in persuading you not to go back."

"You know that I would go even if you had no use for me," she had said.

"I hear Wyman is seriously courting you." He had looked at her keenly.

She had waved a careless hand. "And half a dozen other men too if I gave them the slightest encouragement," she had said. "Wartime conditions are just too flattering to a woman's esteem, Arthur. So many starved men and so few eligible women."

"You are being too modest, Joana," he had said. "Too modest by half."

And so she had come all the way to Lisbon to meet Captain Blake and had met him once, very briefly, at the Count of Angeja's ball. And she had known that he had found her attractive and that he had not enjoyed the feeling and had resolved not to see her again. She knew quite enough about men to know exactly what had gone through his mind during their short encounter.

And the man appeared to stay off the streets of Lisbon, she thought with a sigh of frustration as she strolled beside the river the following afternoon, twirling a white parasol above her head with a white-gloved hand and hoping the dust would not sully the hem of her white dress too noticeably. Her free hand rested lightly on the arm of Colonel Lord Wyman and she laughed merrily at some remark a lieutenant had made. Five officers accompanied her on her walk.

But there was not a sight of Captain Blake all afternoon. It was very tiresome, Joana thought. She might as well have stayed in Viseu. But he would come to her reception the following evening. Of that she was sure.

"Shall I send them all packing, Joana?" Lord Wyman asked her, his voice a murmur against her ear. "Shall I have you to myself for a while?"

She smiled at him. "But I cannot bear to be rude, Duncan," she said. "Or to have anyone be rude on my behalf. And it is such a pleasant afternoon for a stroll in company." She twirled her parasol again. The colonel had proposed marriage to her for the second time the evening before. And she was inclined to accept. Oh, yes, she wanted to accept, all right. The thought of being in England where her mother had grown up and where she had spent many happy years—despite her father's protectiveness—was like the thought of heaven. It would be the pinnacle of joy to marry an English lord and to spend the rest of her life where she belonged.

Joana smiled and unwittingly drew a blush to the cheeks of a young ensign who had stepped off the path to allow her and her entourage to pass, staring at her the whole while and only just remembering to salute his superior officers. She was a strange one to talk about belonging. She belonged nowhere.

Her mother had been English and had been married to a Portuguese nobleman before being widowed and remarried. Joana had two half-brothers and a half-sister in Portugal—*had* had, rather, she corrected herself. Only Duarte was left. Her father was French and was currently back in favor in France and a diplomat again—in Vienna at that particular time. He had been sent back to Portugal after their return from England. It had been a brief stay, but during it Joana had been married to Luis, the Marques das Minas. It had been a political marriage—he had been forty-eight to her own nineteen and they had never particularly liked each other. But he had thought it wise to ally himself to a citizen of powerful France and her father had thought it wise that she have ties with some country other than France and that France show itself to be magnanimous to its friends. He had never encouraged her ties with England and her grandparents there. Joana suspected that her parents had not parted on the best of terms.

She and her husband had gone more or less their separate ways until they had done so entirely in 1807, when he had fled Portugal with the royal family on the approach of an invading French army led by Marshal Junot. He had died of a fever during the passage to Brazil and left Joana free. She might have been with him if she had not been away from Lisbon at the time, as she so often was, visiting friends in Coimbra.

And so where did she belong? Joana asked herself as she talked and flirted with four British officers and one Portuguese all at once and yet gave some preferential glances and smiles to the colonel, to whom she might be married one day if fate smiled on her. In France? But her father was not there himself and was not really happy even when he was, it being now a country he hardly recognized and one of which he secretly disapproved. In England? But both her grandparents were now dead and she had never met her aunt and uncle, her mother's sister and brother. In Portugal? But her husband was dead, as well as the elder of her half-brothers and Maria, her half-sister. Only Duarte was left and she was able to see him only rarely. Not nearly as often as she would have wished.

Besides, Portugal was a dangerous country in which to be at that particular time. The French had been there and the British had driven them out. But the French would be back again, and soon too. Despite the great victory at Talavera the summer before, no one had any great hope that the British would be able to put up another fight this year. It was only a matter of time before the French invaded and drove them back and back until the remnant of their army was driven right into the sea. The fate of the Portuguese was not to be thought of when that happened.

Her very wisest move, despite her French identity, Joana thought, would be to accept Duncan's proposal and to have him send her to safety in England without delay.

Except that she could not go to England—yet. She belonged in Portugal until certain matters had been settled. Very few people even knew that she was half English. It was assumed that she was Portuguese. And she

fostered the belief. Even her name—the name her
mother had given her and her father had later changed
to the French Jeanne—she spelled the Portuguese way.
And fortunately she looked almost Portuguese, though
her hair could be darker and her eyes could be a different
color.

Yes, she belonged in Portugal. Because it was in Portugal during the French invasion, when she had been staying with her brother and sister and her brother's wife
and son, that she had been the horrified and terrified
witness of the arrival of the French army at the village
and the large home of her family. She had been in the
attic, looking for a pair of shoes more suited to walks in
the country than the ones she had brought with her. And
she had looked down through a slit in the ill-fitting trap-
door as soldiers smashed with their bayonets and destroyed everything that was not edible or otherwise worth
stuffing in their packs. And as four of them took turns
raping Maria before one of them ran her through with
his bayonet at a signal from an officer. And as another
shot Miguel at point-blank range as he rushed into the
house to defend his family. She had not witnessed the
slaughter, in another room, of Miguel's wife and son.

Duarte had been away from the village at the time.
He had found Joana still cowering in the attic six hours
after the French had passed on.

Yes, she belonged in Portugal. For she had seen the
French soldiers and in particular the officer who had
taken the first turn with Maria and had stood at the door
watching all that happened afterward, a half-smile on his
lips. Joana had seen him. His face was burned on some
part of her brain just behind her eyes. She would know
him anywhere, anytime, and in any guise.

She could not leave Portugal or Spain until she had
seen that face again. Until she had killed the man to
whom it belonged. He would do the killing, Duarte had
always assured her. She could do the identifying, and he
would do the killing. They had, after all, been his full
brother and sister and his brother's family. And Duarte
was now the leader of a band of Ordenanza, the semimil-
itary organization of partisan fighters who harassed the

French from every hill and along every lonely road. Killing wherever and whenever they could.

Duarte would kill the French officer, and perhaps it was only fair that she allow him to do so. But she would not, for all that. It was something she would do herself. Something she had to do herself. She only hoped that the man would not die in battle before she could find him. But she refused to think of such a depressing possibility. She would see him again one day.

And she had an advantage that Duarte did not have. An advantage that almost no one else in Portugal had. She was half-French. She had made a political marriage with a Portuguese nobleman, now unfortunately deceased. As far as any Frenchman knew, she was a loyal daughter of the Revolution, a loyal subject of the Emperor Napoleon.

Hence her not infrequent visits to Spain—wherever the French happened to be—to visit "aunts." Lately the visits had been to Salamanca. And hence her usefulness to Viscount Wellington and his willingness to trust her despite the fact that she was half-French. And hence her refusal ever to let him talk her out of doing anything as dangerous as going behind enemy lines in order to spy for him.

And hence her willingness to go there again and to act, not alone this time, as she usually did, but in some mysterious conjunction with Captain Robert Blake—who was to know nothing about her except that she was the rather fragile and flirtatious and helpless Marquesa das Minas. One of her disguises.

Not only was it not clear where she belonged, Joana thought ruefully. It was not even clear just who she was. Sometimes she was not quite sure herself.

"You are unusually quiet and serious, Joana," the colonel said, looking down into her face.

She smiled up at him and tapped his arm with her gloved hand. "I was merely thinking," she said, "how sad it is that the afternoon must come to an end. Such beautiful weather and such delightful company. Yes, thank you," she said to a pleased and surprised young lieutenant, handing him her parasol and watching him close it with clumsy fingers. "The sun is no longer as strong as it was. I wish to feel it against my face."

Rather than feeling foolish to be carrying such a feminine confection as a lady's parasol on a public footpath, the lieutenant looked about him with some pity on his companions, whose hands were empty of such a sign of the lady's favor.

During the morning of that same day, the surgeon told Captain Blake that he could return to his regiment in one more week if he absolutely insisted. It would be better, of course, he advised his patient, to convalesce through the summer and forget about that year's campaign. After all, he had been severely wounded and had hovered at death's door for several months, what with the effects of the wound and the killing fever that had set in soon afterward.

"Of course," he added, looking at the war-hardened face of the tall veteran standing before him, "I might as well save my breath to cool my tea with, might I not?"

The captain grinned unexpectedly. "Yes, sir," he said.

"Well, one more week," the surgeon said abruptly. "Come to see me then and I shall discharge you, provided there is no relapse in the meanwhile."

But Captain Blake was released sooner than that, much to his relief. The next day a staff officer from Viseu, in central Portugal, brought him a verbal message from headquarters there.

"Captain Blake?" he said when he was joined in the reception room of the hospital. "Yes, of course. I have seen you before, have I not? I trust you have recovered from your wounds?"

"Well enough to be climbing walls and marching across ceilings for exercise," the captain said. "Is there any action at the front yet?"

The officer ignored the question. "You are to present yourself at headquarters within the week for further instructions," he said. "Provided you are well enough, of course."

"Well enough!" The captain made the words an exclamation. "I could fight two duels before breakfast and wonder as I ate why the morning was so dull. Who wants to see me at headquarters?"

The staff officer looked at him uncomprehendingly. "Who ever wants to see anyone at headquarters?" he said.

Captain Blake raised his eyebrows. "The Beau?" he said. "Wellington?"

"Within the week," the officer said. "You must know very well, Captain, that when the commander in chief expresses a wish to speak with a person as soon as possible, he means yesterday or preferably the day before."

"I shall leave at first light tomorrow." The captain grinned.

"Probably not quite so early." The staff officer frowned. "You are to escort the Marquesa das Minas. Do you know her? It is bound to slow you down to have a lady to escort, and his lordship wants you at Viseu without delay. But both orders come from him, so make your own interpretation."

Captain Blake stared blankly at the other man. "I am to escort the marquesa to Viseu?" he said. "*Into* danger and not out? But why me? Why would the Beau order such a thing? Have the Portuguese put some pressure on him to act nursemaid to all their grandest and most helpless ladies?"

The staff officer shrugged. "It is not for me to ask why," he said. "Just make sure you show your face within the week, Captain, and that the lady is safely delivered to Viseu. I have other errands to run."

Captain Blake stood alone in the room frowning after he had been left alone. What the devil? He was wanted at headquarters? Not at the front, where the Light Division was keeping watch along the line of the Coa? Was there some special job for him to do? His mood quickened at the possibility. He had been used for occasional reconnaissance or special-mission work over the years, both in India and in Portugal. His talent with languages was largely responsible. He had always been able to pick up a language easily, even as a boy when his mother had taught him French and Italian. He hated to be in a country and not know the language. And so after ten years of travel with the British armies, he was multilingual.

More than once he had been offered a permanent position with Wellesley's—now Lord Wellington's—reconnaissance team, with those men who penetrated enemy territory and brought or sent back information about troop placements and movements. He had been tempted. The sheer excitement and danger involved had attracted him. But he belonged with his regiment. He was never so much at home as when he was leading his own rifle company in the skirmish line ahead of the infantry.

But occasionally he enjoyed a special mission. He would especially welcome one now after months of pain and weakness and sheer boredom in a Lisbon hospital, far from the men whom he had come to think of almost as his own family. Perhaps his return to active duty was to be more exciting even than he had anticipated.

But his frown deepened as he remembered his other order. At the request of Viscount Wellington he was to escort the Marquesa das Minas to Viseu. Just at a time when he had convinced himself that he would resist the temptation to attend her reception that evening. Just when he had hoped that he could leave and never have to see or think of her again.

Jeanne Morisette. He could no longer feel any of the hurt and pain of the boy he had been almost eleven years before. It would be foolish to hate her because of cruel and heartless words she had spoken as a girl of fifteen. He did not hate her. But he had glimpsed again during his brief encounter with her at the ball the beauty and the charm and the something else he would not put a name to that drew men to her like bees to flowers. And he had sensed the tease in her that enabled her to keep all those men dangling and panting for just one smile or one mark of favor.

And he had known that he could easily become one of those men if he did not watch himself. What more demeaning fate could there be in life than to become the lapdog of a beautiful and heartless tease?

He would not do it. He would not see her again, he had decided.

And of course there was the fact that she was French. He wondered if anyone knew. Lord Ravenhill had been able to tell him only that she had been married to the

Marques das Minas, a courtier highly favored by the Portuguese royal family and one who had fled with them.

Was the fact that she was French of any significance? he wondered. Her father had after all been a royalist émigré in England. Perhaps he had never returned to France. Captain Blake did not know. Besides, her mother had been English, if he remembered correctly. Her nationality might be of no importance whatsoever. But she had changed her name. She was now Joana, not Jeanne. In order to disguise a truth she preferred to hide?

And yet the Beau had decreed that Captain Blake escort the woman to Viseu, a journey of several days—for a woman traveling by carriage anyway.

Hell and damnation! Captain Blake thought with sudden anger. He filled the empty room with a few other more satisfying oaths. But they changed nothing. He was to spend the next few days dancing attendance on a woman he would rather never see again. For several days he was to be subjected to her beauty and her charm and that something else that he was very much afraid he might not be able to resist if she decided to unleash it on him.

He had better put in an appearance at her reception after all, he supposed, in order to make some arrangements for the following day. He wondered if she had yet been informed of the glad tidings and how she would feel about having to accept his escort.

Probably nothing at all. Probably she would treat him, as she treated any man, as her servant who owed her service and homage as her right. It angered him that his escort would probably mean nothing more than that to her.

And it angered him even more that it mattered to him. Bloody hell!

Yes, he would certainly come to her reception now, Joana thought with some satisfaction. Though there was a little annoyance too after Lord Wellington's messenger had left her. She would have liked to discover if he would have come anyway—she was almost convinced that he would. And she had looked forward to persuading him herself to escort her back to Viseu. It would have been a challenge she could have enjoyed.

But Arthur had not left anything to chance—or to a woman's wiles. He had simply sent an order to Captain Blake.

Well, at least, Joana thought, he would come. And she paused in the act of dabbing perfume behind one ear. She had had a purpose in making his acquaintance, a purpose in inviting him to her reception—indeed, he was the reason for the reception—and a reason for wishing to spend a few days in company with him on the road to Viseu. It surely did not matter how he was persuaded to fall in with her plans. Did it?

He was not, after all, one of her numerous flirts. Anything but. The man as she remembered him—tall, almost shabby in his dress, awkward in his manners, his face marred by the scars of battle, his blue eyes direct and almost hostile, his blond hair cropped close to his head—was not the sort of man with whom she would think of dallying.

And yet his very differentness from her usual type of suitor, his total differentness from Luis, was in itself a challenge. She shrugged and got to her feet. That was not a thought to be pursued.

And yet she looked forward to the evening, she thought as she glanced at herself critically in the looking glass one more time. She was not especially fond of the Marquesa das Minas. She found her rather insipid, rather a bore. Rather like her clothes—all white, always white. She was not sure quite why she had decided to dress the marquesa in unrelieved white after her year of mourning had come to an end. Perhaps the contrast with black? Perhaps the image of helpless fragility that she wished the marquesa to project?

However it was, she always wore white as the marquesa. It was perhaps a blessing, she thought with a private smile shared only with the looking glass, that she was not only or always the Marquesa das Minas.

But perhaps the boredom of her life was not entirely her fault either, Joana thought. Perhaps all the men who worshiped her were more to blame. What challenge was there in worship? What pleasure was there to be derived from compliments that were always so constant and so lavish? What pride was there to be gained from accepting homage, always homage?

Sometimes she longed for more. Her eyes glazed, and she gazed into the looking glass without seeing herself. What was it she longed for? Love? Love was for youth, for young persons who knew nothing of life. Love was for memory and bittersweet nostalgia. Love could not live on into adulthood, just as young lovers sometimes did not. And so she must make do with what remained—with homage that frequently bored her.

She looked guiltily at her image. There must surely be thousands of women who would think heaven had come if they knew just one small fraction of the worship that the marquesa found tedious. But sometimes she longed for a man who would not treat her like a fragile doll, like an angel escaped from heaven.

Perhaps Captain Robert Blake would prove to be such a man, she thought hopefully. Perhaps he would not succumb to her charms. Perhaps he would look on her with dislike and even contempt. Perhaps he would be totally indifferent to her despite that look that had been in his eyes at the count's ball.

Perhaps there would be some challenge in the days or perhaps weeks ahead while she was trapped in the disguise of the Marquesa das Minas.

Joana turned away from the looking glass and descended the stairs to face her reception with a renewed spring in her step.

5

HE came late. She had laughed and talked and drunk and eaten with her guests, outwardly as gay as she ever was in company. The level and quality of the noise about her assured her that her reception was a great success and would be talked about for days to come. And yet inside she seethed. How dare he be late! And perhaps after all he did not mean to come at all, but would merely arrive at some time the next morning expecting her to be standing in the gateway of her courtyard surrounded by her baggage, meekly awaiting his arrival and escort.

How dare he! She was furious with him and tapped an artillery captain on the arm with her white fan and told him, smiling up at him from beneath lowered lashes, not to be impertinent. The man flushed and was pleased. It was so easy to please men.

And then he was there, standing in the doorway of her salon, looking tall and uncomfortable and rather as if he were attending his own funeral. Even across the room she could see the shabby jacket, the hair even shorter than she remembered, the crooked nose, the scar slashing across it and one cheek. And she wondered why she had thought so much about him in the past two days. He was not a handsome man. Perhaps before war had taken its toll on his face he might have been, but no longer. But then, of course, he probably had not been such an overwhelmingly attractive man before his years as a soldier, either.

The marquesa turned her head away before their eyes could meet and informed the amazed and delighted artillery captain that he might escort her to the tables and fill her plate for her. She smiled at him and set a white-gloved hand on his arm. Captain Robert Blake, she thought, might seek her out. She would not seek him.

And yet when an hour had passed and he still stood close to the door, having spoken only briefly with a few of his brother officers, Joana was forced to find an excuse to be strolling past him on the arm of Colonel Lord Wyman and to notice him with a lifting of the eyebrows.

"Ah, Captain Blake," she said, drawing the colonel to a halt. "You came. I am pleased."

He bowed his head to her curtly and she wondered if he knew anything at all about courtly manners. Probably not. He had risen from the ranks. Perhaps he had been a tradesman's son in England or a vagabond or a prisoner. Perhaps he was from the slums of some city and had enlisted merely for the sake of survival—or a survival of sorts. Enlisting as a private soldier hardly brought an assurance of security with it. At all events, he could be no gentleman.

And she smiled inwardly at his discomfort and wished she could add to it. She wished there were dancing so that she could lure him out onto the floor to reveal his awkwardness and his ignorance of the steps. And at the same time she marveled at the spitefulness of her own thoughts. What had the man done to her to make her want to humiliate him?

Perhaps it was that he looked at her very directly with those blue eyes, which were not quite hostile but not quite friendly either. Or perhaps it was that she was ashamed of the fact that he stirred her senses as no man—certainly not Luis—had ever done before.

She was ashamed of the fact that she found a man who had come up from the ranks—a nobody—sexually attractive.

"Duncan." She released the colonel's arm and patted it. "I must leave you for a while. I have business to discuss with Captain Blake."

"Business, Joana?" The colonel looked from her to the rifleman in some surprise.

"Captain Blake has been assigned to escort me to Viseu," she said. "We will be leaving tomorrow. Did I forget to tell you?"

"Tomorrow?" he said. "But you have been here less than a week, Joana."

"My aunt is sick again," she said with a sigh, "and has summoned me. It is tiresome, but she is my aunt, you know, and has been kind to me in the past."

The colonel looked as if he would cheerfully dump her aunt in the middle of the Atlantic Ocean if he could.

"But why Captain Blake?" he asked. "You know that you had but to say the word, Joana, and I would have arranged to take you myself."

"I know." She patted his arm again. And she felt guilty at the knowledge that she was glad it would be the captain and not Duncan who would be escorting her to Viseu. Duncan was, after all, her ticket to heaven, her passport to a life in England. And she was fond of him. "But you have your duties here and Captain Blake is going to Viseu anyway. Besides, Arthur has arranged it all."

"Wellington?" The colonel frowned.

"And who is going to countermand his orders?" she said with a shrug. "It is all very tiresome, but I shall return as soon as I may—to Lisbon and to this room. Have some champagne waiting for me?"

He bowed and looked with some hostility at Captain Blake, who had stood silently watching them the whole time.

"Captain? Shall we go somewhere quieter?" She might have swept past him, led the way to her private writing room. He would, of course, have followed, and would perhaps have been more comfortable to be treated almost like a servant. But she could not resist embarrassing him. She looked at him with slightly raised eyebrows, waited just long enough to see him stiffen with uncertainty, and then lifted her hand. "Your arm?"

He raised it jerkily so that she might place her hand lightly along it. She was surprised by the rock hardness of his muscles, which she could feel even though she put little pressure on his sleeve. One might have expected them to be wasted by injury and long convalescence and soft living. His sleeve, she noticed, was not quite frayed at the wrist.

She led him to her writing room and closed the door

behind her. She did not ring for a chaperone. Matilda would be angry with her but would know better than to scold too loudly or too long. The room opened into a small private courtyard, lit by an almost full moon. But the glass doors were closed, it being a chilly evening for late June.

"I came to ask when you will be ready to leave in the morning, ma'am," he said. Nothing about her convenience or doing himself the honor. No courtly bows or appreciative smiles. Only that look far back in his eyes that she had seen there two nights before at the ball.

But as she looked at him, she had the feeling again of having met him before. Except that it was not that, she realized with a jolt. It was that he reminded her . . . No, it must be the blond hair, the blue eyes, something else indefinable, because really he was nothing like him at all. But perhaps there would have been a real resemblance if the other had lived, if he had not died before his eighteenth birthday.

"Only for that reason?" she asked him. "Not because I invited you to come and because this is *the* social occasion to be attending this evening? There are many disappointed British and Portuguese officers who did not receive an invitation."

He looked back at her silently, his expression unsoftened.

"What may I offer you to drink, Captain?" she asked, crossing the room to a sideboard.

"Nothing, ma'am," he said. "Thank you," he added almost as an afterthought.

"Lemonade?" Her eyes mocked him.

"No, thank you, ma'am."

She walked away from the sideboard. She poured nothing for herself.

"As early as you wish, Captain," she said. "Dawn?"

"It will not be too early for you?" he asked.

She smiled fleetingly. "It will probably be late," she said. "I shall doubtless leave directly from my party. Anything after that, after I had taken some rest, would doubtless be too late. Dawn will be suitable, Captain."

He bowed and looked as if he would take his leave if he could just find a way of doing so gracefully. But she was not ready to dismiss him yet.

"You have a knowledge of many languages, Captain?" she said.

He looked surprised. "I like to be able to communicate with the people about me when in a foreign country," he said. "How did you know that?"

"I make a practice, Captain," she said, "of knowing something of my servants . . . and my escorts. Your knowledge of Indian language enabled you to do some spying work for the British government in India, and you did some here too two years ago when Lord Wellington was first in Portugal. It must be a fascinating life."

He looked uncomfortable. "My place is with my company of the Ninety-fifth Rifles, ma'am," he said. "Leading them against the enemy skirmishers—the *tirailleurs* and *voltigeurs*—is a fascinating life."

"Ah, yes," she said, "you are the simple soldier at heart, it seems. And you were one of those riflemen, Captain, before you donned a sword." She looked down at the curved cavalry saber at his side and was somehow not surprised to note that it gleamed and exhibited none of the shabbiness of his uniform.

"And still am, ma'am," he said. "I still carry a rifle into battle as well as my sword."

"Ah," she said, "so you still like slumming, Captain." She watched his lips tighten and his already firm jawline tense.

"And you feel capable of protecting me during the long journey from here to Viseu?" she asked.

"There is no danger, ma'am." Was that contempt in his voice? she wondered. "The French are still across the border in Spain. All the forces of England and Portugal—the best troops in Europe—will be between you and danger."

"Not to mention the Ordenanza," she said.

"The Portuguese militia?" he said. "Yes, they do a good job, ma'am, of harassing the French and keeping them back, as do the Spanish guerrilleros. You will be quite safe. And I shall protect you from any incidental dangers of the road."

"I am sure you will, Captain," she said. She smiled inwardly. Clearly the man was less than delighted by an assignment that a dozen or more officers of her acquaintance would have killed for. "How could I not feel safe in the care of a man who almost single-handedly held back the French who would have destroyed the British forces during the retreat to La Coruña under Sir John Moore's generalship over a year ago and who did something very similar just last year during the retreat from Talavera?"

He shifted his weight from one foot to the other and looked warily at her. "I do what I must to protect the lives of my comrades, ma'am," he said, "and to destroy the enemy. It is my job."

"And one you do exceedingly well, by all accounts," she said. "Do you enjoy killing, Captain Blake?"

"No one enjoys killing, ma'am," he said. "It is something that, as a soldier, one must do. It is satisfying to kill the enemy during battle. Never enjoyable."

"Ah," she said. "Interesting. So if I were threatened during our journey to Viseu, Captain, you would kill for me if necessary, but you would not enjoy rendering me such a service?"

He did not immediately reply and her eyes mocked him. How could he answer truthfully without appearing ungallant?

"I would do it, ma'am, because it would be my duty to protect you," he said. "I will do my duty. You need have no fear."

"Duty," she said with a sigh. "It would not be your pleasure to protect me?"

That look was there in his eyes again for a moment, the one that could quicken her breathing, the one that challenged her to break him, to make of him merely another abject, easily manipulated follower, like many of the men then proceeding to get themselves intoxicated and merry in her salon. The look that left her hoping he could not be broken. But it was gone in a flash.

"I enjoy my job, ma'am," he said. "To me duty is pleasure."

She almost laughed. Captain Robert Blake might be no gentleman, but he would make an admirable politician or diplomat. It was a masterly answer.

"You are keeping me from my guests, Captain," she said in order to have a little revenge on the only man to have bested her in the game of flirtation—though of course he had not been flirting.

He looked immediately uncomfortable again. "I shall take my leave then, ma'am," he said, "and return for you at dawn tomorrow."

"You will not stay longer?" she asked, walking past him to the door and pausing for him to notice that she waited for him to open it. "You need your beauty sleep, Captain?"

He noticed what she was waiting for and strode toward her. He reached past her to open the door—she had deliberately stood in his way—almost brushing her breast with one hand. He did not answer her question and she mentally scored one point for herself.

"But of course," she said, "if you are to protect me from all the dangers of the road, you must be alert. You are dismissed, Captain."

She stood and watched him before reentering the salon, from which the sounds of boisterous merriment signaled that the more advanced stage of the party had begun since they had left the room. He bowed curtly and strode to the front door into the main courtyard, barely halting long enough for a servant to open it for him. He had said nothing to her beyond a bare good night and did not look back.

Joana smiled in self-mockery at her disappointment. But then, she would see him again at dawn, she reminded herself. And would be as safe with him in the coming days, she suspected, as she would be if a whole squadron of heavy cavalry surrounded her carriage. As if she needed his protection or anyone else's. Dear Arthur. Sometimes he could be quite amusing. But of course the purpose of her journey in company with Captain Blake was not just for her protection, she reminded herself.

The Marquesa das Minas turned toward the door into the salon and prepared to be sociable.

He arrived at the marquesa's palacio when dawn was little more than a suggestion in the eastern sky. He was in a sullen mood purely because he knew that only one small fact held him from an exultant mood. He had been freed from the hospital and the surgeon's care and he was feeling fit after months of convalescence and weeks of private exercising and swordplay. He was leaving Lisbon and heading into the wild hills farther north and toward the bulk of the British and Portuguese armies. Soon he would either join his regiment on the Coa with the certain knowledge that soon the French summer campaign would begin and he would be in the very front lines, or be sent on some challenging mission by Wellington and know all the exhilaration of being in danger with only his strength and his wits to keep him alive.

He could have been in an exultant mood. But there was that one small fact—that one small lady with whom he was to spend the next week. It would surely take them all of a week to reach Viseu, though he could have got there far sooner had he been alone. And Wellington had wanted to talk with him as soon as possible, his staff officer had said the day before. But Wellington had also directed that he escort the Marquesa das Minas. Lord Wellington, of course, had to be careful always to defer to the sentiments of his Portuguese hosts even though he was there risking his life and the lives of thousands of Englishmen in order to save their hides.

She was probably still in bed, Captain Blake thought, hoping that she was, hoping that he would have a definite grievance to excuse his mood. Her reception had not lasted all night. The house was quiet. He would doubtless have to wait while the lady got herself out of bed and dressed and ready to face the world and breakfasted. And by that time it would probably be as well to have luncheon before they set out on their way. They would be fortunate to be well clear of Lisbon before dark. They would be fortunate to reach Viseu within two weeks.

Captain Blake had succeeded in whipping up a mood of sullenness into one of active resentment against the fate that had made him into a nursemaid. He hammered none too gently on the outer door of the *palacio* courtyard. Probably her servants would have to be roused before they in turn could rouse her.

But the door opened almost immediately and all was bustle and activity in the courtyard beyond it. A white-paneled coach, looking more like a coronation coach than a carriage fit for travel along the roads and among the hills of Portugal, stood with its doors open to reveal luxurious golden upholstery. The four horses, which stood obediently in their traces and yet snorted and pawed the ground in their impatience to be moving, were all pure white with golden plumes and golden ribbons plaited into their manes.

Captain Blake scowled as he rode his horse into the courtyard. Jesus, he thought, he was to be ringmaster to a bloody circus. He nodded to the servants and the plump woman dressed all in black who was directing the loading of one small valise on top of several trunks tied to the back of the carriage.

"Good morning," he said curtly in their own language.

And then he saw that he had done not only her servants an injustice in his mind but the marquesa too. She was standing in the doorway, he saw as soon as he had ridden to a place where the carriage no longer obstructed his view of it, looking as bright and fresh as if it were the middle of the morning and there had been nothing to do all night but sleep. She turned her head and smiled at him.

He felt that growingly familiar churning somewhere in the region of his stomach. And the equally familiar hostility. She was dressed—as always, it seemed—in white, from the hat worn at a jaunty angle, its large soft feather curling about her ear and touching her chin, to the supple and dainty white leather boots peeping from beneath her carriage dress. The only part of her apparel that was not white was the gold embroidery on her frogged jacket and the gold fringes on its epaulets.

She looked as fragile as a single swan's feather and as beautiful as . . . Well, he had been of a poetic turn of mind once upon a time. But no longer. She could not be more unsuitably dressed for a rugged journey if she had deliberately studied to be. Christ, it would take them a month.

She was everything that was exquisite and expensive— and trivial. And he had once held her and kissed her and believed her protestations of love. Poor foolish young lad—he looked back on his former self with a tender sort of pity, as if he had been someone else entirely. It was hard to believe that that boy had been he and that that life had been his. That life of privilege and degradation.

He swung down from his saddle and found that his loins were aching for Jeanne Morisette as she had become in almost eleven years. He clamped his teeth together in self-contempt.

"Good morning, Captain." Even her voice was seductive—low-pitched yet clear. He could not remember Jeanne's voice being so. "I thought perhaps you had overslept."

And mocking. She had mocked him the night before and he had felt like a gauche and awkward boy, terrified of saying or doing the wrong thing. Feeling rather like the proverbial bull in a china shop.

"Good morning, ma'am," he said even more curtly than he had spoken to her servants a few moments before. "You are ready to leave?"

"As you see." She held out her gloved hands to the sides and smiled at him. "I have my carriage and my horses and my baggage. And now I have you to protect me from all the dangers of the road." She slanted a smile up at him from beneath lowered lashes. "And Matilda to protect me from you." She indicated the plump female in black.

"You are quite safe from me, ma'am," he said, "I do assure you."

For a moment he was not quite sure what he was intended to do with the slim hand she extended to him. But before he could make an utter idiot of himself by taking it and kissing it—he turned hot with discomfort at the realization that he had been about to do that—he understood the lady wished to be handed into her carriage.

He took her hand and looked down at it as he led her to the open door of the carriage. It was almost lost in his own—small and slender. And warm. It burned him through the white glove so that he wanted to snatch his own away. But she was talking.

"I would guess, Captain," she said, "that your escorting me to Viseu is only a small part of your assignment?"

"Ma'am?" he said.

"I do not imagine that Arthur has directed you to escort me merely for the sake of your health," she said. "You are too valuable to the army to be wasted on such a trivial duty, surely?"

Hell and damnation, he thought, why had Wellington not assigned this task to a man born and bred to gallantry? He was aware that she had given him his cue to bow and simper and lavish her with pretty speeches. She was begging to be flattered and adored and worshiped.

"I am rejoining my regiment, ma'am," he said. "I am pleased if I can be of some service to you."

"Pleased." Her eyes laughed at him as she paused at the foot of the carriage steps. "But your regiment is not at Viseu, Captain. Are not most of the riflemen watching the border?"

"I believe so, ma'am," he said.

"Perhaps you go to Viseu because Arthur is there, then," she said. "Viscount Wellington, that is. Perhaps he has some . . . special mission for you?" It was a question.

He was suddenly reminded forcefully that she was French, and dredged his mind for some pretty words. He was not about to be interrogated by a lovely and wily woman, especially one who was half-French.

"Perhaps he does, ma'am," he said, bowing over her hand. "And perhaps that special mission will be accomplished when I deliver you safe and sound to your friends in Viseu."

"Ah." She laughed outright. "I understand, Captain. But it was nicely said. How far do we go today?"

"I thought perhaps Montachique," he said.

"Montachique?" She raised her eyebrows. "We could go there for an afternoon stroll, Captain. I was merely hoping you would not try to push farther than Torres Vedras. I have friends there."

He felt somewhat cheered as he handed her into the carriage and watched her seat herself beside her plump chaperone. A dove beside a hawk. An angel beside the devil. And he was growing feathers for brains. Unless her words were mere bravado, perhaps after all she was willing to travel and would not forever be calling for stops along the way.

"Very well, ma'am," he said. "Torres Vedras it will

be for tonight. You will inform me if you tire before then and I will make other arrangements.''

She looked at him and laughed, the sound one of pure amusement.

And he was relieved about one other thing too, he thought as he closed the door of the carriage, stepped forward to confer for a moment with her coachman, and mounted his horse again. She had friends with whom she could stay at Torres Vedras. He would not, then, at least for the first night, have to procure her rooms at a public inn.

His scowl returned as he followed the white fairy-tale coach on its slow progress out through the archway from the courtyard and onto the streets of Lisbon.

6

"Ah," Joana said, leaning forward in her seat and peering out through the carriage window, "a royal send-off, Matilda. Do you suppose Captain Blake will be annoyed? I had the distinct impression that he was less than pleased at the sight of my white carriage and horses. He expects nothing but troubles and delays from them, merely because they are white. Do you think he disapproves of me?"

But her companion was given no chance to reply. The marquesa was lowering the window and smiling and extending a hand.

"Duncan," she said. "You have come to see me on my way. And Jack." She removed her hand from Colonel Lord Wyman's and placed it in Major Hanbridge's. "How wonderful."

Captain Blake, she saw with some satisfaction, was scowling at the necessity of drawing his horse to a halt even before they had left Lisbon.

"I have time to ride only a short distance with you, Joana," the colonel said. "As far as the pass, maybe. Hanbridge, the lucky dog, will be able to accompany you all the way to Torres Vedras."

"Will he?" she said. "What is at Torres Vedras, Jack?"

He shrugged. "Unimportant business, Joana," he said. "A mere nuisance, except that it gives me the opportunity to ride beside your carriage."

"Ah," she said, "military matters. I understand. Duncan, do give my coachman the signal to move on. Captain Blake is looking stern and unamused." She turned her most charming smile on her official escort. He did not smile back.

"And so," she said to Matilda, sitting back in her seat again, "the tedium of the journey is to be relieved at least for a while."

And normally it *was* a tedious journey, along a winding road and up hills and down hills. But she had no intention of letting this one be as dull as the journey from Viseu had been no more than a week before. She had planned that already. Now her plan was certain of success.

And so when they stopped for luncheon, she sighed and looked wistful. "Men are so fortunate," she said, "not to be obliged to travel everywhere in stuffy carriages. How I would love to be on horseback, feeling the fresh air against my face, smelling the orange groves and the vineyards. How lovely it would be to ride over the Montachique Pass." She rested her elbow on the table and set her chin in her hand and stared off into the middle distance.

"If I had had the forethought to bring a lady's saddle with me," Jack Hanbridge said gallantly, "you might have ridden my horse, Joana, while I rode in your carriage."

She smiled dazzlingly at him.

"I shall take you up before me, Joana," Lord Wyman said, "so that you may ride over the pass."

"How sweet of you, Duncan," she said, touching her fingers briefly to the back of his hand. "But you do not have the time to ride over the pass. You have to get back to Lisbon."

"I wish I did not," he said. And then he turned to the silent member of their party, as she had known he would. "You must take her up, Blake."

He was not pleased. She could see that. He was not going to be easy to flirt with—a thought that she found stimulating. She looked at him and her eyes laughed at him. The wistfulness was gone.

"You would be more comfortable in your carriage, ma'am," he said.

"But comfort can be tedious," she said.

"Then it is settled," Lord Wyman said briskly. "I must be on my way, Joana, though I hate to leave you."

And so a mere ten minutes later Joana had had her

way—as she always did—though no one seemed particularly pleased about it except her, she thought. Duncan had been dejected over having to take his leave of her, Matilda was sitting in disapproving silence in the carriage, Jack was berating himself as a slowtop for not thinking of suggesting that he take her up before him, and Captain Blake was merely looking displeased.

"You wish me to the devil," she said to him, "so that you could ride without delay to rejoin your precious regiment, Captain. Though I do not believe that is to be your destination, is it?"

But he was not to be drawn on that point, she discovered approvingly. No man who was an experienced spy should fall into the type of trap she was trying to set for him.

She liked the sensation of riding up before his saddle, his powerfully muscled thighs on either side of her, his arms circling her loosely as he held to the reins. But her attention was not all on the man with whom she rode. She looked all about her, and she carried on a bright conversation with Jack Hanbridge, since Captain Blake was nothing of a conversationalist.

"Oh," she said when they were high among the crags of the Montachique Pass and she could see downward, "the orange groves are all black." She had come to Lisbon by the Mafra road the week before.

"A fire, I believe," Major Hanbridge said.

"But in more than one orchard, Jack?" she asked.

"Ah," he said. "An arsonist, I gather."

"How strange," she said, and she began to look about her with renewed interest. The stony crags of the pass were wild and peaked. And yet a few of them had the appearance of an almost manmade smoothness, particularly those that descended to the road. And some looked almost as if they had been leveled off on top.

"One might stand at the top and throw stones down on poor travelers," she said with a laugh, "without any fear of being caught. The rocks next to the road are sheer."

"And so they are," Major Hanbridge said. "Nature's peculiarity, Joana. But you need not fear. I have not heard of brigands in this area. We should increase our pace, perhaps, Bob. Storms have a habit of hitting the pass unexpectedly."

Joana laughed. "There is not a cloud in the sky, Jack."

But Captain Blake obediently nudged his horse to a slightly faster pace. He too had been having a good look about him. And she looked up into his face to find him regarding Jack Hanbridge from narrowed and shrewd eyes.

"We will stop at the next convenient spot, sir," he said, "so that the marquesa can resume her place in her carriage."

Joana said nothing. She had a little skill of her own at observing carefully. She could recognize peculiarities at a glance. More important, she could detect atmosphere with some ease. Jack wanted them through the pass without further delay, and Captain Blake had picked up the message just as she had, and was immediately obedient to a superior officer. She glanced down once more at the blackened orange groves and over her shoulder at the smooth, sheer sides of rock. And she felt an inward shiver. Of fear? Of excitement? She was not certain which.

Joana traveled the rest of the way to Torres Vedras in her carriage. And there Major Hanbridge took his leave of her, and Captain Blake took himself off to an inn after seeing her safely to the house of her friends.

She spent a pleasant evening there, though they had mainly only worries to talk about. The old Moorish castle and the chapel of Saint Vincent, standing on the twin towers of hills that had given the town its name, were being fortified by gangs of peasants, as were other towns round about. But how could fortifying an old castle and a monastery hold back the might of the French armies from Lisbon if the British and Portuguese forces could not do it? It would be all over before the summer was out. The French would be back in Lisbon and the English would be drowning at sea. And pity help the Portuguese who lay in the path of the French armies coming from Salamanca to Lisbon.

It was all very depressing. Joana was in the habit of trusting Viscount Wellington, as she told her friends. But there was, of course, only so much one man could do.

But she thought privately of the arsonist and his blackened groves and of the strangely sheer sides of the normally craggy rocks beside the road through the Montachique Pass. And she thought of Major Hanbridge being fearful of a storm on a perfectly clear day, and of the strange fact that he—an engineering officer—had business in Torres Vedras. And she thought of the penetrating look Captain Blake had leveled on him.

Perhaps there was something, she thought. Perhaps the situation was not after all as hopeless as it seemed. But she kept her counsel. Like Captain Blake, she too could refuse to be drawn when it seemed perhaps wiser to remain silent.

They reached Obidos the following day. They could possibly have traveled farther, but the marquesa had a villa there. Besides, Captain Blake thought, she was probably tired after two days of travel, though to give her her due, she had not complained and had always succeeded in looking fresh—and lovely, of course—whenever he had handed her out of the carriage, and even after that rather dusty ride over the pass. And she had always had a smile for him. And the white of her clothes had remained unsullied by dirt or the incidental smudges of travel.

The medieval town of Obidos rose majestically above the surrounding vineyards, its rust-colored walls topped by the many-colored roofs of its white houses and by the square castle. Captain Blake had not seen the town before. It was sad to think what fate would befall it if the French indeed succeeded in pressing this far into Portugal. And yet the signs that the people—and perhaps more than just the people, too, if he had interpreted correctly the appearance of the Montachique Pass and Hanbridge's agitation as they rode through it—were preparing to defend it, which had been so evident between Lisbon and Torres Vedras the day before, were absent here. The town basked sleepily in the late-afternoon sun, as if its inhabitants had never heard of war, as if its castle had been built only to look picturesque.

The streets of the town were narrow and steep and winding. The marquesa's carriage moved slowly until it

turned sharply to pass through the arched doorway into
the courtyard of a cheerful white villa that fronted on
the street. Captain Blake followed it through, ducking
his head beneath the arch, which was not, after all, as
low as it looked. He dismounted and waited to help the
lady from her carriage.

"Captain," she said, setting a white-gloved hand in his
as he helped her to descend. She looked as fresh and
cheerful as she had when they had left Torres Vedras
that morning. "Welcome to Obidos. You must stay here
tonight."

He cringed from the thought. He would never be comfortable in what was obviously an opulently appointed
villa. And never comfortable under the same roof as the
marquesa.

"Thank you, ma'am," he said, moving to one side as
the coachman handed her companion from the carriage
and she bustled inside the house, "but it would not be
fitting. I shall find an inn."

"And spend half the night fighting off fleas and other
vermin?" she said with a shrug. "But the choice is yours.
Come to dinner at least. You really must. I have only
Matilda to dine with otherwise, and we said all that was
to be said to each other long years ago. You must come
and entertain us with your conversation, Captain." Her
eyes mocked him in an expression he was becoming familiar with.

And she had him at a disadvantage again, he realized.
Almost any gentleman of his acquaintance doubtless had
a whole arsenal of excuses that might be dipped into on
such an occasion. He had no wish to dine with the marquesa and her silent, disapproving companion. And of
course he had no conversation to share with them. She
knew that very well. And he did not doubt that that was
the very reason why she had invited him. She seemed to
delight in setting him up to look like a big dumb ox. But
he could think of not a single excuse.

"Thank you, ma'am." He nodded curtly and turned
away to his horse. But a thought struck him, and he
turned back again. "May I escort you to the house?"

She smiled slowly. She loved to observe his not knowing what was quite good etiquette. "I believe I can walk

alone between here and the house without being set upon by brigands or worse, Captain," she said. "Until later, then. Come early. Come in one hour's time. Not a moment later. I hate to be kept waiting."

He bowed awkwardly and turned away. And felt her eyes on him as he mounted and guided his horse across the courtyard and through the doorway out onto the steep, narrow street.

Joana watched him go and smiled to herself. Any other man she knew would have taken advantage of every possible opportunity that had presented itself during the past two days. He would have ridden in the carriage and tied his horse behind, or at least ridden alongside the carriage and encouraged her to drive with the window down. He would have taken her up before him on his horse more times than the one that had been forced upon him. He would have tried to wangle an invitation from her friends at Torres Vedras. He would have leapt at the chance to stay here at her villa tonight. He would not have looked as if he were drowning in quicksand when she had invited him to dinner.

But Captain Blake was not any other man, unfortunately. Oh, and fortunately too, she thought, her smile growing more amused. She might have saved herself the trouble of coming all the way from Viseu and of returning with his escort, for all she had accomplished so far. Was there a more silent or a more morose man—or a more attractive one—in existence? She was going to have to do something very positive and very fast if the worth of this tedious trip was to be salvaged. She walked purposefully toward the house.

"Matilda," she called to her companion, who was fussing over their bags in the hall, "leave that to the servants. You are banished. Totally and completely. I have not forgotten, you see, that you have a sister in Obidos and that you see far too little of her. You are to take yourself off to visit her now—without delay at all—and you are not to reappear before dawn tomorrow, at which time I have no doubt Captain Blake will be riding into the courtyard chafing at the bit ready to leave."

Matilda argued. Her ladyship would need to have hot water ordered for a bath, and refreshments brought up.

And it would be unseemly for her to spend the evening alone in the house, with only the servants for company. Besides . . .

"Besides nothing," Joana said, waving a dismissive hand. "I shall have my bath and refreshments whether you are here or not, Matilda. And I would be a very dull companion for you this evening, since I am weary and intend to retire early with a book. So there. Go. Now." She smiled her most charming smile and felt only a twinge of guilt when Matilda showered her with gratitude and went. After all, she was no girl to be needing chaperones wherever she went.

Even though, she thought as she made her way to her room and the bath she longed for, she had never entertained a man alone before. Except for Luis, of course, but that did not count. She had always considered that there was safety in numbers. The trouble with Captain Blake was that if there were anyone else present but her and him, he would be likely to fade away into the furniture. He would not be able to do that with her alone. She would not allow it.

She smiled at the prospect. And felt a little breathless with apprehension. She was not at all sure that the captain could be counted upon to behave predictably in a given situation. But then, maybe she did not wish him to do so.

There was no sign of either dinner or her chaperone when he returned to the villa a little more than an hour after taking his leave of her. Only the marquesa, clad inevitably in white, her dress softly flowing, her pelisse embroidered with silver thread, a bonnet swinging from one hand. She was in the low hall of the villa, looking at a painting. She smiled at him.

"Ah, Captain," she said, "you are late. Deliberately so? It is too early for dinner and the weather is too fine to be missed and Obidos is too pretty a town not to be viewed. You are to take me walking, if you please."

"Where is your companion?" he asked.

"Probably talking nonstop with her sister, a niece or a nephew on each knee," she said. "I do not know. I am not her keeper. And don't scowl at me, Captain, as if

I were a naughty schoolgirl about to escape from her chaperone. I will be safe with you, will I not? Arthur recommended you."

He stiffened. "You will be safe with me, ma'am," he said.

"Oh, bother." She laughed lightly. "Shall we go? I shall take you up onto the town walls. There is a lookout path extending right around them. And flights of steep stone steps leading up to it. I hope you have recovered sufficiently from your wounds not to get too breathless."

She had set out to charm him. That was very clear to him. She smiled at him and chattered to him and clung to his arm as they walked. For reasons of her own she was trying to make him her latest conquest. Perhaps it was necessary to the woman to make every man her slave. He looked about him and tried to ignore his awareness of the small, delicately perfumed female at his side. And he wished he had brought Beatriz with him. She had wanted to come, to follow the army about as so many women did. He had said no because he was Captain Blake, not Private Blake. But he wished now he had said yes.

The lookout path provided them with a magnificent view down into the town and out across the surrounding countryside.

She unlinked her arm from his and leaned her arms along the outer wall and gazed outward. She looked as delicate as a girl, he thought—that girl who had thrown her arms wide at the top of the ruined castle on his father's land and turned her face to the wind. But when she turned her head to look at him now, he was reminded afresh that she was now a woman, with all a woman's allure.

"Did you know," she said, "that centuries and centuries ago, when Dom Dinis was passing through here with his young bride and she admired these ramparts twining like ribbon about the white houses inside, he made her a present of the town? And from that time on Obidos was always the wedding present given to Portuguese queens? Did you know that?" She laughed. "And do you feel enriched by the knowledge?"

"History is always interesting," he said, watching the breeze blow the ribbons of her bonnet.

"Do you not think it a wonderfully romantic story?" she asked. "Would you give such a present to the woman you loved, Captain?"

"On a captain's pay," he said, "I could not give anything so lavish."

"Ah," she said, "but would you want to? What would you give the woman you loved?"

She was still looking at him over her shoulder, her eyes sweeping over him in a manner that was clearly meant to make him uncomfortable, and was succeeding. He took a few steps forward and stood beside her at the wall. He gazed out at the lowering sun.

"A length of real ribbon perhaps," he said.

She laughed softly. "Only ribbon?" she said. "It must be that you do not love her enough."

"The ribbon would be beneath her chin when she wore her bonnet, and tied in a bow beneath her ear," he said. "A part of me would be that close to her." He had not thought of love for a long time.

"Oh, well done," she said. "You have exonerated yourself."

"Or a star perhaps," he said. "Perhaps a whole cluster of stars. They are free and bright and would always be there for her."

"She is a fortunate woman," she said, looking sideways up into his face. "Is she Beatriz?"

He looked down at her, startled.

"I told you that I like to know something about the men who are my servants or escorts," she said. "Do you love her?"

"She is—or was—my mistress," he said stiffly.

"Ah." She laughed softly and they fell silent, watching the lagoon—the Lagoa de Obidos—below them and the ocean in the distance. And the growingly lovely sunset beyond.

It was a setting most men would kill to have alone with her, Joana thought with a wry smile. And yet she was not sorry that she did not have to share it with a man who would have ruined it with courtly speeches and abject worship. And certainly Captain Blake could not be accused of abjectly worshiping her. She turned her head and looked up at him. His features were sharpened by the light of the sinking sun. He looked almost relaxed.

And she felt a sudden sharp stab of nostalgia and reached about in her mind for its source. A tower. Ramparts. Wind and sun. A dreamy, gentle, handsome boy whom she had kissed when she came down off the tower.

Robert.

And yet the walls of Obidos were nothing like that old castle at Haddington Hall, and Captain Blake was nothing like Robert, except that they shared a given name and except that they had the same hair and eye coloring. And an indefinable something that escaped her conscious mind. Would Robert—*her* Robert—have resembled him in any other way had he lived? Would Robert have grown as broad and muscular? And would his face have grown as tough and disciplined? Would he have become a military hero? She was sure the answer to all those questions was no. Robert had dreaded being bought a commission. He had thought it would be impossible to kill.

Perhaps, she thought, it was as well that he had died. And yet for a moment she felt a surging of the old grief— for the first and only man she had loved, for the young girl she had been, with her belief in the happily-ever-after. For a long-ago dream.

She was staring at Captain Blake. She realized the fact only when he turned his head and looked steadily back at her. Their elbows were nearly touching on the wall. She could nearly feel the heat from his.

"Do you not love a sunset, Captain?" she asked him. "Perhaps it is another gift you can give your lady."

"I think not," he said, not moving his eyes from her. "The beauty of a sunset is deceptive. It is followed by the dark. A sunrise, perhaps. I would give her the sunrise and what is beyond the sunrise. Light and warmth and life. And love."

"Ah," she said, and her chest still ached with the inexplicable grief she had felt when he reminded her of Robert. "Then we must watch the sunrise together sometime, Captain."

She had perfected the art of flirtation long ages before.

But she realized the flirtatiousness of her words only when she heard their echo. Strangely, she had not intended them that way, although she had brought him up onto the walls with the sole purpose of flirting with him.

"Perhaps," he said, still looking at her so that she felt breathless and almost frightened. She felt not quite in control.

"Perhaps?" she said, laughing. "You missed your cue, Captain. You were supposed to declare that you would move heaven and earth to bring on that day. Are you hungry? Let us return home for dinner."

She took his arm and set herself to talking lightly and ceaselessly to him as they made their way down the darkened steps into the town and back to her villa.

7

HE breathed a sigh of relief when they entered the marquesa's villa. At least now they would be joined by the companion, and while conversation would not be easy, at least the tension would be gone. He had felt ready to explode with it up on the town walls. He had bristled with awareness of her and desire for her and contempt for his own reactions, since her own manner was so deliberately flirtatious. He felt rather out of his depth—again. He hoped suddenly that Lord Wellington would burn in some particularly hot corner of hell for giving him this particular assignment.

"Call Matilda," she told a servant, taking the captain's arm and leading him in the direction of the dining room.

But the servant coughed delicately. Matilda, it seemed, had not returned to the villa.

"How provoking!" The marquesa frowned. "She has forgotten all about the passing of time, I will warrant. It is ever thus when she visits her sister. I daresay I shall not set eyes on her until tomorrow." She sighed. "Companions can be very provoking, Captain Blake. They are not quite servants, and one does not like to scold them. We will have to dine tête-à-tête."

He might have suspected her of scheming that it be thus if he had not noted when they entered the dining room that the table had been set for three.

"I shall return to my inn, ma'am," he said.

But she laughed at him and told him not to be tiresome, and before he knew it they were seated at the table and he was sipping the wine while she sat and watched him, her chin in her hand. And then he had the painful feeling that he had committed a breach of etiquette by lifting his glass before she did. He set it down.

"I am hungry," she said, "and refuse to deliver a monologue all through dinner. You must hold up your end of the conversation, Captain Blake."

There was nothing more sure to tongue-tie him. He picked up his glass again.

She watched him as the servants set out the food on the table. She refused to say another word for a while. She wanted to see how long it would be before he could think of something to say. And she let her eyes roam over his face and wondered what it was about him that made him such an attractive man. His close-cropped blond hair? She preferred men with overlong hair. The crooked nose and the very noticeable scar? But they only took away any claim he might have had to hand-someness. The bronzed skin, perhaps? The light blue eyes? The knowledge that he had killed, that he was a military hero? The awareness that he was from a world and a background alien to hers?

Finally she felt the tension again, as she had up on the town walls. But she was not supposed to feel tension. Only the gentlemen with whom she dealt were meant to feel that.

"Tell me about yourself," she said. "Where were you born? Who was your father? What was your childhood like? Why did you enlist? Speak to me, Captain."

"I enlisted," he said, "because it seemed the right thing to do at the moment I did it. On the whole, I have never been sorry."

He had not answered her first three questions, she thought. But it was what she had learned to expect of Captain Blake. Unlike most men of her acquaintance, he did not like to talk about himself. Or about anything else, for that matter, it seemed.

And so, after all, she did most of the talking as they ate. Or as they picked at the food, to be more accurate. Her appetite was not usually affected by the company in which she ate. But this evening it was. She was aware of every mouthful she lifted to her mouth, of every mouthful he lifted to his. And she was aware of every swallow.

His fingers were long and slim—an artist's fingers, she thought. But his nails were cut short and kept clean—a soldier's fingernails. She wondered what those hands and

those fingers would feel like feathering over her back—
her naked back—and quelled the thought.

The air was fairly crackling with tension.

And Captain Blake tried to eat as if he were dining
with his fellow officers or men but found that he could
not rid himself of the notion that she watched his every
move—as he watched hers. And try as he would to think
of some topic with which to sustain the conversation, his
mind was blank and his only contributions were answers
to questions. She had a habit as she talked of leaning
forward so that her breasts almost brushed the edge of
the table. It seemed that his temperature rose a degree
every time it happened—and it happened frequently.
And she had that way of looking at him that he had
noticed before—her eyes sweeping up at him from beneath her lashes.

He cursed himself for not holding firm about returning
to his inn when he learned that her companion had not
returned. He wondered how long he must sit at the table
before he could decently rise and excuse himself. He had
no idea what was proper form in such circumstances.
Perhaps there was no proper form in a tête-à-tête of this
sort. It was all highly improper.

The room fairly pulsed with tension.

"Let's remove to the drawing room," she said eventually, smiling at him. "If you have finished eating, that
is."

"Yes, thank you, ma'am," he said, setting his napkin
thankfully beside his plate and getting to his feet. "But
I must leave. We should make an early start in the
morning."

She allowed him to pull back her chair as she got to
her feet. And the relief of doing so, of no longer having
to sit alone with him at the table, was enormous. But
she could not let him go. Some foolish stubbornness refused to allow her to do what she knew she ought to do
and what she wanted to do—to let him go.

"It is not even late, Captain Blake," she said, linking
her arm through his. "And I shall be dreadfully bored if
forced to spend the rest of the evening alone. You would
not doom me to loneliness and boredom, would you?"
She smiled and looked at him from beneath her lashes

in a manner she knew drove men wild. And was more aware than she ever had been before of how large he was and how broad-shouldered and well-muscled. And there was a flutter of fear that she was playing with fire. She ignored the feeling.

He did not resist further. She was almost disappointed that he did not. She had half-hoped that he would insist on leaving. They must converse, she thought. They must fill up the silence.

"What languages do you speak?" she asked him as she led him into the drawing room. "I know you speak several. I know that you have been sent on many reconnaissance missions as a result."

"Several Indian languages," he said. "And some European ones too."

She slipped her arm from his and walked about the room, fluffing cushions and repositioning ornaments. He was still standing just inside the drawing-room door, his booted feet slightly apart, his hands clasped behind him.

"Do come and sit down and tell me about some of your spying missions," she said. "Tell me about some you have carried out in the Peninsula." She patted the back of a sofa and felt her heart pounding against her ribs.

"I had better go, ma'am," he said.

He had more sense than she had. It was impossible, she thought that he did not feel the tension between them as she did.

"You do not like the topic?" she asked him. "Then we shall choose something else. I shall tell you about Luis and life at court before the removal to Brazil. There are many amusing stories with which I can entertain you. Come and sit down."

"I must go," he said.

An inner voice told her to let him go. She was in much deeper than she had ever been before. Flirtation had always been a light, amusing, slightly boring game before. And very safe. *Let him go*, that inner voice told her again. But if she let him go, she would be admitting defeat. She could not let him go until she sent him away. She strolled across the room toward him, a smile on her lips.

He watched her come. And he stood there feeling like a gauche boy, wanting to take his leave, desperately wanting to be gone, and not knowing quite how to accomplish such a seemingly simple task. He clamped his teeth together rather than tell her once more that he must go. Almost any other man she might have chosen as an escort would have known how to take his leave, he thought.

She stopped when she was almost toe to toe with him—delicate white slippers almost touching heavy polished black boots. The top of her head was just beneath the level of his chin—smooth dark hair over the crown of her head and styled into a cluster of curls at the back. She wore a soft musky perfume that he had noticed while they were out walking.

"You are not afraid, are you, Captain?" she asked him, long lashes lifting to allow her eyes to travel up from his chin to look into his own. There was a hint of laughter and a hint of something else in her eyes.

He swallowed and wished he could have controlled the action. He was mortally afraid. He had never been in such a situation with any woman who was not a whore and his for the purchase. He had no experience in controlling himself in such situations. There had never been the need. And then one of her hands, for once ungloved—small, white-skinned, smooth—lifted so that one finger could trace the line of a seam beneath the shoulder of his coat.

"Almost threadbare," she said.

"It has seen much service." The heat from her finger burned along his collarbone.

"Some woman will have to mend it for you soon," she said.

"Yes."

Her eyes moved upward again, passing over his chin, lingering over his mouth, pausing at the scar across his nose, looking fully into his eyes. "*Are* you afraid?" Her voice was low, almost a whisper.

The style of her dress, falling in soft folds from beneath her bosom to the floor, made her appear light and slim. Yet she was even slimmer in reality. His hands almost met about her waist—there was a sharp memory of a similar impression from the time when she was fifteen.

He spread his hands downward behind her waist and brought her against him while she arched backward from the waist and set her hands on his shoulders and looked into his eyes with an expression on her face that was almost a frown. She was all light, warm, soft femininity. He slid his hands upward until her breasts touched his coat and flattened against it—he watched and felt their softness yield to the hardness of his chest muscles.

Jesus, he thought, and the blood pulsed through him like a hammerbeat. Lord God in heaven. But she was too small. For as long as they stood, she was too small. He bent at the knees, lifting her against him so that her feet almost left the floor.

And she knew that she had made a mistake. She knew that she had carried the flirtation too far. The fear she had had the moment she had first set eyes on this man was upon her. She had lost control. He had lifted her so that all her weight and all her balance were at his mercy. If he let her go suddenly, she would fall. And he had lifted her sufficiently that she could feel against her womb the hard swelling of his desire for her.

They had moved beyond the area of her own expertise—flirtation—into the realm of his—passion. And she had no experience—no, none whatsoever, not even in her marriage—with passion. She looked up into his light blue eyes, now burning with the fire of his passion, and she felt him with every part of her body and every nerve in it. He was all hard magnificent masculinity.

And she was terrified. Terrified of him: the embrace he had begun was an embrace that led only to one place and to one ending. It was an embrace fully intended to be taken to completion. And terrified of herself: her body was delighting in the sensations and the possession in store for it, and her mind was wanting to surrender.

It would be so good, she thought. She knew it would be good. It would erase, perhaps, the nauseating memories of her marriage bed. She wanted more than anything to surrender. Her eyes fluttered closed and her lips parted as his head lowered to hers. She wanted to know what he would do with her. She wanted to know what a virile, passionate man would do to the woman he desired.

His mouth came down wide over hers so that for a moment she opened her eyes in shock. His tongue outlined her lips until she felt a sharp stabbing ache deep in her womb, and then it plunged warm and hard and deep into her mouth. She gasped and drew it deeper still.

And the terror was back, thrusting its way past the curiosity and the temptation. She had no control over the situation at all. She knew that it was a matter of mere minutes, perhaps less, before she was lowered to the floor and her skirts raised and her body penetrated. She would have surrendered control to a man—a man she did not know or understand. An enigma. Someone she was merely to work with.

She bit down hard on his tongue.

When he jerked back his head, she smiled at him and fought down terror and breathlessness and shaking knees. "Why, Captain," she said, "was that not a little extravagant for a good-night kiss?"

"Why, you bitch!" he amazed her by saying, taking a step backward and frowning ferociously at her.

Terror curled itself into a fist inside her. She raised her eyebrows. "I did not hear that, Captain Blake," she said. "A temporary deafness, I daresay. You had decided not to stay for port?"

"You bitch!" he said again, not taking the cue from her to restore a measure of civility to their dealings. His eyes narrowed on her. "You sent your companion away deliberately, didn't you? You had no intention of there being a threesome for dinner, did you? You do not need a chaperone, ma'am. You need an animal tamer."

She smiled at him. "Alas, the deafness was only temporary," she said. "But I will forgive you, Captain. It seems you misinterpreted the situation entirely. I have been grateful for your escort. I intended to show my gratitude. Pardon me, but I meant no more."

His heels clicked together and his face was again all hard lines, his eyes steely. It was a soldier's face, one which must strike apprehension into the heart of any enemy soldier unfortunate enough to look into it on the battlefield.

"Good night, ma'am," he said. "I shall return at dawn if that meets with your approval."

"I shall be ready, Captain." She smiled at him. "Good night."

He turned and left without another word. A gentleman would have apologized—both for the liberties he had taken with her person and for the unpardonably vulgar language he had directed at her. But Captain Blake was not, of course, a gentleman. And she could not say she was sorry he had not apologized. She would have felt even more guilty than she was already feeling if he had.

And Captain Blake, striding from the villa and the courtyard and up the hill to his inn, cursed furiously beneath his breath and damned her to hell and back. His tongue was throbbing and there were cuts at the back of it that would be sore for days.

The bitch! He could think of no other words to describe her. She had led him on all evening just so that she could make a fool of him and laugh in his face at the end of it all when despite all his efforts he had failed to resist her. But it was a dangerous game she played. He would have been the one laughing if he had been unable to stop despite the bitten tongue.

He felt a prize fool. To have had his tongue bitten! He would never again be able to look her in the eye without remembering how she had set up his humiliation.

Twice. Twice he had been made a fool of by a woman, and by the same woman both times—Jeanne Morisette and Joana da Fonte, Marquesa das Minas. In any language she was trouble, and once she had been safely delivered to Viseu—a task he would complete as expeditiously and as impersonally as was possible—he would have nothing more whatsoever to do with her.

Not that he would have the opportunity to do so, of course—a captain who had once been a private soldier and the widow of a Portuguese marques and daughter of a French count.

How had she once phrased it? He paused outside his inn and frowned down at the ground before his feet. The bastard and the daughter of a French count. Yes, he believed those had been her exact words.

Well, he had just relearned his lesson. From now on

he would confine his attentions entirely to the Beatrizes of this world. Beatriz might take money for services rendered, but at least she was open and honest about what she did. She did not entice a man to madness and then claim, all wide eyes and sweet smiles, that she had merely been offering a good-night kiss of gratitude. Beatriz knew how to give as well as receive. And what she gave was her sweet and ample self for his pleasure and his comfort.

He was sorry in his heart that he had not brought her with him after all. He would have given all the meager contents of his purse at that moment to be able to take her up to his bleak inn room and bury himself in her.

Damn, but she was beautiful, he thought. And warm and slender and shapely. And tasty. But it was not Beatriz he was thinking of any longer.

8

THEIR journey lasted three more days. They stayed at Leiria one night, Joana choosing to sleep at a convent in company with Matilda, and at Coimbra the next—she had friends there with whom to stay. Before the third night closed in on them they had arrived finally at the city of Viseu, high on a breathtaking plateau, its city walls and its churches and cathedral giving it a beauty all its own.

Captain Blake had never been so glad in his life to reach a destination. In three days he had scarcely exchanged a word with the marquesa. And yet she smiled at him as usual, her eyes perhaps laughing at him—he never knew whether she mocked him or not. And it continued to be his task to hand her in and out of her carriage. But during those three days he was more aware of the slimness of her hand and the lightness of her body and that subtle perfume he had noticed first inside her villa at Obidos.

They were days during which he longed to be free of her and back with the army. He regretted the summons to Viseu. He wanted to be back with his company again, relieving Lieutenant Reid from the command of it he had had over the winter. He wanted to be done with women—and one woman in particular—for a while. He wanted to concentrate on his job. It was late June. The French would surely be making their move soon. It was amazing they had waited so long. There would surely be a major pitched battle before many more weeks had passed.

Joana's aunt lived on the cathedral square in the city, a handsome area of noble houses, including the Episcopal

Palace. He dismounted for the last time to hand the marquesa from her carriage.

"Captain Blake." She set her gloved hand in his and smiled brilliantly at him. "We have arrived safely after all. I shall be sure to report to Arthur that you protected me from all the perils of the road."

There was definite mockery in her voice. There had been no perils apart from the one that he himself had posed. And she had protected herself from that. His tongue still pained him when he drank anything hot.

He bowed over her hand when her feet touched the ground. "I hope the journey has not been too uncomfortable or tedious for you, ma'am," she said.

"How could it be," she said, and she laughed aloud, "when I had your conversation to enjoy, Captain Blake?"

Was he dismissed? Or did she expect him to escort her into the house? For the thousandth time he felt woefully lacking in knowledge of the niceties of polite behavior.

"I will not keep you," she said. "You will be anxious to report to headquarters and find your billet. I fear it is too late to talk with the general today, though. Good day, Captain." She had left her hand in his.

"Good-bye, ma'am," he said. And he did what he thought—and hoped—was expected of him. He raised her hand to his lips. And he looked down into her face as he did so, to find her eyes on their hands and her lips parting. Lord, he could taste the sweetness of her still— and feel the sharpness of her perfect teeth. "Your aunt will be pleased to see you safe."

She smiled and raised her eyes to his. "Never say good-bye, Captain," she said. "It sounds so final. I daresay we will meet again." And finally she withdrew her hand from his and signaled, in that quite imperceptible way that ladies were expert at, that he was dismissed.

He swung himself back into the saddle, turned to salute her, and felt all the relief he might feel when being released from a prison cell and certain execution. He hoped not, he thought fervently in reaction to her final words. God, he hoped not.

The French army intended for the invasion of Portugal—the Army of Portugal, as Napoleon Bonaparte liked

to call it—was still stationed in and about Salamanca,
Captain Blake had learned from fellow officers at his
billet the night before. The fifty-two-year-old Marshal
André Massena had just taken over its command. The
bulk of the British and Portuguese armies, both under
the command of Viscount Wellington, were still massed
in central Portugal awaiting the expected invasion from
the east. The Light Division was still patrolling the Coa
River, protecting against any surprise French advance
and preventing any intelligence from getting out to the
French.

Nothing much had changed, although it was early summer already. Captain Blake paced an anteroom at headquarters the morning after his arrival at Viseu and wished
he were at the Coa with his company. There would be
danger, excitement, the feeling of being in an important
place at an important time. He hoped that he would be
sent there, that this detour to Viseu was merely for the
purpose of picking up papers or a message for General
Crauford, in charge of the division.

He was kept waiting for two hours before a staff
officer came to summon him into the presence of the
commander-in-chief

Captain Blake was always struck by two contradictory
impressions of Viscount Wellington. One was how ordinary and unassuming he appeared at first glance. He did
not wear military uniform, but was almost always dressed
in plain, rather drab clothes. The other was how com-
manding a presence he had once one was past that first
glance. His face was stern, with its hooked nose and thin
lips and compelling eyes. And yet an explanation of why
all attention focused on him whenever he was present
was not in either his face or his tall, slim person. It was
more in the man inside that person.

"Ah, Captain Blake," he said, looking up from the
papers strewn over the surface of his desk and acknowl-
edging the other's salute with a nod of the head. "You
have come at last, have you?"

"As fast as I could, sir," Captain Blake said.

"And yet my messenger had returned and was reporting to me yesterday morning," the viscount said,
frowning.

Captain Blake swallowed his indignation. "I was directed to escort the Marquesa das Minas, sir," he reminded the general.

"Ah. Joana." Wellington set his quill pen down. "A delightful lady, would you not agree?"

Captain Blake inclined his head, assuming that the question was rhetorical.

"How is your French?" the viscount asked. "My own is indifferent."

"I can both understand it and make myself understood in it, I believe," the captain said.

"And your Spanish?" But the general waved a dismissive hand. "No, forget that question. I know your Spanish to be fluent. I need you to go to Salamanca for me."

Captain Blake stood still and forced himself to refrain from either raising his eyebrows or repeating the name of the Spanish city. Explanations would doubtless be made.

"Right into the lion's den or the hornet's nest, so to speak," Lord Wellington said. "You are to be captured, Captain Blake. Be sure to wear your uniform. As you are doubtless aware, the French treat their prisoners of war with courtesy, as we do ours. They treat prisoners out of uniform with a barbarity that leaves one wondering if they can be a civilized nation at all."

It was harder this time to prevent his eyebrows from shooting upward. His task was to walk into the enemy camp and allow himself to be captured.

"You will not just walk into the city and surrender your sword, of course," the general said, as if he had read the other's thoughts. "You will be communicating with a band of Spanish guerrilleros—Antonio Becquer's band—you may get the details later from my secretary. And you will be very reluctant to be captured. You will have papers carefully hidden about your person, but not carefully enough, of course."

Captain Blake looked and listened. He knew that questions and comments were unnecessary at this point.

"Sit down, Captain," the viscount said, getting to his feet himself. "I shall explain the situation to you. Suffice it to say that I do not like divulging important information to even a single person more than is necessary. Very

few people, even among my senior officers, know what
I am about to tell you. And before I do that, I must ask
you. You are willing to undertake this mission for me?
I do not need to point out to you that there is danger
involved and that all such missions are voluntary."

"I am willing, sir," Captain Blake said, though he was
not at all sure that he was eager. Captivity? The humiliation of losing his sword to the French? And the tedium,
perhaps the degradation, of a lengthy incarceration?

"This, then, is for your ears only, Captain," the general said. "It must not be repeated even under the stress
of torture, which I do not anticipate to be your fate—
provided you wear your uniform, of course. Did you notice any unusual activity as you traveled north?"

Captain Blake thought. "Very little, sir," he said,
thinking of the Montachique Pass and Major Hanbridge's
uneasiness there. But that had not literally been *activity*.
"Large bands of peasants seemed to be busy on some
fortifications north of Lisbon to about Torres Vedras,
but their efforts would seem to be pointless and rather
pathetic. I saw no evidence of military activity."

"Ah," Lord Wellington said, "your words please me.
My engineering officers are clever in more ways than
one, it seems. Last autumn, Captain Blake, I gave orders
for a chain—three concentric chains—of numerous and
quite impregnable fortifications to be built north of Lisbon, the most northerly to pass through Torres Vedras,
from the ocean to the Tagus River. Old castles and
churches and towers are to be used, mountains are to be
reshaped—I shall not go into full details. These defenses
are almost ready, Captain—with my engineering officers
I have been calling them the Lines of Torres Vedras.
When they are finished and defended by an army of moderate size, they will be quite unpassable. Any army coming from the north can be held from Lisbon indefinitely.
I do not intend, you see, that my army be pushed into
the sea. We will retain our only foothold on the continent
of Europe, and eventually we will have the strength to
nibble away piece by piece at Napoleon Bonaparte's empire. At present we simply do not have the numerical
strength to advance ourselves."

Captain Blake listened in fascination but said nothing.

"When Massena brings his army into Portugal," the viscount said, "as he will surely do soon, once he has subdued Ciudad Rodrigo and Almeida, he will march a long distance through the hills, a long distance from his supply lines. And he will find little comfort in this country. The inhabitants will be encouraged to retreat before him, burning whatever food and supplies they cannot carry with them. He will not be too worried, believing firmly that soon he will be able to supply his troops from the treasure stores of Lisbon. When he reaches the Lines of Torres Vedras, Captain, he will have the choice between a difficult retreat late in the year with a half-starved army, and a pointless digging-in in the hope of blasting his way through the lines and getting to Lisbon. The destruction of a large part of his army should be certain."

Viscount Wellington, who had been pacing about the room, returned to his desk and sat down, looking at Captain Blake.

"Only one thing can spoil my plan," he said, "and that is Massena not doing what I fully expect him to do. He could, of course, march on Lisbon from the south, and we do have lines of defense south of the Tagus too, though they are not as formidable. But I do not expect him to go south. He will, I believe, act predictably—under one condition. An absolutely essential condition. The existence of the Lines of Torres Vedras must remain a total secret. Even my men will believe they are headed for annihilation as they retreat on Lisbon. They will curse me roundly, Captain Blake."

"Yes, sir," Captain Blake said, and watched his commander-in-chief smile arctically. Thank heaven, he was thinking, that Major Hanbridge had rushed them through that pass before the marquesa's questions had become more pointed.

"My army has done a superb job of sealing off the border to French intelligence," Lord Wellington said. "The very positioning of the French army shows that they do not know what they will be facing. But things do leak out, Captain. Three details have somewhat disturbed me in the past few weeks. My own intelligence informs me that small groups of Massena's men are scouting the southern route. And some of our Spanish friends have informed me that the French have their hands on some paper whose description sounds suspiciously like an unmarked diagram of the Lines of Torres Vedras. Are they beginning to suspect the truth? That is the question I have been grappling with. And third, they have not yet moved, though it is almost July. Clearly something is amiss, something troubles them. Again, is it that they suspect the truth? Will they, after all, swing to the south?"

He set his elbows on the arms of his chair and steepled his fingers. He looked broodingly at Captain Blake.

"You have to be caught with a diagram of the lines on you, Captain," the general said. "A misleading diagram, of course, to convince our friends that we are expecting them from the south and have very shaky defenses indeed in the north. It will be up to you to convince the French officers who will interrogate you that the paper is authentic. It will be up to you to convince them that it is plausible for you to have such an important paper on your person as you travel in Spain. You will discuss the matter with my secretary and report back to me tomorrow. I expect you to be on your way within two or three days. Do you understand your mission?"

"It is to make sure at all costs that the French army comes this way, sir," Captain Blake said.

"That they neither stay where they are nor head south," Viscount Wellington said.

"Yes, sir," the captain said. "I understand."

"You will, of course, have questions after you have thought about all that I have said," the general said. "Do you have any now, Captain?"

Captain Blake licked his lips. "Am I to be a hostile prisoner, sir?" he asked. "Or am I to give my parole if offered the chance?"

"Oh, your parole, by all means," Lord Wellington said. "I would not wish your captivity to be an uncomfortable one, Captain."

"You would not wish me to try to escape, then, sir?" Captain Blake asked.

"Certainly not if your parole has been given and your captors do their part by treating you with courtesy," the viscount said with raised eyebrows. "You will be exchanged for a French captive of equal rank in due time, Captain Blake. Are there any more questions?"

"None at the moment, sir," Captain Blake said. His heart felt as if it were in his boots. After months of incarceration in a hospital in Lisbon, he was to have a brief glimpse of freedom only to lose it again quite deliberately for who knew how long. While his company and his regiment and his army prepared for battle, he would be a prisoner of their enemy. And once his parole was given, honor would not even allow him to try to escape.

"If an exchange is made soon enough," the general said, "or if you find yourself freed for any other reason, Captain, I will expect you to help our cause by persuading the inhabitants of the country to burn all behind them as they and you retreat on our army. That task will take precedence over rejoining your regiment."

"Yes, sir," Captain Blake said, but his spirits were not lifted. It was unlikely that there would be any exchange of prisoners before the summer's campaign was over. He rose to his feet and saluted smartly.

"Oh, Captain," the viscount said before he had left the room, "you have received or will receive an invitation to a ball being given by the Countess of Soveral tomorrow evening. She is the marquesa's aunt, you know. I believe the lady wishes to express her gratitude to you for escorting her niece safely from Lisbon. Tiresome affairs, these. But we must maintain friendly relations with our host country. I will expect you to attend."

"Yes, sir," Captain Blake said, and left the room, since there seemed to be nothing else to be said.

And if there were a lower place than his boots for his heart to be, he thought, then that was where it was. He was going to have to see the bloody woman again, and on her territory—a ball at which it was entirely probable that the commander-in-chief himself would be in attendance. And he would wager that she had personally connived at getting him invited just so that she might witness his embarrassment and total discomfort. It had probably never once crossed the aunt's mind to thank him.

Hell, he thought. Hell and damnation! He should have

taken the surgeon's advice and taken sick leave for the summer.

"I do apologize for bringing you into a room that offers so little comfort for a lady," Viscount Wellington said later the same day. "But it seemed safer to talk on such delicate issues here rather than at the countess's house."

Joana laughed. "But you forget, Arthur, that I am not always a lady," she said, "and occasionally know a great deal less comfort than this room affords. So I am to make a mortal enemy of Captain Blake, am I? It will not be difficult, I think. He neither likes me very well nor approves of me."

The viscount looked at her and frowned. "He treated you with discourtesy?" he asked. "I shall have him hanged."

She laughed again. "Oh, no, no," she said. "He did not behave amiss. But I was La Marquesa at her best, you see. You told me that I must get to know him, and I assumed that meant I must flirt with him. I flirted. But I am afraid that your captain is made of stern stuff. He does not approve of flirts—not that he ever said so." Joana smiled rather ruefully as she remembered being called a bitch.

"This is a very delicate and dangerous matter, Joana," Lord Wellington said. "I have agonized over it. But it seems the only idea that might work. Captain Blake must be carrying the actual plan for the Lines of Torres Vedras."

"But it is to be sealed and he is not to realize the truth," she said.

"He is a good man," the viscount said. "He has proved it on many occasions. But I do not know if he adds acting skills to his others. It will be best, I have decided, if he is not acting. Of course he will deny that the papers are real when they are discovered and he sees them. And the French will suspect that he bluffs but will be afraid that the bluff is itself the bluff. They will not know quite what to believe. And that will be where you come in, Joana."

"I will convince them that Captain Blake is your most highly skilled spy," she said, "and that he deliberately had himself captured in order to confuse them, in order to make them believe by his denials that the real defenses are in the north. I understand, Arthur. So even as he realizes that I am unwittingly helping his cause, he will hate me as he would hate poison. Delightful!"

"You do not have to do this, Joana," Lord Wellington said with a frown. "I can still take a chance on what I almost believe, which is that the French have no idea whatsoever of a possible trap awaiting them. I hate to see you put yourself into danger. Is Wyman still particular in his attentions to you? The very safest place for you at present would be England."

"The safest place for Maria and Miguel would have been England too," she said, both her expression and her voice changing. "No, the job will be done, Arthur. The French will come this way and will believe that they have free passage to Lisbon. Perhaps at some time in the future I will have a chance to apologize to your poor captain. And what pieces of useful and useless intelligence may I take with me to Salamanca?"

"Oh." Lord Wellington waved a hand in the air. "You may tell them that I am here, Joana. They doubtless suspect as much even if they do not know for sure. You may tell them that I am poised for flight with the forces stationed in the north to help repel the invasion by the southern route but that I dare not leave here yet for fear that they might come this way. Is that information carrot enough?"

"Oh, Arthur, may I tell them about the pathetic peasant attempts to fortify Torres Vedras?" she asked him, smiling. "They did look pathetic, you know, rather like one small person standing in the middle of a river in flood, trying to hold back the waters. The French would be delighted by my description. I should do it so well. And it will make Captain Blake's 'bluff' seem so much more laughable."

"By all means," he said. "Entertain them, Joana."

"And perhaps this time there will be new troops, new officers in Salamanca," she said with a sigh. "Perhaps *he* will be there this time. I live for the day."

The commander-in-chief looked at her broodingly. "If

he is, Joana," he said, "it will be a job for your brother. You must not try tackling him yourself."

She smiled brilliantly at him. "Once I have betrayed poor Captain Blake, my task is done?" she asked.

"Just one more thing if it can be arranged," he said. "He will doubtless be offered parole and has been instructed to give it. But he is a restless young man and will be most unhappy if he cannot spend at least a part of the summer among his beloved riflemen. Besides, I need at least a few men in uniform—and with a knowledge of the Portuguese language—to persuade these poor people to leave their homes and destroy all behind them. If you can find any way for his parole to be broken without loss of honor to him, Joana . . ."

She raised her eyebrows. "Ah, a challenge," she said. "Accomplishing the impossible. I shall see what I can do, Arthur. And then the marquesa can disappear for a while?"

He frowned. "The hills will be dangerous with the French coming through them, Joana," he said. "They are not kind to captured partisans, you know. And we have never been able to persuade them that the Portuguese Ordenanza is a type of military organization and that its members are therefore entitled to be treated as soldiers. I would prefer that you make for Lisbon with all speed—as the marchioness."

She smiled. "But I do not intend to be captured," she said. "And I shall explode into a thousand pieces if I cannot be free for at least a few weeks."

"I have no power over you at all, of course," Lord Wellington said. "But be sure to proclaim your French citizenship loudly and clearly if you are caught, Joana. Not that you are likely to be believed, of course, unless you have the good fortune to be taken by someone who knows you."

She got to her feet and extended a hand to him. "You will be at the ball tomorrow night?" she asked. "Duarte's godmother will be disappointed if you are not. My aunt." She smiled. "I have so many aunts."

"I would not miss it," he said, taking her hand and bowing over it. "I have instructed Captain Blake to attend."

"Ah," she said. "So I am to work even during a ball, am I? I fear he will dread the evening more than going into battle. Who is he, Arthur? What was he before he enlisted?"

"He is one of my officers," he said, his face quite impassive. "The past is of no significance to me, Joana."

"Ah." She laughed. "A slap across the fingers. I deserved it. But of course I am more intrigued than ever. I shall have to tease the information out of the captain himself. I take it that flirtation would be the best treatment tomorrow evening?"

The viscount smiled. "I do not believe I need to teach you your job, Joana," he said. "Until tomorrow evening, then."

"I shall look forward to it," she said.

But as a staff officer handed her into her carriage a few minutes later, she was not at all sure that she did. She would see him again and have a chance to flirt with him again, and that in itself posed an interesting challenge. Captain Blake was not good at flirtation, perhaps, but she suspected that he was very good indeed at what she had never allowed to follow flirtation.

Though she had almost allowed it with him. She remembered quite vividly that terrifying embrace at Obidos—terrifying because she had almost lost control of both the situation and herself. And she still felt shameful regret that she had not allowed matters to proceed at least one step farther. Though she knew with a woman's instinct—certainly with nothing she had learned during her marriage—that one step farther would have taken them to the point of no return. And then perhaps she would have been lost forever.

She would see him again the following evening. And she would flirt with him. And then in Salamanca she would betray him, laugh at him, make him into a fool, the butt of French humor. And she would have to give him an honorable way out of his parole—his promise given not to try to escape. She already had an idea. It would be the only workable one. And it would be one more thing to give him a disgust of her, to make him hate her.

Joana sighed. She did not want Captain Robert Blake

to hate her. But that was a foolish thought. There was a war to be fought, and she would fight it in any way she could contribute. She would fight against the French, even though she was half-French herself, even though her father was French and in Vienna working for the French government. She would fight the French because one Frenchman deserved to die at her hands.

It did not matter that one English officer would come to hate her even if he did not do so already. She would be helping him accomplish his mission, though he would not realize it. And she would be helping him escape so that he might rejoin his regiment and get himself killed in the next pitched battle.

Perhaps at some time in the future she would be able to explain to him. But if she did not, it did not matter He was just one soldier and she another.

9

"AH, yes. Captain Blake." The Countess of Soveral at least looked relieved that he had spoken to her in her own language. But she smiled vaguely at him, welcomed him to her home and her ball, and turned politely to greet the next new arrivals.

Captain Blake would have grinned if the whole thing had not made him feel so damned uncomfortable. Far from lavishing him with gratitude for having brought her niece safely all the way from Lisbon, the countess had appeared not to know who the devil he was.

It was rather like a repeat of the Angeja ball in Lisbon, except that there were fewer shadowy corners into which to melt and except that he felt less free to withdraw after a decent time. He supposed that he must wait until the end, or, if he were fortunate, until he had been noticed sufficiently by both the marquesa and the Beau that he could make his escape.

He would rather be creeping about Salamanca, waiting to be captured, he thought as he strolled into the ballroom trying to look both casual and inconspicuous. He would rather be going into battle, out ahead of the infantry lines with his skirmishers, waiting for an enemy skirmisher to pick him off. He would rather be anywhere else but where he was.

It was not hard to spot the Marquesa das Minas, or at least the place where she was. It was dense and abuzz with the officers who sported all the most gorgeous uniforms and the most lavish displays of silver and gold lace.

"Bob!" a cheerful voice hailed him as he moved to the other side of the ballroom. "There you are. I heard you were in town."

He turned and grinned in some relief at Captain Rowlandson of the Forty-third, whose gap-toothed smile was welcome in a sea of generally unfamiliar faces.

"Ned," he said, "what are you doing here?"

"Messenger boy," the other said. "Came in last night. On my way out at first light tomorrow. Had to come tonight, though, to pay my respects to the marquesa. Or probably not to pay my respects, actually. 'Worship from afar' is more like it. You were appointed to escort her here from Lisbon, I hear. Lucky dog! Tell me all about it."

"We traveled fast," Captain Blake said with a laugh. "I was only one day later arriving here than I would have been on my own. What is happening on the Coa?"

"Johnny trying to sneak past and the division holding him back," Captain Rowlandson said. "Craufurd in his element. Expect major heroics when the push really comes. He likes to think he is more effective than the whole bloody army put together. Makes for an interesting—and probably short—life, though. You survived, then, Bob? There was a wager on, but no one would wager that you would not. Too stubborn by half to die just because a bullet missed your heart by an inch, Reid said, and he don't want to owe his captaincy to your dying anyway. Are you coming back with me?"

Captain Blake grimaced. "I have some business here first," he said. "Tedious stuff. Save some of the fighting for me, though, Ned. Don't take all of the glory for yourself."

Captain Rowlandson laughed heartily. "I want to dance with the tall dark-haired beauty in green," he said. "Across the room there, Bob. Do you see her? I've met her eyes at least three times in the last half-hour and I don't think it is a coincidence either. Perhaps she fancies red hair, eh? It is a distinct disadvantage not to have any Portuguese, though. Come and speak to her chaperone for me?"

Captain Blake would really have preferred not to, since the beauty in question was seated quite close to where the marquesa was standing, laughing and flirting with a court that was surely larger than the one in Lisbon. Sometimes, he thought, following Captain Rowlandson across the floor, he regretted his handiness with languages.

The matter was soon settled, the tall girl and her chaperone seeming only too pleased to accept the offer of partnership of a British officer despite the fact that they did not have a word of English between them. Captain Blake turned away from the chaperone with a bow as the couple stepped onto the floor for the dance that was about to begin.

The marquesa was in white, he discovered without surprise when he could not resist glancing her way. The gown shimmered with silver thread. Her dark hair was more severely drawn back from her face than usual. The smooth style shone in the light of the candles. The cascade of curls at the back of her head was softer, fuller than usual.

And then he regretted the temptation to look, and even to stare. He caught her eye and inclined his head in some confusion. But before he could look away, she raised her white-feathered fan to her lips and her eyes laughed at him over the top of it and held his. It would be boorish to withdraw his eyes and walk away. And yet without even having to look down, he knew that his carefully brushed green coat and his painstakingly polished boots looked more than shabby in contrast with the gorgeous uniforms surrounding her. He drew a deep breath and walked toward her.

"Captain Blake," she said, and lowered her fan to smile fully at him, "you are late and each of these gentlemen is ready and eager to slap a glove in your face and call you out for having reserved the first dance with me."

"No one deserves to dance with you when he does not deign to stroll up until the music is almost beginning, Joana," a captain of the Guards said, looking at Captain Blake with mingled disdain and amusement. "You should send the fellow on his way with a few sharp words."

"What, Joana?" a lieutenant colonel of the King's German Legion said with a good-natured laugh. "We have all been ousted by a mere captain of the damned Rifles, begging pardon for my German. They all think themselves the elite just because they are the best shots in the army. Blake, is it? The hero of last summer's re-

treat from Talavera? Well, if you must dance with a rifleman, Joana, it might as well be with a hero, I suppose."

She set a hand on the captain's arm, smiling at the
disappointed group of her admirers. "You were late coming, Captain," she said, laughing up at him when they
were on the dance floor. "Do you dance, by the way?"

"I do, ma'am," he said. He did not smile back at her.
He had never danced at a grand ball, and he had no wish
to dance with her, knowing that half the male eyes in
the room would be on them. And he did not like being
maneuvered and made to feel like a puppet on a string
again.

"You see how I am thanking you for your escort?"
she said. "I am granting you the first dance of the evening, Captain, before you could even ask for it. Do you
have any idea how many men did ask?"

"I could probably make an educated guess, ma'am,"
he said. But the music began at that moment and saved
them from further conversation for a while as they moved
into a quadrille.

"Ah," she said after a few minutes, "you *do* dance,
and very well too. You must have had a good teacher."

"My mother," he said.

She smiled. "She enjoyed dancing?" she asked. "She
danced a great deal?"

"With me, yes," he said. "And occasionally with my
father."

He must have been very young. He could remember
watching in delight as they performed the steps of courtly
dances and sprightly ones while his mother hummed the
tune and his father laughed. He could remember pluck-
ing at his mother's skirts and his father's breeches until
one or other of them had lifted him up and continued
the dance. Those were the days when he had considered
their family life normal and happy.

It *had* been happy.

"Captain Blake," the marquesa said, "you are neglecting me. You have gone into a dream. Did they dance at
ton events? And are they both in the past tense? Have
you lost your father as well as your mother?"

He looked at her and wondered that she had not recognized him at all. Had he changed so completely in eleven

years? Or had he meant so little to her that she had
forgotten him as soon as her father's carriage took her
out of sight of Haddington Hall? She had not changed
so very much except that the bright girl with her dreams
of growing up and enjoying life had matured into the
flirtatious woman who perhaps enjoyed life too much for
happiness. He wondered if for all the lovers she must
have had, she had ever loved. He wondered if she had
loved her husband.

Not that love mattered a great deal to him either, of
course.

"Not to my knowledge," he said.

She sighed. "I should have learned by now," she said,
"that you will answer only one question at a time, Captain—the last that I ask. I should have remembered to
ask only one at a time. Did you love your mother?"

"She was the anchor of my happiness and security as
I grew up," he said.

"And your father grieved so deeply after she died that
he went all to pieces?" she said. "That is why you enlisted in the army?"

"I enlisted," he said, "because I wanted the challenge
of making my own way in life."

She sighed again and then laughed. "I did it again,"
she said. "I asked two questions and had the least important answered. I am an inquisitive person, Captain. And
usually it is easy to find out everything there is to know
about men. Ask them a single question and they will
rush eagerly into a life history. I can understand why you
are a spy. Ah, and there is Arthur. I am so glad he came.
My aunt would have considered herself forever a social
failure if he had neglected to put in an appearance. Have
you spoken with him yet since our arrival?"

"I have exchanged a few civilities with him, ma'am,"
he said.

She favored him with her brightest, most charming
smile. "Oh, Captain," she said, "I will wager that you
have exchanged a little more than that. It is difficult talking and dancing at the same time, is it not?"

It was. She was light on her feet and bright-eyed and
beautiful. And she wore the same perfume he had noticed at Obidos. The evening they had spent there

seemed now rather like dream and nightmare all rolled into one. The feel of her, small and warm and shapely in his arms, the smell of her, the taste of her mouth, the desire that had flared in him, the wonder of her response. And the painful ending of the embrace and her laughter and teasing and the knowledge that she must look at him and know that he was just as vulnerable to her charm as any of her numerous admirers.

"You must reserve another set with me, Captain," she said, her eyes laughing with the familiar teasing glow. "Immediately after supper? Yes, that is not yet spoken for. I do not allow dances to be reserved far ahead of time, you know, for I never know with whom I will wish to dance. But in your case I will make an exception. And we will not dance, but walk out in one of the court-yards—my aunt's, which is more private than the main courtyard? Very well, then, I shall risk it without drag-ging Matilda out there too. Matilda hates the outdoors at night. I like your suggestion, Captain. By that time of the evening I shall be tired of dancing and ready for some cool outdoor air. Thank you. I accept." She laughed gaily.

"Does any man ever say no to you?" he asked. He was not returning her smile.

She looked up as if she were thinking. "No," she said. "No man ever does. Are you planning to be the first, Captain? How tiresome. You will not dance with me again or walk out in the courtyard with me? I shall have to find a corner in which to pout. Or better still, I shall stamp my foot here and fly into a passion and have a fit of the vapors. Shall I?"

"I have the feeling," he said, "that if I decided to call your bluff, I should find that it was not bluff at all. Am I right?"

Her eyes danced with merriment. "Ah, Captain," she said, "where would be the fun of the situation if I were to answer that question? You must either play craven and come back to me after supper or you must risk the consequences. Which is it to be?"

For one unguarded moment he grinned back at her. "If it were a gun you were pointing at my head," he said, "which might or might not be loaded, I think I would call your bluff, ma'am, and risk having my brains blown out. But a lady's screams I do not think I could face. May I reserve the dance after supper? And would you perhaps prefer to stroll outside than to dance?"

"Yes and yes, sir," she said. "How kind you are. Is the music coming to an end? How sad. I wanted to ask more questions about your mother." She sighed.

"But alas the music *is* coming to an end," he said.

"Captain Blake," she said, "when you smile—or grin, I think would be the more appropriate term—you are more handsome than any other man in the room despite the fact that someone did not set your nose quite straight after it was broken and despite the fact that someone tried to carve a path across your cheeks and nose with some sharp instrument and had considerable success in doing so."

She laughed merrily at his expression. How did one answer such words?

"I have dozens of questions about those old wounds too," she said as the music ended and he escorted her back to the side of the ballroom where her court was already gathering. "We will not lack for conversation after supper."

He bowed over her hand, feeling his back stiffen as he became aware of at least a dozen pairs of eyes watching him, and withdrew to the opposite side of the room, where he stood cursing his luck. Having danced with her and felt the eyes of Viscount Wellington on them as they danced, he should now have been able to withdraw with a clear conscience. He might have begun to focus his mind on the difficult days ahead and to clear it of a woman who despite the efforts of his will had been using him as a toy ever since their first encounter in Lisbon.

Instead of which he had to wait around for at least two hours until the time came to stroll with her in her aunt's private courtyard—without her chaperone. The very thought set his mind to cursing—and his loins to aching.

Summer was upon them. It was a warm evening and the countess's courtyard was still and shaded, protected from whatever breeze there might have been. There were trees to offer coolness to a summer's day and flowers to add fragrance even to an evening.

"How clever of you to suggest strolling out here," Joana said, her arm linked through Captain Blake's. "It is blessedly quiet and cool." She closed her eyes and drew in a deep breath of fresh air.

"Extremely clever," he said, "considering the fact that I did not know of its existence."

She laughed. She was feeling both exhilarated and sad. Exhilarated because she was to be alone with him for half an hour, and for all his seriousness and incommunicativeness he was more fascinating than any of the numerous gentlemen in the ballroom who would have given a right arm for the privilege of taking his place. Sad because she must deceive him and because she could not be quite herself with him.

Her sadness and the reasons for it disturbed her.

"I suppose," she said, "we will stroll mutely here if I do not rattle off a whole series of questions. You have talked with Arthur, have you not? He has an assignment for you?"

"I am to return to my regiment tomorrow, ma'am," he said, "with letters for General Crauford."

She looked at him and laughed. "The hero of the retreat from Talavera and the occasional reconnaissance officer for the commander-in-chief," she said, "brought out of his way to Viseu merely to deliver a lady safely to the bosom of her aunt and to carry letters from one general to another like a little schoolboy running errands? Am I expected to believe that, Captain?"

"Frankly, ma'am," he said somewhat stiffly, "I do not care what you believe."

"Oh, do you not?" She slipped her arm from his and stopped walking in order to look up into his face. She smiled at him. "Do you really not care? Dozens of men do. Must you be different in that too? Must you be the only one who does not care whether I am alive or dead?"

"You have broadened the meaning of my words," he said. "I did not say that."

"Then you do care?" She ran one finger down his sleeve from elbow to wrist.

"You are playing word games with me," he said. "I

have no skill in them. Your questions presuppose answers, but if I give them, I may be led into saying what I do not wish to say or mean."

"Ah," she said, and sighed. "You will be leaving tomorrow, Captain? Will you not be sorry never to see me again?"

He looked down into her eyes and said nothing. And she knew that he had just given her one reason for her fascination with him. He would not allow himself to be led along in conversation like other men. She could not make him say what she wished him to say.

"Never is a long time," she said, laying a light hand on his sleeve.

He looked down at her hand. "You should not flirt with me," he said. "We do not inhabit the same world or play the same games, ma'am. Socially speaking, I am a nobody, as I have told you before, and you are a somebody. I am dangerous to flirt with, as you should have learned on a previous occasion. I know neither the rules nor the boundaries of the game."

He was right. One part of her was terrified. But another part was excited beyond measure. She remembered the feeling of helplessness and the temptation to surrender when he had lifted her against him until only her toes had rested on the floor. She remembered the feel and taste of his tongue deep inside her mouth. And she knew there was danger, danger that the next time he would not stop, danger that the next time she would not stop him.

"Who said anything about flirting?" she said. Her next words surprised her. They were unplanned. "I wish you were not going. I am not ready to say good-bye."

Her hand was still resting lightly on his arm. She could feel the muscles tense.

"Robert," she said softly. "It is a lovely name. I knew another Robert once."

There was a spark of something in his eyes as they looked intently back into hers.

"He was a sweet and gentle boy,' she said, "quite unlike you. Except that he had your blond hair, which he wore long, and your blue eyes, which dreamed and smiled. He died."

His arm beneath her hand was almost trembling with tension.

"Ah, Robert," she said, "you do not play fair. You warn me not to flirt, but what choice do I have when you just stand there and will make no move of your own? Are we to return to the ballroom and say a civil good-bye and never see or think of each other again?"

"Why would you wish to see or think of me after to-night?" he asked.

"Why?" She looked up into his eyes and shrugged. "Perhaps because you are different. Perhaps because you have been the only man for a long time who does not want me. And yet you did want me in Obidos, did you not?"

She watched him swallow in the darkness. And she felt strangely like crying. She would see him again. He did not know that, but she did, and she did not want it to happen—not in that way. Damn Arthur and his devious schemes. Why could not Robert have everything explained to him? Why could not his own acting skills be put to the test? Why did she always have to play the eternal flirt? And with the last man on earth she wanted to flirt with?

She sighed. "This has not been a good idea, has it?" she said. "We had better return to the ballroom. There are gentlemen enough there waiting to dance with me or to fetch me drinks or to hold my fan while I adjust a curl. I need not be out here trying to make conversation with a silent man or trying to coax a marble statue to kiss me. It is cold." She shivered. "Is it not cold?"

"No." His hands were on her bare arms, large and strong and warm, moving up and down them. "No, it is not cold.' He drew her against him and wrapped his arms warmly about her. She turned her head and rested a cheek against his heart and closed her eyes. And one hand smoothed gently over the top of her head. "And no, I do not want to leave tomorrow, knowing that I will never see you again. But it is a foolish thought. We are from different worlds, ma . . . ma'am."

"Joana," she whispered.

"Joana."

"Robert," she said, and her eyes were brimming with

tears and her throat constricted with them. "Forgive me." But how could she ask forgiveness in advance without telling him all? She was losing control again. She never lost control. That was what made her so good at her self-imposed job and what gave her command of her own life and destiny.

"For what?" She felt his cheek against the top of her head.

"For Obidos." She lifted her head and smiled up at him, hoping that in the night light her eyes would appear merely bright. "I behaved abominably."

He smiled slowly down at her. "Obidos should not have happened," he said. "This should not be happening."

"What?" She gazed up into his eyes, her hands spread across the broad expanse of his chest. "What should not be happening?"

"This," he said, and he kissed her forehead, her temples, her eyes, and her cheeks. And he looked deeply into her eyes as his mouth hovered close to hers.

"But it is," she said.

"But it is." He closed the gap between their mouths, kissing her softly and openmouthed.

She moved her hands up to his shoulders and about his neck. One hand played with his close-cropped hair. And she arched her body into his, wanting to feel his hard-muscled length with every part of her. And she wanted him closer and closer yet. She wanted to feel his tongue, but he would do nothing but lick at her lips with it. Of course, she had hurt him at Obidos.

She experimented, touching his lips with her own tongue, pushing it beyond and up behind his upper lip. She pushed beyond his teeth and felt his arms tighten about her suddenly as he sucked inward and she moaned with mingled fear and desire.

"Robert." She threw her head back, eyes closed, as his mouth moved down to her throat and his hand pushed her gown away from one shoulder and down her arm, exposing one breast. And then his palm was against her nipple, circling it, and his fingers curled in to caress the soft flesh. Her mouth opened in a silent cry and then her fingers twined in his hair as he took the hardened tip of her breast into his mouth and sucked on it, flicking his tongue across it.

She realized in that moment that for all the knowledge and experience she had of sensual matters, she might still be a virgin, though she was not. And she knew why she had both feared and been fascinated by this man since she had first set eyes on him.

And then his face was above hers again, his eyes looking down into her own, and he was drawing her gown back up over her breast and her shoulder.

"A good-bye kiss," he said. "Doubtless you would get more from another man, but you would not remember with pleasure having given yourself in a moment of passion to a man who is not even a gentleman."

She felt blinded by hurt at his assumptions about her morality—assumptions that she had fostered by the part she played. And she ached with disappointment, with a purely physical dissatisfaction. Oh, yes, and with an emotional one too.

She smiled. "A kiss?" she said. "Do you call that a kiss, Robert? It was rather naughty, was it not? Perhaps I should report you to my aunt. Or to Arthur."

"And they will wish to know how I discovered such a conveniently deserted trysting place," he said. "Perhaps it would be wiser to say nothing."

"Perhaps it would." She continued to smile.

"Good-bye, then," he said briskly, straightening up and brushing at his sleeves. "I shall be taking my leave now."

"Will you?" she said. "Kiss and run, Robert? How lacking in chivalry you are. The least you could do is mope in a corner for the rest of the evening, looking lovelorn."

"That is not in my style," he said, grinning at her briefly so that her knees turned to jelly all over again. "I am expected to be silent and morose and rather uncouth, but definitely not lovelorn. I am supposed to be incapable of such a fine emotion. Besides, I must leave tomorrow and need some sleep."

"Ah." She set one hand against his chest and tiptoed two fingers up to his chin. "Take care of yourself, Robert. Don't go getting yourself killed."

"I was told just tonight that I am too stubborn to die," he said, capturing her hand in his and bringing the palm against his mouth. "Don't worry about me, Joana. And forget about me. I am not worth another thought to you."

"You are right." She sighed. "So many new officers arriving here every day, and each one more handsome than the last. It is enough to make a lady wish that the wars will never come to an end." She laughed lightly. "Escort me back to the ballroom, Robert, and then you may make your escape." She set a hand on his sleeve.

The crowds had spilled out of the ballroom so that they were surrounded by people long before he left her at its open doors. She smiled brightly at him.

"Au revoir, then," she said, slipping her hand from his sleeve. "I will not say good-bye, Robert, for I do not really believe in good-byes. We will meet again, I believe, and perhaps sooner than you think. And there are at least half a dozen officers not fifty paces away, all glowering at you, all with itching sword hands. I believe you kept me away for longer than the one set, Captain. For shame!" She tapped his arm sharply with her fan.

And she whisked herself away without giving him a chance to reply. And did not look back to see whether he stood there in the doorway looking after her or whether he hurried away without a backward glance.

She felt, she thought, as she waved her fan before her face and set her eyes to dancing, as if she could sit down in the middle of the dance floor and howl with misery.

Just as if she had fallen in love with Captain Robert Blake or something equally foolish and ridiculous.

10

DESPITE his determination to concentrate on his mission, to put everything out of his mind except Salamanca and what faced him there, Captain Blake found that as he traveled back westward into the hills to meet the Ordenanza leader, Duarte Ribeiro, who was to guide him to the Spanish border, he could do no such thing.

There were two reasons, one trivial to his own mind, the other a heavy weight.

The trivial reason was Joana da Fonte, the Marquesa das Minas. He tried to think of her by her full title, not just as Joana. He tried to distance himself from her. He tried not to remember how she had seemed to move beyond mere flirtation on that final evening into a real fondness for him. He tried not to believe that she had been in any way fond of him.

She was an accomplished flirt and by her own admission he was one of the few men not to fall to her charms. She had been forced by her very nature, perhaps, into using tactics other than her usual ones. She had been forced into trying what had seemed very like sincerity. Sometimes he felt guilty about suspecting her of using just another form of flirtation. And sometimes he called himself fool for wondering if she had been sincere.

He thought of all the questions she had asked, of the way in which she had tried to find out more about him and about the reason for his summons to headquarters. And at such times he remembered that she was half-French and wondered if the commander-in-chief knew that fact and if it were of any significance anyway. After all, she was also half-English and had been married to a Portuguese nobleman.

He wanted to rid his mind of her, but whenever he

was not consciously thinking of something else, there she was in his thoughts and in his dreams and emotions. In his blood. There were times when he regretted pulling back from that final embrace, when he had sensed her surrender. When he might perhaps have possessed her. And perhaps have worked her out of his system once and for all.

He hated pining for what could not be had. He hated himself for reaching beyond his grasp—for forgetting who and what he was.

And then there was the weight and the burden on his mind that made him forget for minutes and even hours at a stretch that he was going voluntarily into danger and perhaps death, that he was expecting the humiliation of capture and the difficult task of convincing his captors that the sealed paper in his boot heel was an authentic diagram of the British defenses of Lisbon. That perhaps many weary months would pass before he was exchanged for a captive French officer.

During his almost eleven years in the army he had heard from his father three times. He had written back only once—with condolences on the death of his father's wife almost eight years before. Another letter had found him at Viseu mere minutes before he had been planning to leave, an old letter that had come to headquarters and been sent on to the Light Division at the Coa and sent back for redirection to the hospital at Lisbon. But someone had had the presence of mind to know that he was in Viseu.

It was not from his father. It was from his father's solicitor informing him that according to his father's will he had been left an estate of moderate size in Berkshire and a sizable fortune. It seemed that another letter informing him of his father's death must have gone astray. The bulk of the property and fortune, of course, had gone to his father's heir, a second cousin and the new Marquess of Quesnay.

His father was dead, and there was no point now in regretting the bitterness and disillusion that had caused him to break off all relations with him. He had broken away because when all was said and done he was to his father only a bastard son, to be provided for because it made his father feel magnanimous to do so.

He did not regret the break he had made. He would not have gone through life with the burden of a humiliation on him, with the knowledge that he owed everything to the generosity of the man who had fathered him. As if one did not have a right to the care of one's father. As if such care were a privilege when one happened to have been begotten on the wrong side of the blanket.

And yet, he thought as he trudged his lone way through the hills, following the route outlined for him at headquarters, there were the memories that crowded his mind now that he was truly alone in the world. Memories of his mother's happiness and of her loveliness on the days when his father was expected. Memories of the two of them, their hands clasped or their arms twined about each other's waists, glowing in each other's company and smiling—always smiling—at him. Memories of his father lifting him above his head and tossing him up toward the sky while his mother shrieked and his childhood self laughed helplessly.

Memories of love. And of innocence. Of a time when it had not seemed odd to him that his father, his mother's lover, did not live with them but in the big house with his wife. Of a time when he had not known that that single fact would make all the difference in the world to him. When he had not realized that he would become something of a charity case to his father.

And now his father was dead and he himself was in a sense a gentleman. At least he had the property and the wealth to set up as a gentleman. He had the wealth to purchase his promotions if he so chose, instead of having to wait for vacancies caused more often than not by death in battle.

He had the position and the wealth perhaps to . . .

No! He had decided years ago that life was to be lived alone if it was to bring him any sense of fulfillment and contentment. There was no room in his life for a woman. No room for the chains of love.

He determinedly did not grieve for his father. It would be hypocritical to do so. But he did grieve for the long-ago loss of childhood and innocence and unclouded hap-

piness. He grieved for the child he had been and the man
he might have been.

He had been a sweet and gentle boy, she had said,
describing that other Robert she had known. A boy with
eyes that smiled and dreamed. Yes, even then, when
innocence had already been fast fading. He grieved for
the boy he had been, the boy she seemed to believe had
died.

And he remembered how she had once called that
sweet and gentle boy a bastard and how she had mocked
him. And he tried again and constantly to put her from
his mind and his heart.

Duarte Ribeiro had left his lands and his home in the
south, laid waste by Junot's army on its advance to Lisbon three years before. Tenants and peasant friends had
restored the land, he had heard, and even seen during
occasional fleeting visits. But he would not go home to
stay until the hated French had been driven finally and
forever from his native soil.

He could not count the number of Frenchmen he had
killed with his own hands during the past three years.
He could not even estimate the numbers killed by his
band of almost forty men and a few women. But it was
never enough. Never enough to satisfy him that the
deaths of his brother and his brother's family and the
brutal rape and death of his sister had been avenged.
Never enough to make him forgive himself for having
been from home that day. And never enough to satisfy
the people of his band for similar grievances.

Duarte Ribeiro lived now, when he was in one place
for any length of time, in the village of Mortagoa in the
rugged hills east of Bussaco. He had been there for most
of the spring, the British army having done an effective
job of keeping even French stragglers out of Portugal.
His men were inclined to grumble about the inactivity.

And yet excitement and anticipation were growing.
The French would be coming soon, they all felt, if they
could get past the forts of Ciudad Rodrigo and Almeida,
if Viscount Wellington did not successfully support the
forts' garrisons. And even if he did, the French would
be on Portuguese soil when they attacked Almeida. And

once on Portuguese soil, they would be fair game to the Ordenanza.

Duarte stood in the doorway of the white stone cottage that he currently called home, idly watching Carlota Mendes, his woman, seated on a bench outside in the late-afternoon sunshine suckling their new son at one shapely and ample breast. Her black hair hung unconfined and appealingly unkempt over her shoulders.

"Will he come today, do you think?" she asked, looking up at him briefly.

"Today, tomorrow," he said. "Sometime he will come. It will be good to have something to do. I am growing restless."

"I know." She grimaced. "And so I will be left here with most of the other women and children. This little one should have waited until the wars were over." She looked fondly down at their son.

"Well," he said, "babies come from what we spent last summer doing with great enthusiasm when we were not harassing our uninvited guests, Carlota. Know that for the future."

She flashed him a wide smile before disengaging the baby from her breast and lifting his sleepy form up against her shoulder. She patted his back gently. "We," she said. "We two. But it is I who must now stay at home fighting boredom instead of my mother and father's killers."

Carlota's father had been a respected doctor, killed with his wife after a wounded French officer he had been ordered to tend had died anyway. Carlota had been away from home, staying with her brother and sister-in-law at the time.

"I'll not be gone long," he said. "I merely have to guide this British soldier to the border and put him into the safe keeping of Becquer and his men. It seems that the Englishman has some secret mission in Spain, lucky dog."

"You see?" Carlota said, guiding the nipple of her other breast to her son's seeking mouth. "You would be gone from me for the rest of the summer if you had your way."

He reached out a hand to run the back of one finger

along her hair. "Not so," he said softly. "I would not be separated from you for a single day if it were not necessary, Carlota. But little Miguel must be given a warm and secure home. And I would not have you in the thick of danger now that you are the mother of my son."

"Oh," she said, bristling with indignation, "but it is all right for the father of my son to be there?"

"Yes," he said quietly. "Our son must be given a country of his own in which to live and grow peacefully, Carlota."

She raised a hand to touch his against her hair, and she looked up and smiled at him.

He nodded his head along the narrow street and pushed his shoulder away from the door frame. "I do believe Francisco and Teófilo have found our man and are bringing him this way," he said. A tall, blond, green-coated British soldier was striding along the street between his two friends, the curved sword at his side and the red sash proclaiming him an officer, the rifle slung over his shoulder suggesting that he was also a fighting man.

"Here he is," Teófilo Costa called, his smile very white in his sun-bronzed face. "And did not get lost among the hills even once. Perhaps his crooked nose would account for his success. Most of the English get themselves lost if they cannot walk a straight line." He was talking in loud and cheerful Portuguese. He turned to Captain Blake as they came up to Duarte's cottage and switched to heavily accented English. "Duarte Ribeiro, sir. The leader of our group."

"Thank you," Captain Blake said in Portuguese. "I believe it had more to do with carefully given directions and a concentration on following them."

Francisco Braga, Duarte, and Carlota burst into loud laughter at the expense of their discomfited friend.

"But it is a very handsome nose nonetheless," Teófilo said, joining in the laughter.

"You have met these two," Duarte said. "This is Carlota Mendes and our son, Miguel." He watched the Englishman's eyes flicker to Carlota's exposed breast and slide away again. The English were prudes, he recalled. And he remembered his mother, always and ever the lady even with that brute of a second husband of hers. "Come inside, Captain Blake. You will be ready for some refreshments. Tomorrow we will start for the border and you may relax. You will be able to rely on native guides rather than the shape of your nose to get you safely there."

Teófilo slapped the side of his head with the palm of his hand. "I will never be allowed to forget that, will I?" he said.

"You have a block of wood for a brain, Teófilo," Carlota said, getting to her feet and tucking her breast away inside her dress again. "Would an Englishman be sent into Spain on a special mission if he did not know both Portuguese and Spanish? I would bet the length of my hair that he also speaks French."

"You are right, ma'am," Captain Blake said with a laugh, setting down his rifle carefully when he stepped inside the house, and reaching into a pocket inside his coat. "Before I forget, Ribeiro. You have been sent your instructions already, I believe, but I do also have a sealed letter for you."

Duarte took it and glanced curiously at it. He did not recognize the handwriting. He opened it while Carlota set down the baby and busied herself cutting cheese and slicing bread and filling cups with wine. He remained standing while the others sat down, and read the letter quickly. It was from his half-sister. She must have had someone else write on the outside.

He was to give Captain Blake every assistance, he read. But he must not reveal their relationship to the captain. She would be coming to Mortagoa herself within a week of his receipt of this letter. Would he be back from the border by then? He must not worry about sending to meet her. She would come in the usual manner. She needed his assistance in some delicate business.

"Some delicate business" was Joana's usual way of referring to her journeys into Spain, going right in among the French in search of Maria and Miguel's killer. He hated her putting herself in such danger, but there was nothing he could do about it. She was not even his full sister to be taking orders from him, and even if she were, he suspected that Joana would be beyond his control unless he were willing to tie her hand and foot.

And now she was going again, it seemed. And coming here first "in the usual manner." That meant that she could be alone and dressed like a peasant and willing and eager to join in all the activities of his band for however long she felt she could stay. And the damnable thing was that she was good at it. The delicate Marquesa das Minas became virtually unrecognizable in the reckless and fearless Joana Ribeiro.

Duarte clamped his teeth together. The devilish woman! She was all he had left in the world. No. He folded the letter back into its original folds. Life was not that uncomplicated any longer. Harassing and killing the French was no longer a simple game of revenge. It was a serious business of survival, a matter of a man doing all that was necessary, even killing, in order to protect his woman and his child and the homeland in which they lived. There were Carlota and Miguel now, closer to him even than Joana, and the sooner the three of them could take themselves off to find a priest, the better he would like it.

"Duarte? Bad news?" Carlota touched his arm while the other three men looked up at him from the table.

"No. Not at all," he said, thrusting the letter into a pocket. "So, Captain Blake, when are the English going to let the French past so that we can have our share of them too?" He sat down at the table and reached for his cup of wine.

It was all almost frighteningly easy. Even the most carefully made plans had a habit of going awry. But not this one. This one happened just as it was meant to happen.

Duarte Ribeiro, Francisco Braga, and Teófilo Costa were cheerful companions and took him to the border and directly to the temporary camp of the Spanish guerrillero leader with a sureness that suggested a long familiarity with the rugged hills and the deep clefts of ravines that tended all to look alike to Captain Blake.

All three of his guides shook hands with him after he had been greeted by the Spaniards and wished him luck in his mission. They did not know what it was and they had not questioned him. They understood the rules of war better than the Marquesa das Minas had, he reflected, finding it impossible not to think of her frequently.

"Good luck," Duarte said to him. "I hope it is our good fortune and yours that we meet again. I have been sent no instructions about conducting you back again." It was the closest he had come to showing the curiosity that he must feel.

"No." Captain Blake smiled rather ruefully. "I shall find my own way. Perhaps my nose will help."

"If someone does not break it in the opposite direction," Teófilo said, and they all laughed.

Captain Blake watched them go with regret. He felt very alone with strangers on the border of another country, enemy territory.

Like the Portuguese, the Spaniards knew only as much of his mission as they needed to know. Theirs was a dangerous task. They were to take him down from the rugged hills of the border into the more rolling hills below and close to Salamanca. There they were to make their presence known so that the French would come in pursuit of them. All but one of them—Captain Blake— were to elude capture.

If they failed, theirs would be a terrible fate. They would not be granted the honorable captivity afforded to enemy soldiers, but would be executed after a suitable interval of torture.

"But, señor," Antonio Becquer, a great mountain of a man with arms and legs like tree trunks, said to him with a smile and a shrug when Captain Blake expressed his concern, "we do the same to our French captives, you see. And we have far more of them to bring us enjoyment than they ever have of us. War is war in Spain. It is not the game you soldiers play."

Captain Blake found himself wishing for the first time in his career that his uniform was scarlet and quite unmistakably British. Not that he would shun a good fight. Indeed he would welcome one to blow away the cobwebs of a winter of inactivity. It was the idea of *not* fighting that was filling him with the jitters.

"We are close to the city instead of being up in the hills because some of your number need to be called out of the city to hear my news," Captain Blake said long before they drew close to Salamanca, when they were reviewing their plans. "That will explain why I am mad enough to venture so close to French pickets. Is it plausible? Is it likely that some of your men would be in Salamanca when it is occupied by the French?"

"Señor." Antonio looked around at his men, who had all chuckled at the question. "We are Spaniards. This is our country. We are everywhere."

"An uncomfortable thought for the French," Captain Blake said.

"We intend it to be." The Spaniard grinned. "We would consider it a personal shame to allow a single Frenchman a good night's sleep on Spanish soil. Not that we are inhospitable, of course."

"So it *is* plausible," Captain Blake said. "And they will know it?"

"They will all have a friend or a friend of a friend who has had his throat cut mysteriously in the night," Antonio said.

Captain Blake shuddered inwardly and was thankful that the British were the friends of the Spaniards.

And so it happened as planned. It had to happen at night—dangerous, everyone agreed, when the French might not immediately be able to see the uniform of their captive, but not unduly so. They would not be anxious to kill a guerrillero too easily.

"Though what your general means by sending you here simply to be captured, I do not know," Antonio said with an expressive shrug. "You are an assassin, señor? But even your uniform will not save you from death once you have killed. Is it Massena himself you are to kill? If it is in his bed, be sure that it is he you kill and not his mistress. She goes everywhere with him, did you know, and is officially listed as his aide de camp? Ah, these French. Such aids they need."

His men all laughed heartily.

"They say he is still in Salamanca, even though the year is already advanced," one of the men said, "because he is too busy in his bed to think of being busy out of it."

Another burst of laughter.

They were on foot on the night in question, making clumsy noises close to a picket line that disgusted Antonio with its lack of subtlety.

"It will be a blow to my pride, señor," he had said the day before, "to have the French believe that I would betray my presence to them in such a stupid manner."

Captain Blake knew how he felt. His ankle turned beneath him as he fled with the rest, and then he tripped over his sword and fell heavily, cursing roundly—in English—lest the pickets pass him by and not even notice him lying among the trees on the south bank of the Douro River, within a hundred yards of the old Roman bridge crossing it to the city.

And so he had to stagger to his feet, hands held high above his head, while a frightened French boy held a bayonet to his chest and another relieved him of his rifle, bumping him roughly and painfully against the side of the head with it, and kicking him hard on the shin of his injured leg.

"He is a soldier," the boy said, his eyes widening as someone else came running with a lantern. "British. An officer."

The soldier who had done the bumping and kicking became considerably more respectful.

"We should take his sword?" he asked the boy in French. "Be careful that he does not grab your bayonet and turn it on you. Were those others British too? Are they invading?"

If he had just said "Boo!" Captain Blake thought, the boy would have turned and run.

"I will surrender my sword to an officer of your army," he said haughtily, "not to a private soldier. Take me to one."

But the commotion of the pursuit of the fleeing Spaniards and of his capture had drawn an officer—a fellow captain—out of the darkness. He directed the lantern holder to shine its light more fully onto their captive.

"Captain?" he said. His eyes strayed up and down the uniform. "A rifleman? Always our greatest enemies and our primary targets in battle. I will accept your sword, sir, and escort you across the bridge. It will be an honor to have a rifleman as our prisoner."

Captain Blake held the French officer's eyes as he unbuckled his sword belt, lifted the heavy sword and scabbard from his side, and held them out. He half-expected that the man would direct one of the gawking private soldiers to take it, but he accepted it himself.

"Thank you, monsieur," he said. "Captain Antoine Dupuis at your service. And whom do I have the honor of escorting?" He indicated the bridge with one outstretched hand, and Captain Blake moved toward it.

"Captain Robert Blake of the Ninety-fifth Rifles," he said. He did not believe there could be a feeling of greater humiliation. He had felt, removing his sword, as if he were stripping himself to the view of the French soldiers. He felt naked now without the weight of his sword at his side.

11

JOANA made her usual stop at the Convent of Bussaco, high in the hills west of Mortagoa. She and Matilda were always welcome to spend a night there. Indeed the nuns kept a small trunk of hers so that her change of person could be made with the minimum fuss.

And so the Marquesa das Minas arrived with some pomp from Viseu early one evening, smiling graciously at her coachman as she was handed from the white-and-gold carriage, and more dazzlingly at the mother superior, who greeted her inside the door. She ate a quiet supper with the nuns and joined them for evening prayer, retiring late to the small bare room she shared with her companion.

The following morning a morose Matilda sat down to breakfast without the marquesa and retired to the small room afterward to put away the white clothes with care and to prepare others of more gorgeous hue. The marquesa herself was nowhere in sight. But the small trunk was empty and one of the footmen who had accompanied the carriage was missing.

Far along the stony track to Mortagoa, the footman trudged behind a young peasant girl dressed in a faded blue cotton dress, sandals on her feet, dark hair hanging in a wavy cloud about her face and down over her shoulders. Her only ornaments appeared to be a wicked-looking knife thrust into her belt and an old musket slung over her shoulder.

It was only José's silent presence behind her that prevented Matilda and Duarte from declaring open war on her, Joana thought as she strode along, so exhilarated by the sense of freedom the morning had brought that she had to exercise the utmost self-control not to jump for

joy and shout out her greetings to the hills. José would
think she had taken leave of her senses if she did either
of those things.

She did not really need José. She had her musket,
though muskets were notoriously poor at hitting any definite target. She thought enviously of Captain Blake's
rifle. And she had her knife to defend herself against
anyone who got past the musket. Anyone who got past
both would doubtless get past José too. But then, men—
and many women too—had a tiresome tendency to believe that a woman was perfectly safe provided she had
some male hovering over her. And José was a large
enough male almost to satisfy Matilda and Duarte.

"We are there," she said, turning to her silent servant
as they approached Mortagoa. "You may go visit your
friends, José."

She approached her brother's house with quickened
footsteps. She had not yet seen the baby. The last time
she had been in the hills, Carlota had been huge with
child and fretting over the fact that Duarte had laid down
the law and forbidden her to go out anymore with the
other members of the band. She was not his wife, Carlota
had argued. He could not give her orders. She would go
if she pleased. She would die if she had to stay at home
with the women and children.

But he could give her orders, Duarte had said, looking
very handsome and very formidable, standing feet apart,
glowering down at his pregnant woman. He was the
leader of the band of which she was a member, and if
he said she was to stay, then stay she would or face
disciplinary measures from the whole band.

Besides, he had added, his voice and expression soft-
ening, and Joana had felt an unexpected and unaccustomed flash of envy for the other woman, she was to be
the mother of his child and she would do whatever he
bade her to do for her own and their child's safety.

Joana knocked lightly on the open door of her brother's house and peered inside, wondering if Duarte had
won that particular war or if Carlota had proved too
much for him. And she wondered if Duarte was back
from the border yet. The thought made her stomach
lurch uncomfortably.

She had tried very hard not to think of Robert since he had left Viseu, or at least to think of him only in a purely impersonal way, as part of the job they were to accomplish jointly. She tried hard to think of him as Captain Blake, not as Robert. She tried hard to forget that she had wanted him to make love to her at the Viseu ball and had felt flat with disappointment all night long after he had left because he had shown more restraint—or less desire—than she.

She tried hard to quell the unwilling pictures of matters gone wrong, of his bloody and mangled remains lying somewhere outside Salamanca.

"Carlota?" she said, seeing movement at the other side of the room onto which the door opened, even though the sunlight outside had momentarily blinded her. "Carlota? And the baby? Oh, he is gorgeous! All that black hair. Just like Duarte." She laughed. "And you, of course."

Perhaps it was as well that Duarte did not return from his journey to the border until two hours later. Much time had to be given to laughing and hugging and admiring the baby, who slept the whole time as he was passed from one woman to the other.

"And you two will be marrying?" Joana asked.

Carlota pulled a face. "Ah, that man," she said. "Now that my body has performed like a woman's and produced a child, I am to be treated like a woman. Nothing but a home and children and safety and boredom, Joana. If I could go back to last summer I would do things a little differently perhaps. Deny him a few times. Leave him panting a few times. But there." She laughed. "I would have had to deny myself too, and done some of my own panting. And I would be without Miguel. I cannot imagine life without Miguel. Yes, Duarte is talking about priests and weddings and baptisms and all that. A typical man."

When her brother did arrive home, Joana discovered that for the first few minutes she might as well have been invisible. Carlota rushed into his arms and he hugged her wordlessly while she showered him with questions and scoldings and news of the baby.

"And Joana is here," she said. "Another woman for

you to bully. There were no French soldiers near the border?"

"Joana?" he said, finally releasing Carlota to cross the room. He bent to kiss her cheek and smooth a hand over the hair of the baby as he lay asleep in her lap. "You are making friends with Miguel? Ah, it is good to be home again. You should be in Viseu or Lisbon. It is not safe to be here now. The summer campaign is about to begin."

"Is he safe?" she asked quickly. "He came to no harm?" She bit her lip. Where had those words come from? She had not planned them at all. "Captain Blake," she said. "We are working together. At least, he does not know it, but we are."

He sat down at the table slowly and looked steadily at her. "Why do I have a terrible premonition of danger, Joana?" he asked. "What do you mean, 'working together'? You are going to Salamanca, I suppose? Is that where he is going? Are you planning to do more there than try to spot a face that has eluded you for three years in addition to soaking up whatever small pieces of information come your way? Is it an active job this time?"

"Yes," she said, her voice somewhat breathless. "I cannot give you details, Duarte. I am under orders from the Viscount Wellington, as is Captain Blake. But—"

"Under orders?" Duarte's eyebrows drew together and he banged the table with one fist so that the baby jumped and opened his eyes to frown up at Joana. "Is the man using innocent women now to do his work? Is that how the English do things, Joana?"

"We are half-English," she reminded him. "And you must know that Arthur is as unwilling as you for me to involve myself in this war. But when he knew that I would go anyway, that I am not easily manipulated by men, then he consented to make use of my talents." She pulled a face. "They seem to be mainly talents for flirting. I am a dreadful flirt, Duarte. The officers at Lisbon and Viseu flock about me. I could be married ten times over each week."

"There will come one eventually," he said, "who will not be manipulated by you, Joana. Then we will see an end to your flirting and to this nonsense of putting yourself in danger too."

"It is not nonsense," she said. "I shall see that face one day, Duarte, I know it. And the long wait will be worth it. Finally Miguel and his wife and children and Maria will be able to rest in peace."

He sighed. "But if you do see him by some miracle, Joana," he said, "you must not go after him yourself. You must send for me. Promise?"

"I shall see," she said vaguely. "Did he arrive safely, Duarte?"

"*He* being Blake this time?" he asked. "I conducted him to Becquer at the border, as arranged. I did not know that his destination was Salamanca. Right among the French." He frowned. "Is everyone mad?"

"I need you, Duarte," she said. "But it will be very dangerous for you."

He snorted and Carlota got quietly to her feet and took the fussing baby from Joana's arms.

"The time will come," Joana said, "at least I hope it will, when Captain Blake will need to be rescued from Salamanca. By that time I do not believe it will be easy for him to escape unassisted."

Duarte scratched the back of his neck and looked up at Carlota.

"He will have given his parole, you see," Joana said. "Then he will have considerable freedom but will be honor-bound not to escape. I will have to see to it that he is released from his word."

"How?" Carlota said. "Men set such store by honor, Joana."

"By seeing to it that he is badly treated," Joana said, "perhaps even imprisoned. Then the French will have broken their part of the bargain, you see. But then, also he may not have the freedom—or the strength—to do it alone. And I think I should be taken hostage at the same time, Duarte. The French will be a little more cautious in their pursuit of you if you have me hostage. I shall make sure that scores of them are expiring with love for me. Besides, I will need to leave, for soon after that they will discover either that I have betrayed them or that I am unbelievably stupid. My pride hopes that it is the former."

"You would not care to go into explanations, I suppose?" her brother asked.

"No," she said. "No, I would rather not."

"He was going to Salamanca, then, knowing that he would be captured?" he said.

"Yes." She drew a deep breath. "If they have not killed him first and asked questions after, that is. I will not know until I arrive there myself. Do you think they would shoot rather than take a captive, Duarte?"

"Joana," he asked, looking at her closely, "does this man mean something to you?"

"Only as a colleague," she said. She frowned. "Although he does not know I am that to him. He is going to hate me dreadfully when he believes that I am allied with the French. But I could not warn him or apologize in advance. It is all part of Arthur's plan, you see."

"He is a very handsome man," Carlota said. "That blond hair and those blue eyes. And the broad shoulders."

"Hey, hey," Duarte said.

Carlota threw him a saucy look. "Of course," she said, "war has spoiled what must at one time have been a lovely face."

"And has made of it a wonderfully attractive one instead," Joana said absently, gnawing on the side of one finger.

Duarte and Carlota exchanged a look over her head.

"Will you do it?" Joana asked, her eyes focusing again and her head coming up. "If I send Matilda home—I think a sister of hers will have to die suddenly or something like that—will you come? I cannot predict exactly when it will be, so we cannot plan on a definite date. But I will send Matilda. Will you do it?"

"To Salamanca and actually into Salamanca?" he said. "It sounds like suicide to me, Joana. Also marvelously challenging. I shall have to seek out Becquer again. He would probably like it less than the French if I encroached on his territory without leave."

"But you will do it?" she asked.

"He will do it," Carlota said angrily, "and I will be left at home to sweep the floors and play with the baby, like the good wife he wants to make me into. He will do it, Joana. Oh, what I would not give for the chance to come too."

"Thank you." Joana breathed a sign of relief. "I have to leave tomorrow, early. It was hardly worth changing persons and walking out here, was it? But how could I resist even one day of glorious freedom? I am beginning almost to hate the Marquesa das Minas."

"So am I," her brother said fervently. "She gives me too many sleepless nights. But then, Joana Ribeiro gives me plenty too."

"This will probably be the end of the marquesa," she said. "She will soon lose her usefulness. I shall have to find someone else to be for the rest of my life." She sighed. "But I so want to see that face first."

"Be careful," her brother said with a frown. "This sounds too dangerous, Joana. I suppose I cannot persuade you to change your mind?"

She smiled at him.

"I did not think so," he said. "Be careful."

"Have fun, Joana," Carlota said. "Have fun while you can."

"Oh," Joana said, and her smile brightened, "I intend to. Yes, I do intend to."

"Have a seat, if you please, Captain Blake," Colonel Marcel Leroux said after introducing himself and the other occupants of the room—except for the two silent sergeants who stood guard at either side of the door.

General Charles Valéry, a tall, thin, aristocratic-looking gentleman, would look more at home in a ballroom than on a battlefield, Captain Blake thought. He stood in front of a window at the far side of the room, allowing the colonel to conduct the interrogation. Captain Henri Dionne was small but solidly built. He looked as if he might be handy with his sword. Captain Antoine Dupuis he had met the night before. Colonel Leroux was a tall and handsome man with dark hair and eyes and mustache. A ladies' man, Captain Blake thought. He sat.

"I trust your night's rest was comfortable?" the colonel said. "It was of course necessary to put you under guard."

"Quite comfortable, thank you," Captain Blake said.

"Do you speak French, monsieur?" the colonel asked. "If you do not, I have an interpreter on hand so that General Valéry may understand what you say."

"I speak French," Captain Blake said, switching to that language. "But I am afraid I have very little to say."

"But you will pardon us if we question you anyway," the colonel said. "Why would an officer of the famed rifle regiment—the Ninety-fifth, is it?—be within a stone's throw of Salamanca last night?"

Captain Blake shrugged and fingered the bruise on his right temple. His right eye was somewhat bloodshot. "I lost my way," he said. "I could have sworn I was approaching Lisbon."

"Ah, Captain," the colonel said as the general turned to look out of the window. His clasped hands beat a tattoo against his back. "Such words are unworthy of you. Your companions, who all escaped, I regret to say, were Spanish partisans?"

"Were they?" Captain Blake said. "That was why I did not understand a word of what they were gabbling, then."

The colonel got to his feet. "Why did you come here, Captain?" he asked. "You are one of the British scouting officers? A spy, in plainer language?"

"Good Lord," Captain Blake said. "Am I? Because I took a wrong turn somewhere in the mountains? Have you noticed how they all look alike? No, perhaps not. Perhaps you do not know Portugal."

"It would seem foolish," the colonel said, "for the British to send a scouting officer so close to Salamanca when they must know that the bulk of our forces and our headquarters are here. And very rash for partisans to come so close."

"I could not agree more," Captain Blake said. "I would not have come knocking on the door had I known whose door I was knocking on, believe me. And I daresay those partisans would have stayed in their, ah, own country if they had known that the might of France was here."

"Unless there were someone inside here with whom

you wished to communicate," Captain Dionne said, speaking for the first time.

"Well," Captain Blake said, "I did hear that there are some quite superior brothels in Salamanca. But I do not look too pretty for the whores at present, do I?" He indicated his eye.

"We are wasting our time, Colonel," the general said without turning away from the window. "You have not been in the Peninsula since the arrival of the British soldiers. They are not as easily cowed as some of our European neighbors. It is a pity he came in uniform. We would have information instead of impudence if he had not."

The colonel shrugged apologetically at Captain Blake. "You are an officer and a gentleman and must be treated as such," he said. "We wish to accord you every honor and courtesy, Captain. But we must of course ask questions. You have papers on you?"

"No," the captain said. "I left behind all the love letters I have received from England. It would be embarrassing to have them read by anyone else."

"You have no papers at all?" the colonel asked crisply.

Captain Blake thought for a moment. "None whatsoever," he said. "I am so sorry. Did you need something to read?"

"We will, of course, offer you parole," Colonel Leroux said. "We would prefer to entertain you as a respected officer of a respected enemy, Captain, than to imprison you like a dog. But first I am afraid we must search you. It is an indignity you may be spared if you will hand over whatever papers you have on your person."

"Lord," Captain Blake said, "if I had just anticipated your offer, Colonel, I would have secreted some scrap of paper in a pocket so that I could now produce it and retain my dignity. Alas, I did not have the forethought."

"I shall conduct him to an anteroom with one of the sergeants for the search, if you wish, sir," Captain Dupuis offered.

"Here," the general said, still without turning from the window. "He will be searched here. And now."

"Ah, regrettably, monsieur," the colonel said, "I must have you searched. Will you cooperate and remove arti-

cles of your clothing one at a time, if you please? Or
shall I give the task to one of the sergeants?"

Captain Blake turned and looked at the silent figures
flanking the doorway. "One of them is not the clumsy
soldier who hit me in the eye with my own rifle last
night, is he?" he asked. "That was a trifle painful, as I
suppose it was meant to be. No, don't trouble yourself,
Colonel. I have been out of a nurse's care for a number
of years and know well how to remove my clothes. Getting them back on again, of course, is a little more tricky,
but since there are no ladies present, I am not shy."

He stood up, removed his coat, and handed it to a
sergeant, who stepped forward at a nod from the colonel.

He was very much afraid half an hour later as he stood
naked in the middle of the room, wrapping about his
waist a towel that Captain Dionne had thoughtfully provided, that Wellington's staff officers at Viseu had been
just too clever for their own good.

"Nothing," the colonel said.

"He had time to get rid of them," the general said.
"Have the area where he was found searched."

"Or one of the partisans took them, sir," Captain Dionne suggested.

"Or there never were any," the colonel said. "All is
committed to his memory, in all probability. And we do
not even know if he came to bring information or to
gather it. Perhaps there is nothing yet in his memory."

"Captain Blake." The general turned away from the
window finally, and his pale gray eyes raked over his
adversary from naked shoulders to bare feet. "You may
be thankful this day that you are a British soldier in
uniform and not a Spanish partisan. We know how to
get information from our friends the Spaniards."

"I can almost feel my fingernails and toenails being
torn out," Captain Blake said.

"It is, I believe, a little painful," the general said. "Information comes long before all twenty are lost."

"His boots are very new in comparison to the rest of
his uniform," one of the sergeants—the one Captain
Blake would have labeled as the less intelligent—muttered to his companion. Captain Blake could have

hugged the man, and wanted to tell him to speak up. But his words had been heard.

"Your boots are new, Captain?" the colonel asked, frowning at them.

"The others walked off my feet one day when I was not watching," Captain Blake said.

"As your coat seems about to do," the general said. "But you have not had a new coat, Captain."

Captain Blake shrugged. "New boots this year, perhaps a new coat next," he said. "One does not make a fortune as a captain in the British army, sir. Perhaps French captains do?" He looked politely at Captains Dupuis and Dionne.

"Nothing behind the leather, sir," the unintelligent sergeant said, running his hands hard all over the surface of the boots.

"The toes," the colonel said. "The heels."

Captain Blake smiled nervously. "How am I to walk home without my boots?" he asked. "Has this not gone far enough? Must you make yourselves look quite ridiculous?" He shrugged and tried to look nonchalant as both the general and the colonel looked keenly at him. But he allowed one hand to open and close at his side.

The colonel nodded to the sergeant.

"We will replace your boots, Captain," he said. "As a gift."

And so the paper was found at last and unsealed and spread on the top of the desk as the general finally walked over from his far window. He bent over the paper with the colonel while the two captains craned their necks from the two sides of the desk for a glimpse of the diagram.

"Ah, Captain," the colonel said, looking up after a silent minute, "you may dress yourself and take a seat again. Your boots, I am afraid, are ruined, but I do not believe the floor is too cold. Is it?"

"Damn your eyes," Captain Blake said from between his teeth.

The colonel shrugged. "Pardon, Captain," he said, "but we have a job to do, just as you do."

Captain Blake was in the process of unwrapping the towel from his waist when the general finally spoke.

"So that other paper *was* correct, though much vaguer than this," he said. "We are expected from the north, and our way to Lisbon is being effectively barred." He banged a fist on the table. "Now the time of indecision is past. Now the marshal will know which route to take." He looked up at Captain Blake, whose hand held a corner of the towel as if frozen to it. "We have that damned Wellesley at last—right where we want him. Or Wellington, as he is called now."

Captain Blake took one step forward and looked down at the diagram. Even upside down he could see at a glance that it was not the paper he had been shown, the one that he had thought to be in his boot heel. What he was looking at was a perfect diagram of the Lines of Torres Vedras.

Oh, Christ, he thought. There seemed suddenly to be no air left in the room. Christ! And he stood perfectly still and expressionless, sending up frantic prayers to a God who could hear in silence.

12

THE "aunt" with whom Joana stayed when in Salamanca was in reality a former governess her mother had employed for the children of her first marriage. If anyone were to try to make a count of the number of aunts she had in the Peninsula, Joana sometimes thought, he would begin to wonder about her grandparents. She could probably discover an aunt in almost every city in Spain and Portugal if she had to.

Señora Sanchez—Aunt Teresa—lived on a quiet street in Salamanca, close to the Plaza Mayor. The white-and-gold carriage of the Marquesa das Minas arrived there late one afternoon, but the marquesa who stepped out of it was a different one from the one who had stepped in at Viseu. This marquesa wore her hair in softer curls about her face and she wore a dress and pelisse of vivid royal blue.

If she must be basically the same, Joana had decided a few years before—rich, spoiled, flirtatious—then at least she would change incidentals. There had to be some variety to add spice to life. In Portugal she was the pale Portuguese marquesa; in Spain she was the flamboyant French marquesa. There must be subtle differences.

It did not take long for word of her arrival to circulate, though the very lateness of the hour forced several impatient officers to cool their heels overnight before they could decently call upon her the next morning.

Colonel Guy Radisson and Major Pierre Etienne were the first to arrive—and they appeared on Señora Sanchez's doorstep almost simultaneously.

"Guy! Pierre!" she exclaimed as she entered the salon where they waited. And she hurried across the room, a hand outstretched to each, and smiled as each lifted a hand to his lips.

"Jeanne," Colonel Radisson said, "the sun has risen on Salamanca again this morning."

"Madame," Major Etienne said, "now our reason for wishing to invade Portugal no longer exists."

She withdrew her hand from his and tapped his arm. "Do not let the emperor hear you say that, Pierre," she said. "But how wonderful it is to be home—home among my people, even if not home in my own land. Portugal grows to be a bore."

"Then you must allow me to escort you home to France, Jeanne," the colonel said. "I shall be returning there soon, I believe. Though if you are to remain here, perhaps I shall request an extended tour of duty."

She laughed and drew her other hand away from his. "But I cannot leave Portugal," she said. "All of the property that Luis left me is there. All my wealth. And how could I live without my wealth? I am afraid luxury is the breath of life to me."

She waved the gentlemen to chairs, sent for refreshments, and resigned herself to a morning of visits and conversation. She was not wrong. She had seven visitors in all—all gentlemen—in addition to four notes and one bouquet of flowers.

"Such a wonderful welcome home," she murmured to her admirers as they finally began to take their leave. "Ah, no, Jacques, I will not be able to attend Colonel and Madame Savard's soiree this evening. How sad I am. But I have just had a note from General Valéry, you see, inviting me to dinner. Wait, Guy, if you please. I have need of your escort."

If Colonel Radisson had other duties to rush back to, he did not show any impatience as he waited for the last of the visitors to take their lingering leave of the marquesa. She turned to him finally with a brilliant smile.

"Everyone is so kind," she said. "Rushing here to pay their respects almost before I have arrived."

"Kindness has little to do with it, Jeanne," he said. "Do you really grow more beautiful every day, or does it merely seem that way?"

She thought for a moment. "I think not," she said.

"Every second day, Guy." And she laughed gleefully, her eyes shining at him.

"Ah, Jeanne," he said, "have you ever regretted your rejection of my marriage proposal? I would renew it in a moment if you were just to say the word."

"I regret it every moment, Guy," she said, reaching out both hands for him to clasp. "But it would not do. I am too restless for you and too . . . oh, changeable. Yes, and too expensive too. I am dreadfully expensive, you know. And selfish. I am enjoying my freedom. Can we not merely be friends?"

"Better friends than nothing at all," he said with a sigh. "How may I be of service to you?"

"Take me to General Valéry," she said. "He wishes to see me before tonight."

"Ah, I have a general for a rival, then?" he asked.

She pulled her hands from his and clucked her tongue. "He is old enough to be my father," she said. "In fact, he is a friend of my father's. We have business to discuss."

"Is it as I have suspected, then?" he asked. "Do you bring information out of Portugal, Jeanne? It is dangerous. I hate to think of such a delicate lady putting herself into danger."

"Bring information out?" She laughed. "How absurd you are, Guy. Who would entrust me with any information that might be of use to an enemy? I should blurt it out without thinking to the very next person to whom I spoke. Papa used to call me a featherbrain. I am afraid, alas, that there was some truth in the insult. Will you escort me?"

"Of course," he said with a bow. "Anyplace, anytime, Jeanne. You have only to ask."

"I shall fetch my bonnet," she said, "and order the carriage."

Less than an hour later she was seated in an elegant room which had been assigned to General Valéry at the French headquarters. He had handed her a glass of wine and they had politely reminisced about her father.

"So," he said, "you have returned, Jeanne. Did you have any trouble leaving Portugal? The English have been guarding the border so diligently that we have been able to gain little idea of what is going on in Portugal itself."

"Oh," she said with a wave of one hand, "I am allowed to come and go as I please. What threat can a mere woman be, after all?" She smiled sweetly at him and fluttered her eyelashes.

"You do it so well, Jeanne," he said. "Anyone who did not know you would think you quite harmless and entirely—pardon me—giddy."

"Sometimes," she said, "one grows tired of constantly playing a part. It is good to be home."

"And what *is* going on in Portugal?" he asked, seating himself opposite her and looking intently at her so that Joana knew that at last the meeting had really begun.

"Oh," she said, "the Viscount Wellington—he allows me to call him Arthur, General. Is that not droll? The Viscount Wellington is in Viseu in the north, as is the bulk of the army. A small part of it is still in the south. They are waiting for you to attack. I am sure you must know all this. I am afraid I always feel inadaquate when I come to report to you. I always wish I could bring more information. But I am just a woman, you see. All I can do is observe and keep my ear to the ground. No interesting documents ever fall into my hands and no one ever confides top-secret information. It is sad."

"But you do very well, Jeanne," he said. "You are a keen observer. Sometimes your observations are more important than you realize. Where have you traveled recently?"

"Before coming here?" she said. "To Lisbon and back to Viseu again. I had to make an excuse to go to Lisbon—I was bored at Viseu, you know, and had to go to seek more entertainment. I wanted to go, knowing that I was coming here soon and hoping to pick up some information for you. But alas, there was nothing."

"Nothing at all?" he asked.

"Only balls and flirtation and endless travel," she said. "It was very tedious and very pointless."

He sat forward in his chair. "We have an English captive," he said. "Recently arrived. A captain. An impudent fellow. A spy, of course."

"Not a very skilled one, if he allowed himself to be caught," she said. "What was he doing?"

"Trying to communicate with some partisans within the city," he said. "Others who were with him escaped, more is the shame, or we would have wrung more information about the whole scheme before they died. We cannot torture or execute a British soldier. And we have been forced to give him parole and return his sword and rifle to him."

"Rifle?" She raised her eyebrows.

"I would have liked to smash it into a thousand pieces," he said. "Damned weapons. Why our own light infantrymen cannot have been supplied with them by now, I will never know. They are twice as accurate as muskets."

"An officer of the Rifles?" she said.

"Blake," he said. "A captain. He had nothing but impudence to throw in our teeth until we found his paper, and then he admitted that he was to show the paper to the partisans in this part of the world so that they could do all in their power to make us behave like Wellington's puppets during the summer campaign in order to give him the advantage."

"Captain Blake " Joana said laughing. "I know him. He was assigned to escort me to Viseu. He came here and you caught him? Oh, he will not like that."

"I gather he was not too pleased," General Valéry said.

"I understand that he is one of Lord Wellington's most trusted and successful spies," she said.

"Is he, by thunder?" the general said. "Now, there you are of value, you see, Jeanne, without even realizing the fact. The man was bumbling, aghast, stuttering, and stammering when we saw his paper, at one moment telling us that it was a bluff and laughing at us for thinking Wellington would send an accurate diagram of his defenses right into enemy territory, and the next moment clamping his lips shut and turning as white as chalk and refusing to say another word except the occasional string of unrepeatable insults."

"Oh, yes," she said. "Doubtless he is a good actor.

He would have to be to have won such a reputation, would he not?"

"There is the problem, though, Jeanne," he said. "What are we to believe? The diagram shows formidable and quite impregnable defenses about Lisbon that would make it madness for us to begin the assault on the northern fortresses that are ready to be begun any day now. And the diagram confirms what we had earlier reasons to believe might be the case. And yet there is the puzzling problem of why the English would allow this diagram to come so close to our hands—and right into them, as it turns out. If the partisans were to be alerted, would it not have made more sense to have Captain Blake merely tell them from memory? We have learned everything and nothing from the capture of this spy."

"Where are these formidable defenses supposed to be?" she asked.

"North of Lisbon," he said. "Three separate lines stretching from the sea to the river. We could take Portugal, Joana. The marshal and I are both convinced of that. But what would be the point if we cannot take Lisbon and drive the English out of Europe once and for all? It seems that we must go south after all and tackle the fortress of Badajoz. But it is getting late in the year to be taking that slower route. The siege may last for months. And perhaps it is all unnecessary if that dratted diagram is a hoax."

Joana was laughing. "North of Lisbon?" she said. "Three lines of formidable and impregnable defenses? Absurd, General. Absolutely absurd. I traveled through that area just two weeks ago—with Captain Blake. Oh, I would just like to see his face if he were to see me here. Would his acting skills hold up, I wonder?" She laughed again and drew a lace handkerchief from her reticule in order to dab at her eyes.

The general looked at her fixedly. "It might work, too, by thunder," he said. "Would you be willing, Jeanne?"

Her laughter stopped as she looked across at him again. "To confront Captain Blake?" she said. She smiled slowly. "Why not? Oh, I think it would be a great pleasure, General. Yes, indeed it would. Oh, let us do it." Her eyes sparkled with mischief.

"It might mean that you will never be able to return to Portugal," he said quietly.

She sobered again. "Ah, but before the summer is out, Portugal will be a part of the empire, as it was always intended to be, will it not?" she said. "I will return, General." She smiled slowly. "I shall enter Lisbon on your arm. I shall give a ball in your honor and in the honor of Marshal Massena. Oh, it will be wonderful to be in Portugal and home all at the same time."

"May I send for him now?" he asked. "Time is of the essence, Jeanne. We must know the truth."

"Oh, by all means," she said. "This I can scarcely wait for."

"It may take a little while," he said. "I do not know just where he is at the moment, the necessity of keeping him under close confinement having passed. And I would wish Captains Dupuis and Dionne to be present, as they were at his interrogation two days ago. And Colonel Leroux, whom I put in charge of it. I find talking with captives tiresome and a little demeaning."

"Colonel Leroux?" Joana said. "Do I know him?"

"He has just returned from Paris," he said. "You will like him, Jeanne. A handsome fellow."

"Ah," she said, smiling, "then you are sure to be right. I always like handsome men."

"I shall have refreshments sent to you while you wait," the general said, getting to his feet. "I shall have everyone here as quickly as possible."

"There is no need to hurry," she said, laughing. "The pleasure of this confrontation is to be anticipated and savored, General."

Her smile held until he had left the room. And then she found that her hands were shaking in her lap and her legs were shaking against the chair on which she sat. And her breath came in uneven gasps.

He was safe, then. Oh, God, he was safe. She had scarcely dared hope that he was still alive. The whole scheme had seemed madder as she had drawn closer to Salamanca. And even now it seemed insane. But at least he was safe thus far. As was she.

She dreaded meeting his eyes. That was going to be the worst part. Once their eyes had met for the first time and he knew, or thought he knew, then it would be easier. But there had to be that first meeting of their eyes.

And she dreaded it more than she had dreaded anything else in her life.

Captain Blake buckled up his sword belt slowly, glanced at his rifle, which was propped carefully in one corner of the comfortable room he had been allotted—unguarded—in the confiscated manor where several French officers had their billets, and decided to leave it where it was. They wanted to talk to him again.

He had had a nightmare of a couple of days and nights, though he had had invitations galore and was being treated far more like an honored guest than like a captive. In all the tortured hours he had not been able to fathom how it had happened. How had the papers come to be switched? Carelessness on someone's part—a quite incredible and criminal carelessness? Or had someone done it deliberately? Did the commander in chief have a traitor on his staff?

Incredibly, he had quite deliberately put himself and his paper into French hands, only to find that he had put there the destruction of the British and Portuguese armies and the whole of the European cause. If the British were expelled from Portugal, then the whole of Europe would be under Napoleon Bonaparte's control again.

And he had unwittingly made that possible almost single-handedly.

He fussed over straightening his uniform, though all the fussing in the world could not make it look anything better than shabby and even though a French lieutenant waited politely outside his open door to conduct him to General Valéry's rooms.

After two days in which to think, Captain Blake still did not know quite how to handle the situation. If he tried to persuade them that the plans were fake, that the French were meant to be misled by them, then they would realize that he lied. If they were fake, then it would be in his own interests to pretend that they were real. And yet if he kept his mouth shut and let them draw their own conclusions, then surely they would conclude that the plans were authentic.

With no time to prepare himself two days before, he had done both—scoffed at their belief at first, until he realized how his scorn would be interpreted, and then closed his mouth and opened it only to utter various obscenities when they pressed questions on him. He had even thought at one point in some horror that he was going to faint.

Damn Wellington, he thought as he strode to the door and nodded curtly to the lieutenant. And damn this spying business. And damn him for ever letting it be known that he had a gift for learning languages quickly. He longed to be with his riflemen again, taking charge of his company, which was what he was trained to do and had some skill at doing. An actor he was not. And even an experienced actor might balk at having to walk onstage without having learned his lines and with no script from which to learn them—and his director a few hundred miles away.

Well, he was about to step onstage—again.

"Do you know Captain Dupuis and Captain Dionne, Jeanne?" General Valéry asked, returning to the room with those two officers fifteen minutes after leaving it. "Jeanne da Fonte, Marquesa das Minas, gentlemen. Daughter of the Comte de Levisse, with the emperor's embassy at Vienna."

"Henri," Joana said, smiling warmly at Captain Dionne. "How lovely to see you again. Have you recovered from the wound to your elbow?" She extended a hand for him to bow over. "Captain Dupius? I have not had the pleasure."

"It is all mine, my lady," he said, clicking his heels together and bowing smartly.

"Blake has been sent for," the general said. "Colonel Leroux is engaged in urgent business, but will be with us in a few minutes' time."

"Well, then." Joana used her most charming smile on the three officers while her heart palpitated with the suspense. Part of her willed the door to open to admit him so that they might get this initial encounter over with. The other part willed someone else to come through the door to announce that he was nowhere to be found.

"Henri will have time to tell me how he recovered from his injury. And Captain Dupuis . . ." She looked at him inquiringly.

"Antoine Dupuis, my lady," he said, flushing and bowing again.

"And Antoine may tell me all about himself." She watched the captain falling for her charms. "But first let me say how wonderful it is to be among my own people again and speaking French."

The door opened again, and Joana, who had chosen to stand and position herself close to a window opposite the door, looked fixedly at the general, her smile held firmly in place, afraid to turn her head. Oh, God, the moment had come. And why she should so wish to avoid it, she did not know. She was, after all, merely doing a job, as was he. It did not matter what he thought of her, provided the job was done successfully.

But it did matter. For some reason that she was afraid to fathom, it did matter.

She turned her head to look with cool amusement at the man who had entered the room and stopped inside the door.

And forgot Captain Robert Blake. And forgot General Valéry and the other French officers. Forgot where she was and why she was there. Forgot everything except one afternoon three years before when she had hidden in an attic, more terrified than anyone ever deserved to be in this life, watching a French officer wrestle her struggling half-sister to the floor and rape her, making animal noises of appreciation as he did so, while three other soldiers stood and watched and awaited their turn, cheering and laughing and making bawdy comments. And then the same French officer, impatient, the sport over, jerking a thumb at one of the soldiers, who raised his bayonet . . .

"But my important business would have waited if you had but told me what beauty waited in your room, General," the man who had entered said, smiling. "You said only that there was a lady here who might help throw light on our dilemma."

A tall and handsome man with dark hair and mustache and experienced charm. A man who was used to getting what he wanted, especially the women he wanted. A man who expected women to fall in love with him and was not often disappointed. A man who raped for sport and ordered the execution of innocents with a jerk of the thumb.

Joana's lashes swept down over her cheeks and lifted again slowly. Her smile reached her eyes and made them sparkle.

"Colonel Marcel Leroux, Jeanne," General Válery said. "Recently returned from Paris, though he was in Portugal with Junot in '07. Jeanne da Fonte, Marquesa das Minas, Colonel. Levisse's daughter. She has just come from Portugal."

Colonel Leroux hurried across the room. "You are the marquesa, by Jove?" he said. "The general has spoken of you. I am charmed, my lady." He reached out a hand for hers.

"Oh, what has he been saying?" she said, setting her hand in the colonel's and feeling the terrible, almost irresistible urge to shudder and snatch the hand away. "Dreadful things, no doubt, and not a one of them true. I shall have to have a good long talk with you myself— Marcel? May I call you that?—and set straight a few misunderstandings." Her lips parted as he raised her hand to his lips.

"I find myself all impatience for the clearing up of those misunderstandings, my lady," he said. "All impatience."

"Jeanne," she said softly, and her eyes fluttered to his mouth before rising to his eyes again.

And then the door opened once more and she remembered in a flash and very nearly panicked in earnest. For she had had no time to prepare herself. She felt naked and exposed. Colonel Leroux moved to one side so that he could face the door. Foolishly she turned her head and watched him, and then it became next to impossible to turn her head back again.

But no one had spoken. She wondered if minutes or merely seconds had passed. She looked toward the door. And her lips pursed slowly and her eyes lit up with amusement.

"Why, Robert," she said. "It *is* you. How very amusing. But why did you not tell me that this is where you were being sent? I might have had the pleasure of looking forward to meeting you again. Perhaps you might even have escorted me here, as you escorted me to Viseu. But do tell me." She took two steps forward and smiled dazzlingly at him. "Did you really come here as a spy, as General Valéry says? How very naughty of you. You swore to me that you were returning to your regiment."

He stood inside the door, his feet slightly apart, one hand frozen a few inches above the hilt of his sword, his face pale and expressionless, looking at her. There was a yellow-and-purple bruise along his right temple and spreading along his eyelid. His eye was bloodshot.

"Hello, Joana," he said finally, when it seemed that the silence must have extended for five full minutes. His voice sounded quite relaxed. "I suppose I might have expected to find you here among your own people. Foolish of me to have been surprised momentarily."

She had guessed a thousand things he might say first. None of them was even close to what he actually had said.

She laughed with light amusement.

13

HE had never seen her dressed in anything but white. Now she was wearing a dress of vivid emerald green and looking more beautiful than any woman had a right to look. Her hair was curled about her face so that her eyes looked shadowed and even more alluring than usual.

Those were the first foolish thoughts that rushed into his mind as he stepped into General Valéry's room and saw her standing at a window directly in his line of vision.

The next thought, which came almost simultaneously, was that she was a prisoner too, that they were going to use her to get the truth out of him, threaten to harm her if he did not speak. His hand moved without conscious volition to his sword.

The third thought stilled his hand. She was French. Of course. She was French.

And then she turned to look at him and she spoke to him with her customary mockery and he knew that the game was up, that he had lost, and that England had lost, and Portugal too. And he felt a curious relaxation now that it was all over, and a reluctant admiration for France's most unlikely—and therefore, of course, it's most likely—spy.

He did not hate her—yet. They were, after all, in the same business. They just happened to be on opposite sides.

"Hello, Joana," he said. "I suppose I might have expected to find you here among your own people. Foolish of me to have been surprised momentarily."

She laughed. "My own people?" she said.

"You were Jeanne Morisette before you acquired your present title," he said. "Daughter of the Comte de Levisse, former royalist."

She laughed again. "I underestimated you, Robert," she said. "I could find out nothing about you, much as I tried. I did not even realize that you were trying to find out about me. Not many people in Portugal know what you know." She turned to smile at General Valéry. "Do you see what I mean about this man being one of Lord Wellington's most able spies?" she said.

Captain Blake kept his eyes on her. What a strange thing to say, he thought, but he kept his face expressionless.

"Shall we all take a seat?" the general suggested. "There are several things to be said, I believe."

"I would prefer to stand," Captain Blake said, not removing his eyes from Joana. She looked back, not one whit abashed by her duplicity, which had just been revealed to him.

"So would I." She smiled slowly at him.

And so all the gentlemen were forced to remain on their feet.

"Captain Blake," General Valéry said, "according to the paper that was hidden in your boot, the main British defenses are centered in three lines north of Lisbon, stretching as far north as Torres Vedras."

No question had been asked, but the general paused.

"Yes," Captain Blake said, "that is what the paper shows."

"And yet you claimed two days ago that the paper was a fake, designed to mislead us."

"Yes," the captain said. "I did say that."

"And what do you say now?" General Valery asked. "Now that we have our own source of information, what do you say?"

"I say that the paper is genuine," Captain Blake said, "as was a previous, less-detailed one that fell into your hands. I say that it is genuine but that you are meant to believe that it must be false. Or is it the other way around? I forget my part in the presence of such dazzling beauty. Yes. I believe I am supposed to say that it is fake so that you will believe that it must be authentic. Devil take it, I really do not know. Perhaps you should ask me again, General, when the lady is not present."

She smiled at him.

"What do you know of this, Jeanne?" Colonel Leroux

asked. "Do you know the truth? As matters stand now, the paper is worse than useless to us."

Her smile turned into laughter. "Robert," she said, "do you not remember escorting me from Lisbon to Viseu less than two weeks ago?"

He said nothing. But it was all over, he knew. She must remember as clearly as he the Pass of Montachique.

"Do you not remember the long tedious days of travel?" she said. "Do you not remember our laughing at the few pathetic attempts the peasants were making to protect themselves against attack? Do you not remember the long evening at Torres Vedras, when you made sure that my chaperone was not present and we talked and talked and then you tried to make love to me? Are you blushing, Captain? You need not. Everyone tries to make love to me." She shrugged. "Only the favored few succeed."

She looked sideways beneath her lashes at the colonel.

Captain Blake stood quite still and chose to say nothing. Her version of what had happened was somewhat distorted, he thought, and she seemed completely to have forgotten that it was at Obidos, not at Torres Vedras, that something similar had taken place. But those details were unimportant. It was the rest of what she was saying or not saying that mattered. Was it possible that she was not now putting two and two together even if she had not done so at the time? He began to see a glimmering of hope.

"I remember our commenting on the peacefulness of the scene at sunset," she said. "And we were at that moment right in the center of the most northerly of these formidable defenses? We had already passed through the other two lines?"

Captain Blake shrugged.

"Oh, come now." She laughed merrily again and took several steps toward him. "It was a very poor try, Robert. There is nothing there at all, is there? Once Marshal Massena takes the border fortresses of Ciudad Rodrigo and Almeida, only the English forces of Viscount Wellington and the sorry forces of Portugal will stand between him and Lisbon. Why else would the English forces be concentrated in northern Portugal? Why would

Arthur himself be there? Would they not all hide safely behind these impregnable defenses or else be in the south to defend the weak route to Lisbon?"

Hope was hammering with the blood through his temples. He had a part to play. He still had a part. But everything depended upon his not overacting.

His nostrils flared.

"What do you say, Captain?" the colonel asked.

"I say nothing," he said curtly. "The lady is undoubtedly right. Ladies always are, I believe."

Joana finally sat down on the nearest chair. She crossed one leg over the other and swung one foot, slippered in green to match her dress. She looked faintly bored.

"But your tone would imply that you know her to be wrong," the colonel said.

Captain Blake shrugged.

"It is a pity," Joana said, "that I decided to journey to Lisbon and back when I did. A pity for the English, that is. I feel almost sorry for you, Robert. Have you ever failed before? This will damage your reputation, will it, and Arthur will think twice about sending you on another such mission? Poor Robert. You may be doomed yet to having to fight with your regiment. But perhaps all will be well. Neither you nor Arthur could have known that I would be following you here, I suppose."

"You devil!" Captain Blake said with quiet menace. "Lord Wellington respected you sufficiently to provide you with an escort from Lisbon."

The general coughed. "I would ask you to remember that you are addressing a lady, Captain," he said.

"A lady!" The captain's tone was scathing. "A woman who would betray her adopted country must be called a lady? I could think of other words that would better describe her."

"You have failed," Colonel Leroux said crisply. "This is war, Captain. We all fail sometimes. Real men learn to take their losses with their gains."

"If I could just get my hands on you for one minute," Captain Blake told Joana, his eyes narrowed to slits.

"Really, Robert." She looked up into his eyes and laughed at him, her foot swinging nonchalantly. "Do you think I would ever have allowed your hands to touch me if there had not been the possibility of information to be had from you?"

"If I could just have that minute," he said, "I would make sure that no other man would ever wish to touch you. Without you I would have succeeded. Do you realize how much destruction you are wreaking? A whole country to fall to the French again, and my own army destroyed? Do you realize? Your husband was Portuguese."

"Luis?" she said. "Luis was a bore and a coward."

"And perhaps you will not win after all," he said. "Perhaps these men will begin to doubt your testimony. What would a woman be expected to see, after all, during a journey? And perhaps they will conclude that what I am doing now is all an act."

"Are there any defenses of Lisbon, Jeanne?" the colonel asked.

"Of course." She shrugged. "My friend Colonel Lord Wyman of the dragoons took me to see the defenses south of the city. Until recently it seemed to the English the only sensible way for you to come. Only recently has it struck them that you would be mad enough to come through the hills to the north. They are desperate to divert you again. Or this is what Duncan said, anyway."

"And you told me earlier that nothing of importance had happened during your visit to Lisbon," the general said, looking fondly at Joana and shaking his head.

"Yes," she said, smiling ruefully. "I suppose what Duncan said and showed me does have some importance in retrospect, does it not? And my very tedious journey back to Viseu. Must I stay longer, General? I am to go shopping with my aunt, but all morning there were visitors—so many kind gentlemen, you know—and now this visit has lasted longer than I expected."

"No, no, Jeanne," the general said. "You have been very helpful, my dear. Very helpful indeed. It may even be no exaggeration to say that you have saved the empire by your observations and by your courage in being willing to confront Captain Blake face-to-face."

Joana flushed with pleasure at the praise and got to

her feet. Colonel Leroux rushed forward to offer her his arm.

"I shall escort you to your carriage, Jeanne," he said. "I shall return within a few minutes, General."

General Valéry inclined his head.

Captain Blake had to move finally so that Joana could pass him to reach the door. He stepped to one side, his eyes narrowed on her.

"I am so sorry, Robert," she said, pausing for a moment as she passed. "But war is war and I have an emperor to serve in any way I can."

He said nothing. But he felt a violent dislike for her, for a woman without a conscience, for one who could flirt with all and sundry merely to serve her own ends. And he disliked her for the fool she had made of him. She had always mocked him. He had known it, and yet he had allowed an unwilling attraction for her to grow into almost an obsession. He had allowed himself to touch her, to be aroused by her. He had even allowed himself to believe on that last night in Viseu that perhaps she felt some affection for him. And all the time her sole purpose had been to try to worm information—any useful information—out of him.

He hated her. Even though it seemed that unwittingly she had helped his cause that morning, he hated her. In fact, she could hardly have done better if she were his accomplice. He felt that his interrogators would now believe beyond a reasonable doubt that the Lines of Torres Vedras were imaginary, that in reality there were no defenses between Almeida and Lisbon except the armies of Lord Wellington.

She had helped him. She had unwittingly done what he had hoped to do himself but had not known how to accomplish. How chagrined she would be when she discovered the truth eventually. And how popular she would be with the French!

But she did not yet know she had helped him. She had wanted to betray both her adopted country of Portugal and her mother's country. And intentions were more important than actual performance.

He hated her.

She left the room on the arm of the colonel, and he was dismissed immediately afterward.

"I shall summon you again if you can be of further help to us, Captain," General Valéry said. "In the meantime, I trust that your quarters are comfortable and that your needs are being adequately attended to?"

Captain Blake inclined his head curtly.

"And I trust that you will still be my guest this evening?" the general asked. "You must allow me to show you hospitality. Such scenes as this are merely the distasteful but necessary business of war, Captain."

"I shall be there, sir," Captain Blake said before turning on his heel and leaving the room, not sure if his elation over the apparent success of his mission despite the switching of the papers and the unexpected appearance of the marquesa was quite sufficient to outweigh his depression over an indefinite captivity, and over the discovery he had just made about Joana.

The Marquesa das Minas. Jeanne Morisette. He did not want to think of her as Joana.

Joana was an occasional spy for the French. She did not believe she was considered of particular importance by them and did not expect to be taken into anyone's confidence in a major way. But Colonel Leroux, clearly pleased by what had happened in General Valéry's room, did confide one thing.

"You were magnificent, Jeanne," he said to her as he escorted her out to her waiting carriage. "You utterly confounded him. He will try to confuse us again. He will try to discredit what you have told us. But the truth came out when he lost his temper with you. There is a saying that there is no wrath worse than that of a woman scorned. I believe it applies equally to men. I suppose he was in love with you?"

She shrugged. "Men are always being foolish and claiming to be in love with me," she said. "I take no notice."

"I could have slapped a glove in his face more than once," he said. "But he is to be considered our guest, you see, now that he has given us his parole. He is not to be mistreated. However." He laid one hand on top of hers and smoothed his fingers over hers. "If he should show you any further discourtesy, Jeanne, you must tell me and I shall see that he is properly dealt with."

"I hope never to see him again," she said. "But thank you, Colonel. You are kind."

"The campaign will be over in no time at all," he said, "now that we have our cue to start. Before the summer is out, we will all be in Lisbon. I enjoyed my stay there last time. I believe I may enjoy it more this time." His eyes appreciated her.

"Before the summer is out?" she said. "So soon?"

"The marshal has been waiting for just such a certainty as this," he said, "before investing Ciudad Rodrigo. The task is to be Ney's. He is just awaiting the order to move. I believe it will come within a day or two. Once Ciudad has fallen, Almeida will not hold out long. And if Wellington brings his forces to the defense of either fort, then we will crush him. This is a great day. The beginning of the end for the English occupation of European soil."

"And I have had a part in it," she said, smiling dazzlingly at him. "How good that makes me feel."

"And you have had a part in it." They came to a stop at the door of her carriage, and he raised her hand to his lips. "A large part, Jeanne. You are to be at the general's dinner tonight?"

"Of course," she said.

"Then suddenly it becomes an occasion to be anticipated with great pleasure," he said, holding her hand close to his lips and looking down at her with smoldering eyes. "Until later, Jeanne."

"You are to be there too, Marcel?" Her smile brightened. "I am so glad."

He smiled at her, revealing even white teeth. It was the sort of smile that was guaranteed to turn feminine knees weak.

"Yes," she said breathlessly. "Until later."

She sat back against the cushions of her carriage and did not look out of the window again, though she knew that he stood there until the carriage moved away. It was a primary rule of flirtation, she had learned years before, to allow the gentleman to be just a little more smitten than she.

She closed her eyes and was thankful that the journey home was not a long one. She rather suspected that her stomach would have rebelled at any great distance. He had touched her and kissed her hand. She had felt his mustache as well as his lips against her flesh. And his breath had been warm. She shuddered, deeply revolted.

She was going to kill him. She had always planned that. She was not going to enlist Duarte's help, though he would be disappointed not to do it himself. She was going to do it. She was going to kill him.

But it was not a simple thing to accomplish. It would have to be planned. She would have to choose the time and the place and the method with care. She would have to think about it.

In the meantime she was going to have to flirt with him. She could think of no other way of keeping him close enough so that she could kill him when the opportunity came. The thought of flirting with the man she had watched rape Maria and give the order for her death had her setting one cold and shaking hand over her mouth. She felt cold all over. And then she had to dip her head sharply forward to save herself from fainting.

And there was Robert. He must hate her now in all earnest. Even though she had helped his cause, supposedly without realizing it, he must still hate her. And it was all so pointless, she thought. It seemed that Captain Robert Blake was after all a fine-enough actor to have accomplished the mission without her help. He had certainly taken full advantage of her apparent misunderstanding of the situation.

She wondered who had punched him in the face and bruised his eye.

He must hate her. And if she was going to have him set free in time to take part in the summer's campaign, she was going to have to make him hate her a great deal more. But she would explain all to him later, she thought. Perhaps it would make a difference. Perhaps it would.

And she was suddenly and unwillingly reminded of the other Robert—*her* Robert—and how she had made him hate her too, though from an entirely different motive. And how she had never had a chance to explain to him.

But she could not dwell on thoughts of Robert at the moment. There was a dinner to attend that evening and some kind of a relationship to set up with Colonel Marcel Leroux. She must concentrate her mind and her energies on that.

She was wearing a gown of shimmering gold, chosen to give herself courage. Finding the courage to face a roomful of people, many of them strangers, was not usually a problem for Joana. But then, it was no ordinary task she had set herself. She had had her maid style her hair in a high topknot with cascades of ringlets trailing down the back of her head and along her neck.

And yet the first person she saw when she entered the general's drawing room prior to dinner was not Colonel Leroux but someone she was equally reluctant to meet again and someone who looked just as shabby and just as awkwardly out-of-place and just as altogether more attractive than any other man present as he had been in that ballroom in Lisbon. She had not thought of his being present.

He could not be avoided. He was standing just inside the drawing-room doors. A French officer and his wife were just turning away from him.

"Ah, Robert," she said, stepping up to him before he saw her, scorning even to try avoiding him, "you are here, are you? French uniforms glitter quite as brightly as English ones, do they not?"

"I daresay you do not see much difference," he said, "or in the men inside them. I do."

"Ah," she said, smiling at him, "that was a setdown, was it not? Are you very angry with me?"

"More with myself," he said, "for having known your secret and for having thought that perhaps it was of no significance. It does not matter to you that your mother was English?"

"You know that too?" she said, laughing. "Why did you find out so much, Robert? Was it that you wished to know with whom you were in love?"

"You would like to believe that, would you not?" he said. "You would like to believe that your charms have never failed. And you did try hard. But you mistake lust for love, Joana. I lusted after you. I wanted to lay you. I wanted to take my pleasure inside your body. Is that being in love? If it is, then I suppose I am guilty."

His blue eyes—one still bloodshot—looked coldly down into hers.

"Ah," she said, setting one gloved hand on his sleeve for a brief moment, "but I could make you love me if I wished, Robert. Even now. And you are not telling the entire truth. If you had wished merely to . . . lay me, as you so vulgarly put it, then you would not have pulled back from that embrace at my aunt's ball in Viseu. It was you, you know. I would not have pulled back. At least, not quite so soon. So I do not believe you. But then, spies never tell the truth, do they?"

"You should know," he said.

"Touché." She smiled at him and remembered that she must flirt with him too—him and Colonel Leroux both. If her plan for effecting his release was to work, she must flirt with him and force a response from him too. He did not look tonight as if he would ever respond to her again.

But she smiled for the first time that evening with something like real pleasure. There was a challenge in making Robert fall in love with her. Flirtation was almost never a challenge. But this time it was. Perhaps for once she would enjoy her work.

"I am going to do it," she said. "I am going to make you fall in love with me. It should not be difficult. I believe you are already more than halfway there."

"Joana," he said, his voice and his eyes perfectly serious, "I suppose the fact that you are half-French saves you from the stigma of being called a traitor. But I see you as such nevertheless. We are on different sides of the fence. We are enemies, and as far as I am concerned, bitter enemies. You betrayed both me and my country—your mother's country—earlier today. You would be well advised not to waste your time trying the impossible. Flirt with the French officers. There are doubtless a few thousand of them who would be only too willing to fall under your spell."

"Ah," she said, "but it is you I want under my spell, Robert."

"Because I am the only man who has ever resisted it?" he asked.

She smiled. "Perhaps," she said. "You are, you know. But not for long."

She wondered why she was giving herself such a challenge and breaking her own rule, the one she had practiced just that day. She was showing him that she was far more smitten than he was. She had told him quite openly that she was going to pursue him instead of letting him believe—as all men she had known had believed—that he was the pursuer.

It was a formidable challenge, one that it seemed she could not win. But there was excitement in it. And somehow, despite everything—despite the dangers and challenges she had already faced and those still to come—she needed this particular type of excitement.

"I believe, Joana," he said, "that you are about to have a far more glittering beau than I. And you would do well to stay away from me while we are both here in Salamanca. I might do you harm, you know, and your loyalty might be brought into question if you are seen to hang around me."

She smiled at him, but a hand at the small of her back caused her to turn her head. She smiled up at Colonel Leroux. "Marcel," she said.

"I hope Captain Blake is acting the gentleman this evening, and not renewing any of the threats he made earlier," he said, taking her hand and bowing over it.

"Oh," she said, laughing, "Robert's temper has cooled and he was being quite civil. But he is not a gentleman, Marcel. He would be far more suited to the French army than the English. He has risen through the ranks and become a commissioned officer entirely through his own merits. Captain Blake is what is known as a hero, you see, but he is not a gentleman. He will not tell me what he was. It is most annoying. Was he a tradesman's son or a runaway apprentice or a convict?"

She laughed again, though she could see Robert's jaw tighten. And when she glanced at Colonel Leroux, it was to see disdain on his face. Oh, yes, she thought suddenly. Of course. That was the way it must be. That was the way she must plan it. Yes. Robert and the colonel must hate each other. She must pit them against each other.

Excitement and a sense of glorious danger built in her and she smiled dazzlingly at both men.

"He is not going to answer, you see," she said to the colonel. "He never does. And that leads me to expect that my last guess is the closest to the truth." She linked her arm through the colonel's. "Shall we walk about, Marcel? You may introduce me to the people I do not know. There are a few. It is quite a while since I was here last."

She threw one final smile over her shoulder at Robert, who was about to be taken under the wing of two officers, she saw. He looked back at her with cold, steady eyes.

14

THERE was so much freedom. So much damned freedom. He could come and go as he pleased in Salamanca, and could have had as active a social life there as he could have had in Lisbon during the winter and spring. He was treated with respect and courtesy and even liking by many of the French officers he met.

Sometimes he felt as if it would be better, more real, if he were caged up in a prison cell. Sometimes he regretted giving his parole. At least if he had not, if he were in a cell, he could dream of escape, plan for it, attempt it. At least there would be some challenge to make life worth living.

As it was, late spring passed into the sweltering heat of summer, and the summer's campaign began in earnest. He had the satisfaction—at least he had that—of seeing the French almost immediately respond to the lie of which he had somehow managed to convince them. Marshal Ney, who had been investing Ciudad Rodrigo with its Spanish force led by Governor Herrasti since May in a halfhearted way, now attacked in earnest, and the fort surrendered on July 10 after the walls had been breached.

The French officers with whom Captain Blake consorted liked to tell him of such things and to tease him good-naturedly about his attempts to deflect the attack southward and away from the easy route to Lisbon. And they liked to scorn Wellington and the English forces in his hearing for not coming to the defense of the fort.

The news about Ciudad Rodrigo he could accept quite cheerfully, since he knew that Lord Wellington was acting wisely and well and since no British forces had been involved in the engagement. The news that followed it, as the French advanced against the Portuguese fort of Almeida, was less easy to take. The Light Division, under General Crauford, was harassing the French advance, the skirmishers worrying Marshal Ney and his soldiers by popping up always where they were least expected.

And among the skirmishers were the Rifles, the men of the Ninety-fifth. His men.

And then toward the end of July the fighting grew fierce as the Light Division became trapped on the Spanish side of the River Coa, with only one bridge at their backs, and the Rifles were again the heroes, along with the light infantrymen of the Forty-third and the Fifty-second. They held back the massive forces of the French while the guns and the cavalry retreated over the bridge and took up a position of strength beyond it.

"You are fortunate," one French lieutenant told Captain Blake with a laugh. "Many of your men were killed in the action, monsieur. Perhaps you would have been too if you had been there. Instead, you are here living a life of ease."

Yes. A life of ease. The captain's right hand opened and closed in his lap. He had been in captivity for a month and it seemed more like a year. Ten years. The French would attack Almeida and probably subdue it within a few weeks—it was doubtful that Wellington would advance to its defense. And then they would advance into Portugal, west to Coimbra, south to Lisbon. Probably somewhere along the way, for very pride's sake, Wellington would make a stand, choosing his spot with care, as he always did.

And if that did not hold them, there would be the retreat behind the Lines of Torres Vedras and the hope that the French army would stand and be caught and decimated by the winter and by hunger while the British passed a winter of relative comfort and prayed for reinforcements from a stingy British government, and with them the hope of waging a more aggressive war the following year—one that would take them through Portugal and through Spain, the French driven before them. One that would begin to eat away at the empire of Napoleon Bonaparte.

And all the while, Captain Blake thought, he would be a captive of the French, he would be away from his own men, away from the excitement. The soonest he could hope for an exchange, in his own estimation, was the following spring.

There were times when the need to be with his regiment, the need to be free, seemed more powerful than the need to retain his honor. There were times when he thought about escape. And it would be so easy. He was not watched at all. There were no restraints upon him, except those imposed by his own honor. He was still in possession of both his sword and his rifle.

But of course he never did make the attempt to escape. For when all was said and done, honor was everything. Honor was what made him into the person he could live with. Honor gave him his self-respect. And so he stayed and chafed at the bit.

It would not have been quite so bad, he often thought, if it had not been for Joana—the Marquesa das Minas.

They were constantly meeting. He had frequent invitations to dinners and assemblies, and found most of them difficult to refuse, much as he would have preferred to live the life of a hermit. And always, wherever he went, she was there too. It was understandable, of course. Like the British, the French army was far from home and their own women. Unlike the British, the local women were, on the whole, hostile to them. It was understandable that all the Frenchwomen who were available should be invited everywhere.

Especially when one of those women was as beautiful and fascinating as Joana.

Captain Blake watched dozens of her countrymen fall under her spell and follow her about with as much abject devotion as had her courts in Lisbon and Viseu. And sometimes his jaw clamped into a hard line as he realized how easy it would be to follow suit. Even though he knew her now to be his enemy—his country's enemy and his personal enemy—he found that this eyes followed her about a room and roamed over her slender but shapely figure and reveled in the rich colors she chose to wear in Salamanca.

And sometimes he caught himself hating Colonel Marcel Leroux and wanting to tear the man limb from limb, not so much because he had been the head of the interrogation against himself as because Joana openly favored him above all her other suitors. And it was easy to see why. The colonel was a handsome devil, and a charming one as well.

And yet she flirted with him too, Captain Blake found. Her strange and impudent claim on that first evening that she could and would make him fall in love with her had not been forgotten, it seemed. She singled him out for attention wherever he went.

"Jeanne," Colonel Guy Radisson said during one assembly, when everyone but her appeared to be wilting from the heat of the indoors. She had stopped to talk to the Englishman while promenading about the room on the colonel's arm. His tone was good-natured. "If you persist in showing such marks of friendship for Captain Blake, there are going to be rumors that you have a divided loyalty."

She laughed gaily. "Ah, but I feel so sorry for him, Guy," she said. "He is a soldier, you see, as well as a spy. And he longs to be with his own regiment now that the fighting is beginning. Do you not, Robert?"

"How could I wish to be anywhere but where I am at this precise moment?" he said in tones so courtly that only she would know how false they were.

She laughed again. "And he so wishes that our army was advancing along a different route, Guy," she said. "And it is all my fault that they are not. I feel guilty. I feel the need to prove to Captain Blake every time I see him that I am no monster."

"Monster!" the colonel said fondly. "No one could look at you and seriously think that, Jeanne."

She looked up at him with large smiling eyes. "Is it hot in here?" she asked. "Or is it my imagination? Be an angel, Guy, do, and fetch me a drink. Something long and cool."

Colonel Radisson clicked his heels and was off into the crowd without further ado.

It was the way she had of getting him alone. She did it frequently.

"On second thoughts," she said, "there would be instant coolness if we stepped outside, would there not? Take me there, Robert."

She never asked for favors. She always demanded them. She slipped her white-gloved hand through his arm—her gown was of a deep wine color.

"The poor colonel will be left holding a long cool drink," he said.

She shrugged. "Then he may drink it himself," she said. "It is very hot in here."

"Joana," he said, "why do you do this?" He led her out into a tree-shaded courtyard, where several people were strolling. He did not elaborate on his words.

She looked up at him and smiled. "Because it is such a challenge," she said. "Because any other man I can have at the snap of two fingers. You have seen that. I need more of a challenge in life."

"And some of it has gone now that you are safely back with your own people again?" he asked. "Did you enjoy the danger in Portugal? Did you enjoy knowing that at any time your French background might be discovered and exposed?"

"Ah, but I have English and Portuguese connections too," she said, "as you know, Robert. And how could a woman like me be of any danger to anyone? My life is devoted to pleasure. And what have I done that was so dangerous? I merely used my eyes on the road between Lisbon and Viseu and reported truthfully what I saw. Does that make me dangerous?"

"You did it quite deliberately," he said. "You have been actively spying for the French, Joana. Except that this time it is the end. I can expose your game if you return to Portugal."

She sighed. "You make it sound as if I have been a highly skilled secret agent," she said. "I almost wish that I had. Perhaps there would have been some excitement in it. Is there, Robert? Is it wonderfully exciting?"

"There are jobs to be done," he said, "and one does them because they must be done."

She looked at him incredulously. "Oh, no," she said, "that is ridiculous. That is not why you do what you do, Robert. I know just by looking into your face that you demand more of life than that. I know it. I know that in

many ways you are like me. It is not enough to let the
days pass by in safety and comfort. Not nearly enough.
There has to be much more than that."

His jaw set hard.

"This month has been dreadful for you, has it not?"
she said. "I know it, you see. I know that it is like a
living death to you. And so I do what I can for you,
Robert." She laughed lightly. "I offer you a different
type of challenge. Can you resist the charms of a lady
whom no one else can resist, even knowing that she is
your enemy—your bitter enemy, as you once put it? Can
you?"

Somehow—he did not know how it had happened—
they had found a secluded part of the courtyard beyond
some vine trees and she was seating herself on a low
wall. The air was cool, though only just, and only in
contrast with the heat of the day and the heat of the
indoors.

He laughed without humor. "How pathetic you are,
Joana," he said. "You know very well that if I once fell
for your charms and crowded up to you just like everyone else, panting for the privilege of holding your fan or
fetching you a drink, you would lose interest in me in a
moment."

"Yes." She smiled up at him. "How right you are. Is
that why you do it, Robert? Is this your way of gaining
my attention? Are you far more clever than any other
man of my acquaintance?"

Her gown looked almost black in the darkness. Her
skin in contrast looked translucent. His fingers itched to
touch her, to rest against her cheek, to caress her shoulder. Her eyes were dark and mysterious.

"I think I must be the most foolish of all," he said.

She continued to smile. "Because you have not thought
until now of how you might turn off my interest by
feigning yours?" she said. "Perhaps it would work. Perhaps it would not. Shall we put it to the test?"

He clasped his hands behind his back and knew that
he had stepped deep into flirtation and could very easily
lose his way. He had never learned how to play that
game with women. He had always been able to get what
he wanted when he wanted it, with money and with his

person and his uniform. But then, he had only ever wanted whores. Only ever the physical satisfaction to be gained from a good bedding.

It had been a long time, he thought suddenly. Almost two months since Beatriz. But then, soldiers were accustomed to going without for long stretches of time. Especially private soldiers, and he had been one for long enough. He had learned to live with celibacy.

"Are you afraid?" she asked him almost in a whisper.

He kept his hands behind his back. "Only uninterested, Joana," he said.

"Oh, no." She got to her feet and took the one step that separated them. She spread her hands on his chest and looked up at him. "Not that, Robert. Never that. Anything but. Perhaps you hate me or despise me. Perhaps you desire me. But you are not indifferent to me. Do you think I do not know enough about men to know that? You are not uninterested."

Her perfume teased his nostrils. And her hands, resting lightly against his coat, burned through to his chest. Something snapped in him.

"Very well, then," he said, and he spread his hands at her waist and drew her against him. He knew that he was holding her too roughly, and tightened his grasp further. Something sparked in her eyes—it might have been fear—as she continued to look steadily up at him. "Let me show you what my interest in you is, Joana."

He was instantly hard. The blood pulsed through his body, through his temples. He wanted to hurt her, humiliate her, frighten her. He wanted to mount her, pound himself into her, have her gasping and crying for mercy.

He lifted her against him, as he had done once before, but higher, so that her feet left the ground. And he backed her against the wall and rubbed himself against her, against her womb, between her thighs, which opened beneath the pressure of his weight. He pushed against her, pumped against her through the barrier of their clothing.

He spoke through his teeth. "Is this what you want of me?" he asked. She was still looking into his eyes, her lower lip caught between her teeth. "And is it excitement and danger you want, Joana? Shall we risk someone's coming around these trees? Would that be a thrill to you? Shall we have you back up on the wall and your skirts up and my trousers open? It will all be the work of a mere minute. I am very hard and ready, as you can feel. Do you want it?"

She continued to stare at him for a few moments. And then she released her lower lip and surprised him by smiling slowly.

"By God, you do," he hissed at her, lowering her at last to the ground. "You are no better than the cheapest whore I have ever had, Joana. Worse. They are willing but not necessarily eager."

"But, Robert," she said, and there was laughter in her voice as she slid her arms up about his neck and her fingers played with his hair, "you are such a gentleman, no matter what you were before you enlisted in the army. Would you have me afraid of you, afraid that you are going to ravish me? And yet you *ask* me? You cannot make me afraid of you, even though this is, I think, the expression you must wear when you have your rifle to your shoulder and are about to fire it."

His anger had not abated. But it had turned against himself. Was he merely playing her game after all, then? Joana's game The woman who had betrayed him, no matter what the outcome of her betrayal?

He splayed one hand behind her head and swooped his own head down to kiss her, opening his mouth wide over hers, thrusting past her lips and teeth, heedless of what she had done to him on a previous occasion, tasting her, drinking her in, withdrawing his tongue and thrusting again, simulating what he had threatened to do to her but knew he would not.

She was sucking inward, he found, one hand pressed to the back of his head as his was to hers, so that withdrawing from her was done under pressure and thrusting inward was swift, almost painful. The sounds he heard came from her throat. No, from his. From both.

And so they fought each other even as they embraced, exchanging desire and pain and the struggle for mastery. His free hand slid across one of her shoulders and forward and down, across warm soft flesh, down inside the silk of her gown, to curl around her breast. His thumb found her nipple and rubbed, swift and hard, against it, until she lifted her shoulders and squirmed. And then he felt shock as her free hand slid down between them and rubbed over the hard swelling of his desire for her.

They were both panting when he lifted his head.

"That is my interest in you, Joana," he said. "No light flirtation. No pretty words of love and adoration. Just a lusting for your body. As I have lusted after countless whores."

"Yes." There was something almost feline about her smile. "But it is not lack of interest, Robert. Never tell me that again. Tell me you hate me and I will believe you. I think you do. Tell me you desire me as you would desire a whore and I will believe you. I can feel that you do. But do not tell me you have no interest in me. I shall pursue you without mercy if you persist in that lie."

His anger was ebbing, to be replaced by contempt, though whether it was directed more against her or himself, he did not know.

"So you want a man who hates you and wants to lay you as he would a whore?" he said to her. "You cannot like yourself very well."

She smiled, her old charming smile. She had taken a step back from him. "Ah, but who said that I want you, Robert?" she asked. "All I have admitted to, if you will recall, is wanting to have you want me, wanting to have you fall in love with me. And you are not far off. Do you hate me? Good. Hatred is very akin to love."

She laughed as he clamped his teeth together, unwilling—or unable perhaps—to continue the conversation, which was moving back again into her area of expertise.

"Take me back inside," she said, reaching out a hand for his arm. "Guy will come running, or else Pierre or Henri, and I shall send one of them for a drink if Guy has already disposed of the first. Now I really need one. I shall not send you, you see, Robert, though I do not believe you would be so ungallant as to refuse. Would you?"

"Probably not," he said. "But I should probably dash it into your face when I had brought it. That would be the fastest way to cool you off."

She laughed merrily. "You would not," she said. "You

are in enemy territory and would be clapped into the
darkest dungeon before you could enjoy my discomfort."

"At least then," he said, "I could honorably escape."

She turned her head to look up at him, and smiled
slowly. "Poor Robert," she said softly.

Things were moving much more slowly than she had
either planned or expected. She had thought they would
be gone within a week, or at most two, of their arrival.
But a month had passed and still she could not put her
final plans into effect. And of course she realized now
that it could not all have happened that fast anyway.

She had left letters behind with Duarte—two of them.
She believed that both she and her servants were above
surveillance by the French, but she wanted to be thor-
ough. She wanted to take no chances. The letters were
to be sent to Matilda, the first to inform her that her
brother's health had taken a turn for the worse, the second to announce his death and beg for Matilda's return.

The timing perhaps would not be perfect. She and Duarte had discussed that. The whole idea of sending Matilda was so that Duarte would know just when to come.
But there was to be a month between the two letters. If
possible, Matilda would leave before the second arrived.
After all, the first letter would give a gloomy picture of
her brother's future. If she could not leave when the
second arrived, then she herself would have to be indisposed. But the letters would eventually give her her reason for leaving.

But the letters, of course, had been traveling from one
country to another, and under wartime conditions. The
first did not arrive for almost a month. And Joana had
not dared to put the final plans into effect before it arrived. Duarte's arrival—or that of the Spanish partisans—would be crucial to their success.

So though she had flirted with both Colonel Leroux
and Captain Blake, though she had drawn Robert into
that one close and indecorous embrace, so that she knew
it could be done, and though she had begun to hint to the
colonel that Captain Blake's attentions were becoming a
little tedious, she had been obliged to hold back and hold
back until she felt she could scream with frustration.

For that same close and indecorous embrace was a trial to her nerves. *He* was a trial to her nerves. She flirted with him and led him on and forced him into an admission of a powerful physical attraction to her. And then she toyed with him and laughed at him.

She wanted to tell him the truth. All of it. She did not like his hatred. She liked his scorn even less. And she could tell him the truth, she reasoned. Now that the French had been misled and now that the chain of events that Lord Wellington had hoped for had been set in motion, there was no need of secrecy any longer. She might have told him.

But she could not do it. Of course she could not. For if he knew the truth, then he would also know that what she was about to do was a daring ruse to effect his honorable escape. If he knew it was a trick, then he would still feel honor-bound to stay. Men were foolish that way.

And so she could not tell him. She had to smile at him and flirt with him and occasionally take him off somewhere where they could be alone. And she had to endure the hatred and the scorn in his eyes—and the desire smoldering behind them. A desire that she could fan and play upon at will. A desire that she must be able to play upon if her plan was to work.

And Colonel Leroux. The very thought of him was enough to make her shudder. She could not glance at his face or his hands or his body without remembering. And she found herself one day early in August after a ride out over the Roman bridge and across the countryside with him and a few other officers, being lifted from her horse's back by him. He did not step back when her feet touched the ground, but smiled down at her and brushed his thumb across her cheek. The very thumb that had signaled Maria's death.

She shuddered convulsively and found herself looking up into a smiling face turning to a frowning one.

"Marcel," she said quickly, breathlessly, "he touched me like that last night. I am afraid of him."

His frown deepened. "Blake?" he said. "Blake again?"

"Oh," she said, smiling, "I am so sorry. I am being foolish. It is just that I had to confront him there in General Valéry's office when I first arrived, and I have the feeling that he hates me, that he would kill me if he could. And who could blame him? He had to listen to me shatter his plans. But he seeks me out, he touches me just as if that unpleasantness had never happened between us. Last night he said he wanted to . . . Well, it does not matter."

"It certainly does," he said. "It matters, Jeanne. What did he say?"

"That he wanted to . . . kiss me," she said, the pause suggesting that the actual words had been rather more suggestive. "I think I would die if he touched me."

"No, he would be the one to die. At my hands," he said, his eyes burning fiercely down into hers. "I shall have him confined, Jeanne, without further delay. This is insufferable."

"No." She caught at his sleeve. "He has given his parole, Marcel. You are honor-bound to treat him with courtesy, to allow him his freedom within the bounds of his own promise. And he has not actually done anything—yet."

"If he so much as lays a finger on you . . ." he said.

"I shall tell you," she said, "if he becomes unmanageable. I do not believe he will. He is, after all a gen . . . No, he is not that either, is he?" She smiled. "But nothing will happen, Marcel. I was merely being foolish. Forget it," She set her hand in his.

She had spoken sooner than she had planned. She had had to think quickly of some reasonable explanation for that shudder she had not been able to control when he touched her. Matilda was still grumbling and flatly refusing to leave her mistress behind. She would have to be forced on her way the following day. And Joana would just have to hope that she would find Duarte without any difficulty and that he would be able to do the almost impossible task she had set him.

She would give him three weeks. She would send that message with Matilda. Three weeks. It was too long. She would like to act immediately. She would like it all to be over within a few days. But perhaps he would have to make all sorts of preparations. She must not rush him in what would probably be a very difficult operation. She would give him three weeks.

"Don't look so worried, Marcel," she said, steeling herself and leaning toward him until she almost brushed against him. "I have you to protect me, I know, and dozens of other officers too if I just ask. But you most of all. I feel better just to have unburdened my mind to you."

"Jeanne," he said, and his eyes strayed to her lips, "you know I would do anything for you."

"Would you?" she said. And she smiled as she passed her tongue slowly across her lips. "Would you, Marcel?"

She thought he would kiss her, and steeled every nerve in her body. But he merely raised her hand to his lips.

"Sometime," he said, "when we are more private, I shall show you."

Her eyes dreamed into his.

15

"YOU." Antonio Becquer pointed one thick blunt finger at Duarte Ribeiro. "You alone. The others wait here."

Duarte looked about at the ten men of his band who had accompanied him to the border and the meeting with the Spanish partisan. Almost to a man they looked disappointed. And they looked fixedly back at him, as if willing him to change the Spaniard's mind.

"It is our fight," Duarte said with a shrug. "We are willing to take the risks. All we need from you is permission to encroach on your territory for a couple of days or so."

"You." Becquer repeated his word and his gesture. "You alone. And forget the stupid talk about doing it with your men unassisted. How would you get inside Salamanca? Huh? And how would you find the people you are looking for once there? How would you get out again?" The Spaniard paused to spit on the ground. "Would you give the French pigs an orgy of torture to look forward to?" He looked about at the Portuguese with a grin. "Eleven victims? Not to mention your sister. She would be a special bonus."

Duarte licked his lips. "It is a dangerous scheme," he said. "Dangerous almost to the point of foolhardiness. If there are any victims to be tortured, it would seem only fair that they be us. I do not wish to put you in danger over something that is not your concern."

The Spanish partisan grinned again. "The scheme is to rescue one of their prisoners?" he said. "And to make a fool of them into the bargain? That is just exactly our business, my friend. And our pleasure too. And the dan-

ger?" He shrugged. "What is a little danger when the
rewards are so satisfying?"

"You believe we can get inside Salamanca?" Duarte
asked.

There was a general rumble of laughter from the Spanish partisans who had accompanied Becquer to the meeting place.

"Let me put it this way," their leader said. "I have a
woman inside Salamanca. She has a hunger that needs
frequent satisfying. She remains faithful to me yet is
never hungry. Have I answered your question?"

There was another burst of laughter from the Spaniards.

"So only I am allowed to go?" Duarte asked.

"Only you," Becquer said. "I am sure your sister will
not be hard to find or recognize, but it will be more
convenient for you to identify her and for her to see
you. Women can become a little difficult around masked
bandits loaded with guns and knives."

"Not Joana," Duarte said. "You will find she is made
of stern stuff. Fair enough, then. When do we leave?"

"Tonight." Becquer grinned once more. "Mention of
my woman has given me a hunger of my own."

"Tonight, then." Duarte found that his heart was
knocking against his ribs. He had never before ventured
outside his own country in his war against the French.
And he had never worked with Spanish partisans rather
than with his own men. The dangers, too, were very real
to him. It was something he had agreed to do for Joana,
and something he would try to do. But he was not confident of success.

All he hoped was that if he failed, Joana herself would
not be implicated. And selfishly he hoped that if he
failed, he would be killed instantly and not taken prisoner. The very thought could cause him to break into a
cold sweat.

He thought of Carlota and Miguel, whom he had left
behind in Mortagoa. At least they would be safe. When
the French advanced into Portugal, as they surely would
within a few weeks at the latest, they would take the
road to Coimbra. Mortagoa was well north of that road,
and safe from their advance. At least he had that
consolation.

He tried not to think of Carlota, who had taken her leave of him dry-eyed and with a stony expression. She had not tried to stop him or, more surprisingly, to plead to go with him. She had merely hugged him hard, pressing herself against him, closing her eyes.

And Miguel, supremely indifferent to the fact that his father was leaving perhaps never to return, sleepy and yawning, had stared up at him with solemn eyes as he had gazed hungrily at his son and kissed him gently on the lips.

Better not to think of them.

"Yes. Tonight," he said, getting resolutely to his feet. And he signaled to his men to draw apart.

More weary weeks had passed. Marshal Ney was besieging Almeida, and the French officers still in Salamanca, polite as they wished to be to their captive, could not help but jeer in his hearing at the British commander in chief, who showed no sign of going to its assistance.

"It seems," Captain Dupuis said at dinner one evening, "that Viscount Wellington was totally dependent upon your persuading us to go a different way, monsieur. He seems now to be paralyzed with indecision and dismay."

"Yes," Captain Blake said. "It seems that way."

"But it is ill-mannered of me to refer to such matters," the Frenchman said contritely. "Forgive me, please. Have you sampled the delights the Spanish ladies have to offer? You are popular with them, being English, and being tall and well-favored too. We French have to pay dearly for their favors, I am afraid."

Captain Blake had not availed himself of the favors that might have been his for the asking. Though why he had not, he could not explain to himself. Certainly the need for a woman was strong on him. Otherwise surely he would not be so obsessed with Joana, a woman he both hated and despised.

He wanted her. It was as simple as that. He had wanted her from his first sight of her in that ballroom in Lisbon. He could remember his feelings on that occasion, his dislike of her even before he had met her, even before he had realized that she was the Jeanne Morisette of painful memory. He had disliked her because she was beautiful and expensive and privileged, because she was far beyond his touch—and because he had wanted her.

He still wanted her, though his dislike of her was ten times intensified. but then, so was his desire. Having experienced the power of her charms directed fully at him, having touched her and enjoyed more than one indecorous embrace with her, he wanted her with a raw passion that he feared no other woman could quell.

Perhaps that was why he had not even tried to taste the charms of the Spanish women of Salamanca. He laughed at himself sometimes—though without any amusement at all—for wanting such a woman. All he should want to do to such as her was kill her.

He did not want to kill her. He did not want her dead. He wanted her . . . Well, he wanted her.

That one embrace behind the vine trees seemed to have satisfied her for the time. Or frightened her. Though he did not really believe that. He was beginning to believe that the Marquesa das Minas was not easily frightened. Or perhaps it had sickened her. Perhaps she wanted no repetition. Though, remembering her fierce participation in the embrace and her panting that had matched his own afterward, he doubted that too. When it came to sexuality, there was nothing of the demure lady about Joana da Fonte.

Whatever the reason, she had not pursued him as actively since. She never ignored him. Whenever she saw him, she smiled at him, or lifted her eyebrows to him, or merely looked and inclined her head. Occasionally she approached, always on the arm of some French officer, to exchange a few words with him. She never tried to get him alone.

Of course, he did not see as much of her as he had done during that first month. He had started to refuse a large number of his invitations. He had always hated grand social occasions anyway, but had felt obliged for very courtesy's sake to accept his invitations for a while. Now he followed inclination and accepted only those that came from people who had been particularly kind to him.

Time was beginning to hang heavily and more heavily on his hands.

He would have refused his invitation to Colonel Marcel Leroux's dinner and reception. Of course he would. He could not stand the man. He supposed that under any circumstances he would dislike the man who had led the interrogation against him and had forced him to stand up and remove all his clothing, an article at a time, while two sergeants had searched at snail's pace. It was hard to retain one's dignity, and even one's sense of identity, he had found, when standing naked to the gaze of several enemy officers in full uniform.

But it was not just that. The colonel had only been doing his job, after all. There was also the fact that wherever he saw Joana these days, Colonel Leroux was not far away. More often than not, she was leaning on his arm and sparkling up at him as if the whole of the universe must rest in his eyes. It was not just flirtation, he sensed. There was something more serious than that. He could not quite put his finger on what it was. But it seemed reasonable to suppose that it must be love. She must be falling in love with the man.

And Captain Blake found himself wanting to commit murder and despising himself for feeling that way and hating the colonel for exposing his feelings so badly to his own view.

And there had been that one occasion when he and the colonel had come face-to-face at someone's reception, both with a glass in hand, and had exchanged polite nods. But the colonel had decided to speak.

"I trust that all is to your liking in Salamanca, Captain?" he had asked.

"Thank you," Captain Blake had said. "I have been made perfectly comfortable."

"Yes." The colonel had smiled arctically. "We treat our prisoners with respect, as you do yours. We expect our prisoners to return the compliment, of course, and to extend that courtesy to our ladies."

Captain Blake had raised his eyebrows.

"I should hate there to be any unpleasantness because you had forgotten to observe that rule," Colonel Leroux had said. "I believe I do not need to say any more, Captain?"

Captain Blake had pursed his lips. "Oh, absolutely

not," he had said. "I see that you fear competition, Colonel. Please feel free to relax and lose your fear."

Colonel Leroux had inclined his head to him and moved on.

A small point. A minor incident. But the warning had been given. And they had given each other notice, without one word of incivility, that they hated each other with a passion.

Yes, certainly he would have refused the invitation. And yet on the very same day it came, there came also a perfumed letter addressed in an elegant female hand. A letter from Joana, urging him to attend.

"I need to speak with you," she had written, "and you have been avoiding me, you naughty man. I do believe you are afraid of me. Are you, Robert? But I do need to speak with you. The matter is very urgent, and I know that your gallantry—oh, yes, and your curiosity too—will bring you. Until tomorrow evening, then. You will be there? You will not fail me? There is no need to reply to this letter. Of course you will not fail me."

For several minutes he tapped the letter against his palm, trying to find the will and the courage to do what he knew he should do. How could he even pretend that she did not have him dangling on a string just as she had countless other men, unless he could resist running as soon as she crooked a finger?

Very urgent? She needed more kisses, did she? She needed to be reassured that he still desired her?

But *very* urgent? What if she meant more than that?

He did not struggle with himself for many minutes. He did not waste his own time. He had known from the moment of reading her letter for the first time that he would go. Of course he would go. Why pretend to himself that perhaps he would resist her demands?

Of course he would go.

It was nerve-racking, to say the very least. She had allowed almost three weeks to pass. Not quite three, as she had planned. The occasion of Colonel Leroux's reception had seemed just too suitable an occasion. But she had heard nothing from Duarte—had she expected to? There was no knowing if he was close or even if he

was on his way. There was no knowing if he would succeed in getting inside Salamanca, not to mention all the
rest of it.

The plan that had seemed so logical to her when she
was still in Portugal now seemed dangerous and chancy
in the extreme. And the trouble was that if something
went awry, if Duarte never came, then it would be Robert who would suffer. And if Duarte came and then was
caught . . . But she dared not let her thoughts move
along those lines.

War was a dangerous business, she reminded herself,
and she was an active player in it for the moment. She
could only move ahead now and hope that all would
work out as she had planned it.

And so she sent her letter off to Robert, guessing that
he would be on the colonel's guest list. There was a great
dearth of British prisoners in Salamanca. Everyone, it
seemed, vied with everyone else to show him the most
courtesy. He was invited everywhere, though she had
noticed that he had not accepted even half his invitations
during the past few weeks. Ever since she had drawn him
into kissing her that way . . .

Hence the letter. She could not take the chance that
he would not go. And yet she was in agonies of doubt
and anxiety all during the day of the reception, even
though she had pondered long over her letter in order
to phrase it in the way most designed to make his coming
inevitable. She knew he would come. She knew him so
well, just as if she were privy to his thoughts. She always
knew what he was thinking, which was a stupid idea, she
admitted when she put it into words in her own mind.

But she knew he would come. And yet there was that
niggling doubt. What if he did not? What if, on this occasion above all others, he did not come? Well, then, she
told herself, she would have to organize something for
the next day. Or the next. She had told Duarte three
weeks, and it was not quite three weeks yet. She had
never been one to be ruled by anxieties. She would not
give in to them now.

And so it was a relaxed and smiling and vivid marquesa—dressed in a gown of startling pink—who arrived
at the house where the colonel was lodged and allowed

him to take both her hands in his and raise them one at a time to his lips. It was possible to endure such contact, she had found, if she imagined his face dead, as it would be when she was finished with him.

"Jeanne," he murmured. "More beautiful than ever. Do I say that every time I see you?"

She looked upward, thinking. "Yes," she said, smiling. "Is it always true, Marcel? Or is it just flattery?"

"How can you ask?" he said, and his eyes assumed that intense look that had been warning her for a few weeks past that the crisis was coming, that soon flirtation would no longer hold him at arm's length. Perhaps that was why she had waited just a little less than three weeks. "If you will just permit it, Jeanne, I will show you just how little my words are flattery." He squeezed her hands tightly.

She laughed lightly and withdrew her hands from his. "Marcel," she said archly, "you have guests to entertain." And she looked casually about, smiling at male faces turned her way, and locating Captain Blake where she had fully expected to see him—in the most shadowed corner of the room. She made no sign, but turned her eyes away from him.

She sat beside the colonel at dinner and ate her way through the meal, each mouthful apparently of the taste and consistency of cardboard, and chattered gaily to the colonel on one side and General Forget on the other and to the gentlemen and one lady across the table from her.

After dinner she allowed herself to be escorted to the reception rooms and spent a whole hour there, at first with the colonel and then without him, circulating among the guests, who were predominantly, as always, officers of the French army. She talked and laughed and flirted— and stayed away from Captain Blake, who made no move to approach her himself.

And then she drew a few steadying breaths, her smile firmly in place, and crossed the room to lay a hand on Colonel Leroux's sleeve.

"Jeanne." He turned to her with a smile. "I thought I had been abandoned in favor of my myriad rivals."

"Marcel," she said, glancing at his companions. "A word with you, please."

He excused himself and moved off a short distance with her. "Is something wrong?" he asked her.

"No." She smiled tremulously. "I do not think so. Just foolishness. I seem to have misplaced a ring, though I am sure it is quite safe. It is just that I cannot stop thinking about it. It was a betrothal ring given me by Luis. It is very valuable."

He took her by the arm and looked down at her in some concern.

"I was wearing it when I left my aunt's," she said. "I know I was. I can remember twisting it around and around, as I have a habit of doing. I remember pushing my hands into the pockets of my cloak so that I would stop doing so. After that I cannot remember. I am sure the ring must be in my cloak pocket."

"I shall send a servant upstairs without delay," he said.

"I would feel so foolish if anyone else knew I had done anything so careless," she said. "It is priceless, Marcel. Would you . . . ? I mean, would it be too much trouble to you . . . ?"

"To look myself?" he asked. "Of course not, Jeanne. You know I would do anything to ensure your peace of mind. The cloak is pink to match your gown? Why do you not come with me?"

But she drew back. "It would be noticed," she said. "Our leaving together and perhaps being away for some time. And perhaps the ring is not in my cloak pocket. Perhaps it fell off in the carriage."

"I shall look there too," he said, squeezing her hand. "You stay here, Jeanne, and enjoy yourself. I shall find it, never fear. I shall be back before you know it."

But not too soon, she hoped as he hurried from the room. He would find the ring between two cushions in the carriage. But the carriage door was locked. He would have to find her coachman.

As soon as he was out of sight, she hurried to the door, where there were two sergeants on duty, one on each side. She spoke to the larger of the two.

"When Colonel Leroux returns," she said, "you will tell him, if you please, to find me immediately. It is most important that he do so."

"Yes, ma'am." The sergeant stood to attention.

"And you are to come with him," she said. "And your companion. Both of you. Do you understand?"

"Yes, ma'am," both men said, and their eyes met over her head.

"The soldier on duty at the main door," she said, glancing quickly across the hallway. "He is to accompany you. I will have need of all three of you."

She swept back into the reception room without waiting for a reply, and looked about her. Her heart felt as if it had leapt into her throat and was beating there at double time. She smiled vaguely at a major with large mustaches who was making his way toward her, and hurried across the room until she reached the corner. Robert was talking with a fellow captain. She smiled sweetly.

"Robert," she said, touching his arm, "I need to speak with you. Excuse us, Captain?"

He came with her without a word and without protest. That was a relief at least. There was so little time. She led him from the room and across the hall to a room that she knew to be an office. She took a candle from a table as she passed and took it inside the room with her.

"Close the door," she instructed him, and he obeyed, his eyes on her the whole while.

She looked quickly about as she set the candle down on the mantelpiece. A large table strewn with papers. An oak desk. Both with sharp corners. A great deal of space in the center of the room.

And she looked at him, standing just inside the door, his legs slightly apart, his hands clasped behind him. Dearly familiar in his shabby green coat with the shining sword in its scabbard at his side. Only his boots were new and shining from the same care he gave his weapons. His face was stern, unsmiling. His hair had grown longer since his captivity and curled enticingly over his collar.

Her heart turned over and she knew again a truth that she had not yet put into words. She could not afford to do so. She had a job to do. And this was the most difficult, the most heartrending part of all. She could not do it, she thought in a flash. But he was so unhappy, so eager to be back with his men, she thought immediately after. And Arthur had asked her to try to effect his freedom if she possibly could.

Oh, yes, she possibly could.

She smiled slowly at him. "Robert," she said softly, "you have been avoiding me."

"You had something very urgent to tell me," he said without moving. "What is it, Joana? How may I be of assistance to you? Or was it a hoax? Am I still to be made to fall in love with you? You become tedious. If it is only that, then I must beg to be excused without more ado."

No, it would not work that way. Or perhaps it would. She had great confidence in her charms, even with Captain Robert Blake. But it would take too long. Clearly he had his heart set like steel against her. She turned immediately to her second plan.

Her smile faded, she looked at him with haunted eyes, and her lower lip trembled. "Robert," she said, her voice matching her lip, "you must help me. Oh, I know you hate me, and I know I deserve your hatred ten times over, but there is no one else who can help. I have no one else to turn to."

His eyes grew more hostile and she felt a small twinge of fear in her stomach. Fear that she would run out of time.

"I am no spy," she said. "And I had no intention of ruining your plans, Robert, and betraying your country. I merely answered General Valéry's questions truthfully, not realizing they were a trap, and then he brought you into the room and I realized it. And I reacted as I always do when confused. I pretended that I thought it all amusing. I did not feel that way, Robert. I am half-English. And my husband was Portuguese." Her voice faltered. "*You* are English."

"My God." She could see his face harden with anger, but he took several steps forward. That was something at least. "Do you expect me to believe such . . . idiocy? Do you think you can make of every man a dupe? Do you expect intelligence to fly out of the brain as infatuation flies in? What is your game, Joana? Why have you brought me here? I do not like being so noticeably absent from the company with you."

"Why not?" She touched his chest lightly with one

hand and felt his muscles contract. "Don't you care for me at all, Robert? Not even one little bit "

"You know what interest I have in you," he said. "All my other feelings are scorn, Joana. And dislike. And I will not allow my body to rule my head merely because you are a beautiful woman and have the gift of enticing men more than any other woman I have known. There are many other women whom I can lust after and from whom I can get more satisfaction. There was no urgent matter, then?"

She swallowed and looked into his eyes with all her soul—her real soul, with no mask whatsoever. She was that desperate.

"I love you," she whispered to him, and the tears formed in her eyes. "I know you will not believe me. I know I am merely opening myself to further scorn. But it is true. I love you."

He looked at her with an incredulity that wounded cruelly, since there was no mask for it to bounce off. "Christ!" he said. "They used to burn people like you, you know. Witches. She-devils."

She set her forehead against his chest and breathed in the warmth and the smell of him. And she raised her head and looked up at him with her unmasked eyes.

"Joana." He gripped her arms in a grasp that was immediately painful. "Stop this immediately. God, woman, stop it."

She took one half-step forward so that she touched him from knees to shoulders. She spread both hands on his chest. "Take me away from here," she pleaded. "When you go, let me come too. I don't want to live here without you." The door was opening behind his back. "Robert," she whispered.

"God," he said, and she could see that he was so furiously angry that he had not even heard the opening of the door, "you are like a fever in my blood, Joana."

"Let me go," she said, her voice trembling again. "You tricked me into coming here, did you not? There is no sick lady here. Do you mean to ravish me? I shall scream and then there will be dreadful scandal. Let me go, Robert." And she began to struggle wildly against the iron bands of his hands, noting at the same time the blank look of surprise and incomprehension in his eyes.

But neither the blankness nor the incomprehension lasted long. And she had been quite right to have estimated that it would need four men, she thought as she stood quietly beside the desk, dying a little with each blow. He easily fought off both Colonel Leroux and the larger of the sergeants and very possibly would have come out on top of a fight against three of them. But after several minutes of silent, desperate fighting, he was finally overpowered and held by all three of the guards whose presence she had demanded, while the colonel pounded him at leisure with his fists.

Captain Blake did not lose consciousness. Nor did he remove his eyes from those of his adversary even when they became swollen and almost sightless. He made no sound except for grunts when fists landed in his stomach.

Joana felt as if every blow had landed on her. They would kill him. They would not be content until they had killed him.

"Marcel," she said. "Enough. Please."

Colonel Leroux stopped immediately and turned toward her. "Jeanne, my apologies," he said. "You should have left the room. This is no sight for a lady."

She was being regarded steadily from two bloodshot eyes that were hardly even visible between the swollen folds of flesh about them. She forced herself to look back briefly. The three soldiers still held him fast.

"I believed him," she said. "He said there was a lady in here fainting and that I should come. I was so very foolish."

The colonel nodded at one of the sergeants, who was unbuckling the captain's sword belt.

"He will not bother you again, Jeanne," Colonel Leroux said. "I have a special dungeon in mind for our comrade here, one that I normally reserve for our friends the Spaniards. We will see if that will cool your ardor, Captain Blake."

He said nothing, but only continued to look at Joana. She could not bring herself to look back, but felt his eyes burning into her conscience.

"His parole, Marcel," she said.

"He has broken parole," the colonel said harshly. He jerked a thumb at the soldiers in a gesture that was so familiar to Joana's nightmares that she felt all the blood drain from her head. "Take him away. Try to avoid upsetting my guests with the sight of him. I shall be with you in a few minutes."

"Oh, dear," Joana said, her hand reaching for the edge of the desk, "I do believe I am going to faint."

It was a good act, she realized afterward. Except that it had not been an act at all.

16

HE had been there for five days, perhaps longer. It was hard to gauge time when there was no daylight. All he could assume was that during the long, long stretches of time when no one came near him, it must be night, and that during the stretches when he was brought meager scraps of food and foul-tasting water and when the brutes came to rough him up, it must be day. Five days, then. Perhaps six.

He was no longer bound by his parole. The thought brought him wry amusement. There had been times when he had wished for just such a situation, when he had wished that he could turn his mind and his energy to escape. Escape! It would be hard indeed to escape from an underground stone dungeon whose single solid door was never opened—except when the ruffians came, two to act guard and three to work him over.

It must be night, Captain Blake thought, or the beginning of night. Some bread had been thrust between the bars of the door grille and dropped to the filthy floor perhaps two hours before, and he knew that long hours would pass before he could expect more. He forced himself to relax on the bare board that was his bed. Long years as a soldier had taught him to endure almost any discomfort and to sleep under almost any conditions. He needed rest. Then rest he would.

He stretched out his sore and aching legs, spread one hand over bruised and perhaps cracked ribs, and laid the back of the other arm over swollen and bruised eyes. He ran his tongue over lips that were swollen and cut inside. Fortunately—very fortunately—none of his teeth had been broken . . . yet. The rest would heal—perhaps, unless Colonel Leroux planned to kill him or have him killed. The colonel had appeared in person only that first night, when he had carried on where he had left off in his house, beating the captain insensible.

At least, Captain Blake thought, he had not been tortured. Beyond the beatings, that was. He did not consider those torture. He had been beaten before. There had been fights that he had lost, though not many of them in recent years, since his weight had caught up to his height and since he had been commissioned to the ranks of the officers.

He tried to sleep. The board was hard. He was used to the hard ground. It was cold. He was used to the cold. He ached all over. He was used to pain. He had been duped by her, made into the ultimate idiot. Christ, she had made a fool of him. For all his apparent incredulity, he had felt himself beginning to drown in the sincerity of her eyes. Sincerity!

I love you.

He turned his head to one side and winced. Lord God! *I love you.* She had done it to him twice, once when he was seventeen and could be excused for falling for it, and now when he was turned twenty-eight and had thought himself worldly-wise. Not that he had quite fallen for it this time, but even so. . . . Even so, he had been hankering after her—even knowing who and what she was.

She was a dangerous woman, one who used her feminine charms with as deadly intent as a man might use his sword.

He tried, as he had tried for five days and nights—or was it six?—to put her from his mind so that he might sleep. But he could forgive Colonel Leroux and his thugs more easily than he could forgive her. At least the colonel thought he had good reason to punish him, even if the punishment was somewhat excessive. But she? What reason had she had for what she had done? He had already been in captivity. There could be only one reason. Although he had admitted to a physical attraction to her and had acted on that attraction more than once, he had refused to fawn on her, to follow her about, to make himself her slave.

It seemed that she needed to enslave men. And he

had refused to be enslaved. And so he had had to be punished. He wondered if she knew about this dungeon and about all the extra beatings since the one she had witnessed that evening. He wondered if she was satisfied, if she ever even thought of him now.

He wished that for just fifteen minutes—ten even—he could get his hands on her.

A key was rattling in the lock of his cell door and he drew a few deep and steadying breaths without moving. The door only ever opened for one reason. Hell! And he thought it was night. Perhaps it was. Perhaps they were going to start on his nights now.

"You—up!" a voice ordered.

"Go to hell," he said automatically. One thing they had not broken yet was his spirit, and he intended to keep it that way.

"You have to come," the voice said. "Now. General's orders. There is no time to waste."

Come? Out of the cell? Jesus, he thought, and he fought to keep control of his breathing. Torture. *Jesus, he prayed silently, help me not to give them the satisfaction of breaking.*

"On your feet, you." The soldier's voice, Captain Blake noticed suddenly, sounded nervous. But then the man stood aside and the cell seemed to fill with them. It was familiar stuff except that they all stood back from him and he could see in the light of some torches in the passageway outside that they were all pointing muskets at him.

He got slowly to his feet.

"Hands on your head," one of them barked at him.

He obeyed slowly, pursing his lips and staring at the barker. And then one of them stepped forward and took his arms one at a time from his head and bound them tightly at his back. Then muskets were poking at his back—at least they did not have bayonets attached, he thought—and he was being ordered to step out into the passageway.

Even though it was night, the light of torches while he was still indoors and then the light shed by the moon and stars when he was outdoors almost blinded him and hurt his eyes like a thousand devils. He was marched along

one street, around a corner, and along another street
to a familiar house—General Valéry's. He was prodded
inside.

Well, he thought, wondering if there were a single spot
on his body that did not ache, the general must have run
out of entertainment for his guests. The prisoner was
now to become an entertainer. Charming!

"Drop them right there," someone said in heavily accented French as soon as he stepped inside the hallway
of the house with his guards. "Yes, in a heap right
there." There was a clattering of dropped muskets behind him. "They communicated with no one, Emilio?
And had no chance to load their guns? Good. And this
is he?" The speaker switched to Spanish and nodded
toward Captain Blake. "Step this way, señor, if you
please."

Captain Blake looked around and noticed for the first
time that one of the five men who had brought him there
was not dressed in the uniform of a French soldier. The
man grinned.

"Only my gun was loaded, señor," he said with a
shrug, "and it was trained on the French pigs, not on
you."

Captain Blake looked back to the first speaker, who
was motioning him toward the open door of the drawing
room in which he had been entertained on more than
one occasion.

The man wore a handkerchief up over his mouth and
nose.

Four days passed after the incident at Colonel Leroux's
reception before Joana heard from Duarte. She was almost at the point of panic, but she spent her days as
before, strolling in the splendid Plaza Mayor, surrounded
by her court of admirers, riding out over the Roman
bridge with them, attending evening entertainments, and
always smiling and gay and flirting.

She turned her charm with particular force on Colonel
Leroux himself, and even allowed him one kiss on the
lips—closed lips—when he escorted her home one evening. She thought she would surely die, but she spent

the few seconds before she pushed him gently away and smiled dreamily up at him picturing his dead face.

"Jeanne," he said to her, catching at her hands, "have I offended you? I do apologize if I have. But you must know how I feel about you."

"Must I?" She looked up at him with large innocent eyes.

"You must know that I love you," he said, his own eyes burning back into hers. "I have made no effort to disguise the fact. Tell me that you are not indifferent to me."

"Marcel." Her lips parted as she gazed up into his eyes. "I am not indifferent to you. Oh, no, you know I am not. But do not force me to say any more. This is moving too fast, I believe."

"Any day now," he said, taking her hand and holding it close to his lips, "Almeida will fall and the advance on Portugal will begin. Perhaps I will not see you for several weeks or even months after that. Forgive me for rushing you, Jeanne. Soldiers are not the most patient of men, I am afraid."

"If you are forced to leave in a hurry," she said, raising her free hand and running it lightly over his wrist, "then perhaps I will be persuaded to say more, Marcel. But not now."

He kissed her hand.

Duarte's messenger, a thin and none-too-clean Spaniard who came to the kitchen to deliver eggs, arrived on the fourth day. Duarte needed to know that all had gone according to plan so far. And he needed to know the time and the place. By good fortune there was to be a dinner at General Valéry's house the following evening, to which both Joana and Colonel Leroux had been invited. Also fortunate was the fact that it was to be a private dinner rather than a large assembly, with no more than a dozen guests.

Ten o'clock on the evening of the following day, she told the Spaniard. At General Valéry's house.

That evening she allowed Colonel Leroux to kiss her again, and she smiled warmly at him when he told her again that he loved her, and opened her mouth as if to return the words, but closed it and smiled apologetically at him.

Dinner the following evening was interminable, and again the food seemed to be made of cardboard. Joana listened to her own voice and her own laughter as if she were observing from a long way off. The other two ladies present were far quieter than she. She was seated next to Colonel Leroux—they seemed to have been accepted as a couple, though other officers had certainly not ceased their attentions to her.

It was almost half-past nine, she saw in a nervous glance at a large clock in the hallway, when they adjourned to the drawing room. Her heart was beating so fast that she was feeling breathless. She was laughing too much, she thought. But she was always laughing. It would seem strange if she stopped.

There was no clock in the drawing room. The half-hour dragged by. Surely a whole hour must have passed, she thought eventually, and a little later she was certain it must be so. Madame Savard was even suggesting to the colonel, her husband, that it was time to leave.

And then Joana thought that she heard noises in the hallway beyond the drawing room, and then she was certain.

The drawing-room door burst open.

There must have been at least a dozen of them, though when she tried to count she found that her mind was not functioning rationally. There were more who stayed out in the hallway. They all wore scarves or handkerchiefs up over their noses and would have been difficult to recognize anyway. But she knew a moment of panic when she realized that they were all strangers. She could not recognize even one member of Duarte's band among them.

And then she saw Duarte himself and she felt herself sag with relief before the tension and danger of the moment grabbed at her again. Perhaps five seconds had passed—perhaps not so many—since the door had burst open.

One of the other ladies—perhaps both—was screaming. The men had all scrambled to their feet. Joana felt her arm being grabbed and she was pulled firmly behind Colonel Leroux.

"Stand exactly where you are," a voice said in heavily accented French, and Joana located with her eyes a great mountain of a man, his black hair wild about his head and shoulders, his dark eyes fanatic. "Move a muscle and you die."

They were all carrying firearms.

"Do as you are told," the large man said, "and no one will be hurt."

General Valéry took one step forward, and something exploded at his feet.

"That is your warning that we are serious, señor," the Spaniard said. "We have come for an Englishman. Captain Robert Blake."

"I have never heard of him," the general said. "The English are in Portugal."

"You will have him fetched, if you please," the partisan said. He chuckled. "Or if you do not please. Here is a sergeant." One stepped into the doorway, his arms raised above his head, a musket at his back. "Send him."

The general pursed his lips. One of the ladies screamed again and was instantly silenced.

Duarte took a step forward, and Joana felt her breathing grow ragged. He looked directly at her and stabbed a finger at her. "You," he said. "Come here."

"Leave the lady alone, you cowardly bastard," Colonel Leroux said.

"Come here." Duarte kept his eyes on Joana and ignored the colonel.

"Stay where you are, Jeanne," the colonel commanded.

"Come here."

Joana threw back her head and stepped out from behind the colonel. "I am not afraid of him," she said. "You will find, monsieur, that Frenchwomen do not cringe easily before scum." She stepped forward just before the colonel's arm came out to prevent her.

The next moment she had been swung around, her back against Duarte, his arm tight about her shoulders, his knife at her throat. She could feel the edge of it against her bare flesh as she swallowed. He had killed with that knife. She knew that he kept it razor sharp.

"I suggest, monsieur," he said quietly, addressing General Valéry, "that you send for the Englishman without delay. My hand might grow unsteady after a while. And I am sure that your digestion and that of your guests would not be helped by the sight of the lady's blood." He leered down at Joana. "And such a lovely lady, too."

Joana closed her eyes, her head resting on Duarte's shoulder, the blade of his knife grazing her throat.

Very little was said during the interminable minutes that passed after the French sergeant had been sent about his errand, presumably under guard. They all stood like statues, the masked partisans at one side of the room, all of them except Duarte with pointed firearms, the French at the other side. Colonel Savard was granted permission to allow his lady to be seated.

"You will not get away with this," General Valéry said after a few minutes.

"Will we not, señor?" the mountain of a man asked politely.

"I will kill you," Colonel Leroux said steadily a few minutes later, looking intently at Duarte.

"Will you, monsieur?" Duarte asked politely.

That was the extent of the conversation.

And then there were voices in the hallway and the clattering of dropped guns. Joana held her breath. She swiveled her eyes sideways—she dared not move her head—and within seconds he appeared.

She drew in a sharp breath. He was almost unrecognizable. He looked thin—surely he had lost weight even in five days—and dirty. His hair was a darker blond than usual, and there was a heavy stubble of beard on his cheeks and chin. His face—every part of it—was swollen and raw. But surely in five days he would have recovered somewhat from that beating, when he had been cruelly outnumbered, thanks to her.

The truth dawned on Joana, and she closed her eyes again.

The first thing he saw, though he was instantly aware of the whole tableau, was Joana, her back hard against the chest of one of the masked partisans, the blade of a knife resting against her throat. His first foolish instinct was to rush forward to her assistance, though his arms were still bound behind his back. But at the same moment he recognized Duarte Ribeiro, and beyond him, the mountainous form of Antonio Becquer.

What the hell? he thought. Joana had closed her eyes, but he did not believe she had fainted. He felt a reluctant admiration for her, uncowed by even such terrifying circumstances.

"Ah, señor," Antonio Becquer said, glancing his way quickly. "I see the French pigs have been using your face as a punching ball. They have done nothing to improve your looks." He chuckled. "Free his hands." He nodded to someone behind the captain, and a few moments later Robert's arms were free and he was rubbing his wrists and looking warily about him.

"We will be leaving, señores and señoras," Becquer said, also looking about the room, "now that we have what we want. No one has been hurt, you see? And no one will be hurt if you do not try to pursue us or raise the alarm against us."

A French colonel laughed shortly.

Duarte Ribeiro spoke, and Captain Blake's eyes returned to Joana. "If there is pursuit," Duarte said, and he grinned unpleasantly down at Joana, "some harm may come to the lady."

Captain Blake watched her close her eyes again and swallow. And he felt a surging of exultation. Yes, of course, these men would need a hostage. And who better than Joana? Oh, yes. Perhaps he would get his fifteen minutes with her yet. Perhaps longer.

Colonel Leroux took one step forward, and instantly half a dozen muskets were leveled at his chest.

"Let her go," he said, his voice tight. "If you must have a hostage, take me instead."

Antonio Becquer laughed heartily. "But who would think twice about a colonel having a bullet shot between his eyes when the alternative would be to capture a band of Spanish partisans and an escaped British officer?" he said. "Remember, señor—señores—that the lady dies if anyone tries to prevent our leaving Salamanca."

"Marcel," Joana said, and Captain Blake felt that twinge of admiration again when he heard not a tremor of fear in her voice, "I am not afraid of them. You will come after me?"

"Never fear otherwise, Jeanne," the colonel said, his hands opening and closing into fists at his sides. "This is now my personal war. The man who holds you will die slowly. Every other man will die, including Captain Blake."

"Come after me," she said, and she gazed across the room, seeing no one but the colonel. Her voice dropped almost to a whisper. "I love you."

"Very affecting," Duarte said as the other partisans withdrew from the room.

Captain Blake stood where he was until Antonio Becquer caught at his sleeve. "Come, señor," he said. "We have come for you. Never tell us now that you are reluctant to leave."

Duarte was backing slowly from the room, the last to leave, his knife still at Joana's throat. Her eyes were open, Captain Blake saw, and they turned and met his as she drew level with him. He smiled slowly at her, though he doubted that his damaged face registered his expression as a smile.

"So, Joana," he said, "we are to be traveling companions for a while. How pleasant—for me."

And he turned and strode into the hallway. The only unmasked Spaniard, the one who had accompanied him from his prison, was holding out his sword to him in one hand and his rifle in the other. He was grinning, just as if he had conjured them out of thin air.

"You will not wish to be naked on your travels, señor," he said.

Captain Blake grinned back.

"You will be sorry," Joana was saying in a clear voice behind him. "You have made a powerful enemy tonight, monsieur. He will come after me, you see. He will not rest until he has found me and rescued me—and killed you."

Captain Blake strapped on his sword belt with hasty fingers—God, but he was sore all over—and wondered at the strange good fortune that had brought both Antonio Becquer and Duarte Ribeiro right inside Salamanca to rescue him. And for the first time he blessed the woman's spite that had unwittingly helped release him from his parole. And he exulted at the chance that had made her their hostage—*his* hostage.

Joana da Fonte, the Marquesa das Minas, would rue the day she was born before he had finished with her, he decided.

Within a matter of seconds they were all outside the house and had divided up. At least half of the partisans melted into the darkness. The reason for the masks, Captain Blake guessed, was that several of the men actually lived in Salamanca. They were the ones he had not recognized. The others strode at a brisk pace through the darkened streets of the city. It was not easy to keep up when every bone in his body ached, but keep up he did. He was, after all, accustomed to pain.

Duarte Ribeiro's knife had disappeared. He had an arm about Joana's waist, hurrying her along with them. Captain Blake kept behind them. He would not risk her escaping, and with Joana nothing was impossible. If he had to carry her every inch of the way beneath his arm or slung up over his shoulder, he would do it. He did not intend to take his eyes off her until they had reached safety, wherever that happened to be, and he could deal with her at his leisure.

They left Salamanca on foot, mounting onto horseback only when they reached an old monastery beyond its walls. And they rode all night and on into the morning, frequently at a gallop, always at a trot.

Joana rode up behind Duarte, her arms firmly about his waist.

"You are all right?" he asked her as he led his horse at a walk from the monastery courtyard.

"I am all right," she said. "What took you so long, Duarte?"

"I came," he said. "That is what matters."

"They will come after us," she said. "He will, at least. Colonel Leroux."

"You do not really love him, do you, Joana?" he asked. "Lord, it was a most affecting scene. Did you have to say that, knowing that now he will move heaven and earth to rescue you?"

"I had to convince them that I was reluctant to come,"

she said. She had decided long before that she would not tell Duarte who Colonel Leroux was. The pleasure of killing him was going to be all hers. She would not deny herself that. Not after having suffered for the privilege. She thought of the colonel's kisses and shuddered.

There was no chance for further conversation. There was no sign of pursuit, but they had to reach the mountains and Portugal before they could breathe with any ease.

It was a long, long night. At first she was cold. Later she was cold and stiff and sore. Eventually she was cold and stiff and sore and tired. Very, very tired. A few times she even almost nodded off to sleep.

"Bite on your lips," her brother told her as he felt her arms slip from his waist and lifted a hand to restore them there. "Flex your toes. Open your mouth wide and gasp air. Sing. Stay awake, Joana."

"Oh, I shall," she said. "Never fear."

And she concentrated her mind on the horse and its rider just behind them. Always just behind. Tomorrow— in just a few hours' time—she was going to be able to tell him all. And she was going to help bathe his wounds. Were there wounds on his body too? She shivered at the thought, though not with cold this time. Yes, there were bound to be. They would not have worked only on his face.

She was going to bathe and bandage his wounds and apologize for having been the necessary cause of them. And he would forgive her. Once he knew all, he would forgive her.

And then . . . ?

Joana shivered again at all the possibilities.

She had said something to him just before she had caused him that dreadful and savage beating. She had said it out of desperation, out of the urgent need to draw him into an embrace before Colonel Leroux came through the door. She had said it out of desperation and yet she had frightened herself with the truth of her words.

Perhaps she would be able to say them again to him.

Perhaps he would say the same words to her.

How pleasant—for me, he had said. She shivered

again. But of course it would all be different once she had told him everything. He would know that she had done it all for him, that her loyalty had never wavered from her half-brother's country and from her mother's.

She could feel his presence at her back almost like a large and menacing hand.

17

IT was still early morning, though the sun had been up for some time, when they rode into a deep wooded gorge between bare and rugged hills. They passed two men on guard—Captain Blake recognized one of them as Teófilo Costa—and paused while Duarte exchanged a few words with them, and then rode on to the welcome sight of several rough huts built in the shelter of the trees. Even more welcome to the captain was the sight of a stream bubbling its way down the center of the gorge. He had not washed even so much as his hands in almost a week.

"Portugal. Home," Duarte said, a note of relief and elation in his voice.

But the Spanish partisans who had ridden with them drew back. "Safely delivered," Antonio Becquer said. "Now we must safely deliver ourselves to the northern hills, señores, before the avengers discover our tracks." He saluted Captain Blake and grinned broadly. "It has been a pleasure, Captain. It is a long time since I and my men enjoyed ourselves more."

Captain Blake extended his right hand, and the Spaniard caught it in a strong clasp.

"I shall not forget," the captain said. "Thank you, my friend." He held his horse still and watched the partisans ride out of sight up one hillside. They had not even stopped for a rest or a bite to eat.

And then he turned his head back to watch a crowd of Duarte's band gather around their leader as he dismounted and reached up his arms to lift Joana to the ground. She set her hands on his shoulders and slid along his body until her feet touched the ground. And then she wrapped her arms about his neck and kissed him on the cheek.

"Duarte," she said, "you are wonderful. It is so good to feel Portuguese soil beneath my feet again." She looked around at the other men with a dazzling smile. "You are all wonderful."

Duarte Ribeiro caught her in a close hug and swung her once around while Captain Blake watched, as if turned to stone. The devil! She must have been whispering sweet nothings into his ear all through the night, and he had fallen under her spell—as all men did. He had fallen despite the feisty woman and the dark-haired baby he had left behind in Mortagoa. All the men were falling under her spell. They stood around watching and grinning.

"Aren't we, though?" Duarte said, looking down at her with a grin and bending his head to kiss her firmly on the lips. "You owe me a number of favors in return, Joana."

She smiled at him almost impishly and turned to address the other men. "Which hut is mine?" she asked eagerly.

Captain Blake felt his jaw tighten. She would probably expect a feather bed and a case full of perfumes and jewels inside too. She was soon hurrying toward the closest hut.

He swung down from his saddle, schooling himself not to wince, and not sure that he had succeeded. "Ribeiro," he said sharply.

The Ordenanza leader looked around with a smile. "You will want a bath and a shave and a meal and a sleep," he said. "In that order? Are there any broken bones?"

"No," Captain Blake said, "and in that order, yes, please. Keep an eye on the marquesa. More than an eye. Keep ten eyes on her. She must not escape."

Duarte's smile turned to a grin. "She is a handful, yes," he said. "You have realized that too? But she is mortally tired and will not be going anywhere alone. At least, she had better not try if she knows what is good for her."

One of the other men—Francisco Braga—had just

come out of another hut and was holding out soap, a towel, and a razor to the captain.

I am afraid we cannot supply warm water," he said with a grin. "But this water will wake you up for your breakfast at least."

The need for a bath and a shave overcame all other needs, Captain Blake found. He glanced uneasily at the hut into which Joana had disappeared and around him at the half-dozen or so men who were there to guard against her escape. She would not be able to do it. And if she did somehow get away, then he would go after her. There was no way on this earth she was going to get away from him until he could deliver her to headquarters for imprisonment as an enemy agent.

"Thank you," he said, and he took the articles gratefully and looked about him for a secluded part of the stream where he could strip off all his clothes and bathe at his leisure.

The cold water caught at his breath ten minutes later when he plunged into a deep part of the stream. But it felt strangely good against his bruises, at first soothing and then numbing them. And the luxury of water and soap against his skin and in his hair was more delicious than he could have imagined possible.

He shaved with care. His jaw was sore and bruised, his lips still swollen. But he put up with some discomfort for the sake of being able to rub his hands along smooth jaws and chin. He flexed the shoulder that had been so badly wounded the year before. It felt no stiffer than the rest of his body—which was not saying a great deal, he supposed.

He floated on his back, feeling clean and pleasantly cold all over, and marveled at the freedom the morning had brought. Looking about at the trees and the hills and the blue sky, one would not have thought that war was not far off and all around. But he was free at least, free to fight the enemy again—after a few hours' sleep. It struck him suddenly that he was bone weary. And hungry. Hungry enough to eat a bear. And Francisco Braga had said something about breakfast?

He waded out of the water, shaking his arms and legs before toweling himself dry and rubbing at his hair, which had grown longer than he had worn it in years. And of course, he thought, the enemy was right at hand. There was an enemy to be fought that very day. And she was within his grasp. The thought brought renewed energy. He strode back toward the Ordenanza camp as soon as he had dressed.

And stopped short when he was still several yards away. He had not realized that the men had brought a woman with them. She was wearing a faded blue peasant dress, which reached barely to her ankles, and leather sandals. Her dark hair was in a wavy cloud about her head and shoulders. She was small and slender. The musket that was slung over one of her shoulders looked as if it must be very much too heavy for her.

And then she turned and looked at him with dark eyes from a beautiful face. There was a wicked-looking knife tucked into her belt, he saw at a downward glance.

It was only when he looked up again into her face, startled, that he recognized her. Christ Almighty! She was looking at him rather warily, but when his eyes met hers for the second time, she smiled slowly.

Joana! What the hell?

Joana had stepped outside the hut, where she had changed from the trappings of the Marquesa das Minas into the self she enjoyed most, and threw back her head and closed her eyes.

"Ah," she said to no one in particular, "fresh air and freedom. Blessed freedom." And then she lowered her chin and looked about her. "Where is Robert?" She was talking directly to Duarte.

"Having a bath," he said. "I guessed that it would be more important to him than either eating or sleeping."

"He is going to kill me," she said cheerfully, "unless I can explain everything to him first. He must have a dreadfully low opinion of me, don't you think? I had him imprisoned just so that he would be freed from his parole. I did not imagine that he would be so severely beaten."

"He does not know anything of your part in all this?" Duarte asked, grimacing.

"As far as he knows, I am a hostage," Joana said. "He

does not know that you are my half-brother. Don't say anything, Duarte. I want to tell him in my own way." She laughed lightly. "Unless he kills me first, of course."

"I don't think the knife and gun are necessary at the moment, are they?" Duarte gestured toward her weapons and grinned.

But his words merely made Joana shade her eyes and squint off along the valley and up the hillsides in the direction from which they had come.

"He will come after me, you know," she said. "And he will bring men with him. He fancies himself in love with me. He was on the verge of proposing marriage to me. I know. I can sense these things. He will come, Duarte, and soon."

"But not too soon," he said. "He does not know this country as we do. And Teófilo and Bernardino are still on watch back there. There will be time to eat and to sleep for a few hours. Before nightfall we will be gone from here."

"But he will find us," she said almost anxiously. He had to find them.

And then she turned at the sound of loose stones being displaced behind her. Robert was standing some distance away, looking quite magnificent, she thought, his face clean and shaven, his hair wet and waving close to his head. His face also looked as if he had come out at the wrong end of a fight, but it was a look that somehow enhanced the tough soldier quality that was uniquely his—and his virility.

She felt self-conscious and naked to his gaze. He had never seen her in her peasant clothes. He had never seen her with her hair down. And she knew that he was looking with some incredulity at her weapons. She felt breathless suddenly, and peculiarly uncertain of herself.

She reacted in the only way she could under such circumstances. She met his eyes and smiled. It was totally against her nature to show anxiety.

He did not smile back. But then, she did not expect him to.

"Your breakfast, Joana," Francisco Braga said, holding up a plate to her from his squatting position at the fire. "And yours, Captain." He held up another plate to Captain Blake. Duarte was already eating.

They both accepted their plates in silence and took their places on the ground beside Duarte. Joana was between the two men.

"I hope the knife is blunt and the musket unloaded," Captain Blake said over her head to Duarte, just as if she were deaf and dumb or did not understand the Portuguese language. "She is a hostage, Ribeiro. A hostile hostage. And if she has spun you a tale about really belonging here and really being loyal to your cause, don't believe a word of it. The woman is incapable of telling the truth."

Joana lifted a piece of fish to her mouth and chewed on it steadily.

Duarte grinned. "But women's wrists are weak," he said. "And muskets are notorious for never hitting what they are aimed at."

"Nevertheless," Captain Blake said, "I would not like to wake up to find either one pointing at my stomach from two feet away. Keep a guard on her, Ribeiro. I warn you she is dangerous."

Duarte shrugged and grinned down at his half-sister. "Perhaps I will take them before you go to sleep, Joana," he said. "I would not, after all, like to have you roll over onto the point of your knife."

It was not the time for explanations. They were both very tired and everything was too public. She would suffer the humiliation of handing over her gun and knife, she decided, and explain later. She was so very tired. She did not believe she had ever felt more tired in her life. There was a broad and green-clad shoulder close to her cheek. How wonderful it would be to rest her head against it and close her eyes. But one glance upward showed her the hardness of his expression and the hostility in his eyes.

She laid both her knife and her musket on the ground before her. It would have been just too shameful to actually place them in Duarte's hands.

"There was a message from Lord Wellington," Duarte was telling Robert. "One of my men brought it on here while I was in Salamanca. He is hoping that Almeida will

hold out for another month and that after that the autumn rains will come early. They will slow down the
French and make things that much worse for them."

"Almeida has not fallen yet, then?" Captain Blake
said. "Good. I was afraid that I was going to miss all the
fun. Whose idea was it, by the way, to come to rescue
me?"

Duarte ignored the question. "Our task, apart from
the usual," he said, "is to visit as many of the farms and
villages between here and Coimbra as we possibly can
and persuade the people to flee west with as many of
their possessions as they can carry, and to burn everything else, including their homes. It will not be a pleasant
or an easy task, I think." He shrugged. "But Wellington
swears that he will not abandon our country or leave us
to occupation by the French. And against all the odds, I
believe him. I suppose there is nothing else I can do and
remain sane."

"It is essential that the French armies be unable to live
off the countryside in Portugal as they usually do on their
advances," Captain Blake said. "They must be stranded
far from their supplies. It is the surest way to defeat
them."

"You have your part too," Duarte said. "Lord
Wellington specifically mentioned you and directed that
if your escape from Salamanca was effected in time, you
must join us in our task. A soldier's uniform may do
much to convince the doubtful, he feels. And who
knows? Perhaps he is right."

"I am not simply to rejoin my regiment, then?" the
captain asked.

"It would seem not." Duarte smiled at him apologetically.

But Joana could concentrate no longer. The words had
drifted a long way off, so that she could hear only sound
but no meaning. Her head was just too heavy for the
rest of her body. The side of it touched something warm
and solid and she gave in to the temptation to relax and
to sleep.

"She is very tired," Duarte said, looking at his sister
asleep against Captain Blake's shoulder. The captain had
not moved a muscle except to harden his jaw. "As we
are too. I don't know why we sit here talking when time

is so short. We must be well away from here before dark. In the meantime, let's sleep."

He scrambled to his feet and leaned down to pick up Joana. But she awoke with a start as soon as he touched her, and looked up, startled, at Captain Blake, who was not even looking down at her. She was glad he was not. She was not one for blushes in the normal course of events, but she knew she was blushing now.

How unspeakably mortifying.

"Go to bed, Joana," Duarte said. "And that is an order."

Normally she would have had to refuse out of mere principle. But now she scurried toward her hut rather like a frightened rabbit, she thought in disgust. But she could not think. It was almost painful to think, too much of an effort. She lay down on the blanket spread on the ground and slept.

It was late afternoon. Almost all of them were squinting off to the east, but if Colonel Leroux and the men he would bring with him were coming, it was not yet. The two sentries had just been withdrawn from the entrance to the valley and had reported that all was still quiet.

Even so, camp had been broken and they were to be well on their way from the ravine before nightfall. They would split up into small groups, Duarte had ordered, there being many places to visit if they were to carry out their orders from Lord Wellington with any thoroughness. Besides, small groups would form a smaller target for the French to spot.

"And we must never forget what our primary reason for existence is," Duarte said, his eyes narrowing in an expression that made his face look cruel for a moment. "Our purpose is to keep Frenchmen out of our country and to kill those who try to enter it."

Captain Blake, Duarte directed, should move south, toward Almeida. There was no particular hurry in persuading the populace until the fort fell, it seemed, but there might be very little time afterward. And there was no real doubt that Almeida would fall eventually. Perhaps it would hold out for a week or a month, but it would never withstand a determined siege by the French armies.

"She comes with me," Captain Blake said, jerking his head in Joana's direction.

Joana lifted her chin as Duarte and all his men looked at her.

"It is I the Frenchmen will be looking for most determinedly," Captain Blake said. "It is only fitting that I have their hostage with me. Besides"—his swollen eyes narrowed on Joana—"I have a score of my own to settle with her."

Joana half-smiled at him and made no appeal to her brother.

"Very well." Duarte shrugged. "Joana goes with you. I suppose she will be as safe with you as with any of us, even though the two of you will be on foot." The southern route was the steepest. It would be impossible to take horses up the slope.

And so the huts were destroyed and dust kicked over the ashes of the fire—there was no point, the men had decided, in wasting time trying completely to camouflage what had so obviously been a camp—and hasty farewells were made and good-luck greetings exchanged.

Duarte took Joana in his arms and hugged her hard. "You will not let me send you back directly to safety?" he asked her for the last time.

"When life is suddenly so full of meaning?" she asked, her face hidden against his shoulder. "Never, Duarte."

"Then stay close to him," he murmured into her ear. "He will protect you, I believe, once you have explained to him, and probably even if you do not."

"And I shall protect him." She lifted her face to his and grinned impishly at him. "I shall see you and Carlota and Miguel at Mortagoa, Duarte. Be careful."

"Yes. And you." He gazed into her face as if to memorize it, and then kissed her on the lips. "There is no half-relationship in my feelings for you, Joana. You are as dear to me as Maria and Miguel were. As dear as our mother was."

She smiled and touched his face with one palm before pulling away and turning to face Captain Blake, who was standing a little distance away, stony-faced. She smiled at him.

"Well, Robert," she said, "shall we go?"

He motioned her to the southern slope, steep and rocky and bare across the stream. The day was still blistering hot despite the advanced hour. Soon they were scrambling upward, using hands as well as feet in places. Their weapons and the food and blankets strapped to their backs were an encumbrance, but a necessary one. They were traveling as lightly as they dared.

He reached a hand across to help her in one particularly difficult place. But she turned her head and smiled at him.

"I can manage, Robert," she said. "You do not have to play the gentleman."

"I am no gentleman, as you know," he told her, his voice and his eyes cold. "What I am playing, Joana, is guard. You will answer to Lord Wellington when I have got you to headquarters, probably with your freedom until the wars are over. You should be thankful that the British do not treat their prisoners out of uniform as your countrymen treat theirs. And in the meantime, you have to answer to me. You will be sorry you did not beg your new lover back there to take you with him."

"Duarte?" she said with a laugh. "Duarte is my brother."

"That was not even an intelligent lie, Joana," he said. "We both know that your father was French and your mother English. Remember? Duarte Ribeiro is Portuguese."

"My mother was married to his father," she said, "before she married mine. He is my half-brother."

He clucked his tongue impatiently and reached across to smack her rather painfully on the bottom. "Move!" he ordered. "We are wasting time. Or rather, you in your usual way are forcing me to waste time. He has a woman who adores him, Joana, and a plump little baby on whom they both dote. Does it not touch your conscience at all that you forced him into being unfaithful today?"

"No!" She ground her teeth together and scrambled upward out of reach of his large hand. "I will not be

satisfied until I have enslaved every man I have ever
encountered, Robert, and slept with as many as it is possible to sleep with. Let their wives and women beware.
And if any man resists me, well, then, he will be sorry,
as you were sorry in Salamanca. They hurt you, did they
not? I am glad. Very glad. I am only sorry that it did
not last longer than five days."

"Ah," he said, moving up beside her effortlessly despite her burst of speed, "at last we have stripped away
layers and come to the real Joana. I think I prefer her
to the one everyone else knows. At least she is honest."

They climbed the rest of the way to the top in silence,
needing every breath to accomplish the steep climb.

Captain Blake paused at the top to look back down
into the valley and away to the lower hills to the east.
He shaded his eyes and reached out to take Joana's wrist
in his grasp. Then he swore and jerked her down to lie
on the ground beside him. He pointed.

"There comes lover-boy," he said, "together with a
whole company of horsemen. Panting with frustration
after a whole night without your favors, doubtless. And
I was stupid enough to stand against the skyline. Well,
Joana, it would be strange indeed if they did not see us.
But don't allow hope to soar. I have no intention of
relinquishing either my freedom or my life yet. I have
even less intention of relinquishing you."

"Am I to be flattered?" she asked sweetly.

He wormed his way back from the crest of the hill,
drawing her with him, before pulling her to her feet and
half-running with his hand still grasping her wrist over
the barren, uneven country above the ravine. The
horsemen had been miles off and perhaps had not spotted them. But he intended to find a safe hiding place
before night fall.

He found what he was looking for a few miles farther
on when the gamble of climbing a lone peak paid off and
offered a low cave that sloped inward for some distance
and would hide them completely from the view of anyone
below. He pushed Joana inside none too gently.

"They will not catch up with us tonight," he said, "or
even tomorrow, at a guess. And we will be difficult to
track in this country. But we might as well establish a

few ground rules from the start. You will not try to attract the attention of any Frenchman, Joana. If you do, I may be forced to slit your throat. And you will not try to escape from me. If you do, I shall use your belt to bind your hands and attach it to my own belt. And I shall have your weapons—now."

"Don't be tiresome, Robert," she said, turning to face him. "Do you not realize that I am on your side? That Lord Wellington sent me after you to make sure that your paper was believed to be a hoax? That I arranged for you to be freed from your parole? That I arranged for Duarte to come to rescue you and to take me hostage? That I am as much a British spy as you are?"

"Your weapons," he said, standing in the entrance of the cave, his feet planted firmly apart, his expression implacable. "And I might yet have to bind your mouth too, Joana. You must think me more of a fool than I have already proved if you think I will believe any more of your lies. And such outrageous and stupid lies. Your weapons!"

"Very well." Her voice was quiet, sweet. "If you think I am going to beg and grovel and plead with you, Robert, then you are sadly mistaken. You will believe what you will, and you may go to hell with my blessing into the bargain." She hitched the musket off her shoulder and dropped it with a clatter to the stone floor of the cave. "But don't expect me to be a docile prisoner."

He scarcely saw her hand move, but the next moment her knife was pointed at his stomach, and she was crouched in a defensive stance.

"You want my knife, Robert?" she asked him sweetly. "Then come and get it."

He was furiously angry—with her for trying after all she had done to him to make a dupe of him yet again, and with himself for expecting her, against all the evidence of his experience, to act as one would expect a woman to act and lay down her arms meekly.

"By God, Joana," he hissed at her from between his teeth, "you are asking for trouble."

She smiled at him that feline smile that he had seen once before. "Are you afraid, Robert?"

The foolish, the idiotic part was that he *was* afraid.

Afraid of hurting her. He should go in, twist her wrist, and allow her to stab herself. That was what he should do. He cursed himself for being unable to do it. And so he circled her in the confines of the cave, feinted one way and then the other—and both times found the knife still trained on the very center of his stomach, and was finally forced to grab for her wrist at the same moment as he reached out with one boot to catch her smartly behind one ankle.

She went down with him on top of her and they wrestled soundlessly except for their labored breathing, while he slowly forced her hand up over her head and to the ground and then cut the circulation from her wrist until her hand opened and the knife fell with a soft clatter to the stones.

"Bastard," she said to him.

"Slut."

"Coward and brute."

"Traitor and siren."

She snarled up at him.

He snarled back.

And then suddenly and quite unexpectedly she smiled at him, her eyes sparkling, her mouth curving appealingly. "Oh, God, Robert," she said, "I would rather fight with you any day of the year than make love with another man. I don't know when I had such fun."

He looked down at her guardedly. Always when he thought he had her finally figured out she ducked around and came at him from another angle. "You might have killed yourself with your own knife," he said.

"Never." She continued to smile and pant. "You would not have allowed it. Do you think I did not know at every moment that you were completely in control of that struggle? But only physically, Robert. Physically you can overpower me. But you can never overpower my will. Never. You will lose if you try. So don't try laying down rules for me. I never obey rules. When I left school at the age of sixteen, I vowed that never again would I obey a rule I did not like. And sometimes I break rules I do like just because they are there. You are heavy."

"Am I?" he said. "But you do not have a mattress at

your back, Joana, as you usually do when you have a man on top of you."

"Do you think I would care?" she asked, and her eyes sparked up into his. "If we were making love, Robert, do you think I would care about a stone bed at my back or your weight on top? But we are not making love, are we? And you are heavy."

He moved off her slowly, not taking his eyes from hers. He reached up, took the knife, and stuck it into his own belt. And he moved the musket over into one corner and stood it there with his rifle.

"We had better eat," he said, "while we have the dregs of daylight in which to do so. And then I will give you five minutes to go outside to make yourself comfortable. Five minutes. No longer. And I would advise you not to defy me by trying to escape, even if defiance is in your nature. Try to escape this time and you will never be allowed privacy again. Understood?"

She merely smiled at him as she sat up and smoothed her dress over her knees.

"Are you going to have the bedroom on the left or the one on the right tonight?" she asked. "There is so much choice."

"We occupy the central bedroom," he said, "together. You do not think I would allow myself to sleep without my arms firmly about you, do you?"

She made a kissing gesture with her mouth. "I am that irresistible?" she said. "I told you you would fall in love with me, Robert."

He unpacked their food without either replying or looking at her. There had been definite advantages to that prison cell, he thought. Despite the daily beatings, he had had long hours alone with the peace of his own thoughts.

18

SHE had dozed and woken again. But she knew that she must sleep. She was unaccustomed to the life of Joana Ribeiro, and the first few days would be tiring, she knew. More so than usual—there was not usually quite so much traveling as there was likely to be in the coming days. And the traveling would be filled with tension, for they would be journeying not only *to* various places but also *from* the pursuit of Colonel Leroux and his company.

Colonel Leroux, she thought. He must come. He must find their tracks and follow. And she must be ready for him when he came. It struck her suddenly how suicidal her plan was and how dangerous for Robert. She might as well have killed the colonel in Salamanca, where only her own life would have been forfeit as a result. But for some reason she had wanted him on her own territory. She wanted him in the country where Miguel and Maria had died.

But she would need her weapons. They were in the back corner of the cave with his sword, though his rifle, she knew, was at his back, within his reach. She could reach none of them, imprisoned as she was. One of his arms was beneath her head and curled about her shoulder, a comfortable-enough pillow but really only a chain of captivity. The other was firmly about her waist. One of his legs was thrown over hers. He would awaken, he had told her earlier when she had protested, if she moved so much as a muscle during the night.

It was hard trying to sleep on a stone floor without moving a muscle.

There was no way she could get to her gun or her knife without waking him. And even if she could, she would never get away without being caught by him again. She thought with some indignation of her belt binding her wrists and attached to his belt, and knew without a shadow of doubt that that would be her fate if she tried to get away. She would never get to her gun again if that happened.

No, she would have to have patience and await her chance. It would come. She had never wanted anything that she had not got. And he could be made to fall in love with her. Despite everything, she could have him wrapped about her little finger within days if she tried. She clamped her teeth hard together when she recalled the scorn with which he had greeted her attempt at explaining the truth to him. Not that she had tried very hard. It went against her pride to beg and plead. If he chose not to believe her, then so be it.

But she could still make him fall in love with her if she so chose. They were kindred spirits, she and Robert Blake. They sparked desire off each other, and yet neither would ever fawn on the other. She knew she could never make him her slave, and she exulted in the knowledge, difficult as it made her task. If she ever called him bastard again, then he would call her slut again. He would give insult for insult. He was not a gentleman and did not know that one did not insult a lady no matter what. She was glad he was not a gentleman.

She lifted one hand to rest against his chest, and his boast proved to be no boast at all, but the simple truth. He had been fast asleep just a moment before. Now he was looking down at her. She knew it even though she did not tip her head back to look.

"It is impossible to lie still for a whole night without moving a muscle, Robert," she said with a sigh. "Especially when you have me in such close embrace. But of course, it is not an embrace, is it? It is captivity." She tipped her head back and looked up at him. There was moonlight coming into the cave. Even so, she could sense him more than see him.

"It is captivity," he said. "Do you want to turn onto your other side?"

"No," she said. "I am quite comfortable as I am. One has but to have a powerful imagination. A feather mattress. A pile of soft blankets. Feather pillows. Mmm. Can you not feel them?"

He caught her wrist in a tight grasp as her hand slid downward from his chest to his waist.

"Cut it out, Joana," he said. "Go to sleep."

"You would have me believe that you are made of stone like this floor?" she said. "I know differently, Robert. Do you not desire me even just one little bit?"

"You will be sorry," he said, "if you continue this. I warn you, Joana, that you will not be able to control the situation if you continue to play the tease. And I will not even try to do so. It is a while since I had a woman and I am hungry."

She could hear her heart beating. She could see it pulsing behind her closed eyes. Luis had bedded her six times in all—she had counted—each more horrid and nauseating than the one before, until she had told him that if that was what marriage was all about, she would rather do without it, thank you very much. He had not even been offended. Relieved was more the word. She had discovered why later.

And Robert talked of hunger!

But she had never deliberately pressed flirtation beyond the point at which she could control it. And even with Robert on those two occasions there had been no great danger. But this time she knew he spoke the truth. They were alone together—very alone in the middle of the night and very close to each other because he thought there was the necessity of guarding her from flight. And perhaps he was right too.

She felt him relax. He thought she had gone back to sleep. But how could she sleep now that her blood had been aroused? More to the point, how could she back off when he had issued such a challenge? It was not in her nature to resist a challenge, much as she feared picking it up.

"Is it food you need, then?" she asked, her voice low. "I am hungry too, Robert. Do you have food? Shall we share it?"

He swore, a word she had not heard in the English language before, though she had heard its Portuguese equivalent among Duarte's men.

She thought he was going to unleash his anger on her in words. She braced herself for the tirade, prepared herself to give as good as she got. Instead he pulled her against him with such force that she felt the breath slam from her body, and found her mouth with his, forcing it wide with his own, plunging his tongue inside so that she was sure she must choke.

And she knew the terror of helplessness, of having unleashed a passion that she could in no way control and that would violate her and perhaps hurt her before it was sated. But terror could be fought, she thought while she still could, and a fight could be fought even if it was to be inevitably lost. She had fought such a fight for her knife. Now she would fight for her very self.

She sucked inward on his tongue, pulsed her teeth against it, pressed herself to him, rubbed her breasts against him, twisted her hips, wrapped her free arm about him, pushing it beneath his coat, dragging at his shirt so that she could touch the bare skin of his back. And when he rolled her over onto her back, her other arm joined the first in its task.

He had pulled her belt free and flung it from them, and her dress came up with one jerk of his hand to her breasts and above. Other garments came down over her legs and feet and were flung to join the belt. She felt cool night air against bare skin for a moment before the weight of his body became her blanket.

His hands were between his body and hers, on her breasts, moving hard over them, squeezing them, his thumbs rubbing roughly over nipples that were hard and tender. His mouth was at her throat and moving below her bunched dress to her breasts, his tongue taking the place of his thumb at one nipple, his lips surrounding it. He sucked inward as he worked his knees between her legs and pushed them wide, lifting himself to a kneeling position.

The only thing to do with her legs was lift them and twine them about his. The fabric of his trousers was rough against the soft skin of her inner thighs. His mouth on her breast was driving her to madness. But her hands were up inside his shirt and moving from his back to his sides to his chest, as her palms pushed over warm ribs and chest muscles and her fingers sought his own nipples.

She could hear the rasping of both their breathing as he lifted his head again, twined his hands painfully in her hair, and brought his mouth to hers again. He lowered his weight once more and she could feel between her legs the hardness and hugeness of his arousal through his trousers. Her whimper of fright and desire took her completely by surprise.

His hands moved from her hair down her sides and beneath her buttocks to lift her against him. He ground himself against her. And she drew up her knees and hugged his waist with them. The aches, the blood pumping through her, were equal parts terror and desire, she knew, pushing her hands up between them to undo the buttons of his coat and wrestle it open. But she would not give in to the terror. She was going to be taken. Nothing could stop that now. But he would not take her, for all that. He would never be able to boast of that. She would give herself, and then she would be as much the victor as he.

But he went still suddenly, and as suddenly rolled off her to lie on his back, one arm thrown over his eyes. He was panting. "No!" he said. "No, I will not give you the satisfaction of ravishing you, Joana. That is what you want, is is not? The joy of knowing yourself irresistible even to a man who despises you?"

She lay for a moment bewildered, stunned, humiliated, naked from the breasts downward, before surging over onto her side and raising herself on one elbow.

"Bastard!" she hissed at him. "Impotent bastard. Eunuch."

"Bitch in heat!" he said without removing his arm. "You want it, Joana? You are going to have to take it."

She stared down at him, her eyes blazing, her breathing labored, taking in the implications of what he had said.

"Oh!" she said then, coming up onto her knees, leaning over him, her hair falling forward over her shoulders to touch his shoulder and his chest. "And you think I will not, Robert? You think I am too timid, too ladylike?

You think you can play with me like this and leave me bruised and humiliated and . . . and . . ."

"Unsatisfied?" he said.

"You bastard!" she said. "I hate you."

"Then the feeling is mutual," he said.

Her hands opened the one remaining button of his coat and pushed it wide. She undid the buttons of his shirt and opened it wide too after fumbling to remove his stock and throw it up behind his head. And she leaned over to feather her mouth over his chest and down to his waist. She feathered kisses back up again until she found his nipple, and she licked at it and drew it into her mouth.

He was lying quite still, his hands spread flat on the stone floor on either side of him. But she could hear his heart thumping erratically. And she hated him with a passion that pounded in her ears. Her hands went to the waist of his trousers, unwrapped the red sash that denoted him an officer, worked at the buttons.

He did not move until she pulled at his trousers. Then he raised his hips while she drew them downward to his knees—she did not feel equal to tackling the removal of his boots. He still desired her, she saw with satisfaction. And she ran her hand over him lightly and quickly, gasping, and sure that she would never be able to expel the air from her lungs again.

Her eyes had grown quite accustomed to the darkness. He was looking up at her, she saw when she straddled his body and set her hands on his shoulders beneath his open shirt.

"You did not think I would dare, did you?" she whispered to him, lowering her head so that her hair formed a curtain about their faces. "I will dare anything, Robert. Even this. You do not have the courage to ravish me? Very well, then, I shall ravish you."

And she brought her mouth down to his, at the same moment lowering her body and impaling herself on him.

She could do no more. She was in shock. She was deeply, deeply occupied and waiting for a pain that did not come.

When she came somewhat to herself, he had one hand spread against the back of her head and the other down behind her waist. And his mouth was soft and warm against hers and his tongue licking at her lips and sliding up behind.

She had not panicked, she thought in some surprise. But she did not know what to do next.

She lifted her head. "It's your turn," she said. "Unless you are afraid, of course. Or do not know what to do."

She could see his grin in the darkness. His hands moved down to grasp her hips, to raise her a little, and then he began to move in her, his thrusts swift and deep so that she raised herself up on her knees again in panic, her fingertips at his waist, her head thrown back. Every muscle in her body was tightening. Even her own body was beyond her control, she thought with one of the few rational thoughts left to her.

And then even the semblance of control left her, and her head jerked forward until her chin rested against her chest, and all the air whooshed out of her lungs in a long and audible sigh. He continued to move in her while she felt herself begin to shudder, the shock waves spreading upward and outward from the point of his deepest penetration.

There was a blank of time somewhere after that—whether seconds or minutes long, she did not know. But the next time awareness reached her mind, she was lying full-length on top of him, her legs spread on either side of his, her hands and one cheek against his bare chest. Both his arms and one of their blankets were about her. Their bodies were still joined.

"I will be too heavy for you," she said, and was surprised by the sleepiness of her own voice.

"Don't talk nonsense, Joana," he said. "Go to sleep. This is as good a way as any of holding you prisoner."

"Guards are not supposed to have sexual relations with their prisoners," she said, moving her cheek until it was quite comfortable. She could hear his heart beating steadily against her ear.

"Neither are prisoners with their guards," he said.

"But prisoners will do anything to be free," she said.

"You are not going to be free." One of his hands caressed the back of her head. "Nothing has changed. Nothing at all. We have, after all, always admitted to a physical attraction to each other. We have merely acted on that attraction—to our mutual satisfaction, it seems. Whoever calls you a lady, Joana, has obviously never had you between the sheets. But I did not know there was such a man left."

"Go to the devil," she said.

"Go to sleep."

He knew with that extra sense that had developed during the past ten years that dawn was not far off. They should be up soon and on their way. If Colonel Leroux and his men intended to bring their horses on the pursuit—even assuming he and Joana had been seen against the skyline the day before—they would have to make a wide detour. And then they would have to do some careful tracking. It was unlikely that they would be a threat that day. But even so . . .

He stared out at the night sky, one hand propped beneath his head, the other playing absently with Joana's hair. He must have slept quite soundly for several hours. And so must she. She had not moved since she had told him to go to the devil. And she was still deeply asleep.

Her legs were going to be stiff, he thought, feeling them against the outside of his. But at least he had been able to give her a softer bed than the stone floor of the cave. He smiled grimly into the darkness. And was it important that she be shielded? He thought of the underground cell in which he had recently spent five days, courtesy of the Marquesa das Minas, and of the daily exercise several French soldiers had taken there at his expense. Making love to her the night before had not been a painless experience.

Making love to her! He closed his eyes again. His one hand still fondled her hair. And he thought of Jeanne Morisette, that beautiful eager young girl who had sworn that she would always love him, who had sworn that she would marry him one day. And of the gentle young dreamer who had lain beside her there at the lake at Haddington, swearing to ride off with her on a white charger on her eighteenth birthday to the land of happily-ever-after, only half in jest.

And he thought of the same young girl laughing at him

and calling him bastard and scorning him because he had dared to lift his eyes to the daughter of a count and weave dreams about her.

And he thought of the Marquesa das Minas as he had first seen her in a ballroom in Lisbon and of his first impression of her as lovely and expensive and far beyond his touch. And of the warm, disheveled woman who lay on him now, no longer smelling of expensive perfumes, but only of woman.

All woman and no lady at all. He thought of the way she had undressed him and caressed him the night before after fighting him like a wild thing when he had had the initiative. And of the way she had mounted him while he had lain passive, terrified that because she was his prisoner any violation of her person would be rape.

No lady at all. All bold and voracious woman.

And such thoughts were not to be indulged in. Already he was aware again of every soft, shapely inch of her against him. He was still inside her. If he was not careful, he would be growing again. Once was enough. They had both made their points. But when all was said and done, they were enemies. Bitter, implacable enemies. Once her French lover caught up to them—if he did—she would be doing all in her power to have her jailer killed or returned to that cell in Salamanca. And in the meanwhile he would be doing all in his power to deliver her to Lord Wellington and certain incarceration for what remained of the war against France.

Joana would hate imprisonment. She would rage against it, like a bird in a cage. He would not think of it.

"Hey," he said, "time to wake up."

She stirred. "Nonsense," she said sleepily. "It is not even daylight yet. You are comfortable, Robert." She sighed.

Damn the woman. She always said the wrong thing. And did she think she could lie abed until noon?

She wriggled against him and sighed again. He gritted his teeth and willed his body to calmness.

"Will you give me my gun and knife back today?" she asked. "If I promise faithfully not to use them on you, Robert? I shall use them against the French. I do not wish to go back with them anyway, you know. I want to stay with you."

"I see," he said. "Instant love from one bedding, Joana? I was that good? And now you intend to follow me about, the meek and faithful little woman, for the rest of my life?"

She snorted. "You can forget that pleasant masculine dream," she said. "I will never be meek, Robert. But I will kill Frenchmen with you. May I have my gun?"

"Yes, certainly," he said, "and my rifle and sword too, Joana. When hell freezes over, that is."

"I hope you are there when it happens, then," she said. "So that you cannot claw your way upward to fresh air and freedom. I thought you would trust me after last night."

"As I would a deadly snake," he said.

"Would you believe me if I told you that you are the only lover I have ever had apart from my husband?" she asked.

"Not for a single moment," he said.

"I did not think so," she said. "And he was dreadful, Robert. He preferred young boys, you know. Is that not ironic and a little lowering? You were wonderful. Are we to be lovers during this journey of ours—until Marcel catches up to us and cuts you into a thousand pieces?"

You were wonderful. Are we to be lovers . . . ? The words of a practiced flirt and compulsive liar. But of course they were having their effect, as she must have known they would. God damn the woman. God damn her to hell and back.

"We mated last night," he said. "We were not lovers, Joana, and never could be. We coupled."

"Ah," she said, and sighed and squirmed against his chest again. "Are we to be mates for a while, then? A couple? You are growing hard again, are you not?"

"Damn you, Joana," he said. "Do you always blurt out whatever embarrassing observation leaps into your mind?"

She lifted her head and looked up into his face. And she smiled slowly in that way that could always raise his temperature a degree. "Are you embarrassed?" she asked. "I think it feels rather lovely. Are we to mate again?"

He lifted her off him and set her on the floor beside him. He could see her face clearly—another sign that dawn was approaching. "Is that what you want?" he asked her harshly. "To be used as my plaything until I can deliver you over to proper captivity? That is all you would be, and that is what I will do with you in the end, Joana, no matter how many times I may have taken my pleasure of you in the meanwhile."

Her smile was dreamy. "And you shall be my plaything," she said. "I shall draw pleasure from you, Robert, and give you infinite pleasure too—oh, yes, pleasure to infinity; it is a promise—until Marcel does with you whatever he has in store for you. Make lo . . . No, mate with me. Couple with me."

"Joana." He leaned over and kissed her fiercely on the mouth. She had an insatiable appetite, it seemed. He might have guessed it. But whereas she was normally surrounded by countless men only too willing and eager to satisfy it, now there was only he. And he, poor fool, was flattered by her need for him, excited by it.

He spread his hands beneath her buttocks when he came over on top of her, intent on cushioning her against the floor as he drove his desire into her. But she showed no signs of discomfort. She set her hands on his shoulders and closed her eyes, her lips parted, and lay uncharacteristically still.

"Oh," she said as she was coming to her climax. And she bit on her lower lip and opened her eyes to look up into his while it happened. "Oh," she said afterward when he finally lay still on her, and one of her hands played gently with his hair. "I had no idea it could be beautiful like this, Robert. I had no idea."

It was unfair, he thought—but since when had he expected Joana to play fair? She spoke when he was at his most vulnerable, when he had just spilled his love—no, not his love, his seed—into her and was sated and tired again. She spoke at a time when he most wanted to believe her.

It was time to be up and on their way. Time for day-

light. Time for sanity. Time to see her and know her for
what she was again.

But God, she was a beautiful woman to love—to mate
with, to couple with. He used a more obscene word in
his mind to set in perspective what had happened between them twice in the night.

"Get up and dress," he said, rolling off her and slapping her sharply on one bare buttock as he did so. "It is
time we were on our way."

She sat up. "You know, Robert," she said, "one day
I am going to do that to you. It is not very pleasant."

"I am not your prisoner," he said.

"Oh, I think you are." She smiled up at him. "Though
you will never admit it, I suppose." She shrugged. "And
that is what I like most about you." She got to her feet,
ignoring the hand he stretched down for her assistance,
and brushed at her dress. "Ugh! Creases. The Marquesa
das Minas would have a major fit of the vapors if she
were expected to wear this."

She looked up at him and laughed. "But then, the
marquesa is a tiresome bore, is she not? Nothing to do
all day but flirt and look helpless and invent errands for
besotted gentlemen to run. I think I would go mad if
there were not Joana Ribeiro to become occasionally."

"Joana *who*?" he said.

"Joana Ribeiro," she said. "My fantasy self, Robert.
The self who mated with you a few minutes ago and last
night. You do not believe the marquesa would ever have
done that, do you? She is at home only in the world of
flirtation. Besides, you are not a gentleman and she is a
lady. And besides again, she would have demanded a
feather bed. Joana Ribeiro is a wonderful fantasy."

She could be so enchanting, he thought, watching her
in the growing light as she fastened her belt about her
waist and frowned down at the heavy creases of the dress
she had worn up about her breasts all night. Her hair
was in wild tangles about her head and shoulders. She
was barefoot. He did not believe he had ever seen her
look more beautiful.

Yes, so enchanting if one allowed oneself to forget.
And it was so easy to forget with Joana, to live for the
joy of the moment with her. So easy to forget, even

though he still bore fresh on his body the bruises that proved just how cruel and ruthless she was in reality.

He belted on his sword, slid her knife inside his belt, and hoisted both his rifle and her musket onto his right shoulder. There was only a little food left. They had better postpone their breakfast in case they did not find anywhere to replenish their supplies during the day.

"Ready?" he asked.

"For anything," she said, smiling dazzlingly at him. "Lead the way, sir."

He led the way, wondering when the novelty would wear off and aching muscles and blistered feet would wipe the smile from her face. And when the heat of the day would have her begging him to stop. And when hunger would make her cross and irritable. But for the moment, all was adventure for her.

He looked back to make sure she was following him closely down the slope. She smiled at him again.

And God, it was hard not to smile back. It was hard not to revel in the feeling of relaxed well-being that the night's two lovings had brought to his body.

19

B Y early evening they had reached another ravine, more shallow than the one where Duarte's band had been camped, less wooded, with the stream narrower and more shallow. But nevertheless it provided welcome shelter from the sweltering hot late-August day. They had passed two remote farms, but had stopped at neither. They were close to Almeida, Captain Blake had said. He wanted to have a look at it before proceeding with his orders.

"There is no point in forcing these poor people into leaving their homes and burning everything they leave behind them," he had said, "until it is necessary to do so. Perhaps Almeida will hold out until the autumn rains and the French will decide not to advance into Portugal this year after all."

And so they had trudged onward, not even stopping to replenish their food supplies. But in the heat of the day they were not hungry. Only thirsty. And so the sight of water was welcome indeed.

Joana sank down on her knees beside the stream and drank deeply and gratefully before lifting her head to find that the captain was doing the same thing.

"I thought we would not stop," she said. "I thought you would force me on. That is partly what today has been all about, is it not, Robert? To see how much endurance I have? To see how loudly I would lament the absence of my carriage and my servants?"

She knew it was the reason. There had been no sign of pursuit all day, and they really should have stopped at those farms, if only to warn the inhabitants of what might be expected of them at any moment. When he sat on the bank, cross-legged, and did not look at her or smile, she was even more certain. He would love to hear her whine and complain and beg for mercy.

She slipped off her sandals and lowered her feet into the water, wincing with the cold and—yes—with some pain too. She wriggled her toes.

"What are you planning to do at Almeida?" she asked. "Raise the siege single-handed?" She swished her feet in the water and wriggled her toes again. She could see that he was watching them.

"See if Cox and the garrison there are holding out,'" he said. "If they are, Joana, and we move off to the west, I will be safe and you will be doomed. Your lover will not dare follow you deeper into Portugal until the fort has fallen."

"Then I shall have to hope that it falls without delay," she said.

"I would not count on it." He turned his head to look at her. "Cox is a stubborn devil and Almeida not an easy fortress to storm."

She shrugged and looked back at him. "Marcel will come," she said. "I know he will. No matter what the danger." And she believed her own words. He would come. He had to come. She would not believe that she had found him at last and ensnared his heart, only to lose him because she had wanted to kill him in Portugal rather than in Salamanca. "Are we going to stay here tonight?"

He looked about with narrowed eyes. "Yes," he said. "It seems as good a place as any. There, I think." He pointed to a group of trees that was denser than any other. "We will be well-hidden and well-sheltered. We will find a more comfortable bed there than last night's."

She smiled at him. "My bed was very comfortable last night," she said.

He was not pleased by the new turn their relationship had taken. She could tell that by the way he had walked all day a little ahead of her, saying nothing beyond purely mundane remarks concerning their journey. Nothing personal. No looks that revealed his awareness that they had become lovers the night before.

She had been glad all day long that she was walking a little behind him. For her looks had revealed that awareness. She had watched him as he walked, his long power-ful legs and slim hips and waist, his broad back and shoulders, his blond wavy hair curling over his collar, his effortless carrying of two heavy guns as well as his sword. And she had shamelessly undressed him with her eyes and liked what she had seen. And she had deliberately relived his lovemaking and knew, inexperienced as she was, that he was an expert lover and that he knew far more than he had shown her the night before.

She wanted more. She wanted all his expertise. And she wanted soft looks from him and soft words too. But for the time being she would settle for the expertise.

"Are we going to make love again tonight?" she asked him.

He picked up a stone and sent it splashing into the stream. "We had better eat what remains of our food," he said, "and move our things into the trees."

"Is that yes or no?" she asked him, smiling. "Robert, may I borrow my knife for a minute?"

"No," he said, getting to his feet.

"Are you not going to ask why I want it?" She sighed. "Must you assume that I want to carve my initials into your chest?"

"If you have a legitimate need for a knife," he said, "I will use it for you."

"Will you?" She looked up at him. "You will be pleased at this, Robert. It will confirm all your suspicions about me and my soft living. I have a blister that needs to be burst. And it hurts like a thousand devils."

"Show me," he said, and he stooped down on his haunches beside her.

She lifted one foot out of the water and showed him the large blister on the inside of her heel, just below her ankle, where the strap of her sandal had been rubbing her all day.

"Joana." He sounded angry rather than sympathetic. "That must have been giving you agonies for hours. I suppose you were too proud to complain."

"Too stubborn," she said. "It is just what you ex-pected of me, is it not? I slipped the strap down so that it was no longer rubbing."

He took her foot in his hand and touched gently the

tender skin around the blister. "You should have told me," he said.

His hand was warm against the chilled flesh of her foot. His head was bent close to her own. He smelled of dust and sweat. He smelled rather wonderful.

"What would you have done?" she asked. "Carried me?"

"We might have stopped at one of the farms," he said.

"And you could have had a marvelous time scowling and sneering with an I-told-you-so look all over your face," she said. "No, thank you. A little pain does not quite kill."

He tested his thumb to the blister. It was sore and definitely needed bursting.

"Lend me the knife," she said. "If you wish, you may stand ten feet off and point your rifle between my eyes."

He drew the knife from his belt with his free hand and felt its tip. "You could do real damage with this," he said.

"That is the whole idea." She smiled up at him.

"You had better look away," he said.

She continued to smile at him as he frowned in concentration, pricked the blister, and lowered her foot into the water again. His face was still looking somewhat battered from his week's ordeal, but the bruises succeeded only in making him look even more tough and attractive.

"We will bind it tomorrow morning before continuing on our way," he said.

"With what?" She laughed lightly. "Oh, but I know the answer. You are going to be unutterably gallant and tear strips from your shirt, aren't you?"

"Actually," he said, and she knew him quite well enough to know that he almost grinned, though he caught himself in time, "I was thinking of the hem of your dress."

"So that it would be shorter and you could brighten your days by staring at my ankles," she said. "For shame, Robert."

He reached for his pack and handed her some bread and cheese, both of them rather dry. But after a day's abstinence, the meal tasted marvelously satisfying.

"A glass of wine, sir?" she asked when they had finished eating, pointing to the stream. And she knelt again and lowered her mouth to the water. He stayed where he was and she knew he was watching her. She cupped her hands and washed her face and neck and her arms to above the elbows.

He was moving their packs back among the trees when she finally got to her feet. He returned with a leafy bough to obliterate traces of their presence at the bank of the stream.

He spread one blanket beneath the trees, and they sat down on it, side by side, peering outward to the stream and the opposite sloped bank.

"Why did you do it, Joana?" he asked softly after a few minutes of silence. "How could you betray your mother's people and your husband's?"

"My father's people are the French," she said. "My father is an ambassador in Vienna. It seems I have to betray one side or the other."

"You could have been neutral," he said. "You could have decided to be a typical lady."

"Typical? Me?" She smiled quickly at him. "I could never be that, Robert. And neutral? It is not in my nature to be neutral."

"And so," he said, "you were willing to see your adopted country destroyed and your mother's countrymen driven from the continent."

"Ah," she said, "but I still hold to my story that I am one of Arthur's spies, as you are, that I was in Salamanca working for the same cause as you."

"A strange way you had of doing it," he said. "If you were on my side, Joana, I would hate to have had you against me."

"I did not know you would be beaten again," she said. "I did not think they would dare. You would have beaten off Marcel and two of the soldiers, I do believe. I was glad I had had the forethought to make sure that there were more than just the three there."

"Thank you," he said. "And you were on my side?"

She smiled. "Would you have left Salamanca with Duarte and the Spanish partisans if that had not happened?" she asked.

"Of course not," he said. "I had given my parole."

She turned her hands palm-up. "I rest my case."

"I believe you could persuade most people that black is white if you set your mind to it, Joana," he said. "What about the Lines of Torres Vedras?" He looked at her with narrowed eyes. "Are they real or are they a myth?"

"You know the answer as well as I," she said. "I do not need to answer your question, Robert."

"There, you see?" he said. "You will not give me an answer because you fear that it will be the wrong one and that I will know beyond the shadow of a doubt that you are a liar."

"There *is* a shadow of a doubt, then?" she asked. "You would like to believe me, would you not, Robert?"

"I would like to believe that there is no such being as the devil," he said. "But I know that there is."

"You would like to believe it," she said, "because you have made love to me and because you love me just a little, even though you will not admit as much even to yourself. And because you want to make love to me again tonight. You feel disloyal making love to the enemy, don't you?"

"I can see how you have salved your conscience through the years," he said. "You have persuaded yourself that sex is love, Joana, that all your sex partners have been lovers. I suppose I am a lover too. I suppose you persuade yourself that you love me—just a little."

"I told you so once," she said.

"Yes, I remember it well." He looked across at her, his expression stony. "And a moment later your thugs were upon me. They would still be amusing themselves with me every day if things had not turned out as they did."

She reached out to touch his arm, to run her hand down the rough fabric of his sleeve. She could not resist working on his vulnerability—or giving in to her own. And she knew suddenly, as perhaps she had known unconsciously for some time, that she had found in Robert Blake what she had been searching for all her adult life.

But she was given no chance to wallow in the thought. He flinched away from her hand and turned on her, his face fierce, his blue eyes blazing.

"Listen, Joana," he said, "we may be together for days or even weeks. I have no intention of living with this tension between us all that time. I have no wish to spend every day and every evening debating the question of whether we should or whether we should not, of whether we are going to or whether we are not. Let us have it settled once for all. Are we to be sex partners or are we not? The choice is yours. But let me warn you. If the answer is yes, it will happen, daily and nightly, without any pretense of either seduction or romance. And with no pretense of love or even tenderness. It will happen because we are a man and woman alone together and because we both consent to the physical pleasure to be taken from uniting our bodies."

"And if the answer is no?" She smiled at him and touched his arm again. She was not afraid of his anger. It would be unleashed in only one way if he lost control. He would never hurt her. She knew that with the instinctive knowledge she seemed to have of him. "Would you be able to live with the daily tension, Robert?"

"There would be none," he said. "If the answer is no, then there is nothing to cause tension. I will not take what is not freely given."

"You think we could be together and celibate and feel no tension?" she asked him. "I think you are a liar, Robert. Or else you have no imagination."

His jaw tightened. "Then you had better try me," he said.

She grimaced. "I wish you had not said that," she said. "You know I cannot resist a challenge, Robert. But on this occasion I believe I must. My answer is yes, you see. I think we had better be lovers while we are together. Or sex partners, if you prefer the term. Yes, that is my choice. Are you glad or sorry?"

He was removing his coat. And then unbuckling his sword belt, holding her eyes with his own the whole time. And she knew what he was doing, what he was going to do. He was not going to wait until darkness fell, until the right moment came for love. He had meant it when he said no romance and no seduction. He was going to take her then, quite dispassionately, to prove to her that they were to be in no way lovers. Only sex partners.

Well. She smiled slowly. Two could play at that game. And if he cared to throw down the gauntlet—as he was in the process of doing—then she would pick it up even before it touched the ground. She unbuckled her belt and dropped it beside the blanket. Then she got to her feet, pulled down her undergarments and stepped out of them, and crossed her arms to draw her dress up over her head. She dropped it on top of her other garments. And she lay down naked on the blanket and looked at him.

He was angry. She knew it, though he said nothing. She had stolen his fire. He had meant her to be dismayed, disconcerted, embarrassed—any number of negative things. He had not expected her to prepare herself in as matter-of-fact a way as he was doing. She almost asked him what the delay was, but that would have been going too far. He would have known if she had spoken the words that she merely mocked him. He would have known that she was indeed dismayed. She did not want to be taken with no semblance of love at all.

But she would win eventually, she decided. If he thought that he could be intimate with her for days or even weeks without his feelings being in any way engaged, then clearly he did not know her even half as much as she knew him. She would allow him his daily and nightly couplings if they gave him a feeling of power over her. But all the time she would be weaving a golden spell of love about him. Oh, yes, she would.

He had changed his mind, she saw. If he had meant to completely undress, he would have removed his boots first. But now he was removing them, and his shirt, and his trousers too. And oh, yes, she thought, watching him, he was every bit as magnificent as she had been picturing him in her imagination all day. Except that she had not pictured the scars, especially the large and still-purple one below his left shoulder, only just above his heart.

Like his facial scars, the ones on his body did nothing to detract from his overall attractiveness. He was beautiful. She wanted to tell him so, but this was supposed to be a dispassionate sexual encounter. So be it, then. And so it would be.

There was to be no kissing, no caressing, it seemed.

She felt regret, but she parted her legs for him at the first nudging of his knees and watched him as he positioned himself and came into her in one swift thrust. She smiled up into his eyes.

"If this is to be for pleasure only, Robert," she said, "then I expect to be pleasured."

"Oh, you will be." His voice and his eyes were hard as he brought his body down on hers and she was reminded of the weight of all those muscles bearing down on her, the ground at her back. "You will be, Joana."

"And I expect to give pleasure," she said, her hands sliding over warm flesh until her arms were about him and her legs slid up the sides of his and over the tops of them until she wormed her feet between. "I will not give pleasure merely by lying like a fish until you have finished inside me."

"Do what you wish," he said. "We have a mutual agreement."

Undressing in front of him and watching him undress had excited her quite as much as kissing and fondling would have done. When he had come into her, he had come into wetness, and she was throbbing there, and her breasts were tender and aching and hard-tipped, and her desire for him was pulsing through her.

Her love for him.

She held him with her arms and legs, all his hard-muscled magnificence, and moved against him, twisting her hips and her shoulders, drawing on him with inner muscles, feeling him hard and deep, wanting him and wanting him, and keeping her teeth firmly clamped so that she would say nothing. He had not moved.

"Does that feel pleasurable?" she asked him in a whisper. "Does it, Robert?"

"Yes." He braced himself on his elbows, and his face was above hers suddenly, his blue eyes gazing down into hers, expressionless. But she could see deeper than his eyes and she knew that he spoke the truth.

"Give me pleasure too," she said. "I want to be pleasured too, Robert."

"Like this?" He withdrew very slowly and reentered as slowly. "Does that give you pleasure?"

"Yes," she said, and he did it again, his eyes holding hers, and once more.

She wanted his mouth on hers. There was nothing more intimate than what they were doing. But the meeting of mouths brought the closeness of love. She wanted his mouth on hers, his tongue inside. But of course this was to be an experience without love. This was about intimacy and not closeness. About sex and not love.

She moved her hips again so that together they set up a slow rhythm.

"It is good?" she asked him.

"Yes."

"It is very good," she said. "You are larger than most men, Robert?"

"You should know," he said. "Is the ground hard? Would you prefer to come on top?"

"No." The ache of her need was in her throat. She closed her eyes. He would surely know the truth if he continued to look into them. How could he not know the truth? Was it possible to do this—this, in just this way—only for physical pleasure? Perhaps it was for a man. Perhaps it was for some women. But not for her. She could not do this purely for pleasure. She could do it only for duty—though when it had been duty she had been able to stomach it only six times—or for love.

Did he not know that? And that she owed him no duty at all?

And was it not so for him? Was it always like this with his whores? With Beatriz?

"Is it like this for you with Beatriz?" Her eyes flew open and she found herself looking up into his again. "Is it as pleasurable with her?"

"Have done, Joana," he said. "Hush." And he lowered his weight onto her again, reached down with his hands to cup her buttocks as he had early that morning so that she would not feel the hardness of the ground, and built the rhythm of their loving to a faster speed.

She thought she would surely go mad. It took him forever to finish. Not that she had any complaint about that. She wished they could be joined forever. But he would not allow her her pleasure. When she felt it coming, recognizing the signs from the night before, and knew as she had not the night before what glory, what peace awaited her, he must have felt it too and stroked her more shallowly so that though she twisted and pushed against him, she could not bring him to the core of her aching, to the center of her being.

And so despite everything she was losing this particular round of their struggle. She had to bite down on both lips not to whimper and plead. And he knew it. He was using an expertise she could not compete with. He was playing with her as one would play with an opponent one was absolutely sure of defeating. She could not fight him, not even the hopeless fight she had fought with him before. For she could not play mind games with him when her body was crying out its love and its need to be loved.

"Now, Joana!" he ordered against her ear, though he might as well have spoken Greek for the amount she understood the words. But she understood the language of his body. He had slowed and deepened, and then he drove urgently into her so that she shouted out and came against him with a shattering force that obliterated all thought and even consciousness for endless moments.

She was lying on her back, gazing up at tree trunks and branches. The warm air of evening was cool against her bare skin. Her cheek was close to a shoulder that radiated heat and that drew her like a magnet. She rubbed her cheek against it, and the shattered pieces of her mind came together again.

"Thank you, Robert," she said. "That was indeed pleasurable."

"What the devil did you mean," he asked, "mentioning Beatriz in the middle of all that? Do you have no sense of decorum whatsoever? And what about all your lovers? Do I measure up against them?"

"Very favorably," she said, closing her eyes. "Very favorably indeed, Robert. I think you may have spoiled me for them all."

"Well," he said, "Leroux and countless dozens of the others can give you a fortune and a lifetime of luxury as well as a damned good time in bed, Joana. I do not believe you will pine for me for long."

"I never pine," she said. "Except once. That was before I learned to cope with life."

"Was there ever such a time?" he asked.

"People laugh at the love between children," she said. "They call it puppy love, just as if it is not love at all but something merely to cause amusement. I believe it is the best love, the only love. It is pure and innocent and all-consuming. I would never belittle such love."

He had turned his head to look at her. She was staring across his chest to the trees beyond him.

"He was beautiful," she said. "He was seventeen years old, but very grown-up to my fifteen-year-old eyes. He was the first man I danced with, the first man I kissed. He was the first to touch me." She smiled dreamily. "He touched my breast and I felt sinful and wonderful. I loved him totally and passionately, Robert—he was that other Robert I told you about. I vowed that I would love him always, that I would never marry anyone but him."

"And yet," he said after a short silence, "you have loved countless others and married someone else."

"For political reasons," she said. "And no, I have never loved anyone as I loved him." Except you, she thought, the thought sweeping at her, and she turned her head into his shoulder and closed her eyes. "It lasted for only a few days before my father caught me—he was ineligible, you know—and took me away. But I pined for him for months. Foolish, was it not, at the age of fifteen?"

"Yes," he said. "Foolish."

"But it was not foolish," she said. "He was the one beautiful thing in my life, my Robert. But he died. When Papa wanted to take me back to France, I did not want to go. And perhaps he guessed the reason why. So he told me what he would otherwise have kept from me— my Robert died of smallpox only six weeks after I left him."

"Did he?" he asked after a pause.

"I thought I would die too," she said. "Is that not foolish? Are not young people foolish to believe that a broken heart can kill? Instead I went back to France with Papa and I learned that I am beautiful and attractive—I am, am I not? And I learned how to keep men at bay so that I would not have to experience that pain again. Love is painful, Robert."

"Yes," he said.

"I just wish . . ." she said.

"What?"

"I just wish," she said, "that I had not believed the lies my father told me about him. I did not for very long, but it was too late when I admitted to myself that my Robert would never have boasted about me to the servants and called me a French bitch. You might call me that, Robert, but he would not have. He was a gentleman despite his birth. And I taunted him with his birth because my own feelings had been shattered. I think I hurt him. There was hurt in his eyes when I left him."

She heard him swallow.

"You see?" She smiled against his arm. "I was human once too, Robert. I loved. You would not think me capable of love, would you? But then, of course, I was only fifteen years old. It was only puppy love. Not the real thing at all. Rather amusing really. But you remind me of him. Is not that absurd? He was a tall and slender boy, and gentle. He hated the thought of having to kill, once his father bought him his commission. Nothing like you at all. And yet you remind me of him. Perhaps he would have matured into a man like you, had he lived. Perhaps not. I suppose it is as well I will never know."

"We must dress, Joana," he said, "and then sleep. I would not like to have to get up in a hurry dressed as I am now."

She did not want to move. She felt a deep grief, as if time had just rolled back eleven years. "There," she said, dashing a hand over her eyes to wipe away a spilled-over tear, "my memories are reducing me to a watering pot. Have you ever known anything more ridiculous?"

He sat up suddenly and linked his arms about his spread knees. She felt bereft and very lonely and frightened by her feelings. Normally she guarded herself carefully against any vulnerability. The most negative of emotions she would allow herself normally was boredom.

"There is nothing ridiculous about it," he said. "It is quite natural, I think, at times to crave the innocence and joy of childhood and youth. And to grieve for their loss. There is nothing foolish about your story, Joana."

She felt warmed again, reassured. And her love for

him was almost a tangible thing. She stretched out a hand and would have touched his side, but she did not do so. He would have misunderstood. He would have thought she was asking for pleasure again. He would have thought it a purely physical gesture.

"Get dressed," he said, and began to pull his own clothes back on. "You would not wish to be found like that, Joana, even by your French lover. He has a whole company of men with him."

He might as well have told her to get dressed and slapped her face to hasten her along, Joana thought ruefully as she drew her dress toward her. His words were more painful than a slap. Her French lover? Did he not have that extra sense that she had? Did he not know that she had no lover but him? That there *could* be no one but him now?

Apparently not. And it seemed that her second love was destined to bring her as much grief as the first.

"Actually," she said, "it would not bother me, Robert. I am quite accustomed to being gazed at naked by all the men who desire me—though usually one at a time, I must admit. But I would hate to see you blush. Will you let me have my gun if Marcel and his company of men come up with us? You will be horribly outnumbered. Perhaps I can kill a few for you."

"Forget it, Joana," he said. "I will be giving you a great deal of pleasure during the coming days and nights—according to your decision. But I will not give you the pleasure of killing me, I do assure you."

"Then I shall kill Marcel instead," she said. "I am tired of him and he is not as good a lover as you, Robert. Not nearly. I shall kill him for you, and all his men will go running back to the safety of Spain and the waiting arms of the partisans."

"Lie down," he said. "I want to be on our way by dawn, and this has been a long day. How is your heel?"

"Sore," she said. "You must give me a bullet to bite upon during tomorrow's march, Robert. Are you going to hold me imprisoned in your arms with your leg thrown across mine as you did last night?"

"Yes," he said. "Lie down."

"You know, Robert," she said, obeying him and wriggling against him to find a comfortable position while his arms came about her and one leg came over hers, "I could grow quite comfortable with being a prisoner. Do you think Arthur will appoint you my guard? But you are going to have to let me up again."

"Forget it," he said.

"You did not allow me my five minutes of privacy," she said. "I am afraid I need them."

He swore and released his hold on her. "Five!" he said. "Not one second longer."

"Robert." She laughed lightly as she got to her feet. "You really should not have said that. Now you must realize that I will have to be away for six minutes. Oh, yes, and for one second longer than that too." She whisked herself off through the trees. What a delight it was to tease him, she thought. And she felt almost guilty, considering all the circumstances she might have enumerated in her mind, to be feeling so wonderfully happy.

20

HE was not sure at first what had woken him. But whatever it was had woken Joana too. She stiffened in his arms, and he set three warning fingers over her lips.

"Sh," he murmured against her ear.

But it had not been voices or the sound of footsteps or hooves. He knew that as soon as full consciousness returned.

"What was it?" she breathed against his fingers. "The earth shook."

"An explosion," he said. "A great one. Quite a long way off, I think. It must be Almeida."

"Shelling?" she asked.

He frowned. "It was just one big boom," he said. "It would be continuing if it were shelling. Come on. It's time we were on our way."

It was not quite dawn and he had planned during the hour or so after their second loving—when he had lain awake thinking about her and about himself, about them as they had been eleven years before and as they were now—he had planned to have her again before they set out on their way to find Almeida and to find food. The best way to quell his disturbing thoughts, he had decided, was to take her again and again and again for his pleasure, to use her as the whore she was. A high-class whore who did not take money for what she did, but a whore nevertheless.

But there was no thought now to delaying for pleasure. God, the earth had shaken. Whatever it was, it had been one hell of an explosion.

Joana was rolling her blanket and pointedly leaving his for him to roll. She might have agreed to be his sex partner for as long as they were together, he thought with a grim smile directed at himself, but she was not going to play the part of his woman. He could expect no favors from Joana other than the sexual. And even in that she demanded as many favors as she gave.

God, but she was wonderful to make love with, he thought, bending to roll his blanket and turning to lift his weapons into place on his shoulder. He had to use all his willpower when having sex with her not to lose himself in emotion, not to be murmuring sweet nothings in her ear, not to be wooing her with his hands and his mouth and his body instead of merely concentrating on pleasure given and received.

Wouldn't she just love that? he thought, straightening up and looking to see if she was ready to go. Wouldn't she love to know how very close she was to having total power over him? Fortunately she would never know. He would die rather than give any part of his inner self to such a woman—or to any woman, for that matter.

Though she had really loved him at the age of fifteen, he thought suddenly, and the thought almost weakened him as it had very nearly done the evening before. She had spoken those words to him all those years ago out of hurt, because she had thought that he had hurt her. But she had since recognized the fact that her father had lied to her over that incident without in any way suspecting that he had lied to her about the other too. She had been told that Robert was dead—because she had been pining for him. But that had all happened a long, long time ago, during another lifetime.

"Ready?" he asked. "How is the heel?"

"It is all right," she said. "I shall keep the strap down. I shall not slow you down, Robert, or ask to be carried. And if I feel the need to scream, I shall bite down on my lower lip until it is raw."

She smiled that dazzling, teasing smile that could make his heart somersault inside him. And it was true, he knew. She had boundless courage. She had to have in order to be a French spy. But now he knew that she had physical courage too. She had not once complained the day before about the heat or the dust or about hunger or the deliberately killing pace he had set. She had not once lagged behind. He felt an unwilling admiration for her.

"Let's go, then," he said. But the words were no sooner out of his mouth than he reached for her, whirling her around so that her back was against him, and clamped one hand hard over her mouth. "Hush!" he whispered harshly.

This time the sound was definitely that of horses' hooves, and many of them. And voices. He pushed Joana to the ground and came down beside her. He hooked one leg over hers and kept his hand over her mouth. He shrugged the guns off his shoulder until they were lying on the ground beside him.

He would not have a hope in hell, he thought, if they were seen. But at least he would take two Frenchmen down with him if he was to go, one with the rifle and one with the musket. And if he were fortunate, perhaps one or even two with the knife or his sword if he had a chance to draw it.

Someone cursed in French. "We were camped just a mile or so away without even realizing that this was here," the same voice said.

"All right," Colonel Leroux said. "Give the order for the men to drink and water their horses. Ten minutes. That explosion must have come from Almeida. The bastards must have been blown to glory."

"Ney will be inside the walls by now?" the first voice asked. "Lucky dog. Plunder and wine . . ."

"And women," the colonel said. "Women by the dozens while they live. Give that order. We must move on. They came this way, I am certain of it. Probably heading for the safety of Almeida."

The first man sniggered and turned to give the order to fall out.

Captain Blake was easing a handkerchief from his pocket. He lifted himself half over Joana and brought down his weight on her. He set his mouth to her ear.

"Not a sound or a movement," he murmured, "or you may be the first to go." And he folded the handkerchief into a thick strip, covered her mouth with it, and tied the ends firmly at the back of her head. His hand went beneath her to unbuckle her belt. He brought her hands one at a time to her back and bound them firmly with the leather band. And he moved off her again, keeping one leg across hers. She had not struggled at all, he thought in some surprise.

The eastern sky was beginning to lighten, he noticed for the first time. When he peered cautiously through the trees, he could see horses and men at the water's edge, and Leroux, still on his horse's back, a short distance away. The captain lifted his rifle silently from the ground, braced himself on his elbows, and sighted along it, training it on the right temple of the colonel. Another horse sidled up on the far side of him.

"It would make more sense to travel alone or with only one or two others," Colonel Leroux said. "We can never hope to surprise them with the noise this company makes, can we? God, I hate this sort of warfare. They have all the advantages in this type of country, those damned partisans."

"But traveling in a large group is the only way to protect ourselves," the other man said. "They would think twice before attacking a whole company, Colonel. Your life would not be worth the snap of two fingers if you traveled alone."

"If they have touched one hair of the marquesa's head," the colonel said, "they will all die—very slowly. The Englishman most slowly of all. I will strip him of his uniform and swear, if there are any questions, that he was not wearing one. And then I shall strip him of his flesh, one painful inch at a time. I shall do it personally."

Joana had turned her head to one side and was looking at him, Captain Blake knew, though he did not take his eyes off the colonel for even one moment. Doubtless she was gloating over what she was hearing.

"They could even be hiding here," the other man said. "They know the country better than we do. They would have known about this water."

"There is not enough cover," the colonel said as Captain Blake tensed and his finger steadied on the trigger of his rifle. "There are at least a dozen of them."

"Unless they split into smaller groups," the other man said.

"With a whole company of the best soldiers in the

world after them?'' the colonel said scornfully. "They would have to be foolish in the extreme."

"Or clever," the other man said.

"Time is up," the colonel said impatiently. "We must move on. We need food and there were only the two farms yesterday. Besides, I intend to pick up her trail today. It has been too long. She is such a delicate little thing."

He moved his own horse down into the water as the rest of his men were recalled and formed up to resume their journey. Captain Blake's rifle followed the colonel. They were mad not to search, he thought. It was such an obvious camping place. But there was very little shelter. He owed his survival, he knew—if he did survive; the Frenchmen had not moved off yet—to the fact that Colonel Leroux assumed that he and Joana and Duarte Ribeiro's band had stayed together. All of them could not possibly have hidden in this valley.

He did not lay his rifle down until the last man had disappeared over the top of the opposite bank and until the sound of hoofbeats had died completely away. Then he laid it down carefully and set his forehead against it. He knew from long experience as a soldier that the cold sweat and the thumping heart and the weakened knees and the dizziness came only after the danger was over. He knew also that they were best dealt with by giving in to them for a brief spell. He drew deep slow breaths.

The darkness was lifting fast. It was easy to see the hatred and the fury in Joana's eyes when he raised his head to look at her. He released her wrists from the leather belt first and then undid the knot of the handkerchief.

And she was on him like a fury, her fists pounding his chest and crashing into his face, her legs and feet kicking him, her teeth bared in a snarl.

"You bastard!" she hissed at him. "You bloody, bloody imbecile. I hate you. I wish they had cut you down with a hundred bullets. No, I wish they had taken you alive. I would have asked Marcel to let me watch them strip away your flesh. I would have listened to your screams. I would have laughed at you while you were still sane enough to know that I was laughing."

The words came jerking out of her piecemeal while

they fought. He tried to imprison her arms at her sides, but she was kicking him painfully in the shins, and then he squirmed away only just in time when she brought up her knee sharply.

"Have done, Joana," he ordered her. "You have me at a disadvantage. I cannot hit you back."

"But you can bind my hands behind me and gag me," she said, lifting her head to try to bite the hand that had clamped onto one of her wrists. "You bully. You bloody coward. Hit me! Fight me properly. Don't hold me. *Don't hold me!* Hit me if you dare. I want to fight you. Coward. Bully. Bastard."

He released his hold on her wrist and slapped with stinging force at the leg that was kicking him. His anger was up at last. Perhaps they both needed release from the tension of the past half-hour. He jumped to his feet, grasping both her arms firmly and lifting her up with him. He unbuckled his sword belt and threw it from him with her knife.

"If it is a fight you want," he told her grimly, "then I am your man, Joana. Hit for hit. Come on."

She came at his chest with her fists and he reached around her to smack her ungently on one buttock. She drew back and punched his chin with a closed fist. He slapped one of her cheeks smartly. She kicked at his shin and he caught her leg before she could return it to the ground, almost throwing her off-balance, and slapped it with an open palm.

She stood before him panting loudly, her bosom heaving, her eyes flashing, looking for an opening through which to attack him.

"I wish . . ." she said after a few moments. "Oh, I wish I could have the strength of a man for just ten minutes. I would not stop until I had beaten you insensible." Her hands were opening and closing into fists at her sides. "But this is humiliating. You are not fighting me. You are playing with me. I should have a broken jaw and two black eyes by now. Hit me, damn you! Fight, you coward."

He looked at her reddened cheek and took her suddenly by the shoulders and drew her hard against him. "I can imagine how it must feel, Joana," he said, "to have been so close to freedom to have seen and heard your chance gallop away into the distance. Have done now. There is no point in raging.''

"Oh, God," she said, her face pressed to his coat, "he was so close. I could almost have touched him. And my musket not two feet off. I may never see him again. I may have lost my chance forever.''

"Hush," he said, one hand coming up to stroke the back of her head.

"Hush?" Her head came up and her eyes were still blazing. "How can I hush? I want to fight you, and you will not fight. I wish I were not a woman. Oh, I wish and wish I were a man. You would regret the day you were born if I were a man.''

"Yes, I would." Both his tension and his anger had dissipated, he realized suddenly, and he could not resist grinning down at her. "I would be embarrassed and horrified too to be holding you like this if you were a man, Joana, and feeling as I am feeling.''

She was still panting. Her breasts were heaving against his chest. "You might have been dead," she said, "and I was trussed up so soundly that I could not have lifted a finger to help you or uttered a word in your defense. And now all you can think of is making love, you fool. You imbecile!''

"Where did you learn your language?" he asked her. "You must have made a few trips to the gutter, Joana.''

"I wish I knew more," she said. "My repertoire of foul words is lamentably small. I need more to hurl at your head. If we cannot fight, let us make love, then. But don't you dare try to do it quickly or gently, Robert. I want it rough. And I don't want you asking if the ground is hard. I want to fight you—for pleasure.''

It was madness. There was a war to be fought and orders to be carried out. There was an explosion to investigate and a whole company of French soldiers not far off, all looking for him so that their colonel might have the pleasure of parting him first from his uniform and then from his skin and finally from his life.

It was madness. And yet all he could think of for the next several minutes—he had no idea how many passed— was rolling and panting and growling on the ground, giving and receiving pleasure and pain in equal portions, making love with his bitterest enemy. Making love for the fifth time in little more than twenty-four hours—and trying to convince himself that it was merely a physical thing, that it was just sex, that there were no feelings involved at all.

He wondered if he was fooling her as poorly as he was fooling himself.

"Oh, Robert," she said, flat on her back on the ground a few minutes after it was all over, turning her head to look at him, "you do that most awfully well, you know. I must be bruises all over, inside and out. I feel wonderful."

"And better?" he said. "The anger worked off?"

"He will find me," she said. "And in the meantime I have you to give me pleasure. I must go and wash. Permission to absent myself for five minutes, sir?"

"I'll come with you," he said, sitting up and wishing for a bath or at least for a bathe. But alas, there was not enough water—or enough time. The day was going to be a tricky one now that they would be pursuing their pursuers.

"I was planning to take my clothes off," she said, smiling archly at him. "You will not be embarrassed, Robert?"

He snorted and she laughed lightly before turning to run down to the stream. Like a faun. Like a light-footed beautiful faun, without a care in the world, perfectly in tune with her surroundings.

God, she was a strange woman, he thought, going after her. A strange and wonderful woman. Equally at home as the refined and exquisite Marquesa das Minas and as the earthy and wild Joana Ribeiro, as she liked to call herself. A lifetime would not be long enough even to begin to know her. And all he had was a few days. Well, he would make the most of those days. He would pack a lifetime of experience into them.

He frowned as he caught the direction of his thoughts

They had not gone far before they could hear the steady booming of guns. Almeida was being bombarded with a constant shelling. Only one hill had stood between them and the sound, faint at first, felt more than heard, and then quite distinct to the ear.

"Is it like this in battle?" Joana asked, hurrying up beside Captain Blake. "Someone told me that the sound of the guns is the most frightening part."

"Especially when they are directed right at you," he said, "and you cannot step out of the way because if you do the line will break and the enemy infantry will be through it and will win the day. You have to stand—like a sitting duck."

"But at least there is the line," she said. "Other men to either side of you for a sort of protection. But you go out in front of the line, do you not? You and your riflemen are skirmishers? That must be far more terrifying."

"No," he said. "At least we have something to do instead of just standing waiting for the enemy column to come up so that the guns will stop and the real killing begin."

"It is madness," she said. "War is madness."

"But a necessary one," he said. "There is no point in saying, as so many people do, especially ladies who spend their days in perfumed drawing rooms, that we should all love one another and learn to get along with one another. Life is not like that."

"And would it not be dull," she said, "if it were? We would not have had that delicious fight this morning, Robert. I did enjoy it, though I did not enjoy what provoked it. I have no taste for being bound and gagged. Have you ever struck a woman before?"

"No," he said. "And don't expect me to apologize, Joana."

She chuckled and fell back a few paces again. Her foot was hurting like the devil, but she would not allow herself the luxury of limping while she was in his sight.

They saw no sign of Colonel Leroux and his company of horsemen, though they approached the crest of every hill with caution. The Frenchmen must have galloped straight to Almeida and joined Marshal Ney's forces, he told her.

"Perhaps they imagine you are inside, Joana," he said. "He will be preparing to rescue you."

"Those poor women who are inside," she said, "if the

fortress is taken and does not surrender. It will be sacked and they will all be raped before they are killed." She shuddered.

"Perhaps Cox will surrender," he said. "Though I doubt it. He has a reputation for stubbornness."

"And Marcel will be in there with the rest," she said, "raping them and then ordering them killed. You should have shot him this morning, Robert."

"And offered my body to the rest of the company for target practice?" he said. "He'll not harm any woman, Joana. He is an officer and bound to try to impose discipline on his men, not lead the way into savagery. Besides, he has a mission. He is looking for you."

"Yes." She shuddered again and was once more glad that she was behind him.

They approached the crest of one more hill cautiously. The sound of the guns was almost deafening. Joana felt a deep, knee-weakening terror, though she would not have admitted as much for worlds. Captain Blake reached back a hand and drew her down to the ground. And they edged up side by side and found themselves looking down on hell.

The plain before the fortress was thick with the blue uniforms of the French, just beyond the reach of the guns on the walls—what was left of them. A good half of the city was either in flames or in smoking, blackened ruins. No simple shelling could possibly have done such damage, surely. But something had happened. Something that had woken them that morning, even though they had been out of earshot of the guns.

"Jesus!" Captain Blake said beside her. "The main magazine must have blown. The bloody fools must have had the ammunition in a place where a French shell could set it all off. It must have been the grandest fireworks display the world has witnessed."

"They must all be dead," she said, gazing at the ruins and at the gaping breaches in the walls with mingled horror and fascination. "And yet some are alive and fighting on. Why do they not surrender?"

"At a guess, because Cox is one of the survivors," he said. "Bloody magnificent fool. But it cannot hold out long. Hours, probably. A day perhaps. No longer. So much for the Beau's hope that Almeida would hold up your countrymen until the autumn rains. August is not even quite out yet, and the rains are at least a month off."

She was gripping the scrubby grass on either side of her. "Do you think there were children inside there?" she asked. "Or would they have been evacuated? There are dead children in there, Robert."

He turned his head sharply to look at her. "Are you all right?" he asked. "Put your head down. Stop looking."

"And that will make everything all right?" she said. "It will not matter that there are dead children down there as long as I do not look? I live a frivolous and pampered life, Robert. I have never been this close to death on a large scale before."

She scrambled down behind the hill suddenly on all fours and retched onto the ground. And humiliation took the place of horror and grief. She could not seem to stop her stomach from heaving.

"Go away!" she said sharply when she heard him come up behind her. "Leave me alone."

"Joana." One broad hand came to rest against her back. "It is all right to vomit. There is nothing shameful about it. I don't know a soldier, myself included, who did not chuck up his last meal at his first encounter with death. Some do it routinely at every battle. There is nothing unmanly—or unwomanly—about it."

"It is just disgusting," she said, her face cold and clammy. "Go away."

He was sitting just below the top of the rise, facing away from her, when she had cleaned herself up as well as she could and felt that the moment of facing him again could be avoided no longer.

"You were stupid to turn your back," she said. "How did you know I would not be running down the slope toward the army?"

"It did cross my mind," he said, turning to look at her. "Except that I don't think you could run if hounds were at your heels, Joana. Let me see that foot."

"It is all right," she said with a shrug. Don't fuss, Robert, like an old nanny."

"I think I would prefer 'bastard' and 'imbecile,' " he

said, "and even 'coward.' And 'eunuch,' I believe it was once? Your foot." He held out a hand that was not to be denied. She placed her foot next to it and he lifted it and clucked his tongue. "So you *were* limping. I thought you were, but I knew I would have a fight on my hands if I commented on the fact."

Her strap had kept slipping up all day so that the inside of her heel, from ankle to sole, was red and raw. He drew his handkerchief out of his pocket.

"It is clean," he said, "unless you spat on it this morning." He bound it snugly about her foot as if he were used to administering such services—and he probably was, she thought. "It will not help a great deal, but it will prevent any more rubbing or any more dust getting at it. Perhaps the woman at the farm where we stopped for a meal earlier—a pity you could not keep that meal down, Joana, considering the fact that it was our one and only today—perhaps she will have some ointment. And perhaps we can stay there for the night."

"We just walk away?" she asked, looking to the top of the hill and marveling at how one quickly became almost accustomed to the booming of the guns.

"There is nothing we can do for those poor bastards down there," he said. "There is no point in wasting energies where they can do no good, Joana. In the meantime we have work to do—*I* have work to do. And there is no time for delay. By tomorrow Almeida will either fall or surrender. Perhaps even today or tonight. I have to make sure that the people between here and Lisbon get safely away and destroy the supply lines ahead of the French. They will be on their way soon—once they have done some suitable rejoicing over the fall of Almeida. The gates into Portugal are wide open. We can hardly expect them not to come pouring in, can we?"

"And Marcel too," she said. "He will come."

"Doubtless," he said.

"Good," she said. And then her tone sharpened. "What are you doing? Put me down at once!"

"If I do," he said as she kicked her legs on air, "it will be to give you a sharp slap where it most hurts, Joana. Now that I have started, I will not find it nearly so difficult the next time."

"Oh, I wish you would," she said. "I feel so humiliated, what with one thing and another, Robert, that I would like nothing better than the chance to smash your nose. I would feel loads better if I could break it for you again. That farm must be two miles away at the very least. Is it not amazing that those people had not even ventured out to discover what the explosion was all about? It must have been deafening at the farmhouse. They were frightened, I suppose. Put me down."

"When I collapse beneath your weight," he said, "you may pick yourself up off the ground, Joana, and walk the rest of the way. In the meantime, save your breath. And keep your hand away from those guns."

"Damn you," she said. "Where am I supposed to put it?"

"Try about my neck," he said.

"Oh," she said after a few minutes of silence, "this is humiliating. I have never lived through a more humiliating day."

"It's good for you," he said. "Prisoners are supposed to feel humiliated."

"Go to the devil," she said.

21

SOMEHOW, Joana found, everything happened much more slowly than she had expected. She had expected that they would rush westward toward Coimbra within a few days, warning as many people as they could to evacuate and burn all behind them. She had expected that the French armies would hasten along at their heels. She had only hoped that in all the rush and confusion Colonel Leroux would find her and she could complete the task that had obsessed her for three years.

Things did not turn out that way at all. Governor Cox in Almeida surrendered the day after losing almost the whole of his ammunition supplies and half of his fortress and the people within it in the process. But the French did not immediately sweep through the open gate into Portugal. Marshal Massena and the main French forces had to come up from Salamanca. He had to consult with advisers and guides on the best route by which to advance on Lisbon, although the route he would take was a foregone conclusion. There was only one good road west to Coimbra, the one that followed the Mondego River toward the sea.

Their own retreat westward, Joana found, took them weeks rather than days, weeks that she shamelessly enjoyed despite everything. Yet they were not easy weeks. Every day they trudged from farm to farm, from village to village, Robert talking and persuading endlessly. It was not easy. How did one persuade men and women with homes and families to leave for an unknown part of the country with only what they could carry with them, and to burn everything that was left behind, including their homes and the crops that were still in the field?

The peasants were heroic. They accepted the argu-

ments given them with stoic calm and followed orders
with dogged determination and lack of complaint. On
more than one occasion Joana watched them with a lump
in her throat, their packs heavy on their backs, their
children gathered about them, trudging away from the
burning remains of all that was home to them. Very often
the burning building was the one in which she and Robert
had lain and loved the night before. It was as if their
love was to have no roots, no past, just as it was to have
no future.

Not that they ever called it love, of course. It was
pleasure that they took together. But even their pleasure
was burning up behind them, and destined to end soon,
as soon as they came up with the bulk of the British
army and Robert could rejoin his regiment.

She tried not to think of the future.

The wealthier people of the towns, particularly the
merchants, were harder to persuade. They were angry at
the incompetence of their government and the armies,
which could not protect their property as well as their
lives. They were defiant. Sometimes it took longer than
one day to convince them that starving the advancing
French, who always lived off the land over which they
marched, was the surest way to their eventual defeat.

Captain Blake and Joana were not alone. They met a
surprising number of British officers during their travels,
some of them on the same errand as Robert's, some of
them scouting officers whose job it was to estimate
enemy forces and watch their movements and constantly
report back to headquarters.

They heard news from these officers, sometimes confused and out-of-date, but nevertheless received eagerly
by two people starved of news for a long time. Headquarters was no longer at Viseu. Wellington had moved first
to Celorico, closer to the border, and more recently back
to Gouveia.

There was unrest in Lisbon, they heard, and loud
grumblings in England. The governments of both countries were being blamed for the imminent disaster of all
their expensive hopes. Viscount Wellington, in particular, was being called incompetent. There were loud clam-
ors for his removal from the command.

As a result, they were told, Wellington was planning to silence his critics with one last final battle during the retreat to Lisbon. He had chosen a strong position on the southern bank of the Mondego at the Ponte Murcella on the road to Coimbra.

Robert ached to hurry there to rejoin his beloved riflemen, Joana knew. And the thought saddened her. What would she do when that time came? Return to Lisbon? Become the Marquesa das Minas again? She supposed she would do both. And in the meantime, would she see Colonel Leroux? Had she been mad to assume that he would search for her and find her? It seemed madness during those weeks. Finding her would be like finding the proverbial needle in the proverbial haystack.

She tried not to give in to such depressing thoughts.

Occasionally they came across small bands of the Ordenanza, and those men—and some women—were excited by the prospect of action at last. It seemed almost as if they welcomed the approach of the hated French, even though it meant invasion of their country. Once Joana and Captain Blake even met Duarte briefly, when they had strayed north of the road to call at a village in the hills. He found them there.

"Rumor had it that there was a stray rifleman roaming the hills," he said with a grin, extending his right hand to Captain Blake before setting an arm about Joana's shoulders and kissing her cheek. "How goes the battle?"

He was elated because the French advance had finally begun. "We will not attack their main forces," he explained. "We will let them pass on in peace to the burned and barren countryside, and then attack their supply trains. We will catch them in a giant nutcracker. And their advance will be slowed while they release large detachments to try to catch us." He grinned. "How is Joana? Still in the path of danger? You should come with me perhaps and let me send you to safety." He still had an arm about her shoulders.

Robert, she saw with some satisfaction, was scowling.

"Let's talk about it," she said, and she walked off a short distance with Duarte while two of his companions exchanged news with the captain. "How are Carlota and Miguel? Have you heard from them?"

"I sent to let them know we had got safely out of Spain," he said. "Carlota is doubtless grinding her teeth with frustration at the inaction, but she is safe and far to the north of the advance. You are looking about as unlike the marquesa as you possibly could."

"Yes." She looked down ruefully at the dress, which was even more faded after its weeks of wear and several washes.

"I did not mean just the clothes," he said. He looked at her critically for several silent seconds and then frowned. "Where are your knife and gun?"

"I am a prisoner," she said. "They have been confiscated. This is the farthest from his person he has allowed me since we reentered Portugal."

His frown deepened and then he chuckled. "You are serious?" he said.

"He will not believe my story," she said. "Not that I begged and pleaded with him to do so. I would not so demean myself. He does not believe you are my brother. He thinks we became lovers the morning after you rescued us from Salamanca. He even gave me a scold about coming between you and Carlota and Miguel. He is taking me to Arthur to have me imprisoned as a French spy until the end of the wars."

He chuckled again. "Well, that is all easily remedied," he said. "I shall have a word with him, Joana."

"No, you will not," she said firmly. "Either he must believe me or he can believe what he wishes for the rest of his life. I do not care."

"Joana." He looked at her closely again. "Yes, now I know what it is. It is neither the clothes nor the absence of weapons. It is you. Your face—what is in it and what is behind it. You love him?"

She snorted. "Oh, certainly," she said, "I am going to love a man who thinks me a liar and a slut."

"Does he?" he said. "He has not fallen for your famous charm, then?"

"He actually tied me and gagged me once when Colonel Leroux and his men came close to us," she said indignantly.

He laughed. "Ah, yes," he said. "He is just the man you would fall for, Joana. I approve, by the way."

"How foolish," she said. "There is no possible future, Duarte. I am Luis' widow and the Comte de Levisse's daughter and he is a nobody who enlisted in the ranks of the English army. His life is the life of a soldier."

"You would like there to be a future, then?" he said, squeezing her shoulder. "Poor Joana."

"What nonsense you talk," she said. "Kiss me. On the lips. He will be incensed."

He kissed her on the lips and smiled at her. "You are sure you don't want me to explain?" he said.

"Captain Robert Blake can go to hell with my blessing," she said. "Don't you dare tell him anything, Duarte."

They strolled back to join the others, Duarte's arm still about her. He kissed her again when he and his companions took their leave a few minutes later.

It was evening already. She retired almost immediately with Robert to the small and none-too-clean inn room they had taken for the night—and had a thoroughly satisfactory quarrel even though it had to be conducted in lowered voices.

"I want one thing understood, Joana," he said, taking her by the upper arm and turning her to face him as soon as the door closed behind them. "For as long as you are my woman, you will remain faithful to me. There will be no flirting with other men or old lovers, and no kissing them. Your behavior was disgusting."

She shrugged. "In England perhaps it is not the thing for brothers to kiss their sisters," she said. "In Portugal it is."

He shook her roughly by the arm. "It is no joking matter," he said. "Perhaps it seems not greatly distasteful to you to kiss another man and allow him to keep his arm about you for all of twenty minutes while your current lover looks on. But it is distasteful to think of that woman and child awaiting his safe return in the mountains."

"You are jealous," she said, making a kissing gesture with her mouth. "Poor Robert. I think you love me just a little."

"You disgust me," he said. "You have no morals at all."

"But I stayed with you," she said, daring his wrath by reaching out one finger to run down his sleeve. "I might have gone with him, Robert. He wanted me to go."

"I would like to have seen you try," he said.

"He wanted to tell you the truth," she said. "He wanted to tell you that he is my brother and that everything else I have told you is the truth."

"You would not know the truth if it formed a fist and punched you in the nose," he said.

"I don't think you would either," she said, stung at last. "You are a pompous, opinionated ass, Robert. You enjoy the image of yourself as the wronged man and the jailer. It gives you a feeling of power to walk about loaded down with your own weapons and mine. You are afraid of losing that power if you believe me."

"It stings, does it not," he said, his voice icy, "to know one man, and that man your jailer as you so rightly put it, who will not hang on your every word and believe every foolish piece of nonsense you speak? It angers you to have one man who can resist you."

"Resist me?" She raised her eyebrows and looked at him haughtily. "What you have been doing to me every night and day for weeks except for those four days when nature forced you to stay away from me has not seemed much like resistance, Robert. If that is resistance, I wonder what capitulation would feel like. It might be interesting."

"You confuse respect with lust," he said. "I have no respect for you whatsoever, Joana, and no liking. I would not trust you if my life depended on it—especially then— or believe a word that came from your mouth. All I feel for you is lust. I have never made a secret of that fact."

"And I for you," she said. "How could I like or respect someone so inflexible and so humorless? How could I like an Englishman, and one who came out of the gutter? How could I respect someone who sneers at every word I speak? But you have a body to die for and you know what to do with it in bed, and so I lust after you. Do you think I will even deign to look at you once

I have been restored to civilization? You will be beneath my notice."

"You will be a prisoner and beneath mine," he said.

"I will be the Marquesa das Minas," she said, "and you will be remarkably foolish. I shall have all of Lisbon and the whole of the British army laughing at you."

"Lie down," he said, his face set into angry lines as he unbuckled his sword belt. "I have had enough of you for one day."

"Have you?" she said. "Do I take it that I may sleep peacefully throughout the night, then? A night of rest? That will make a change."

"Hush, Joana," he said. "You have an answer for everything."

"Would you like it if I did not?" she asked him, pulling her dress off over her head before lying down on the narrow lumpy bed. "Would you not be bored if I were a meek mute? Yes, sir, and no, sir, and if you please, sir, and if I can be of service, sir?" She batted her eyelids at him.

"Hush, Joana," he said, removing his coat and his shirt and his boots before lying down beside her. "I grow mortally tired of your taunting."

"Please, sir." She turned over onto her side and spread a hand on his chest. "Will you put your arms about me so that I do not take it into my head during the night to try to escape? And your leg over mine so that I will resist the temptation to kick you where it most hurts and then escape?"

"God, woman," he said, "you are making me angry."

"Making?" she said. "I thought you were made already." She lifted herself on one elbow and rested the side of her head on her hand. She looked down at him, wooing him with her eyes. Her anger had passed long before. She was enjoying herself. "Please, sir, will you take off your trousers and come inside me? That is the surest way to prevent my escape."

His anger had not abated. Not quite. "You like being taken in anger, then?" he asked her, his eyes firmly closed. "You like being hurt, Joana? Sex is not for punishment. It is for pleasure."

"Let it be for pleasure, then," she said, laying her

head on his shoulder and gazing up into his face as her
fingers tiptoed their way up his chest and over his chin
to rest against his lips. "You are not really still angry,
are you, Robert? How foolish you are. Do you think I
would seriously flirt with Duarte Ribeiro or any other
man while you and I are still together? Perhaps soon I
will indeed be a prisoner or perhaps I will indeed be the
marquesa again and looking down my nose at you. But
not just yet. Now we are together. Tonight we are together. Take me for pleasure, then. Pleasure was never
more pleasant than with you."

"God!" He turned his head to look at her. "Sometimes
it takes the devil of an effort to remember that you never
tell the truth, Joana. You want me? Very well, then. I
want you too. Let us have each other. Let us take what
pleasure is to be had." His hands were undoing the buttons at his waist.

Sometimes, Joana thought, she was frightened by the
force of her love and her need for him. Even after several
weeks of frequent and lusty lovemaking she could not
get enough of him. And yet it was not just the pleasure.
It was not just his body or the ecstasy he could create
on and in her own. It was he. She could not have enough
of him. Her mind shied away again from the future as
he freed himself from the last of his clothes and tossed
them from the bed and as she opened her arms to him.

"Of course," she said, smiling up at him, "if you are
still angry, Robert, you may be a little rough. I like it
when you are rough."

She longed to have it slow and tender. She yearned
for tenderness.

"You are shameless," he said, his weight coming down
on top of her.

"And how glad you are of it," she said. "Ah, Robert,
I don't believe anyone else will ever feel as good as you
there. Ah, yes, there. You feel so good."

And since there would be no love and no tenderness,
she abandoned herself to sheer wonderful sensation—
both given and received.

They were within one day of rejoining the army when
the shocking, almost unbelievable news reached them.

They had done about as much as they could do. Almost every farm and village and town had obeyed the order eventually and the French would advance along a road denuded of food and other supplies, harassed in their rear by the Ordenanza, and facing a battle in a place of Lord Wellington's choosing.

He had done enough, Captain Blake thought. He had been away from his regiment for a whole weary year, and for much of that time he had languished, idle and fretting and longing to be back. The next day he would be back, and within a week or two at the latest he would be fighting one more grand battle against the French. He was excited by the prospect. The days could not go fast enough for him. It had been such a long time.

And yet he was reluctant too. Part of him did not want these weeks to end. The next day he would seek out Lord Wellington and turn Joana over to him. His duty would be done at that point. What happened to her would not be his concern. He could leave her and forget about her.

Forget about her! That was one thing he would never do, he knew. She had warned him that they could not become lovers without his feelings becoming involved, and she was right, of course. His feelings had become very much involved. For, her physical attractions aside—and they were many—there was Joana herself, flirtatious, teasing, untruthful, deceitful, occasionally foul-tongued, charming, smiling, and always stimulating. He had never known anyone quite like her. There *was* no one quite like her.

He found her irritating beyond bearing more often than not. He lashed her with his anger almost every single day, and she lashed back just as viciously and even more so. When Joana wanted to wound, she went straight for the jugular vein. And he found her enchanting almost beyond bearing too. It could be put simply into words, though he avoided the words in his mind. He wanted to love her and knew that he never could. He hated her too much, despised her too much.

And so he loved her without ever putting his feelings into words even in his mind. For once he verbalized them, then he must despise himself too. He would be no better than all the other men who had fallen under her spell. Worse. Those other men did not know her for what she was.

He dreaded the next day, when he must part with her forever. No more days of quarrels and nights of love. Only memories. And he knew that the memories would haunt him for a long, long time—if he had a long time to live. There was to be a major pitched battle within weeks.

And then came the news with returning scouts just the day before they would have reached the army. Massena and his forces were approaching, not by the main road along the Mondego toward the awaiting army, but by the narrow and incredibly difficult trail to the north, leading through Viseu. It could not have been planned that way surely, one scout with whom Captain Blake had a former acquaintance said. They had to be mad to come that way with a huge army and all the heavy guns and baggage. Their progress was considerably slowed and their susceptibility to attack by the Ordenanza increased tenfold. It had to have been an accident.

But that was the way they were coming. Lord Wellington would have to be informed so that he could move his position and find a new one in which to meet the French when they came up. And the people farther north who had not evacuated their homes must be warned to do so and persuaded to leave nothing behind.

It was great news. But there was no further thought to making straight for the army. Captain Blake had work to do farther north. And since he could not spare a day in which to take Joana to headquarters, then she must come with him. Or so he persuaded himself.

"Christ," he said. "If they push onward from Viseu, they will pass through Mortagoa."

She was very pale, he saw when he looked at her. Perhaps the reality of the situation was coming home to her. Her countrymen were coming closer, and if Wellington was quick enough, they would meet him on ground favorable to him. Thousands of them would die.

"Mortagoa?" she said.

"Many of Duarte Ribeiro's band live there," he said. "Their women and children are there now. Including his own."

"Then they must be warned," she said. "We will warn them, Robert?"

"We will cut straight north," he said, "and work our way gradually westward. We will warn them if Ribeiro and his men have not already done so."

"What are we waiting for, then?" she said.

He looked at her with reluctant admiration. "You thought all this traveling was almost over," he said. "Doubtless Wellington will have you sent directly to Lisbon and perhaps on to England once I turn you over to him. At least you will be comfortable then, Joana, and safe. Are you sorry this has happened?"

"Robert," she said, "you do not know how excruciatingly tedious comfortable living can be. There is nothing to do but sleep and eat and go to parties. And flirt for excitement. I am not sorry that our adventure is to be extended."

He did not believe a great deal of what she said. But he did believe those words. Amazingly she had seemed to thrive on the hard living they had done in the past several weeks. She had never once complained about heat or dust or dirt or sweat—or blisters. She had had one on the other foot after the first was almost healed, and had threatened him with a long and sharp twig and swished it wickedly in the direction of his arm when she had thought that he was going to carry her again.

"Besides," she said now, smiling dazzlingly at him, "I have not yet had enough pleasure from your body, Robert. It is such a wonderful body."

For all her lady's upbringing, she seemed to feel no embarrassment at all at the outrageous things she frequently said to him. Sometimes he was thankful that he was past the age of blushes. And yet her words always drew a powerful—though quite private—response from him too.

No, he had not had enough of her either. He would never have enough of her. He quelled the thought.

"North we go, then," he said.

North into the greatest danger and the deepest emotional experience they had yet encountered together.

22

MARSHAL Ney entered Viseu on September 18 after a laborious march over a stony, narrow, and precipitous track that had strung out the army into a dangerously thin line. The guns, supplies, and horses had fallen behind the infantry, and two thousand militiamen of the Ordenanza almost succeeded in capturing all the heavy guns. They narrowly failed, but they took a hundred prisoners and they harassed an already suffering French army almost beyond endurance.

Viseu was deserted when the French entered it. Its inhabitants had put up little resistance to the persuasions to leave. The vanguard of the French army was very close, and those people had not expected invasion. They were frightened by the prospect.

Captain Blake and Joana lay flat on their stomachs on top of a wooded hill to the west of Viseu, watching its occupation by the French. They had seen Joana's "aunt" and Matilda on their way to Coimbra earlier in the day. Matilda had been disapproving and tight-lipped, her aunt openmouthed with shock at the sight of Joana. But she had flatly refused to accompany them. Not that she would have been allowed to, of course. But while they had argued with her, Captain Blake had stood by and said nothing.

They should have moved farther away from Viseu. But they both felt a strange reluctance to do so.

"Part of my life is caught up in this place," she said. "And yours too, Robert. If you had not been ordered to escort me here, we would never have met. Do you wish we had never met?"

"Yes," he said.

She turned over onto her side and looked up at him. "Do you? Why?"

He turned his head and his blue eyes gazed into hers. "The answers should be obvious," he said. "Do you want me to spell them out? Do you want to hear insults when I am not even angry?"

She smiled at him. "I believe it is because you have fallen in love with me and feel that it is the wrong thing to have done," she said. "Am I not right?"

"Joana," he said, "will you never give up on that idea? Do you think yourself so irresistible even to someone who knows you? And what about me? Am I irresistible too? Have you fallen in love with me?"

She smiled slowly. "A lady never tells," she said.

He grinned at her, an expression that was so rare with him that it could always succeed in turning her weak at the knees. "Which happens to be one of the greatest whoppers you have ever told, Joana," he said. "You are not shy about telling everything else."

She laughed. "But I am not sorry that I made that tedious journey to Lisbon just to meet you," she said. "And I am not sorry that we traveled back together or that I agreed to let Arthur send me after you to Salamanca. And I am not sorry that I maneuvered your escape and mine or that we have had these weeks together. I am not sorry, Robert. There will be many pleasant memories."

His grin held. "You came to Lisbon to meet me?" he said. "All the way from Viseu. I am flattered, ma'am. I did not realize that my fame had spread so far."

"And you do not believe a word," she said. "But you will. And then you will feel foolish. And then I think your feelings for me will come flooding up when you realize that I am not what you think me."

His grin had faded to a smile. "And Duarte Ribeiro is still your brother?" he asked.

"Half-brother," she said. "Yes, he still is and doubtless always will be."

"And yet," he said, "you did not know that his wife and child were at Mortagoa? The place name meant nothing to you when I mentioned it."

"She is not his wife—yet," she said. "And it delights

me to see you plagued by doubts, Robert. Of course I knew they were there."

"What is her name?" he asked.

She reached out to touch a finger to his nose. "You probably know it," she said. "You do not need me to tell you."

"Meaning that you do not know?" he asked. "Or is it that you are still teasing me with doubts?"

"That is for you to decide," she said.

He shook his head. "I have no doubts, Joana," he said. "You lose."

"Perhaps," she said, "and perhaps not." She rolled onto her stomach again and looked down onto the distant roofs and church spires. Blue-coated soldiers by the thousand were camped to the east of the city. "It feels dreadfully real, does it not? The French here and the British not many miles behind us, waiting. Will it be soon, Robert? Tomorrow?"

"Oh, no," he said. "Ney will wait here for the rest of the army and the guns to come up and then they will have to try to scout ahead and make plans. A week at least." He looked across at her. "Does it excite you to see your countrymen so close?"

"And freedom?" she said. "I don't think I particularly like the thought of my father's people fighting my mother's. I grew up with my father and loved him. I still do. And I returned to France with him after our exile in England. He did not like the new order and was happy enough to be sent away on an embassy. But he loves his country nevertheless. I do not remember my mother. I was taken from her at a very young age. I think she and my father had a dreadful quarrel and he did not take her from Portugal when he and I left. But I feel I know her nevertheless. Miguel and Duarte and Maria told me a great deal about her."

He turned his head sharply to look at her. Her chin was resting on her hands and she was staring sightlessly down at Viseu and the French army encamped before it.

"Miguel?" he said. "Maria?"

"Duarte's brother and sister," she said. "They are both dead."

"How?" he asked.

"Junot's men," she said. "In 1807. My mother's son and daughter were killed by my father's people. Is it any wonder that I have never known quite who I am or where I belong, Robert?"

He stared at her, his eyes boring into hers.

She smiled suddenly. "Careful, Robert," she said. "You are in grave danger of believing me, are you not? And if you believe this, perhaps you will have to believe everything. Perhaps Miguel and Maria are figments of my imagination. They are quite common Portuguese names, after all. And perhaps there is no division in my loyalties. After all, I never knew my mother and I hated Luis."

"We had better move away from here," he said abruptly. "We are too close. We will find somewhere a little farther away to spend the night. Tomorrow we will call at as many farms as possible and head for Mortagoa. The British are forming at Bussaco, not far from there."

"I know Bussaco," she said. "There is a convent there."

"Come, then." His tones were abrupt as he got to his feet below the level of the skyline.

"I hope Marcel is down there," she said. "Do you think he is, Robert?"

"Quite possibly," he said. "But I would not get your hopes too high, Joana. I am not going to lose you after keeping you with me for so long."

"Just once," she said longingly. "If I could see him just one more time." Her eyes strayed to the two guns slung over his shoulder.

"And I am supposed to wonder if you are in love with me?" he said. "I don't believe you have ever been in love, Joana, or ever will be. Your appetite for men is too insatiable."

She smiled at him as they strode down the hill side by side. "And for you especially so," she said. "We are going to sleep outdoors?"

"We have no choice, I'm afraid," he said.

"I like sleeping outdoors," she said.

"Even in September when the nights are brisk?" he asked.

"Especially then," she said. "We have to hold each

other particularly close in order to share body heat. But I do have an unfair advantage. You make a larger blanket than I." She laughed up at him.

He knew as soon as he woke that he had made a mistake to stop for the night so close to Viseu. He still felt sure that the bulk of the army would wait there for several days until all was organized to march into pitched battle. But of course scouting and foraging parties would be sent out. He had said as much to Joana just the evening before.

There was such a party out now. He could feel it with that sixth soldier's sense he possessed, even before he heard it. And long before he saw it.

"Joana." He had slid his hand between his chest and her mouth before speaking into her ear. He shook her shoulders at the same moment. "We have company, or will have soon if we don't move." He looked down into her open eyes. "Do I have to gag you?"

She shook her head slowly and he slid his hand away.

They had slept in a partly wooded valley behind the hill that shielded them from Viseu. Now the choice did not seem a wise one at all. The hill ahead of them was almost bare. There were only a few clumps of trees to provide cover. And yet if they continued along the valley, the scouting party or whatever it was that was approaching would be upon them before they could round the far side of the hill.

"We are going to have to run for it," he said. "We need to be at the top of the hill and over it before they have a chance to see us. Hold my hand, Joana. We are going to rush from one clump of bushes to the next. And for God's sake, don't prove difficult."

He picked up the guns, which he had kept close to his hand throughout the night, grabbed Joana's hand, and began to run. She kept pace with him, making no attempt to impede his progress. She did not waste breath in speaking.

But it was hopeless. He knew that before they were even halfway up the slope. He could feel Frenchmen coming over the crest of the hill behind them. They would not be quite within musket range yet, but his back bristled nevertheless. The trees were thicker toward the top of the slope, but they would never make it that far.

He ducked behind one small clump of trees briefly and sank to one knee, dragging Joana in behind him. But he could see from pointed arms that they had been spotted. And there must have been fifty horsemen coming over the crest of the hill.

"Damnation!" he muttered. He knew that they had no chance at all. For even if by some miracle they succeeded in reaching the top of the hill before being gunned down, they would be caught beyond it. It was death or captivity they were facing, only relatively few miles from the British army. A fine choice.

"We are not going to make it, are we?" Joana said calmly from behind his shoulder.

He knew a moment of indecision. Only a moment, and then he drew his handkerchief from his pocket and tied it quickly to the end of her musket before thrusting the weapon into her hands.

"Here," he said. "Hold it high above your head and step out from behind these bushes when they reach the valley. They will not shoot. I am going on. Good luck, Joana." And he wasted no time, but raced on upward away from the shelter of the bushes, his back bristling even more than before. For now there was one musket within easy range of him, and it was loaded too.

And then shots were being fired—ahead of him and behind. And there were voices—English voices—shouting at him.

"Come on, sir," someone yelled. "This way. We'll cover for you."

"Faster, Blake, you bastard!" someone else was calling. "You don't want to die with a bullet in your back. It would look bad on your record."

He almost grinned except that he was still too intent on the fear clawing at his back. What more opportune time could there be to run into—literally run into—a party of his own snipers? It was rifles that were being fired from the trees above and ahead of him. One swift glance over his shoulder showed the French horsemen in the valley pulling up uncertainly. Viscount Wellington was famous for the deadly ambushes he hid behind the crests of hills.

The same glance showed him Joana at his heels, the musket, minus his handkerchief, slung over her shoulder.

"What the hell?" he said, and he reached back to grab one of her arms and drag her upward with him until they could duck behind a reassuringly thick clump of bushes only just below the level of the British snipers.

"I felt a little nervous about being caught between two fires," she said, panting and throwing herself down onto her stomach before peering downward between the bushes.

Captain Blake meanwhile was also on his stomach beside her and readying his rifle with hasty fingers and pointing it down the hill to the horsemen, who were milling about, still undecided whether to attack or not. They looked alarmingly close.

"Trust Captain Blake to have with him the only lovely woman left in this corner of Portugal," one of the green-jacketed soldiers called loudly. Sergeant Saunders. Captain Blake grinned. He felt suddenly very much at home despite the deadly danger. There were perhaps a dozen of them against fifty French cavalrymen. He knew beyond a doubt that there was no ambush waiting over the crest of the hill.

"Just keep your head down," he said to Joana, "and you will be quite safe."

But she was peering downward quite as intently as he.

He supposed afterward that it all happened within a few seconds. So much happened. At the time it seemed to go on forever, as if time had been slowed to one-tenth its usual speed.

Before he knew what was about to happen, long before he could do anything to prevent it, Joana had scrambled to her feet so that she was in full view of the horsemen below, and she was waving both arms above her head.

Before she opened her mouth—and she shrieked at almost the same moment as she jumped up—he knew what she was going to say and he understood what was happening.

"Marcel!" she shrieked. "I am here. It is Jeanne. Marcel!"

And she was back down behind the bushes, pulling feverishly at her musket before Captain Blake reacted.

"Jesus Christ!" he exclaimed, and he threw himself on her, knocking the gun from her hands, catching at her wrists and twisting them behind her back without any thought to gentleness. "You vixen. You devil!"

"No!" she cried, her voice frantic. "Give me my gun. Give me my gun, Robert. I have to kill him. Oh, please, you don't understand. I have to kill him."

Rifles were firing from both sides of them. The horsemen must be coming up the hill. He did not look to see. He rolled her over onto her stomach, dragging her belt from her waist, and bound her hands as he had on a previous occasion. There was no point in a gag this time, even if it had been possible to gag her with his handkerchief fluttering halfway down the hill.

"And don't even think of using your legs," he said from between his teeth, rolling to her side again and grabbing for his rifle. "You are like to find one of them broken. You have probably got us all killed."

Some of them, he saw, had ventured up the hill, Colonel Marcel Leroux in the lead. But the riflemen of the British army did not have their deadly reputation for nothing. Two of the horsemen were down and their horses running loose, and the others were clearly hesitant. Attacking a group of riflemen uphill was much like committing suicide, even if they could be sure that there were not hundreds or even thousands of silent troops awaiting them over the crest of the hill.

Joana did not stop pleading with him, though he did not listen. Most of her words went over his head.

"Please, Robert . . . oh, please . . . you must trust me. I must kill him . . . I have waited three years for this moment . . ."

Colonel Leroux was the last to retreat to the valley. His men had withdrawn behind them and stood their horses uncertainly in the valley. But it would have been unnecessary madness to attack. Even Colonel Leroux must have realized that. It was doubtless only Joana's presence at the top of the hill that held him there so long, motionless even though he was well within range of the notoriously accurate rifles.

Finally he turned his horse and joined his men in the valley. A minute later they were returning the way they had come, taking their two wounded with them.

Joana had told him once, Captain Blake reflected, that her knowledge of profane vocabulary was lamentably small. One would not have thought so for the next minute or so. She swore with blistering venom in a grand mixture of English, French, and Portuguese.

"You!" Captain Blake turned on her, his eyes blazing fire, his voice contrastingly icy. "You could not have shot me in the back, could you? You had to endanger all these innocent men. And, yes, those men too. Two of them were injured, perhaps badly. Did you notice that? Merely so that you could make a theatrical gesture for the benefit of your French lover?"

"I hate you." All the frenzied anger had gone from her voice and her eyes and her body. She lay facedown on the ground, her head turned his way, and looked up at him with lifeless eyes. "I will never forgive you for this, Robert. Never."

And then other green-clad figures, each clutching a rifle, his comrades, came running and sliding down the hill toward them.

"It has been so long, I wouldn't have thought to recognize you, sir."

"Who could fail to recognize that crooked nose?"

"Trust you to have a whole company of French cavalry at your heels, you bastard, and to survive it."

"Nice to see you again, sir. There are bets on as to whether you will make it back for the battle or not."

"I'm certainly glad I bet on you, sir."

"You have all the fun, you bastard. I bet the story behind this one would fill a book. Where is she going? Christ Almighty!" Captain Rowlandson had had a good look at Joana. "She's the marquesa, Bob." His eyes were almost popping out of his head.

Joana was walking slowly up the hill, her hands still tied behind her back.

"She won't get far," Captain Blake said grimly. "She is French."

All the riflemen were gazing after Joana with fascination. Captain Rowlandson whistled. "French?" he said.

"Your prisoner, Bob? Well, I always knew you had all the luck. Where the hell have you been?"

"Where I am going is more important," Captain Blake said. "The army is making a stand up ahead?"

The captain grinned at him. "Wait until you see it, Bob," he said. "It's a beaut. Johnny will surrender after one look at it. They thought this was an uphill battle! It's a good thing we were out on patrol in this direction, by the way. Are you coming back with us?"

"I have a few things to do first, Ned," Captain Blake said. "But I'll be there. I would not miss this battle for worlds." He was squinting up to the top of the hill. Joana had disappeared. "I have to go. I'll see you fellows within the next few days. And thank you."

Noisy comments and friendly profanities followed him to the top of the hill.

She had not gone far. There was a pile of large boulders partway down the other side of the hill. She was seated on one of the lower ones, her arms pulled tightly behind her, her head bent forward so that her forehead rested almost on her knees.

By God, Captain Blake thought, striding down toward her, he would have to be careful not to kill her. What he wanted to do was give her a good sound thrashing.

She was not running away. She did not know quite where she was going. She sank down onto the boulder without even consciously choosing the spot. She tried to move her arms and remembered that they were tied. She did not struggle. She let her head fall forward until it almost touched her knees.

It was against her nature to despair. Very rarely was she even depressed. To Joana there was almost always hope, almost always something she could do. She was not a person to admit defeat—normally.

But she admitted it now. Total defeat. Total despair. There had been all those journeys into Spain, in among the French, looking always for one face. And she had found it finally and made her plans. Plans that were far too clever and far too unlikely to succeed. She could see that now. She should have killed him in Salamanca. She must have had dozens of chances there.

She had had another chance ten minutes before. The perfect chance. The one she had dreamed of. And she had failed again because of her own cleverness. She had had several weeks in which to get Robert to believe her story. She could have done it easily. As recently as the evening before, she could have done it. She had sensed then that he had been on the brink of believing her. But no, she had never liked anything to be too easy. She had enjoyed teasing him, keeping him in doubt.

And so she could not blame him for what had just happened, even though she had told him that she hated him and that she would never forgive him. Of course, hearing her yell out like that and seeing her grab her gun like that would have forced him to pounce on her, wrestle the gun from her, and bind her hands. She could not blame him.

And so it was all over. Her chance to avenge Maria's and Miguel's deaths and those of Miguel's family. All over. And all through her own fault. Joana sank deeper into despair. And she watched, fascinated and puzzled, as large drops of water fell onto her knees and darkened the fabric of her dress. She was crying! Misery washed over her.

She did not hear him come up. She saw his boots, a little apart from each other, to one side of her. She knew that soon she would be ashamed of herself and furiously angry with him for having witnessed her misery. But at the moment she was too miserable to care.

She felt hands at her back, deftly freeing her from the bonds of her own belt. She let her hands fall limply to her sides.

"Joana," he said. His voice was as gentle as the hand that came to rest on the top of her head. "I am sorry."

She sniffed and was aware that her nose was dripping as well as her eyes.

"I am a spy," he said, "and therefore deal in the business of deceit. I can hardly blame you for doing the same. And I can hardly blame you for being on the opposite side from me. Your father is French and he works for the French government. And you love him. I am sorry that this has had to happen to you. But this is war and I cannot let you go. You were so close just now. I'm sorry."'

She sniffed again.

"Perhaps the wars will be over soon," he said. "You will be able to go home and marry your Colonel Leroux."

"Robert," she said, "you are so very blind." But her voice sounded abject. She was ashamed of it. "So bloody blind," she said a little more caustically.

"You would have me believe that you really wanted to kill him?" He came down on his haunches and peered up into her face. "But that makes no sense. Why would you want to do that?"

"It does not matter," she said. "You would not believe me anyway."

"Try me," he said.

"I did not want to kill him," she said irritably. "I wanted to kill you so that he would admire me and love me more. Or perhaps I did want to kill him. Perhaps I am offended that he did not prevent my being taken as a hostage. Or perhaps he insulted me in Salamanca. Perhaps he was dallying with me when he already has a wife and I found out. Jealousy can create murderers, you know."

"Looking into your face is like looking at the surface of a shield, you know," he said. "How well do I know you, Joana? Do I know everything? Or do I know nothing? I begin to suspect the latter."

She rubbed at her nose with the back of one hand. "Your shocked friend below the hill should see me now," she said. "I look worse than a fright, don't I?"

"You do rather," he said.

"Thank you," she said. "A gentleman would be pouring out reassuring compliments, Robert."

"Would he?" he said. "But you would know that they were all lies. You lost my handkerchief."

"Then I shall just have to sniff and use the back of my hand," she said.

He drew a rather dirty-looking rag from his pack. "I wrap the muzzle of my rifle with it when it rains," he said. "To keep it dry. You are welcome to it."

She took it from him. "I wonder if there are any lower

depths to which I can sink," she said, drying her eyes and blowing her nose firmly. "I have not bathed in four days or washed my hair or my clothes in a week. I must . . . stink."

"If you were your usual perfumed self," he said with a grin, "you would not be able to stomach me within twenty yards of you, Joana. Perfumes are much overrated, you know."

"And soap too?" she said, wrinkling her nose.

"I would probably sell your musket for a bar right now," he said, and drew a laugh from her. "That is better. I thought that I had lost you."

"I thought you would have been pleased to see me in tears and defeat," she said. "It is what you have always wanted, is it not?"

His smile faded. "I don't want to see your spirit broken, Joana," he said. "These past weeks would have been very dull if you had not been . . . you."

"Well," she said, getting to her feet, "that was almost a declaration of love after all, Robert. Is that as close as you will get?"

"It was a declaration of respect," he said quietly, straightening up too.

She sighed. "This is almost over, is it not?" she said. "I will be sorry. But then, all good things come to an end, just as bad things do. And life goes on. Where do we go now?"

"A zigzag trail to Bussaco," he said, "to make sure we have not missed anyone."

"Lead the way, then," she said. "I am still your prisoner, it seems, but a woman never had a more desirable jailer, I believe. There will still be one more night, Robert? Perhaps two? I am going to make you remember these nights more than all the others put together. I promise."

"Sometimes," he said, "I hope that not everything you say is a lie, Joana."

She laughed. "You will find out," she said. "Tonight. And if I have told the truth about this, then perhaps I have told the truth about everything, Robert. By tomorrow morning you will be tortured by doubts—again—and by guilt. For by tomorrow morning you will be all the way in love with me."

She challenged him with her dazzling smile. Although he never responded openly to it as all other men of her acquaintance had always done, she knew instinctively that it had had its effect.

23

By late afternoon Captain Blake realized that they had walked farther north than they needed to go. They had called at a cluster of houses, too few in number to be dignified by the name of village, and found the inhabitants either gone or on the point of leaving. It seemed that their own people had been there before him, members of the Ordenanza. Nevertheless he decided to continue yet another couple of miles farther north before looping back south again into what would more definitely be the path of the French advance. One of the villagers had mentioned a farm farther north.

"We will rest soon," he told Joana, "and make our way to Mortagoa tomorrow. We will spend one more night there if it is still safe to do so, and then finally we will get behind British lines."

"And I will stay there safely until the end of the great battle," she said with a sigh, "and you will go out in front of it with your riflemen. It is not fair, Robert. Life is not fair to women."

"Or to men," he said. "Depending on which way you look at it."

"The way that men look at it is the only way that counts," she said. "Men believe that women like to be protected and kept safe from all harm."

"And they do not?" he asked her.

"Bah!" was all she would say.

And then, almost before they could lapse into silence, they were both reaching for the sky after Captain Blake had sent his guns clattering to the ground, and they were surrounded by men variously armed, most of them grinning.

"Captain Robert Blake of the Rifles, English army,"

Captain Blake said loudly and distinctly in Portuguese, cursing himself for walking like a novice into an ambush.

"And the woman?" one of the men asked, jerking his head in Joana's direction.

"The mar—" he began.

But she interrupted him. "Joana Ribeiro, sister of Duarte Ribeiro," she said. "And unarmed, you imbeciles. Since when have you begun ambushing your own allies and countrywomen?"

"Jesus!" Captain Blake muttered. There was a curved and wicked-looking knife pointed right at his stomach, no more than four feet off, and a woman beside him who was almost openly inviting its owner to make use of it.

The small, wiry man who appeared to be the leader of the group grinned and looked about at his men, who lowered their weapons. Captain Blake dared to draw breath again.

"The English are all fools," the man said. "They wear scarlet uniforms and expect to blend into the countryside. Almost all the English, at least. Some are sensible enough to wear green. I was not sure, Captain. My apologies."

One of his men picked up both the rifle and the musket and handed them, grinning, to Captain Blake.

News and plans were exchanged during the following hour as the two newcomers shared an evening meal with the Portuguese.

"The French will stay at Viseu for a day or two," the leader told them, "and then they will march west through Mortagoa to Bussaco, where the English and our own army will be waiting for them. It will be a massacre— our own men will have the heights."

It seemed that the men were heading for Viseu that night to harass the French in any way they could. When the army marched from the city, then the Ordenanza would be on their tails as they had been all the way from the border, doing as much damage as they could, trying to prevent their enemy from organizing properly for the battle ahead.

"There is no point in staying up here," one of the men said. "We are too far north to clap eyes on a single

Frenchman. We will miss all the fun. You should come with us, Englishman."

Captain Blake smiled. "My way lies toward the army," he said, "via Mortagoa."

"Ah, yes," the leader said. "That is where Duarte Ribeiro and several of his men live. And their women. The lady will wish to rejoin her kinfolk." He nodded at Joana. "And I daresay Ribeiro will miss the fun for the next day or two. He will be busy moving everyone out ahead of the French. That is your job too, Captain?"

The group of Portuguese were heading south without further delay. But their leader stopped and looked thoughtfully at Captain Blake and Joana before he left.

"I have a small farm and a house not far away," he said, nodding off to the northwest. "I have not burned it, since it is not on the route of the French army, though I have sent my wife and mother and my children away with everyone else just to be on the safe side. You are welcome to stay there for the night, Captain." He grinned. "I did not consider it necessary to lock the doors."

"Thank you." Captain Blake stood to watch the men on their way. "We might just do that."

And the men were gone about their appointed task, a spring in their step, their spirits high now that they were about to get their hands on at least some of the hated enemy at last.

"Well." Captain Blake looked down at Joana, who still sat, her hands clasped about her knees. "Do you want a roof over your head tonight, Joana? It is going to be a chilly night."

"It is so real, is it not?" she said. "The might of France not far to our left, the strength of England and Portugal not far to our right. Battle is inevitable. All within days. No longer weeks, but days. So many men are going to die. Thousands. And perhaps you too, Robert. Are you afraid of dying?"

"Yes," he said as she looked up at him. "I have yet to meet the person, man or woman, who is not. But it is something that we must all do sooner or later. It would be foolish to live our lives in fear of it. It will come when it comes."

"Ah," she said, smiling faintly. "A fatalist. I hope you do not die in this battle."

"Thank you," he said. "So do I."

"Yes." She got to her feet and smiled more fully up into his face. "A roof over our heads, please, Robert. A whole house to ourselves with no one else there at all. We can play house. Shall we?"

"We will spend the night there," he said, "and leave early in the morning."

"But it is still only early evening." She set her fingertips against his chest. "Robert, let us play house for a few hours. Let's find this house and pretend it is ours. Let's go inside and shut out the world and pretend that the whole world is inside with us. Just for a few hours, shall we? We will pretend that we are a very ordinary couple very much in love. Are you good at pretending? But of course you are. You are a good spy. I saw that in Salamanca. Will you pretend this with me?"

"Joana," he said, looking down into her eager, beautiful face, "we are in a dangerous place at a dangerous time. We are in the middle of a war. We are on opposite sides."

"And I am your prisoner," she said. "You forgot to add that detail. Play house with me for one night. For one night let's treat each other just as we would do if nothing else existed or mattered in the whole wide world but the two of us. Will you?"

"Joana—" he said, but she set three fingers over his lips.

"When you say my name like that," she said, "I know you are going to say something stuffy and sensible. Tomorrow or the next day we will be parted. Perhaps we will never meet again. *Probably* we will never meet again. We have been granted the gift of this night, far from the course of the armies, an empty house in which to stay, and no plans to leave until dawn. It is a gift, Robert. Are you willing to throw it away?"

No, he was not. He was tired of fighting her, holding her always at arm's length—even though for the past several weeks he had slept with her almost nightly. He was tired of the barrier between them, tired of always thinking of her as the enemy. And he was quite as aware as

she of the fact that time was running out and that within
the next day or two he would have the difficult and unpleasant task of turning her over to Viscount Wellington
as a French spy. Sometimes he longed to be able to step
outside his life into one more congenial to him.

Not permanently. He liked his life. It was one that he
had made for himself by sheer effort, and he was pleased
with what he had done. But just for a short while. Just
for a few hours.

"Very well, then," he said, his harsh tone at variance
with his words. "For tonight, Joana—until dawn—we will
play house. Let's see if we can find this farm, shall we?"
He shouldered the two guns almost as if he had a quarrel
with them.

And just what had he done now? he wondered as he
strode off in the direction of the deserted farm, Joana at
his side. Had he finally succumbed to her charms just
like all those other poor fools who dogged her footsteps
wherever she went? Was he really going to bare his heart
to her and risk having it hurt? And risk her ridicule?

But it was for only a few hours. Just a short time out
of time. At dawn everything would be back to normal
again.

She had rubbed and rubbed at her hair with a spare
towel until it was almost dry. She felt it with her hand,
felt its dampness and softness, dropped the towel, and
used both hands to work through the tangles and push it
into some style. She felt so deliciously clean that she
closed her eyes and breathed in the smell of herself. And
she smiled.

When they had come into the house, she had turned
to wrap her arms about his neck and kiss his cheek. He
had not offered to kiss hers in return or do more than
pat the sides of her waist with his hands. She had felt
cheated for a moment. He was not going to play after
all. But she knew that men found it more difficult to play
such games than women. And at least he had not put
her away from him.

She had wrinkled her nose. "Robert," she had said,
"I think you stink. I am not quite sure because I believe
I stink too. There will be water here—and a bathtub. Let

us have a bath, shall we? With warm water? Can you imagine a greater luxury?"

"Not without having to think very hard," he had said, and she had smiled more brightly at him. It was the closest Robert had come to joking with her. "So you are going to set me to work hauling water?"

She had smiled dazzlingly. "But think how wonderful it will be in bed tonight," she had said. "Both of us clean and smelling sweet." She had had the satisfaction of seeing his eyes kindling. "And I will work too. I will get a fire going. And to think that usually I bathe every day and take it very much for granted."

That had been more than an hour before. She had bathed first, undressing and stepping into the warm water in the bathtub in the middle of the kitchen without at all worrying that he was in the room too. She had sighed with satisfaction and looked up at him from beneath her lashes. And she had known that he was after all going to play. She had never seen such a naked look of desire on Robert's face.

Now he was bathing and she was waiting for him in the main bedchamber, a towel wrapped about her. Her clothes were hanging above the stove, drying. She bounced once on the bed where she was sitting and found that, yes indeed, it was soft and well-sprung. It was going to be a wonderful place on which to make love.

And then the bedroom door opened and he stepped inside. He was wearing only a towel wrapped about his waist. He looked almost unbearably masculine and virile. His hair, still wet, curled close to his head as it had when she had first met him.

"Robert," she said, swinging one foot, "are you clean again and sweet-smelling?"

He stopped inside the door. "You had better come and find out for yourself," he said.

She smiled and got to her feet. If that was not an irresistible invitation, coming as it did from Robert, then she did not know what would be.

She was indescribably beautiful, he thought, her damp hair in unruly waves about her head and down over her shoulders, her shoulders and arms and legs bare. Her skin had been darkened by the sun during the past weeks, so that many English ladies would have been horrified at the sight of her. But to him she looked healthy and vivid and lovely.

She looked even lovelier when she got to her feet and discarded the towel, dropping it carelessly to the floor. His eyes roamed over her, over the slim legs and rounded hips and small waist, over the firm high breasts to her finely boned shoulders. And to her face, alight with mischief and something else too.

She came up to him and set her nose against his chest and sniffed. She set two cool hands against his shoulders. Her breasts brushed tantalizingly against his chest. He inhaled slowly.

"Mm," she said. "You smell good, Robert." And her hands moved downward to his towel and tossed it backward onto the floor. "This is our own home and our own bedchamber, and the night is ahead of us. What shall we do?"

"This for a start," he said. And he gazed into her dark eyes while he twined his fingers in her hair and lowered his mouth to hers, his tongue reaching out ahead of him. He saw her open her mouth before closing his eyes.

He had not kissed her since the night they had become lovers. He had been too intent during the weeks since on convincing both himself and her that what he did with her was done merely to satisfy a physical need. Kissing implied more than the physical. There was something very personal and intimate about kissing—more intimate, strangely enough, than the actual act of coupling.

Her mouth was soft and warm. Inside it was hot and wet and inviting. She moaned.

She had wanted him to kiss her. For so long she had wanted it. Intimate as they had been for weeks, there had always been something missing. Some closeness. Some tenderness. And now suddenly it was all there—because he was kissing her deeply and because they were naked together and because they were in their bedchamber in their own house, a whole night ahead of them.

"Robert." She stroked one hand through his hair as his mouth burned a path down over her chin and along her throat to find the pulse at its base. "Robert, this is more than physical, is it not? Tell me that it is more."

And his face was above hers again, and he was gazing down into her eyes. There was depth in his, so that she knew her answer with almost frightening intensity. She had never wanted this of any man, had never expected it. She had wanted always to be in control. She could never be in control if she allowed him to look at her like this and say the words that accompanied the look—and if she responded to both.

And yet always, always in her dreams she had wanted nothing else but this. Oh, surely far back in dreams she had wanted this. This was all she could ever want of life. There was nothing else. Oh, there was nothing.

And he looked down at her and saw the vulnerability, heard the words she had spoken and the ones she had not yet spoken but perhaps would if he replied as he wished. And he was terrified. For if the words were spoken, then they were not playing house at all. There would be no game involved, but only naked reality.

And he did not want reality. He wanted a night of make-believe. That was what he had agreed to. But, God . . . oh, God, she was beautiful. And not just the more-than-lovely body that he held naked in his arms. *She* was beautiful.

"Hush, Joana," he said, his mouth against her ear. "Let's not talk. Let's make love. Sometimes the body can speak more eloquently than words."

"Make love?" She turned her head and smiled slowly into his eyes. "We are going to make love, Robert? At last?"

"Yes." His mouth was on hers again. "We will make love, Joana. On the bed, if you please. We are too different in height to be comfortable standing."

"It is such a lovely bed," she said, drawing away from him and leading him by the hand toward it. "It is large and soft. And look at all the warm covers we may pull over ourselves afterward."

"Afterward?" he said. "Who said anything about afterward?"

She had never heard him tease so. She lay down on the bed and smiled up at him. She still held his hand. "I thought perhaps I might exhaust you before dawn," she said.

"Now, that," he said, lying down on his side next to her and propping himself on one elbow, "is a challenge pure and simple. We shall see who exhausts whom."

Her breath was coming fast. She had never seen him like this, relaxed and teasing, a smile lurking in his eyes. Ah, she had never seen him like this. He was wonderful almost beyond bearing. She lifted a hand and set her palm against his cheek.

"Robert," she said, "you have had much experience with women, have you not? No, don't answer. It was a rhetorical question. Use all that experience on me tonight. Will you? All of it? I want all. Please?"

"On one condition," he said. "That you use all your expertise on me. We will see who has the most to teach, shall we?"

Oh, dear God, if he only knew! Joana smiled. "And who can learn more quickly," she said. "Robert." She was whispering. "Make love to me."

"Joana." He was smiling at her as his head lowered to hers. "Make love to me."

God, he should never have agreed to her insane suggestion, he thought. For he knew even before his mouth touched hers and she turned on the bed to set her full naked length against him that dawn would come far, far too soon. A lifetime too soon. For pretense had only succeeded in opening the door wide to reality. And reality frightened and grieved him. He should have stayed out in the hills with her and taken her for his pleasure again beneath the inadequate warmth of their blankets. He should have kept telling himself and kept telling himself that it was purely for pleasure.

He touched her with his hands, and his hands could not do enough touching. And he touched her with his mouth, and his mouth and his tongue and his teeth could not have enough of her. And she was touching him, her hands and her mouth roaming over him as freely as his own over her. His arousal, his need to plunge his seed into her, was a painful throbbing. And yet he did not want to stop the touching. He did not want to be past the glorious anticipation—not yet.

His hand parted her legs, his thumb pushing at one, his fingers at the other. And he was touching her there, where she had not expected him to put his hand. And at first she was embarrassed to have him touch her there, and embarrassed at the knowledge that she was wet, embarrassed by the sound of wetness. But he sighed with satisfaction and she relaxed and knew that the sound was erotic and that the wetness was a part of her female response, an invitation to an easy penetration of her body. She set the soles of her feet together and let her knees drop almost to the bed.

And she stopped touching him in the wonder of what was happening to her own body. Fingers feathering over her, sliding up inside her, and then his thumb, so light that at first she did not feel it, rubbing over one small spot, arousing an instant and almost unbearable ache that spread inward and upward into her throat.

"Robert." She whispered his name. Her eyes were closed. "Robert." Her hands pressed down hard against the bed.

He had not expected her to surrender so totally to the caressing of his hand. And yet he found her total absorption in what he did to her more exciting even than her hands on him had been a few moments before. He raised himself on one elbow again and watched her. He watched her mouth open and her head tip back.

"Ah," she said, and she drew in breath audibly through her mouth.

He watched her whole body tense.

"Robert," she said again, and there was agony in the sound.

And there was agony in him too as he stroked with his thumb and brought her to climax. She was Joana, he thought. She was not just any woman whom it was his pleasure to pleasure. He had always enjoyed bringing his women pleasure as well as himself. But it was not that with Joana. That was not it at all. She was Joana. He was not just pleasuring her. He was loving her.

She shouted out suddenly, agony and ecstasy in the sound. He set his hand flat against her during the minute or more while she shuddered into stillness.

The feelings of relaxation and well-being were almost not to be fought against. The urge to slide into a delicious sleep was almost overpowering. Except that his hand remained over her and she could feel that he was still up on his elbow looking down at her. And except that nothing had happened—nothing that she normally associated with making love. He had not been inside her.

She turned her head and opened her eyes. She looked up at him and smiled lazily. "You won that round," she said. "How did that happen? How did you know to do that?" Her eyes strayed downward. He was still fully aroused, she could see.

He bent his head and kissed her warmly on the lips. "You are not going to give in to defeat quite so easily, are you?" he said. "How disappointing."

But she did not know what to do. She knew nothing except what she had learned with him. But even under present circumstances she was not about to resist a challenge. She smiled into his eyes and reached down a hand to touch him. Then she reached down the other hand and cupped him in her two hands, rolling them lightly about him, touching the tip lightly with her thumb. She heard him inhale.

"Come inside me," she said. But there she could only allow him to complete his pleasure.

She turned onto her back, opened herself for him, lifted to him as he slid into her wetness. And she wished she knew more. She wished she had experience to match his own.

She acted from instinct. She nudged her legs beneath his so that he was forced to widen his own about her. And she held her legs together and moved, twisting her hips rhythmically against him, drawing him tight into her with inner muscles.

"God, Joana," he said urgently, his arms coming up to grip her shoulders, "do you want me to come like a schoolboy?"

She kissed the underside of his chin. "How does a schoolboy come?" she said. "Show me."

"Very fast," he said with a gasp, and he moved in her with a frenzy of need.

God, he thought. God, the witch! And he had been beginning to imagine that perhaps she was not as experienced as he had thought after all.

He exploded in her with a cry and lost himself for the

following few minutes, or hours—he could not be at all sure which. She was stroking one hand over his back and one through his hair when he came to himself. He was still embedded in her, her legs tight together about him.

"I must have squashed every bone in your body," he said.

"Have you?" She turned her head to kiss his shoulder. "Then it feels wonderful to have every bone broken. Did we do equally well on that round, Robert? And are we going to compete for the rest of the night? I would prefer simply to make love."

He moved to her side and set his arms about her. She snuggled into him and sighed.

"Joana," he said, "we ought not to have started this."

But she lifted her head sharply and kissed him on the mouth. "There is no such thing as reality before dawn," she said. "No such thing at all, Robert. You must not spoil this night. Oh, please, you must not."

But it was spoiled nonetheless. For somewhere not far behind the pretense was the reality. A reality that was perhaps not painful for her, for reality for her was an artificial world where she piled up conquests for her own amusement. But for him reality was going to be painful indeed.

"Reality?" he said against her mouth. "What is that?"

"I don't know," she said. "I have never heard of it. Robert?"

"Mm?" he said.

"Will you give me the sunrise tomorrow?" She lifted a hand and set it over his mouth. "Don't you remember at Obidos? What you said about ribbons and stars and the sunrise?"

Yes, he remembered. God, he remembered.

She should not have asked that question. She closed her eyes and buried her face against his chest. She should not have asked. Because the ribbons and stars and sunrise were what he would give his love, and his answer could bring her pain. *Oh, Robert,* she pleaded with him silently, *please give me the sunrise. Please give me the sunrise.*

But she knew he could not. And she knew she had spoiled the night for herself.

"The sunrise comes after the dawn," he said quietly, and his hand smoothed over her head.

"And so it does." She lifted her head and smiled at him. "But what comes before dawn, Robert? Anything else? Or have I succeeded in exhausting you already?"

A great deal came before dawn. They loved and dozed and loved and dozed. And each privately gloried in their love and each privately grieved at the imminence of dawn. And finally they lay together, passion spent, waiting for the moment when daylight would begin to gray the windows and there would be nothing to do but get up and dress themselves and resume their roles as jailer and prisoner.

She might have pleaded with him and tried to persuade him of the truth. It would not have been impossible, she believed. But she would not do it. Dawn had still not come and she was jealous of their one night of love. It was he who finally spoke.

"Joana," he said, one arm beneath her head, his hand playing with her hair. "That first love of yours?"

"Robert?" She smiled and turned her head to him. "Is it not a coincidence that you have the same name?"

"Not really," he said. "Joana, he did not boast to the servants about you. He did not call you a French bitch— not at that time, anyway."

She looked at him and frowned slightly. "You think not?" she said. "I don't think so either."

"He loved you totally," he said, "as perhaps only a seventeen-year-old can. He did not lie when he said he loved you, though he did not want to say it aloud. And he did not lie when he said he would come for you on a white charger on your eighteenth birthday and ride off into the sunrise with you. I suppose he knew he would never do any such thing, but he spoke the heart's truth. That is what he passionately wished he could do."

She was staring at him in the near-darkness, wide-eyed.

"If he is precious to your memory," he said, "then know that the memory can be unsullied. If you have ever harbored doubts, however faint, you can discard them. He did not do those things."

Still she said nothing.

"He was deeply hurt," he said, "at being told that you would never seriously have given your love and your troth to a bastard. Even though he knew your words to be true, he was hurt. And hurt by his father's laughter that he had dared raise his eyes to the daughter of a count. He decided on that day that he would never again lay himself open to people's contempt. He decided to make his own way in life, starting at the bottom and ending there too if he could not raise himself up by his own efforts. He has not done badly. You can console yourself with that knowledge, Joana, if he is still of any importance to you. Your Robert is well-satisfied with what he has done with his life. There was no smallpox, you see. He did not die—at least, not yet."

"He had his mother's name," she said, "not his father's." She was whispering as if she thought they might have been overheard. "What was it? What was his mother's name?"

"Blake," he said. "Her name was Blake." He closed his eyes.

The silence seemed to stretch forever.

"Robert," she said at last, and he hardly recognized her voice. It sounded lost, hurt. "Ah, Robert."

"It was a long time ago," he said. "A very long time. He is a different person, Joana, except in name. And you are a different person. It was all so long ago. Way back in the age of innocence. But he is alive. And he did love you."

"Ah, Robert," she said again. And there was such pain in her voice that he could think of no way of comforting her.

They lay waiting for the dawn in silence.

24

"JOAQUINA gave it to me," Carlota said, setting the large and battered gun down carefully in a corner. "She said she would never have the courage to use it, and I said I would, and so she gave it to me. Don't laugh at me, Duarte. Anything but that. *Don't laugh at me.*"

Duarte laughed. "It must surely be one of the first guns ever made," he said. "You would probably blow yourself to bits with it, Carlota, if you ever fired it. So you chose to stay and fight, did you, instead of running for safety? I must admit I would have been surprised not to find you here when I came."

"And now you have come," she said warily, "you are going to try to shoo me off westward with Miguel, aren't you? But you can forget it, Duarte, and if you are planning to argue, then I am sorry that you came home at all. I have known nothing but boredom and inaction for weeks—though it seems more like months—and now by some good fortune the French have stumbled on this ungodly route to the west. And you expect me to miss the opportunity of a lifetime? You do, don't you?"

"Carlota—" he began.

"You do," she said, hands on hips. "Well, I won't go. I will go up into the hills with you and see what I can do to trouble the army as it passes. And Miguel will come too. This is his country, his birthright, as well as ours. And if you do not like it, then I shall go alone. I shall find another band to which to attach myself. And if you will not provide me with a decent weapon, then I shall take this one and blow myself into a million pieces with my first shot. Stop laughing at me."

"I love you," he said, silencing her effectively. "And there is no fight left in me—not for you anyway. Up into the hills we go together, then. Joana has not been this way, you said? Nor Captain Blake? I thought they would have come to warn you."

"Two dozen men at the very least have come to warn us," she said. "There have been nothing but warnings. And always the French are at the very heels of those who warn. And yet I have not set eyes on a blue uniform yet."

"The foolish woman has not told him the truth," Duarte said. "Or at least she has not insisted that he listen to the truth. She is teasing him with the impression that she is a spy for the French."

"Yes," Carlota said, "Joana would tease. Good for her. If that man did not believe her the first time she told him, why should she beg and plead with him?"

"She is his prisoner," Duarte said with a grin. "I would bet that a jailer has never been so plagued."

"Ho," Carlota said, "and what a jailer. I would bet that Joana is enjoying every moment of her captivity."

"I think she is," Duarte said. "But if they do come this way, Carlota, we must follow her lead. I believe she does not even know you. She has been accused of flirting with me and trying to take me away from you."

"And that handsome Captain Blake is pitying me, I do not doubt," Carlota said, hands on hips again. "Men! Why must they always assume that women are poor helpless cringing creatures?"

"Probably because they do not all know you or Joana," he said, still grinning.

The French were still at Viseu, and there were enough men between there and Mortagoa to sound the alarm if they marched unexpectedly early. There was all day in which to pack what must be taken and to destroy what must be left behind. There was no great sense of rush, although a home was to be broken up within twenty-four hours. But then, both Carlota and Duarte had known homes broken far more bitterly just a few years before, and since that time they had lived with impermanence. They felt no great unhappiness on this occasion.

"It is so good to be back with you and our son," Duarte said, catching Carlota to him at some time during the afternoon. "You cannot imagine, Carlota, how lonely it has been without you."

"Can I not?" she said, and her voice became indignant. "Oh, can I not indeed?"

But he hugged her and kissed her and refused to quarrel. "We have each other and Miguel," he said when she finally returned his kisses. "That is all that really matters, isn't it?"

"Yes," she said fiercely against his mouth. "And having a country in which to live together freely."

Captain Blake and Joana arrived late in the afternoon, the former knocking at the open door and peering into the dark, bare interior. Duarte strode to the door and clasped his hand.

"You made it safely this far, then," he said. "Good. You are only a few miles from Bussaco, where the army is gathered. Did you know?"

"I will be with them tomorrow," Captain Blake said. "I guessed you would be here, but we came to warn Carlota just in case she had not heard."

"Had not heard?" Carlota said, raising her eyes to the ceiling, but crossing the room nevertheless to greet their guest. "I have heard nothing else for the past week. I am so delighted that the French have proved stupid enough to come this way that I hardly know how to contain my excitement. I am glad you got safely out of Spain, Captain."

"With Duarte's help," he said, and he stood aside to reveal a smiling Joana. "Do you know the Marquesa das Minas?"

Carlota knew that he was looking at her keenly. "Everyone knows the marquesa," she said. "Welcome."

"Carlota?" Joana said, smiling more broadly. "And where is the baby?"

"Miguel?" Carlota said. "Sleeping and quite unperturbed by the fact that his first home is being destroyed around him. Come and see him."

Joana took a step forward, but she turned first to Duarte before following Carlota into the inner room. "Duarte," she said, stretching out both hands to his. "How lovely to see you again."

He grinned at her and squeezed her hands. "Hello, Joana," he said.

"Is she your sister?" Captain Blake asked abruptly when the women had disappeared to look at the baby.

"Does she say she is my sister?" Duarte grinned.

"Yes." Captain Blake looked grim. "Half-sister. She says that you have the same mother. Do you?"

"If Joana says it," Duarte said, "then it must be true, mustn't it? Would she lie? She must be my sister if she says so—pardon me, my half-sister."

Captain Blake looked somewhat exasperated. "Very well," he said. "I'm sorry I asked. What news have you had today?"

"The French are still at Viseu," Duarte said. "But they will surely move tomorrow, unless they are cowardly enough to turn tail and run. Since they have come this far through impossible country, I think that unlikely. And Lord Wellington has moved all his forces up from south of the Mondego, where they were expecting to do battle. They have such a good position at Bussaco that one almost feels sorry for the French. Almost." He grinned again. "But not quite."

"God," the captain said, "it is so long since I was in an all-out battle. I missed Talavera last year by a day. A forced march from Lisbon in a time that still has people gaping in wonder, and still we missed it by a day."

"And thereby perhaps you missed your death by one day too," Duarte said. The women had come back from the inner room. "You will stay here with us tonight? You can have the inner room, Joana. Captain Blake can sleep out here with us."

Joana smiled dazzlingly. "But I am Robert's prisoner, remember?" she said. "He is not willing to let me out of his sight for longer than five minutes at a time, especially at night. Are you, Robert? We will share the inner room. Are you outraged, Duarte?" She turned her smile on the captain. "Brothers sometimes are, at such situations."

"The inner room is yours, then," Duarte said. "Carlota and I will sleep out here with the baby. Tomorrow we will all leave early. With any luck, some real action will begin tomorrow."

They sat eating and quietly talking among themselves and with other members of the band and their women who were still at the village, until darkness fell, and then retired to hard beds on the floor.

"Duarte," Carlota whispered, curling up close to him after she had soothed a fussing baby, "did you see her? Did you see Joana?"

"I have not had my eyes closed all day," he said. "I would say that those who worship the Marquesa das Minas would simply not recognize her now. A dress more faded and ragged than ever. Hair tangled and unkempt. Skin bronzed like a peasant's. That unladylike stride."

"Oh, yes, yes," she said impatiently. "But I meant *her*, Duarte. Her eyes. It has finally happened to her, hasn't it? I always said it would one day."

"I would say they are certainly lovers," he said. "They would both have to be made of stone not to be, since it seems they are compelled to spend their nights together."

"Oh, not just lovers, you fool," she said. "She loves him, Duarte. She worships him. It is there in her face for all the world to see. Joana has never loved anyone, for all her hordes of worshipers."

"Yes," he said, "I see it too, Carlota. And the same look in his face, for that matter, hard and disciplined as it is. But it will not do, you know. She is an aristocrat both by birth and by marriage. He is apparently a nobody and has made the army his career. They are from two worlds that can never meet, except briefly and under strange circumstances like this."

"Oh, fool," Carlota said. "Idiot. Men can be so stupid. As if such things matter when the heart is involved. You are a nobleman and I am a doctor's daughter. Does the difference keep us apart? Or perhaps you don't intend to marry me after all."

"You must admit," he said, "that the difference between us is somewhat less extreme than that between them. And I intend to be married by the very next priest we encounter—whether you like it or not."

"Well," she said, "I will think about it. Are you intending to spend our first night together since I-don't-remember-when talking?"

"Not I," he said, turning toward her. "Talk on if you wish, Carlota, but I have better things to do."

"I too," she said. "I have missed you."

"Mm," he said. "Show me how much."

The high ridge of Bussaco ran ten miles northward from the great perpendicular cliff rising from the Mondego River. Its top was bare apart from some heather and spiky aloes and the occasional pine tree, and apart from a few stone windmills and the Convent of Bussaco, two miles from its northern end.

Viscount Wellington had taken up quarters at the convent, together with his staff. The two armies under his command, the British and the Portuguese, were strung out in a somewhat thin line across the entire ten miles of the ridge.

But the apparent weakness of the lines was deceptive. They were on top of the heights, or, to be more accurate, beyond the top, out of sight of anyone approaching from the east. There would be no way of an advancing French army knowing for sure that they were there or of estimating their exact position or numbers. And the French now had no other way of advancing westward and ultimately southward to Lisbon. Their way lay over the ridge of Bussaco.

And finally Massena and his army were on the move. On September 25 they passed through Mortagoa, only eight miles from Bussaco.

Somehow, Joana thought, trudging after Captain Blake over the rugged and wooded country below Bussaco on that same day, the news had filtered through. They met few people between Mortagoa and Bussaco, but all those people knew that the French had left Viseu, that the battle would take place very soon, perhaps even the next day.

She was feeling unaccountably depressed. They were nearing the English and relative safety. Soon, before the day was out, she would be back where she had started from, reporting success to Viscount Wellington, the Marquesa das Minas again. Matilda would be waiting for her, she would wager, or at least would have made some arrangements for her comfort. The following day, while the battle was being fought, she could be making her way farther back into safety. And it would be safety—she knew about the Lines of Torres Vedras.

She had nothing to feel depressed about. But of course she did. Did she hope to fool herself by claiming that she was *unaccountably* depressed? Of course she was depressed.

Captain Blake turned back to look at her. "You are all right, Joana?" he asked.

She smiled brightly at him. "Am I likely to complain of blisters or fatigue at this late date?" she asked.

But he did not walk on as he had done after several similar stops that day. "Joana," he said, "it is possible to respect and even to admire an enemy, you know. I respect you and admire you. You have an indomitable spirit."

"Ah," she said, "but I am not an enemy, Robert."

"Your supposed sister-in-law did not know you yesterday," he said quietly.

"Perhaps she was playing my game," she said. "Duarte has a strong sense of fun."

He looked at her and nodded slightly before turning to walk on. She flexed aching legs before following along after him. And she felt so mortally depressed that she did not know how she would smile if he turned to her again.

She was in love with him—deeply, irrevocably in love. And not just in love. She loved him. He was the man she had looked for unconsciously all her life, her gentle, poetic Robert transformed by time and circumstances into a tough, self-reliant man of firm principle and hidden passion. Robert—her long-dead, bitterly mourned Robert—resurrected. And the uncanny resemblance she had always noticed was uncanny no longer. And her attraction to him was no longer a mystery. Or her love for him. She had always known that she would never stop loving her Robert—Robert Blake. And she had not.

And yet the tough, scarred body and the hard, damaged, attractive face! They were Robert's? Her Robert's? She felt somehow like crying for the lost boy, for his shattered dreams, for the pain she and his father had caused him between them. And yet she could not cry for the man he had become. For though tough and hard, he was proud and sensitive too. He was not a bitter man. And alive. Her father had lied to her. Robert was alive!

She loved him. And later on this very day she would be saying good-bye to him—again. The thought was enough to make her feel panic. He would discover his mistake, of course, and would know that they were not enemies. But he would be mortified—and she would not be innocent. She had shamefully misled him because it had been fun to do so. Fun! Her stomach felt like a lead weight in her. He would be angry. He would not be able to leave her fast enough.

And even if he were not, even if he were willing to forgive her and shake her by the hand, still they must part. For she had the life of a marquesa to resume and he had a battle to fight. Perhaps a battle to die in. She stumbled against one of the rough boulders on the hillside and went down painfully on one knee, and he was beside her in an instant, catching her beneath her elbow with one firm hand.

"Oh, Robert." She snapped at him in quite uncharacteristic fashion and snatched her arm away. "Don't fuss. I shall survive."

He stood looking down at her silently while she rubbed her knee. She looked up at him and swallowed.

"Will you?" she asked, and she could hear that her voice was not quite steady. "Will you survive?"

"I always have," he said.

"And does 'always' include tomorrow?" she asked him.

He said nothing, but looked down at her broodingly. And then she was in his arms, her face hidden against his coat—she thought that she had probably put herself there.

"Oh," she said, "I hate situations over which I have no control. I don't care how difficult or dangerous something is, provided I can control it or at least have a good chance of doing so. I have been able to control almost everything else in my life. Except leaving you that first time. And except marrying Luis. I could control what happened in Lisbon. I could control what happened in

Salamanca. But this I cannot control. I wish I were going into battle too. Then I would feel better."

"Joana . . ." he said.

"I would," she told him passionately. "If I could fight alongside you, Robert, I would not be afraid at all. I would laugh with the excitement of it all. I swear I would. I hate being a woman!"

"I love your being a woman," he said, and his arms were about her and he was hugging her tightly to him.

"And I hate this," she said. "This womanly hysteria and clinging. I hate myself. Let me go at once." She pushed at his chest and tossed her hair back from her face. "If you would not be hovering over me just like a guardian angel every time I cough or stumble, Robert, I would do very nicely indeed. Kindly walk on and let me follow you in my own way. I promise you that I will get there under my own power or die in the attempt. Go!"

He went after looking steadily into her eyes for several uncomfortable moments. She wished his eyes were not blue—so gloriously blue. She hated his eyes. She kicked at the rock that had tripped her, grimaced, and climbed on.

And even if he forgave her, and even if he survived, there could be no possible future for them. None. They were who they were and nothing had changed since he was seventeen and she fifteen. Though he was the son of the Marquess of Quesnay, he was as much a bastard now as he had been then. And she was as much her father's daughter. And now she was Luis's widow and carried around with her her ridiculous title and was burdened with her enormous wealth and consequence.

Even if he forgave her and even if he survived, there were realities to be faced. They would not meet after today, or if they did, it would be as remote strangers.

"Well," she said crossly, speaking much more loudly than she needed to, "you don't have to walk so fast just to prove to me that I am not your equal and cannot keep up." They were climbing a particularly steep part of the hill.

He stopped immediately and turned to look at her and wait for her to come up with him. "Joana," he said, and there was a smile lurking in his eyes, "I have never heard you complaining so much."

"I am not complaining!" she said. "I am merely out of breath."

He took her by surprise by cupping her face with both hands and lowering his head to kiss her softly on the lips. "I know this is difficult for you," he said. "More difficult, I daresay, than for me, though I do not know how that could be. I'm sorry. Believe me when I say I am sorry."

"Are you forgetting," she said, "that I had you beaten in Salamanca and arranged it so that there were four against one? Are you forgetting that I had you thrown in a prison cell and beaten daily?"

"No." He took his hands from her face. "That all seems such a long time ago. Have you caught your breath again?"

"Robert," she said, and she looked at him with unaccustomed earnestness, "I have deceived you dreadfully and quite deliberately. But not maliciously. Will you remember that? It is just that I must always take up a challenge. I cannot seem to help myself. And I can never resist teasing, especially those I like best. Will you forgive me when you remember this conversation?"

"This is war, Joana," he said. "There is no point in bearing grudges. We have both done what we must do in this conflict."

She sighed. "But I of course have done a little more than that," she said. "Continue on your way, Robert, and don't you dare move like a funeral procession merely because I just accused you of walking too fast. You were right. I am in a bad mood and I am never in a bad mood and do not know how to handle it. We are almost at the top. Is there really an army just the other side? It looks almost deserted."

"Just the way the Beau wants it to look," he said. "I believe the French will be suspicious of every bare and silent slope before these wars are at an end." There were some pickets on the slope, but no sign of a whole army.

He strode onward, a little more slowly than before despite her warning, and she kept pace with him.

And there was that other thing too, the thing that had dominated her life for three years and had only recently paled in significance beside her growing love for Robert and her equally growing knowledge that only an inevitable parting awaited them.

She had failed. She had persevered against all the odds until she had seen him again, the man who had raped and killed Maria, and then she had failed to kill him. She had had her chance—the perfect chance. And yet she had failed. And now it seemed that she could never succeed. Soon she would be behind the whole of the British and Portuguese armies in their seemingly impregnable position, and there was no chance that she would see Colonel Leroux again.

Unless she went back to the French side. She could still do that, she supposed. They still thought her loyal. They still thought she had been taken against her will, as a hostage. It was probable, though, that they would not think so for very much longer, not once they had come up against the solid barrier of the Lines of Torres Vedras. Then they would know that she had deceived them, that she worked for the British, not for them.

She had failed. Joana hated to fail. She had never yet given in to failure. And yet it seemed that on this occasion she must. She was mortally depressed.

And then suddenly they were on the crest of the hill and her eyes widened in shock even though prior knowledge had led her to expect the sight. An army—a whole vast and busy army—was stretched out for as far as she could see on either side of her, just out of sight of anyone even a few feet down the eastern slope.

"Jesus!" she heard Captain Blake say.

The Convent of Bussaco was about a mile to the north of them.

No one recognized her and she recognized no one. Not that she looked at anyone to recognize him despite the cheerful comments and catcalls and whistles that were thrown her way as she passed beside Captain Blake. All the other women—wives and camp followers—were well away from the crest of the ridge, in the rear with the baggage.

This was it, she kept thinking. The end. And she could not even say a proper good-bye to him. All would be done in public from this moment on.

The convent looked familiar and yet strange too, bustling as it was with military men and activities instead of basking in its usual quiet peace. Joana smiled at one man, a major, who had favored her with an openly appreciative glance as he hurried past and then returned his gaze, startled, for a second look.

"Yes, it is I, George," she said gaily. "A wonderful disguise, would you not say?"

But the major said nothing—or not in her hearing, anyway. She whisked herself onward to keep up with Captain Blake's lengthened stride. He looked grim and remote, and she was reminded of an earlier impression that she would not like to be his enemy facing him in battle.

Headquarters was incredibly busy. No one walked, it seemed. Everyone ran. At first Joana thought that no one would take any notice of either of them, and she smiled at the thought of how everyone would have stopped at least to take notice if she were dressed as the marquesa. Oh, yes, they would, she thought, even if every sign about her indicated that something of great significance was about to happen.

But finally they were admitted to the presence of Lord Fitzroy Somerset, Lord Wellington's chief secretary, and he nodded to Captain Blake and expressed his satisfaction at his safe return, and he smiled at Joana despite her appearance and made her a courtly bow and offered her a chair.

"His lordship will be pleased to see and hear from both of you," he said. "But not today, I am afraid. You will understand, Captain, that there are a thousand demands on every moment of his time. Ma'am, your companion insisted that a room be reserved here for your convenience. A trunk of yours is there, I believe. I shall have you escorted there."

"That cannot happen, I am afraid," Captain Blake said stiffly. "The Marquesa das Minas is my prisoner, sir. She was taken as a hostage from Salamanca and has been in my custody ever since. She is or has been a French agent."

Lord Somerset's eyes looked to Joana in some surprise and she smiled dazzlingly at him. "I think perhaps, my lord," she said, "we should become the thousand and first demand on Arthur's time."

25

SHE did not want it to be this way. She did not want him to discover the truth in front of other people, least of all Viscount Wellington. Arthur would look through him with those piercing eyes of his and explain the truth in a few succinct words, and Robert would be humiliated—a British spy who had made such a foolish mistake. She did not want him to be humiliated.

She should have forced the truth on him when they were alone together, she thought. She could have done it if she had set her mind to it and if it had not been so delightfully amusing to lead him astray. She could have done it at Mortagoa, with Duarte and Carlota to back her story. Instead of which she had allowed them to play along with her. How dreadful she was.

Lord Wellington really was very busy, it seemed. Lord Somerset took them into a more private room, and she seated herself with all the grace she would have shown if she were dressed in her marquesa's finery—it was amazing how one reverted to habit when one's environment changed—while Robert stood stiffly, his back half to her, telling the secretary all about her. She frowned when Lord Somerset's eyes strayed to her, and she rubbed a finger across her lips, silencing his comments.

"My lord," she said, getting to her feet when Robert had finished his story, aware that her regal bearing and manner must seem remarkably ridiculous when combined with her wild and rather ragged appearance, "I believe Captain Blake is eager to return to his regiment. He has given enough of his time to guarding me. Perhaps you have a moment to convey me to my room. You will, of course, set a suitably strong guard outside it until Arthur can deal with me himself."

Perhaps he need not know at all. Not yet, at least.

"That would seem to be the best idea," Lord Somerset said, frowning. "Wait here, Captain Blake, if you please."

She swept from the room ahead of the secretary. Robert was still standing in the middle of the room, like a marble statue, looking away from her. They did not even exchange a good-bye.

"Joana?" Lord Somerset spoke as soon as the door was closed behind him. "Your deception was so good that Captain Blake still does not know the truth?"

She turned to smile brightly and apologetically at him. "Oh, I did tell him," she said, "but he did not believe me and I did not insist that he lay to rest his doubts. It was too amusing to foster them, I'm afraid. He must not know, Fitzroy. It would be too dreadfully mortifying for him." But it was so hard to smile when she felt as if her heart was breaking.

As fortune would have it, a distant door opened at that moment to reveal a flurry of voices, and Viscount Wellington himself strode into the long corridor in which they stood, three aides hurrying after him. He stopped.

"Ah, Joana," he said, his eyes sweeping her keenly from head to toe, "you are safely back, are you? That is a relief to know. I had heard, of course, that you were safely out of Spain. And events have proved that you must have been successful there. Captain Blake is safe too?"

"Yes," she said, "and itching to return to his regiment, Arthur."

"You must leave without delay," he said. "Before nightfall. This is going to be too dangerous a spot for a lady by tomorrow."

"I thrive in dangerous spots," she said with a smile.

"But not this one," he said. "I shall get someone to escort you to safety. Fitzroy, look to it, will you? Send Blake. He deserves something of a break from active duty."

"Captain Blake believes—" Lord Somerset began, but Joana laid a hand lightly on his sleeve and smiled her most dazzling smile.

"Oh, very well," she said. "I will not argue, Arthur,

as I can see that you are dreadfully busy. Fitzroy will get Robert to escort me to Lisbon."

Lord Wellington nodded briskly and hurried on his way, his aides close at his heels. Joana stared after him for a moment before drawing a deep breath and turning back to Lord Somerset, her smile still firmly in place.

"You must be frantically busy too, Fitzroy," she said, her hand still on his sleeve, "and wishing me a thousand miles away. Let us return to Robert and tell him of his new assignment. But I shall do the talking. Will you bear me out?"

"Certainly," he said, and he turned back to the room they had just vacated and opened the door. She preceded him through it.

Captain Blake was standing where they had left him, staring fixedly at the floor. He looked up at the opening of the door and his eyes met Joana's blankly. He looked as hard as nails, she thought, as if he were quite incapable of any human feeling. He looked like the quintessential soldier.

"We ran into Arthur in the hallway," she said with a sigh. "Literally ran into him. He was very vexed with me, Robert, but of course he has no time to deal with me today and no soldiers to be spared to guard me." She smiled. "It seems that I am a prisoner whom no one wants. What a dreadful fate! I thought I would be hailed as the most dangerous spy of the wars and put on public display surrounded by a score of guards all armed to the teeth or something like that. It is quite lowering to find I am nothing but a nuisance. You are to keep me tight and safe, it seems, until this battle is over."

"Joana—" Lord Somerset said. But she swung around to face him and widened her smile.

"Oh, you need not be apologetic, Fitzroy," she said. "It was a good game while it lasted. And Captain Blake will look after me as well as he has done since we left Salamanca. I am quite sure he will not let me escape, alas. You may go about your business. I know you are anxious to do so."

He looked at her frowningly for a few moments, hesitated, and then nodded curtly to both of them and left the room, closing the door behind him.

Joana turned and smiled at Captain Blake. "I am sorry, Robert," she said. "You must be wishing me in perdition."

He still looked like granite, standing in the middle of the room, staring at her. "Lord Wellington has not made arrangements to send you back to safety?" he asked.

"He knows I will be safe with you," she said. "But I will not be a burden to you, Robert, you will see. I know that you want nothing more than to return to your company now and prepare them and yourself for tomorrow's battle—I believe it really is going to be tomorrow, is it not? You shall do that, and I shall sit quietly in your tent—do you have a tent? If not, then I shall sit quietly on the ground, and I shall spend tomorrow with the other women at the rear. What do you say? Are you very vexed?"

He stared at her for a few silent moments. "Bloody hell!" he said finally.

Joana smiled.

Normally he had no trouble sleeping even under the most adverse of conditions. He had trained himself over the years to sleep even on muddy ground with the rain beating down on him and danger all about him. It was a simple matter of survival, for a man who had not slept was a weaker man than one who had, and strength was everything when it came to soldiering.

But he found it difficult to sleep the night before the Battle of Bussaco. His brain teemed with too many thoughts and feelings.

His company had been expecting him. Nevertheless they had given him a boisterous good welcome and he had felt a surging of joy to be back with them, almost as if he had come home to a family. He had inspected them and watched critically their methodical preparations for battle and made his own. He had reported to General Crauford, who had called him a tricky bastard for absenting himself during weeks of almost eventless marching and turning up just in time for the great show. But the general had slapped him heartily on the back while saying so.

All the preparations were made as quietly as possible,

and no one was allowed to show even the topmost hair on his head over the crest of the hill. The French were not to know that the whole of the army awaited them the following day. With luck they would believe that the skirmishers who were on picket duty on the eastern slope were part of a rear guard of merely a few companies set there to delay their advance.

For the same reason, they were to camp in darkness that night. No fires were to be lit. There was to be no hot food.

The long-expected news came during the evening—and excitement stirred up and down the quiet lines—that the French were moving up, that they were camping below the heights, a mere three miles away. Apparently the lights of their fires shone brightly. The men had to take the word of the privileged few who had been permitted to look for themselves.

It would begin the next day. Probably at dawn, perhaps earlier. The pickets would be watching very carefully for a night attack, and the men would sleep close to their lines, fully clothed, their loaded arms at the ready.

Captain Blake had fought in many battles and had lived through many battle eves. There was nothing different about this one. He felt all the usual tense excitement—part exhilaration, part fear. And here there was nothing to allay those feelings. The Light Division was stationed close to headquarters, within sight and sound of the convent, Cole's Fourth Division to their left on the other side of the ravine that held the main road to Coimbra, Spencer's First Division to their right.

It was not the imminence of battle that made sleep difficult. And his night was relatively comfortable. Although most of his men slept on the ground in the open and he would normally have joined them there, someone had erected a tent for him, as tents had been erected for most of the officers and for some of the men with wives. And he had not scorned to occupy that tent as he would normally have done—with a few choice words of explanation for the soldier who had thought him grown soft. He slept in the tent with Joana.

He had set a guard over her while he was busy with his company—an eager private who knew him only by

reputation and had a tendency to gaze at him worshipfully with a mouth that gaped. Not that a guard seemed
necessary. She had shown no sign of wanting to escape.
She had even helped erect the tent, apparently. And she
had chattered brightly with several surprised officers of
her acquaintance—and with a few she had never met
before.

"Lucky bastard!" Captain Rowlandson had said to him
when he realized that Joana was to share his tent.

But he did not feel lucky. He had steeled himself to
parting with her at the convent, had not weakened at all
there, but had told all he knew about her, concisely and
dispassionately, and then had escaped lightly—or so it
had seemed. She had left the room without a word of
good-bye—something he had been dreading for days.

But she had come back again. And he had felt a great
upsurging of joy when he knew that he would have her
with him for at least another day, and a corresponding
resentment that it was all to be gone through again, that
it was not yet over after all. That perhaps good-byes were
yet to be said.

He had wanted to be free to concentrate on the battle
ahead. And he had wanted to stride across the room to
her after Lord Somerset had left it and sweep her up
into his arms.

He did not want this confusion of feelings on the eve
of battle. He resented her and he resented Lord Wellington for sending her back to him because for the moment
there seemed to be nothing else to do with her.

"Joana," he said when he joined her in their tent for
the short night ahead—he was to be up long before
dawn, ready to lead his men in the skirmish line on the
hill. He stretched out beside her, turned onto his side to
face her, and slid his arm beneath her neck—such familiar actions that he wondered how he would sleep at all
at night once she was finally gone. "I will not be making
love to you tonight."

"I know," she said softly, cuddling up against him and
setting an arm about his waist, without indulging in any
of her usual wiles.

"I will need all my energy tomorrow," he said.

"I know." She rested her cheek against his chest. "I

know, Robert. You do not have to explain. Go to sleep now. And don't spare me a thought tomorrow. I shall not try to run away. I promise—on my honor. And my honor is dear to me."

He kissed the top of her head and wondered if he would even be alive after the battle to know if she spoke the truth. He normally did not wonder such things. Fearing that one might die in battle was a useless expenditure of energy.

And yet he spent the next half-hour—valuable sleeping time—thinking about the morrow and wondering if he would die and hoping that he would survive to see her one more time, to hold her once more. Just so that he would have the pain of saying good-bye to her at the end of it all and of watching her taken away to captivity! His brain would not cease its activity, no matter how hard he tried to quiet it.

He began to wish that he had made love to her after all.

"Robert." She whispered his name. "You need to sleep."

He laughed shortly.

"When you were a boy," she said quietly, and he could feel her fingers in his hair, "I loved you because you were tall and handsome and because I had never known a young man. And because you had a way of smiling that reached all the way to your eyes and because you were willing to listen to the dreams and ramblings of a girl. And because you could dance and climb and run and kiss. And because . . . oh, because it was summertime and I was young and ready for love."

Her fingers were moving lightly over his head.

"You were a sweet and gentle boy," she said. "But you were not weak. You were incredibly strong. Most men would have put up with a great deal of degradation and many insults too for the comforts of the privileged life you were offered. But you gave it all up so that you could retain your integrity and your dignity. And then you made for yourself a life that you could be proud of."

She made him sound like a bloody saint, he thought with lazy amusement.

"I was stunned when I realized that the two Roberts

in my life were one and the same person," she said. "I could scarcely believe it at first. For so long I had thought you dead. And you looked and seemed very different from the boy of my memory. But it is fitting that you are one and the same. I am glad that you are, and I am glad that you grew into the man you have become. I am glad you lived. Did you know that you are a hero to your men and very popular with them? Allan—the young private you set to guard me—looks upon you as some sort of god. And you are highly respected at headquarters. You have done wonderfully well, and all on your own, without anyone's help at all."

Her fingers continued to smooth through his hair.

"Robert?" she whispered after several moments of silence.

But there was no answer.

"And I love the man quite as dearly as I loved the boy," she said, her voice no louder than a murmur. "More so. For now I know how hard love is to find, just how difficult it is to find a man worthy to be loved. I will always love you, no matter what happens tomorrow."

Captain Robert Blake slept on.

There was something almost eerie about the predawn scene. Thousands of men were woken without the aid of bugles and adjusted their clothing and checked their firearms and ate a cold and hurried breakfast with almost no sound at all beyond the inevitable rustlings and bustlings. There was no sign of open fear, only of a heightened awareness, of a suppressed excitement.

The tents had been dismantled and taken back to the rear. The women who had come up to spend the night with their men were kissing them good-bye without fuss or hysteria and were also taking themselves back.

Joana watched all the activity as if she were a long way off, as if she were not part of it at all. But then she was not. And she hated her lack of involvement. For she felt sick and mortally afraid, feelings that she despised in herself and usually went out of her way to avoid. If only she were preparing for battle alongside the men, she felt, she would not be afraid.

Whoever had decreed that women should not fight was stupid in the extreme, she thought.

The same young private was to guard her that day too. Captain Blake was giving him instructions, crisply, impersonally, as if she meant nothing to him whatsoever, as if she were nothing more than his prisoner. She wondered if the soldier minded missing the battle, if he resented her. He looked proud enough of himself, as if his captain had singled him out for a deed of extraordinary valor.

She tried to fill her mind with such details and thoughts. She tried to ignore the ball of panic that was lodged deep in her stomach.

And then it was time to go. And time for him to go.

"Joana," he said, looking at her at last. Dawn had still not provided them with enough light to see each other clearly. And there was a mist. He was his granite self, she thought, looking at him too at last. "Go with Private Higgins. And remember your promise of yesterday, if you please. I shall see you later."

The ball in her stomach exploded and she found herself fighting her legs and her breathing. She wondered if this was what women called the vapors. She lifted her chin and looked steadily at him.

"Until later," she said, and she gave him her most dazzling smile before turning away.

He was swinging his rifle up onto his shoulder when she whirled back to face him again. "Robert," she said, and she did not care that the young private was there beside her listening, and perhaps half a dozen other men within earshot. "I love you. I want you to know that." *In case you never return.*

His hand stilled on his rifle. His whole body stilled and tensed. And then he nodded curtly, unsmilingly, and turned and strode away.

"Well." She laughed lightly. "One has to say such things when a man is going into battle, Allan. Now, where are you going to lead me? I hope not right back to the baggage carts and the other women. It would be tedious to hear no news of the battle as it is fought, would it not?"

"Yes, ma'am," he said.

She smiled at him. "You would hate that, would you not?" she said. "You came here to be a part of it all and would be justly annoyed if a mere woman kept you so far beyond the action that you did not even know what was happening. Some of your friends might even call you coward. That would be quite unjust, would it not?"

"Yes, ma'am," he said uncertainly. "But I am following orders. I am proud to follow Captain Blake's orders."

"Of course you are," she said. "And tonight he will be proud of you. For you will have done your job well. I shall even make it easy for you by not trying to escape. I would not do so, you know. I must stay here to see his safe return. I meant what I said to him just now, you see." She smiled confidentially at him.

"Yes, ma'am," he said.

The boy was falling under her spell. She knew that if her next statement had been "Black is white, you know," he would have replied, "Yes, ma'am." And she had to ruthlessly press her advantage. She would die of boredom and frustration—and fear—if she had to spend the day right at the rear with the supplies and the baggage and the women. She would not know how the battle went and she would not know how Robert did. And she would be far from the French army. It was just beginning fully to dawn on her that the French army would be close throughout the day.

Perhaps she would have one more chance . . . But, no, she must not expect as much. It would be too good to be true. Besides, she still did not have either her musket or her knife. The former was over Private Higgins' left shoulder, balancing the rifle over his right. The latter was probably still in Robert's belt.

"I think," she said when they were in the no-man's-land between the front and the baggage train, "this would be a good place to stop, Allan. From here we can watch the action for ourselves, or what can be seen of it from this side of the hill, anyway."

She stopped and gazed back up the way they had come, to where the thin lines of the British and Portuguese infantry were forming in two lines just behind the crest of the hill. But very little could be seen. The darkness was only just beginning to lift, but the mist had not yet decided to follow suit. Whom would the mist favor? she wondered, and she felt that unfamiliar fear clutch at her again as she pictured Robert, out in front of the lines with his skirmishers, unable to see exactly who or what was advancing on them.

"But if the French take the hill, ma'am," Private Higgins said, "you will be in danger. You will be safer farther back."

"But, Allan—" she turned the full force of her charm on him—"I have complete faith in the courage and strength of our gallant men. Don't you? Of course they will hold back Marshal Massena's men. And if by some chance they do not, then you will protect me." She set a hand lightly on his sleeve. "I have complete trust in you. Were you not personally chosen by Captain Blake? I know you would distinguish yourself in my defense."

He gazed at her with the same worship in his eyes as she had seen there the day before for Robert. Poor boy, she thought. He had probably completely forgotten that he was to guard her as a prisoner and not defend her as his captain's lady.

"We will stay here for a while, then, ma'am," he said, "until the action gets too hot. Then I shall escort you farther back." There was a suggestion of a swagger in his voice, Joana noticed.

She had never been near a battlefront, but she imagined that this no-man's-land, crossed from north to south by a wide cart track, would be used later by riders carrying messages back and forth between Lord Wellington and the various divisions. Perhaps she would hear news of what was happening.

But her sense of triumph was swallowed up by fear as she heard distant drums and fifes sounding the advance.

French drums and fifes. Sounding the French advance.

26

MARSHAL Massena made the mistake of assuming that if Wellington's forces were on the ridge at Bussaco at all, they were concentrated in the northern half of the hills. He did not believe that Wellington would be daring enough to string them out the whole ten-mile length of the ridge. His plan was to launch General Reynier's corps against a low ridge in the center of the hills so that when his men took it they could circle behind the British while Marshal Ney attacked the higher northern front of the hill, up from the road to Coimbra, toward the convent. Marshal Massena intended to surround his enemy.

The first attack came perilously close to success as the French attacked in dense columns behind the brisk skirmishing of their *tirailleurs*, who cleared the hill of British skirmishers. The early-morning mist was in their favor. It was only the dogged determination of the British infantry and the steady courage of the Portuguese, involved in their first pitched battle, and the timely arrival of General Leith's forces, brought up from the idle right, that averted disaster and sent the French columns hurtling back down the hill in disarray, leaving their dead and wounded behind.

Marshal Ney began his attack soon after seven o'clock, sending General Loison's division to take the village of Sula and then to push upward along the paved road to the convent and Ross's battery of twelve guns and the Sula Mill, the allied command post commanded by General Crauford of the Light Division. It was a difficult task, and the lifting of the morning mist gave some of the advantage back to the British.

Joana stood with Private Higgins a little way back from the lateral track that ran the length of the ridge, behind its crest. All was movement and noise and apparent confusion once the fighting had begun, and she knew all the agony of her own helplessness. In Salamanca there had been danger, but there she had been able to control it, to manipulate it. She had not been afraid. Indeed, if the truth were known, she had enjoyed herself there. Here she felt impotent.

Not only was there nothing for her to do, but there seemed to be no way of knowing how the battle was going. No way of knowing if he were still alive. There was all the frustration of the mist and the top of the ridge, which would have hidden her view of the action even without the mist, and the deafening and terrifying sounds of the drums and the guns, coming all from the south at first.

At the start she made no attempt to stop any of the riders who galloped back and forth along the path, obviously carrying important messages from one command post to another. But she bristled when one yelled in passing.

"Women to the rear!" he roared. "Goddammit, soldier. Get her out of the way." He rode on without pausing.

Private Higgins coughed nervously. "For your own safety, ma'am . . ." he began.

But the insult had been all Joana had needed to bring her out of the near-paralysis that the sound of the guns had imposed on her. She stepped out onto the path and yelled epithets after the departing and oblivious staff officer that had the poor private gaping in astonishment.

"Men!" she said finally. "God's gift to the animal kingdom. He made such a number of ghastly errors creating them that he had to create women to set all to rights again. Ah, this is better."

Someone else was galloping toward her, someone she knew. She set her hands on her hips and lifted her chin while Private Higgins, she could see from the corner of her eye, appeared to be hopping from one foot to the other.

"Jack!" she called in a loud, clear voice.

Major Jack Hanbridge reined in so quickly that his horse reared and he had to fight for a moment to keep his seat. He frowned at the woman who stood her ground on the path, and then peered more closely.

"Joana?" he said at last. "Joana? Is it really you?" His eyes swept over her. "Good Lord. But what in the name of thunder are you doing here? Allow me . . ."

But Joana held up an impatient hand. "Tell me what is going on," she commanded. "Are we winning?"

"Oh, assuredly," he said. "You may trust the Beau, Joana. We have sent them back from the center with their tails between their legs. They think to gain the convent here, but Bob Crauford will hold them. And see what awaits them if they do reach the top?" His arm swept a wide arc over his shoulder.

Joana had already seen. Lines of quiet, disciplined infantry had already taken their places behind the skyline. They would send a deadly volley into any Frenchmen unfortunate enough to come charging up over the hill.

"But what on earth are you doing here?" the major asked again. "You must get back, Joana. You should be far from here. Let me— "

"Jack, don't be tiresome," she said. "The French are fighting their way up this hill, then? Who is stopping them?"

"Oh, they will be stopped," he said. "Have no fear. We have the best of our skirmishers down there."

"The Ninety-fifth," she said, her stomach performing a somersault.

"And the *cacadores*," he said. "The very best. Now, let me— "

"And which French forces are coming up?" she asked. "Do you know, Jack?"

"Ney's corps," he said. "But we will—"

"Ney's?" she said. "Who in particular, Jack?"

"General Loison's division, I believe," he said. "Joana, I have to go. Is this private your escort? Soldier . . ."

"Yes, yes," Joana said. "Be on your way, Jack. I would not keep you. I shall be quite safe."

He looked at her doubtfully and frowned at Private Higgins. But he had already been delayed longer than a minute. He touched his spurs to his horse's sides and galloped off to the south.

General Loison. Colonel Leroux was in his division.

Perhaps his battalion was among those coming up the hill. Perhaps, oh, perhaps . . . Joana looked hastily about her. All was businesslike organization. And yet it sounded as if all hell had broken loose beyond the hill. Perhaps Colonel Leroux was just beyond the hill. And Robert was there—amidst all the thunder of the guns and all the deadly smoke. Perhaps he was already dead. Perhaps Colonel Leroux was even now in the process of killing him. Perhaps . . .

Perhaps she would go insane if she had to stay inactive one more minute. No, there was no perhaps about it.

"Allan," she said, turning on the boy who was her guard. She looked wild, afraid. "Give me my musket. Please give it to me."

"I can't, ma'am." He took one step back from her, but she advanced on him.

"You can and you will," she said. "How would you like to be weaponless at this moment? The French may burst over the hill at any moment, and I am defenseless. And don't tell me that you will defend me or that you will take me back to safety. I am talking about now— this moment. Give me my gun at least. Do you think I am about to take on the whole of our own army with it? *Do* you?"

Private Higgins took one more half-step back. "No, ma'am," he said.

"Give it to me, then," she said, her voice trembling. "Captain Blake would not want me dead, I do assure you."

"But, ma'am," he said, protesting as she reached out and took her musket, checked it quickly with hands that were somewhat out of practice but nevertheless skilled with the weapon. "But, ma'am . . ."

She felt sorry for him—almost. Robert would crucify him at the very least. But there was no time for conscience. She leveled the musket on the boy, whose eyes widened in a kind of hurt astonishment.

"I am going forward," she said. "I must see for myself what is happening. You may follow me if you wish, Allan. Or you may shoot me in the back—I shall turn it on you in a moment. But you will not stop me. This is my battle too. It is more my battle than anyone else's, I daresay."

"But, ma'am . . ." Private Higgins protested, his voice high-pitched and frantic as she turned her back on him and broke into a run. Her back was tense for the first few yards, though she knew that he would not shoot. The noise of the guns was too intense for her to hear whether he shouted anything more at her or whether he was running up behind her. But she would not stop.

She would not stop for anyone or anything. A few of the infantrymen of the Forty-third and Fifty-second, standing in line below the skyline, looked back and saw her. General Crauford saw her and roared something as she passed the mill. And the gunners saw her as she circled past the battery and ran downward into hell.

But no one tried to stop her. No one was going to stop a battle or take any extra risk to prevent a mad peasant woman from hurling herself into certain death.

And strangely, once she was over the brow of the hill and all was noise and smoke, and guns were firing both behind her and in front of her, once she could see the British and Portuguese skirmishers down in the heather and rocks before her, strung out across the hill, firing down on the approaching *tirailleurs*, the masses of the French columns coming up behind them, she felt no more fear at all. Only a heart-pounding excitement and a sharpened awareness.

It was almost as if time were slowed, as if she had all the leisure time in the world to observe details. The British and the Portuguese were on the hillside, quite close. The French had already pushed them back through the village of Sula and were themselves on the slope. They were moving inexorably upward. Her mind took in the larger picture almost immediately.

She went down onto her stomach behind a boulder. She could shoot only once with her musket. She had no ammunition with which to reload it. She must choose her shot with great care. Not that she had any interest in killing Frenchmen—only one Frenchman. And surely, oh, surely she would not be fortunate enough to see him.

But she saw Robert suddenly below her and was glad that she was down on her stomach. He was crouched

down aiming his rifle at the enemy and firing it. His face
was black with the smoke of his gun, and there was a
smear of blood down one temple. But he was still alive.
Oh, God, he was still alive.

He flung his rifle behind him for a sergeant to reload
and picked up his sword from the ground beside him. As
a captain he was not expected to use a gun at all, but only
to lead and guide his men with his sword. But Robert was
doing both. He was both leading and fighting. The sergeant reloaded the rifle and set it back on the ground.

Captain Blake and his company were stubbornly holding one rise of ground, she could see, refusing to give
ground until they were forced to do so despite the fact
that companies around them were already edging back
up the hill. But the columns were coming closer and
closer behind their own *tirailleurs*. Soon the riflemen and
the *cacadores* would have no choice but to retreat or die
needlessly.

Joana saw everything in just a few seconds. She saw
Robert's danger and his stubbornness. And she looked
beyond him to the advancing blue columns, scarcely visible as more than a dense mass through the smoke. And
yet one sharp detail burned its way through her eyes and
she stared, unbelieving, convinced for a moment that she
saw only what she wished to see.

Colonel Leroux was at the head of one of the columns,
urging it forward, his sword raised. Her hands suddenly
felt cold and clammy against her musket. They shook.
But they would not shake. By God, they would not. He
had killed Maria. Worse. He had done those unspeakable
things to her before ordering her death, and she, Joana,
had seen it all. For that he would die. For that she would
keep her hands steady or die herself in the attempt.

He was too far away. She knew it even as she sighted
along the gun. Not beyond range of the musket, but beyond sure range. For the musket was notoriously poor at
hitting any definite target at any distance. And yet she
could not wait. Her heart was pounding up into her
throat and against her eardrums, more powerful even
than the noise of the French drums. She would be
helped. Some power above would help her. She could

not miss. Not now, when fate had given her this one last unbelievably coincidental chance. She could not miss.

She fired the gun and watched Colonel Leroux march onward, still urging his men on, still waving his sword in the air. He was quite unaware that she was there and that she had just fired on him. She dropped her face to the ground and gave in to momentary despair while hell continued to rage about her.

And then her head snapped up and her eyes focused and widened on the loaded rifle still on the ground behind Captain Blake below her. At any moment he would pick it up. At any moment he would signal his men to move back—all about them had done so. At any moment her very last chance would be gone and Miguel and Maria would be unavenged for all eternity.

The battle was nearing and intensifying. But all Joana saw was the rifle on the ground below her. All she thought of was reaching it before it was too late. She abandoned her musket, pushed herself into a crouching position, and launched herself downhill.

It all happened in seconds. And if a higher power had not guided her aim a few moments before, certainly one was looking after her now. The only wounds she could count after it was all over were the scratches and bruises she had acquired from the ground.

She hurtled down the steep hillside somehow without stumbling, and the rifle was in her hand before Captain Blake whirled around and regarded her from astonished eyes that looked remarkably blue against his bloodied and blackened face.

"Jesus Christ!" he said.

But she did not even hear the blasphemy. She was on her feet and hoisting the unfamiliar rifle to her shoulder and sighting along it and screaming out against the thunder of sound around her.

"Marcel!" she shrieked.

Whether he heard her, or whether his attention was caught by the unusual sight of someone—a woman—standing up straight despite all the shells and bullets whizzing about her, she did not know. But he saw her. And he recognized her, she knew. And he saw that she had the gun pointed at him. It was all the matter of a split second, but she knew that he had seen her and that he knew, and she knew that this time she could not miss.

She fired the rifle.

And watched him stop mid-stride, an expression of surprise on his face, and twist sideways before going down.

She laughed in triumph.

And then the strange feeling she had had since coming over the top of the hill, that time had been suspended, left her as she came crashing down onto the ground, two powerful arms about her waist.

"Jesus, woman!" he said. "Jesus!"

She lay panting on her face beneath the full weight of his body. And she felt a chilling terror at the steady beating of the French drums and the heavy thunder of the British guns and the harsh cracking of the skirmishers' firearms.

"I killed him," she said, her voice a gasp of triumph. "I killed him."

But he was not listening to her. He was on one knee beside her, his sword sweeping the air, his voice a great roar. "Back," he yelled. "Back, you bastards."

He kept a bruising grip on her arm as they retreated up the hillside, his men shooting as they went. The sergeant had grabbed his gun and was reloading it, Joana saw. And she prepared her mind for death. There was no way of avoiding it, she decided, caught as they were between two vast armies in all the chaos of a living hell.

"Give me the rifle," she said, reaching for it. "I'll help."

But he pushed her roughly behind him so that she stumbled. He spoke with a snarl. "You are not going to escape," he said. "You will remain my prisoner or die with me. Get down and stay down."

She did as she was bidden. Their very lives depended upon her being meek for once in her life, she knew, even though she could have helped if only he had allowed her to use his rifle. But it was no time to argue.

Every inch of ground was hard-fought, and on every inch of ground Joana prepared herself to die. She would not mind dying, she told herself, now that she had avenged the deaths of her half-brother and half-sister—if only Duarte could know. And she would not mind dying with Robert beside her. She felt strangely calm after the first bone-weakening terror.

But if she was to die, it was not to be just yet, after all. As the skirmishers neared the top of the hill, the French columns hard upon them, the great guns were withdrawn to avoid capture and General Crauford sat quietly on his horse outside the mill assessing the moment. Joana caught a glimpse of him as he was in the act of sweeping off his hat. And then she heard his high-pitched bellow, quite audible above all the noise.

"Now, Fifty-second! Avenge the death of Sir John Moore!" he roared.

"Company!" The bellow was Robert's, in her ear. He had a grip on her arm that cut the circulation from her hand. "Join the line!"

"Charge! Charge!" the general roared. "Huzza!"

The British lines that had been waiting behind the sky-line were stepping forward to make their presence known to the unsuspecting French, their muskets leveled, their bayonets fixed. The skirmishers fell in at the end of the line and joined the charge.

Captain Blake flung Joana back behind the lines. "Go back!" he yelled at her. "Get yourself to safety. I shall find you later and beat the living daylights out of you."

And he was gone to join his men in their charge back down the hill. Joana heard the murderous volley of musketry and knew that the French advance had been halted, that hundreds had died in that first moment. She got wearily to her feet and retired to the far side of the lateral track.

She felt mortally weak, mortally tired. If she could just sink down to the ground and close her eyes, she thought, she would surely sleep for a week. But she would not do that. Not yet. Not until she knew that he was safe. Not until she had given him the chance to beat her black and blue. There was a thin thread of amusement in her smile.

Until she remembered that she had just killed a man.

And then she began to shake.

It was all over. The French had been routed, and there would be no more attacks that day. As usually happened after a battle, or sometimes even in the midst of a battle when a temporary truce had been sounded, the French and the English mingled on the hill, all hostility gone, gathering together their dead and wounded. Some men even exchanged greetings and drinks of precious water with men they had been shooting at just minutes before.

It was perhaps the strangest part of war to those who were not accustomed to it.

Captain Blake toiled uphill with his men. He could drink two brooks dry if they would just present themselves, he thought. But his main duty was to find his own dead and arrange for their burial—always the most painful part of a day of fighting—and to see that his wounded were tended if their wounds were slight or carried away to the hospital tents if they were in need of amputation.

And yet he made one detour from the path that he had taken with his company earlier in their retreat uphill. He walked over to where a larger-than-usual group of Frenchmen was gathered, a sure sign that an officer of high rank was about to be carried away. And he found that he had not been mistaken. He had wondered—though he had not had a great deal of leisure in which to wonder. But that strange out-of-time, slower-than-time experience had seemed unreal. He had doubted the evidence of his own senses.

But he had not been mistaken. The French officer, who had died from a bullet wound just above the level of his heart—roughly in the same spot as his own wound had been the year before, Captain Blake thought—was Colonel Marcel Leroux. And Joana had killed him.

Hadn't she?

Had he imagined it? She had stood up, quite recklessly exposing herself to harm, yelled out his name, quite deliberately taken aim, and killed him.

Captain Blake frowned and made his way off to join his men again and to direct the burials and the removal of their wounded.

Almost at the top of the hill he knelt down beside a sobbing boy and touched him reassuringly on the shoulder before recognizing him. Private Allan Higgins turned his face away as Captain Blake's jaw tightened.

"You will live," he said as another private cut the trousers away from the boy's leg to reveal the bullet hole. "We will have to have the bullet removed, but you will keep your leg. It is hurting badly?"

The boy made an effort to control his sobs. "No, sir," he said, obviously lying. "But I could not shoot her in the back, sir. She ran, but I could not shoot her."

"No." Captain Blake squeezed his shoulder. "A man does not shoot a woman in the back even if she *is* the devil's dam. Well, lad, you have had your first taste of battle and you have acquitted yourself well. You came forward when you might have stayed back."

"But I let you down, sir." The sobs resumed.

"Get a hold on yourself, soldier," Captain Blake said, straightening up and nodding to the two privates who had come to carry the boy up the hill. "We will discuss that matter later. It is sufficient now that you have survived."

The boy did not seem in any way consoled.

Captain Blake felt bone weary. It was a feeling he recognized as one that always succeeded the excitement and even exhilaration of battle. A ball had grazed his temple. He felt the soreness suddenly and lifted a hand to touch the crusted blood on the side of his face. But there were no more injuries. He was fortunate. Hundreds of men—thousands, if he counted the unfortunate French—had died that day in a battle that was, after all, indecisive. The French would either attack again the next day or find a way past the hill, and the British would resume their retreat on Lisbon.

They had played one more hand in the deadly game of war. That was all.

He wondered where Joana was. If she were wise, she would have taken herself off back to the convent and thrown herself on the mercy of Lord Wellington or whatever senior staff officers were likely to defend her against him—and all of them, to a man, would be only too happy to do so. Though he was far too weary to do to her the things he had contemplated doing when he last saw her.

And far too puzzled as well. She had killed Colonel Leroux.

He came up over the crest of the hill alone, his task done. And amidst all the milling masses of men and guns and horses there, he saw her immediately. She was standing on the far side of the track, and was apparently sending a staff officer reluctantly on his way to the convent without her. She was favoring the man with her usual beguiling smile.

He stood and watched her with narrowed eyes until she looked about her again and saw him. She smiled as he approached.

"I was afraid to come to the top of the hill," she said. "I was afraid to look down. I was afraid that perhaps you were dead."

"You were not afraid earlier," he said harshly. "Not when there was a chance of escaping to your own people."

"Robert." She was no longer smiling. She set her head to one side and looked very directly into his eyes. "You know that was not what I was doing. You saw me shoot him. I did kill him, did I not?"

He stared back at her. "Yes," he said. "He is dead."

And then she did something he least expected her to do. She bit at her upper lip, and her eyes filled with tears, and her whole face trembled.

"Well, I meant it," she said, her voice a whisper. "I meant to kill him. That has been the sole purpose of my life for the past three years. And I am glad that it is done at last. I just wish I could have told him the reason why."

"Joana," he said as her hands came up to cover her face. "Oh, Joana."

And she was in his arms while noise and confusion swirled about them, gulping and sobbing against his chest, beating against it with the sides of her fists.

"Fighting to the end," he said. "The battle is over, Joana. And your private war too, whatever it was."

27

"WHAT was it all about, Joana?" he asked her, and she stopped pounding at his chest and stopped the stupid crying and looked up at him. His face was powder-blackened, the dark blood crusted down one side of his face.

"You were hit," she said, raising one hand but not quite touching the wound.

"Grazed," he said. "It is nothing."

"You must bathe it," she said. "I shall do it for you."

He surprised her by grinning. His teeth looked very white in contrast to the rest of his face. "You behaving like a normal woman?" he said. "I never thought to live to see the day."

"Had you been standing one inch farther to your right," she said, "you certainly would not have. Is it sore?"

"Excruciatingly," he said. "What was going on, Joana? There is a great deal about you I do not know, isn't there?"

She opened her mouth to answer, but a group of horsemen passing along the track reined in suddenly, distracting her attention, and she found herself looking up into a stern and frowning face.

"Joana?" Viscount Wellington said. "Whatever are you doing here?" His stare shifted to Captain Blake, who had swung around to salute him. "Captain? Did you not have orders to escort the Marquesa das Minas with all haste to Lisbon?"

"No, he did not, Arthur," Joana said quickly. "I passed your orders on to him, you see, but I somewhat twisted them in the telling."

Lord Wellington's lips twitched. "I can imagine," he

said. "Well, it seems I have the two of you to thank for a job well done. Marshal Massena has certainly been tricked into coming this way. I am sorry I could not take you more fully into my confidence before you left for Salamanca, Captain Blake. But I thought your behavior would be more convincing if you really did believe that the marquesa was betraying you and us."

"It worked wonderfully well," Joana said, glancing hastily at the stony face of the captain. "Didn't it, Robert?"

"Yes, sir," he said. "It worked well."

The viscount nodded curtly. "This victory today is little more than a booster of morale," he said. "Might I beg you to leave without further delay, Joana, and make for the safety of Lisbon?"

She smiled brightly at him. "Yes, Arthur," she said. "I shall withdraw with everyone else."

"*With* everyone else, not ahead of them," he said with a sigh. "Well, I shall not waste any more breath on someone who is not directly under my orders. But take care of yourself. You had no more success than usual with your other mission?"

"Oh, yes," she said. "Full success, Arthur. I hope you will not need me to make any future visits to my aunts in Spain. I have no plans to go there again."

He looked at her keenly and nodded once. "I am pleased for you," he said. And he saluted her, nodded to Captain Blake, and continued on his way to the convent, his aides in close attendance.

"Have you seen Private Higgins?" Joana asked, turning back to the captain. "I lost him, I am afraid."

"I plan to take him apart limb from limb once he has recovered from his bullet wound," he said. "He will wish the bullet had lodged in his heart rather than his leg before I have finished with him."

He was deadly serious, the steely soldier from the crown of his head to the soles of his feet. She smiled at him and linked her arm through his.

"But, Robert," she said, "you know how difficult it is for any man to obey orders when I am involved. I am a match for any man, am I not? It would be unfair to chastise an inexperienced boy for allowing me to get away. He is a very sweet boy and was very concerned for my safety."

"He had a strange way of showing it," he said curtly. "And I have no room in my company for sweet boys."

"And yet," she said, smiling up into his face, "you were one yourself no more than eleven years ago, Robert. It took time and experience to mature and toughen you. And what about your orders to take me to Lisbon yesterday? They have not been obeyed. We are still here."

"For the simple reason that I did not receive those orders," he said.

"And why not?" she asked. "Because of me, that is why. But they were orders nevertheless, Robert—and from no less a personage than the commander in chief. If I had not spoken up just now, Arthur would have been very vexed with you. Perhaps he would even have torn you limb from limb and made you wish that you had been standing one inch to your right earlier this morning."

He looked down at her, his granite look broken only by exasperation. "All right, Joana," he said, "you have made your point. I shall go and kiss the boy and tuck him up in his bed while he rests his leg."

"Don't kiss him," she said. "He may be embarrassed." She laughed gaily.

But he was not to be teased out of his vexation. "And what sort of a fool have you been making of me?" he asked. "You have been, haven't you, and enjoying every minute of it?"

"Not quite every minute," she said. "There have been times when I have been remorseful, Robert. But yes, on the whole it has been fun. Are you going to forgive me?"

He drew his arm away from hers without smiling. "You are a dangerous woman, Joana," he said. "You will get any man under your power somehow, won't you? If not by fair means, then by foul. Well, you have made me your fool just as you have every other man on whom you have ever set your sights. But I have provided you with amusement for longer than most, I believe. No more, though. Enough is enough. It is time for you to find someone else on whom to practice your wiles. I don't suppose you have ever failed, have you? Well, perhaps one day you will. Excuse me. I have important matters to attend to."

And he strode off away from her, leaving her standing staring after him—and feeling less confident than she could ever remember feeling. If only Arthur had not come along at that precise moment. Robert had known already, but she had not had a chance to explain fully to him. She had been about to do so, but she had been too late.

And so he had learned the truth from Viscount Wellington and felt humiliated and betrayed. Drat Arthur!

I don't suppose you have ever failed, have you? he had just said to her. Well, she just had. And she felt a chill somewhere in the region of her heart and a feeling that must be very close to panic. He had been very serious. Perhaps too serious. Perhaps he would never forgive her. And even if he did, there was very little left for them. Only the retreat behind the Lines of Torres Vedras and the inevitable parting of the ways—a week, perhaps two.

Joana shrugged and looked about her at all the moaning wounded being carried up over the hill and in need of tending. She would help tend them even though she had never done such a thing before. Later she would think about Robert and how she might smile her way back into his good graces again. Later she would think about the future. But not now. Now there was plenty to keep her busy.

But she would think about those things later, and do something about them too. For never in her life had she been able to resist a challenge, and she was not about to start now.

He lay on his back in his tent, one arm thrown across his forehead, staring up into the darkness. He was exhausted. The battle seemed days ago, not just earlier that same day. There had been so much to do since—writing up reports, gathering his men together and making sure they were prepared for further action in the unlikely event that the French should attack again, writing to the relatives of those who had been killed, visiting the sick of his company again.

Visiting Private Higgins and arriving just at the moment when a surgeon's assistant was digging the bullet out of his leg. Standing watching as Joana cupped the boy's face in her hands and smiled at him and talked soothingly to him as sweat broke out all over his face and he gritted his teeth and refused to shame himself by screaming.

She had moved off after the ordeal was over and the boy had fainted, without looking his way at all. She had moved off to another, even younger boy—not of his regiment—who was screaming for his mother. She had been incredibly dirty and untidy—incredibly beautiful.

He had waited by the boy's side until consciousness came back, and talked quietly to him until he saw hope and pride come back into the pain-filled eyes. And then he had squeezed his shoulder and moved on. Perhaps after all, the boy would make a good soldier. He had thought of a lieutenant, long dead, who had talked quietly to him when he was blubbering with terror after coming under fire for the first time and had made him feel that perhaps his behavior was not quite shameful after all.

He had caught sight of Joana several times during the day. But he had not approached her, nor she him. He felt bruised and hurt. She had been laughing at him the whole time, playing with him. While he had been falling in love with her and fighting his feelings because she was the enemy, she had been enjoying herself immensely. She had even admitted it.

He was as much a fool as any of those men in that ballroom in Lisbon whom he had so despised. More of a fool because he had allowed her to make him so much more her toy than she had any of those men.

He closed his eyes but he knew he would not sleep. Where had she gone? he wondered. To the convent? To some other man's tent? But he did not care. He would not think of her any longer. His mission was at an end, and everything else along with it.

Against his closed eyes he saw her, standing straight and reckless in the midst of battle, aiming his rifle at Colonel Leroux and shooting him almost through the heart, though she had probably never used a rifle before.

She never had told him what that had been all about. But he did not care.

He saw her quietly watching him that morning as he prepared to leave to join his men. And telling him that she loved him. He felt sick. But he did not care. She was not worth caring about. She was not worth a sleepless night. Not when the coming day promised to be almost as busy as the one just past.

There was a rustling suddenly at the opening of his tent, but he did not open his eyes. He only stiffened slightly. He did not move as she settled beside him, her arm brushing against his in the close confines of the tent.

"I had nowhere else to go," she whispered to him.

"The convent," he said harshly. "The arms of any other man in this damned army."

"All right," she said. "Perhaps I did not quite tell the truth. I meant that there was nowhere else I wished to go. Not that I wished to come here either. You are as cross as a bear."

"Joana," he said, "go away, or at least be quiet. I have no desire to be teased into a more congenial mood. Or to listen to any of your lies or wiles."

"Would it help," she asked, and he could feel her turning onto her side to face him, "if I promised never ever to lie to you again?"

"Not at all," he said. "You would not be able to keep the promise for five minutes."

She was quiet for a while as he lay beside her rigid with tension. "Did you think I was lying this morning?" she asked.

He drew in a slow breath. And he cursed himself for not having the courage or the good sense to order her from his tent.

"I was not," she said. "I was never more serious in my life."

"Don't, Joana," he said. "It will simply not work this time."

She touched his arm but removed her hand immediately. "You are not relaxed," she said. "I would be mortally afraid if you were. As it is, I am only afraid. Robert, is there nothing I can say?"

"Nothing," he said.

She sighed and he felt her forehead against his shoulder. It was impossible to move away from her in the tent. But she seemed to have nothing more to say. There was a long silence, a silence during which he listened to the rustlings of the camp about them.

"He killed Miguel and Maria," she said quietly into the silence. Her voice was toneless. "Duarte's brother and sister, my half-brother and sister. Or at least he ordered their killing—with a jerk of a thumb."

He could feel the rigidity of his own body. He could scarcely draw breath.

"He raped Maria first," she said. "On the floor while some of his men looked on. And then they took their turns. And then the jerk of the thumb."

Breathing had become a conscious effort. "How do you know?" he asked her at last.

"I watched," she said. "From the attic. His face will be forever burned on my memory. I searched for that face for three years. Thank God I could go among the French because I am French. But he had returned to Paris and only recently came back again. Duarte wanted me to tell him when I saw that face again. He wanted to be the one to kill him. But it was something I had to do myself. I always knew I had to do it myself or carry the nightmares with me to the grave."

He opened his mouth to suck in air.

"I had to make him follow me here," she said. "I thought it would be easy. I thought he would catch up to us early, and I thought I would have my musket and my knife. But when he did come, I had no weapon and you tied my hands. But he did come eventually, and justice has been done. A measure of justice. There were those other men too, but I do not care about them. Only him. For he was their leader and honor-bound to uphold decency. I am not sorry I killed him, Robert, even though I know that the horror of having killed someone will live with me for a long time. I am not sorry. He deserved to die—and at my hands."

"Yes," he said. "He deserved to die."

He heard her at his side trying to bring her own breathing under control. "You believe me?" she asked.

"Yes," he said, his voice dull. "I believe you."

"You will forgive me, then?" Her voice was still toneless.

"No." He tried to fight her story from his mind. "I might have helped you, Joana. But you were having too much fun making a fool of me. Men are only idiots to you, not people. I don't believe you could resist trying to enslave a man if you tried. I have no interest in being any woman's slave."

Her forehead pressed harder against his shoulder. "It was partly your fault," she said. "I told you the truth but you would not believe me. It has never been in my nature to beg and plead. If you would not believe me, then you would not. But I could not resist keeping you always guessing. I was teasing you, Robert, not trying to enslave you."

"Well," he said, "I cannot see much difference, I'm afraid, Joana. I'm sorry about your family. And I'm glad that you have avenged them at last, though how you did not lose your life in the attempt, I will never know. Don't you know that it is sheer suicide to stand up in the skirmish line?"

"No," she said. "I know nothing about skirmish lines except that you fight in one and this morning I thought I would die until I came over that hill and saw that you were still alive. But I will not keep you awake. If you will not forgive me, then so be it. I will not beg or grovel. Don't ask it of me, Robert. It is not in my nature to do so."

She turned her back on him and wriggled into a comfortable position—leaving him still rigid with tension and now furiously angry as well.

"Oh, no, you don't," he said, pushing one arm beneath her and rolling her to face him again. "You are not going to put me in the wrong like this, Joana, and then think you can turn away from me and sleep the night away in my tent. Why did you do it? Tell me that. To show your contempt for me and for all men?"

He heard her swallow in the darkness. "No," she said. "I think it was to set a barrier between us, Robert. If you thought me your enemy, or if you were not quite sure, then there would be a barrier there."

"Some barrier!" he said. "We have had each other

almost every night and several days too since leaving Salamanca. Heaven help me if you had wanted no barriers."

"There has always been a barrier," she said. "With everyone. I have never wanted it otherwise. I have never wanted anyone close. Except you. And when we became close physically it was wonderful and I was happy—and terrified. I was afraid of what would happen if there were no barriers between us at all. I was afraid of losing myself, of never being in control of my life again. So I think that was what I was doing—keeping you at arm's length so to speak."

"And all the others?" he said harshly. He wished he had not given in to anger and turned her to face him again. He wished he had not invited these words, which were weaving their lying web about him.

"The others?" she said. "You have always seen me as promiscuous, have you not, Robert? I sleep with every man I smile at? I was with Luis six times. I counted and I hated every encounter a little worse than the one before it. And I have been with you I don't know how many times. I have not counted. And it has been wonderful, every encounter a little more wonderful than the one before, if that is possible. That is the extent of my experience, Robert. And now I wish I had not begun this speech, for of course you will not believe me. You will scorn me and throw all my other imaginary lovers in my face. Go to sleep. You must be tired."

Her hair smelled dusty. Her skin smelled clean. She must have found somewhere to wash herself, as he had. He breathed in the warm scent of her.

"Joana," he said, willing himself not to believe, wanting more than anything else to believe her. "Why? If your experience was so limited, why me? Why did you give in to me so easily? *You* made love to *me* that first time, I seem to remember."

"Oh," she said, "you will make me say it again, will you, and totally humiliate myself? I am not used to humiliation. Very well, then. I suppose I owe it to you. It was because I loved you, Robert. Maybe I fell in love with you when I first saw you in Lisbon, looking shabby and morose in the midst of a glittering ball, and looking hostile and determined to resist my charms and my invitation. Or maybe at that time I was only intrigued. Perhaps I fell in love with you at Obidos when you frightened me by taking away my control and I bit your tongue. Did I hurt you badly? I'll wager I did. Or perhaps then I was only fascinated by a man who did not dance to my tune as other men did. Perhaps . . . Oh, I don't know. Whenever it was, I fell in love with you, and I wanted you and decided to have you when the opportunity presented itself. But I wanted a barrier between us nevertheless. Love terrifies me."

He said nothing for a few moments. "God damn you to hell, Joana," he said at last.

"For loving you?" She laughed rather sadly. "I never expected to love. Not once I was past the age of fifteen and knew that the world was not made up of knights in shining armor and damsels waiting to be carried off into the happily-ever-after on their chargers. It is ironic that I have done it with the one man who would rather see me in hell than in his tent. Or perhaps it is not ironic at all. I suppose I would never have fallen in love with you if you had not glowered at me in Lisbon. It was something quite new to my experience, to be glowered at."

"I did not glower," he said. "I was just damned uncomfortable."

"Were you?" she said. "You did not show it. You looked as if you held everyone, and me in particular, in the utmost contempt."

"You were beautiful and charming and expensive," he said. "And I wanted you and hated myself for wanting someone so far beyond my grasp. If I felt contempt, it was against myself. As it has been ever since. I have always despised myself for loving you."

"Robert." Her breath was warm against his neck and her arm twined itself about it and her body came full against his. "Say that another way. Oh, please. And if you think I am begging and groveling, then you are right. I am. Say it another way."

He licked dry lips and closed his eyes tightly and folded her in his arms as if he intended to break every bone in her body. "I love you," he said. "There. Are you satisfied now?"

"Yes." The single word against his neck.

He had not made love to her the night before. It was difficult to make love in a tent. It was small, easily toppled. Besides, there were people all about them, some also in tents, many more on the open ground. It felt almost like making love in public.

He lifted her dress carefully to her waist, eased himself free of his trousers, lifted himself on top of her, and put himself inside her. And she lay uncharacteristically still and quiet beneath him while he moved in her with slow care.

"I love you," she murmured against his ear while he wondered if anyone could hear them coupling.

And God help him, he thought, burying his face against her hair and feeling release coming despite the caution with which he moved in her, but he believed her. He had to believe her. It was there in her body as well as in her voice. She held him silently cradled in her arms and in her body, giving. He knew she was nowhere near climax herself and would not reach it. But she was giving nevertheless, and telling him with words what she gave with her body.

Joana was giving. Not taking, but giving. Giving herself. And he was not imagining it. He would swear to God that he was not imagining it.

"I love you," he told her against her mouth as he spilled himself into her. But he said worlds more than just the three words. And he knew as he relaxed down on her and her arms came about him and she kissed his cheek that she heard him, that she heard all the other words that could never be spoken.

There were no barriers. None at all.

28

IT was not morning. All was relatively quiet and still beyond the tent. And yet they must have slept for several hours. The night felt far advanced. But as often happened, they both woke together. She could tell that he was awake, that like her he had just awoken. She stretched against him, rather like a cat.

"I told you it gets more wonderful each time," she said. "Tonight was no exception."

"And I told you you could not stop lying if you tried," he said. "Do you think I was so intent on my own pleasure that I did not know it was no good for you?"

"Because the universe did not shatter into a million pieces about me?" she said. "How little you know about women, Robert, or about me anyway. Sometimes it is wonderful beyond words just to feel what you do to my body, just simply to relax and enjoy. And this last time it was especially good because you told me that you love me and your body proved that the words were true. Say them again." She reached up a hand to touch his mouth and sighed with contentment.

"They were a dream, Joana," he said. "An unrealistic dream, just as they were that other time when we were children."

She hated him suddenly. "But dreams can sometimes be more true than reality," she said. "Let's dream for a little while longer. I love you, and that will be true even when reality takes over from dreams again and tears us apart. It will, won't it?"

"Yes," he said. "But before it does—I do love you."

She snuggled against him and closed her eyes. But it was impossible to recapture her mood of lazy contentment. "I am going to stay with you as long as I can," she said, but there was a feeling of desperation in her already. "Will you be going all the way to Lisbon?"

"Probably not," he said. "I don't know what is planned, but I would imagine that these lines of defense, though formidable, will not keep back the French without a little human help. I am sure I will be manning those defenses with my men."

"Ah," she said. But her mission was at an end. All of it—what she had done for Arthur and what she had done for herself. That latter had occupied her mind for three years. And now it was over, and in its place was a void, a certain feeling of anticlimax and dissatisfaction. He had something still to do. She had nothing.

His hand was stroking lightly through her hair. He kissed the top of her head. "And you?" he said. "What will you be doing?"

"Oh, I will go to Lisbon," she said, "and dazzle all and sundry again. I shall return to my pure white. Don't you think that is a masterly touch, Robert? It becomes tedious sometimes, but I know it intrigues my admirers."

"So you will stay in Lisbon," he said. "That will be wise."

Oh, wise, yes, and dull, dull, dull. "I may not stay there," she said. "I think I will go to England. It has always been my dream to go there, to become English. You cannot know how tiresome it is, Robert, not quite to belong anywhere." But she had a sudden memory of a boy who had lived at his father's house but had not been invited to join or even to meet his father's guests. "Ah, yes, perhaps you can too. I want to be English. I want to live in England and marry an English gentleman. I want to have English children."

"Do you?" he said, kissing the top of her head again.

"Lord Wyman—Colonel Lord Wyman—has asked me more than once to marry him," she said. "He is sure to ask again when I return to Lisbon. I think I may accept his offer. I think I may."

"You love him?" he asked.

"Fool!" she said scornfully. "I love you, Robert. How can I love two men? He is rich and handsome and amiable and charming and a whole lot of other good things. He can offer me what I have always wanted."

He said nothing, but merely turned his head to rest his cheek against the top of her head.

"I could not follow the drum," she said. "There are too many uncertainties, too much moving from place to place, too many discomforts, too much danger and worry. I could not do it, Robert."

"No," he said. And very quietly, "I am not asking you to."

His words stung. She had not realized how much she was hoping that he would do just that, until he spoke. She was dreaming of impossibilities as she had not done since she was a girl.

"I am very, very wealthy," she said suddenly, though she knew how useless it was to try to fight against reality. "You would not believe how wealthy I am, Robert. I could buy property in England. We could live there together—"

"Joana," he said. "No. I have made a career for myself in the army and this is where I stay for as long as I am needed. This is my life. This is what I like doing."

She hated him for being so inflexibly the realist, for refusing to enter her world of make-believe for even a few moments. "It is more important to you than I am?" she said, but her hand shot up to cover his mouth again before he could reply. "What a stupid, stupid thing to say. Forget I said it. Of course this is where you belong. I would like you less if you could give in to the lure of wealth and comfort—and love. So of course we must part when we reach Torres Vedras. That is a fact of life. How long will it take? One week? Two? We will make them the most wonderful weeks of our lives, shall we, Robert?"

"Yes," he said.

"Retreating with an army," she said, "and sleeping and making love in a tent each night. It would not sound much like heaven to anyone who was not you or I, would it?"

"We will make it heaven," he said. "Why do you wear perfumes normally? You smell wonderful as you are."

She chuckled. "I believe there would be a significant empty space about me if I appeared in a Lisbon ballroom smelling like this," she said. "And I would hate that.

Can we make love again, Robert? Would we wake everyone?"

"If we have only two weeks left, or perhaps not so long," he said, "I think we had better perfect the art of making love without arousing the whole camp. Come on top of me."

"I promise not to scream," she said, bringing herself carefully astride him and hugging his hips with her knees and setting her hands on his shoulders as he mounted her and she felt the beginnings of pleasure even without full arousal.

And she began to memorize him—the feel of warm and slender hips against her inner thighs, the feel of strong hands spread on her hips, holding her steady for his upward thrusts, the feel of him in her, long and hard encased in her own wetness and softness, the feel of his muscled shoulders beneath her hands. She brought the upper part of her body down on him, feeling his shirt and chest muscles beneath her breasts. And she sought out his mouth, opening her own and fitting it to his, feeling the familiar inward push of his tongue.

She began to memorize him and knew that she was thereby destroying some of the pleasure. For loving was not something that could be calculated and hoarded. It was in the here and now, to be enjoyed here and now. It could not be stored up for future pleasure or for future pain.

She wanted to die, she thought suddenly, and the absurdity of the wish struck her. She wanted to die while she was still with him. She wanted to die now while his arms were about her and he was murmuring sweet nonsense into her mouth and while their bodies were still joined and they were about to relax, sated, into each other.

"Robert," she whispered, "I wish I could die. Now. I wish I could die now."

"We still have more than a week," he said. "Perhaps two. An eternity, Joana. Now is all we ever have, and perhaps the next week or two. One learns that fast as a soldier. A day, a week, is a whole precious lifetime."

"But I am not a soldier," she said. "Ah." She rested

her forehead against his shoulder and closed her eyes. "That feels wonderful. Oh, yes, Robert. Oh, yes."

He lifted her head and covered her mouth with his own so that she would not cry out. But she would not have done so. It was not ecstasy she was feeling as he pulled her down hard onto him and held her while she felt the hot gush of his release. It was just the quiet force of love and union, far more powerful than even the wildest physical passion.

She turned her head against his shoulder and knew that they would both sleep again for the short remainder of the night. But she was memorizing him again, and there was sadness mingled in with the drowsy relaxation and feeling of physical well-being.

"Robert," she said, "I will always love you. When you are eighty-two years old, know that there is an eighty-year-old woman somewhere who loves you. Isn't that a delightful thought to keep you going for the next fifty years or so?"

"You will probably still have a court of admirers," he said, "and will not be interested in knowing that there is also an eighty-two-year-old man who loves you."

She sighed. "I could sleep for a week," she said. "I am so tired."

"Sleep, then," he said. "But not for a whole week, please, Joana."

She found herself wondering, as they both drifted off to sleep again, why it was that time could not just be stopped. If one was enjoying a particular moment, why could one not make it last forever? Life was a stupid business, she thought. She could have done so much better if she had been God.

Marshal Massena learned his lesson quickly. He had underestimated the size and strength of the allied forces and had attacked them in a position that gave them all the advantages. He would not attack again. Instead he looked for another way past to the heart of Portugal. And he found it in the mountains of the Sierra de Caramula to the north, where a rough track led to the coastal plain a few miles north of Coimbra.

Lord Wellington knew of the track and had sent orders

for the Portuguese militia to defend it. But they were not quite equal to the task of holding back a whole army on the move. The French moved inexorably into Portugal.

And so the allied forces began the inevitable retreat to the grumblings and complainings of those who had thought their victory more decisive than it had been. The army felt defeat and despair as they marched south across the ridge of Bussaco and down onto the main road to Coimbra. They felt betrayed by a commander who was snatching defeat out of the jaws of victory.

The retreat began on the evening of September 28, the day following the battle. Most of the army moved out, leaving behind them a rear guard and many blazing fires so that the French who remained would not know that they had gone. They marched westward to Coimbra and south at last on the road to Lisbon.

Miraculously the autumn rains held off. Or perhaps it was not a good miracle either, for while the rains would undoubtedly have slowed them and made of their march a dreary business, it would have been worse for the French, who were following a rougher and more difficult route.

The riflemen formed part of the rear guard, sniping at the few French who followed at their heels, waiting always for the main body of the army to catch up to them. But the forced marches did not allow for such a disaster.

The inhabitants of Coimbra, who had largely ignored the orders to follow Wellington's scorched-earth policy, realized too late the danger in which they were being placed, and were soon fleeing along the road to the south ahead of the army, loaded down with those possessions they could salvage, while their remaining possessions had to be left behind to be looted, possibly to burn. It was essential that the French continue to feel the full effect of their penetration into a virtual desert.

The Light Division were among the last to leave the old university town, much of which was burning. And it was there that Joana met her half-brother again. He had come there deliberately, he said, to find her, to see that she was safe. Carlota was with the baby up in the hills, he explained, much against her inclination.

"But she saw the wisdom of not bringing the baby

here," he said with a grin. "And where Miguel is, there Carlota has to be too for at least the next few months, whether she likes it or not."

He hugged Joana and shook Captain Blake's hand before slapping him on the back.

"I heard about the fight," he said. "Lucky devils. What I would not have given to be there. You had to stay close, Joana? You could not be persuaded to go back to safety?"

"Go back to safety?" Captain Blake said scornfully. "Joana? She actually came into the thick of the fighting. The shells and bullets could not kill me, but the sight of her waving my rifle almost did." He set an arm about her shoulders.

Duarte smote his forehead with the heel of his hand. "My sister and my woman both," he said. "Two of a kind."

"Duarte," she said, "I had to go into that battle. I had to kill him."

"Him?" He looked at her, at first blankly and then with gradually widening eyes.

"I recognized him in Salamanca," she said. "It was Colonel Marcel Leroux, the one who said he would kill you, the one I begged to come after me. I had to kill him, Duarte, and I did—with Robert's rifle. I have never fired a rifle before, but I knew I would not miss. I could not miss. He was mine."

"Joana," he whispered, and all the carefree vitality had gone from his face. "Oh, my God, I might have lost you too. Why did you not tell me, madwoman? It was my job to do, not yours."

And he pulled her from Captain Blake's arm and hugged her to him.

"He is dead," she said, "and they can rest in peace. They can finally be at peace. I killed him, Duarte."

Captain Blake turned away tactfully and watched a sergeant nod to him to confirm that all buildings in that particular street had been checked and found empty of food and other supplies. Brother and sister wept in each other's arms behind his back.

"So you are on your way to Lisbon?" Duarte asked Joana when they finally drew apart.

"Yes." She smiled at him.

"I hope you will be safe there," he said. "I hope Viscount Wellington plans to make another stand somewhere between here and there. And you, Captain?"

"Not as far as Lisbon," Captain Blake said. "I will be a part of that stand you talk about."

"Ah." Duarte looked from the captain to his half-sister. "Joana has finally convinced you of the truth about herself, I gather? But fate and circumstances are about to take you in different directions. Well, that is the way of the world—or of this particular world in which we are living. I had better be taking myself off. I just wanted to see that Joana was safe."

He hugged her again and shook Captain Blake by the hand, looked once more from one to the other, and shrugged.

"I shall see you," he said. "Both of you. Together perhaps. Perhaps separately. I will not be happy until this bloody war is at an end and the French back in the country where they belong and our lives back to normal. I don't like what war is doing to our lives. But enough of that." He grinned. "On your way, or you will be having a grand French escort."

They continued on their way south with the Light Division.

The rains held off until October 7, the last full day of the march for the bulk of the army, and then they came down with full fury, lashing the long line of refugees and the longer line of weary, ragged soldiers into misery as they dragged themselves through mud that was knee-deep in places. And the French drew ever nearer, their cavalry sometimes within sight of the Light Division as they rode up into the hills to left and right of the road.

The men trudged on, expecting ignominious defeat.

And then the allied army reached Torres Vedras, and the lines were there in the mountains to greet them—one of the closest-kept secrets in military history and one that was not even then immediately obvious to the eye. Every pass through the mountain had been barred, every road made impassable to an enemy. Guns hidden behind earthworks or set up in old towers and castles and redoubts pointed down from every height. Trenches had been dug, streams dammed to form bogs, houses and forests leveled to allow no hiding place for an approaching foe, hillsides smoothed out into glacis or blasted into precipices—the story went on.

The defenses stretched from the sea in the west to the River Tagus in the east, three solid concentric lines of them. And the British navy was on guard both at sea and on the river.

It was only as the regiments were met on the road and directed to their new posts that they began to realize what had been awaiting them and what would be awaiting the enemy hot on their heels. It was only then that elation began to replace the deepest depression.

And it was only as the French came up, drenched and miserable from the rains, hungry from the lack of food, far from their own supply lines, cut off from retreat by the fierce Ordenanza in the mountains, totally barred from a forward advance, that Massena realized finally how he had been tricked, how his advisers had made the wrong guess and given him the wrong advice. It was only then that some men realized whose side in the conflict the Marquesa das Minas was really on.

All Massena could do was settle his men in for a long siege and hope that something before them would give way.

The Light Division arrived in Torres Vedras, drenched, muddy, and miserable—and not yet in a place where they could rest. They were to march south and east to a position at Arruda, not far from the River Tagus. They were to rest for only a few hours before resuming their march.

"Well," Joana said, smiling at Captain Blake, "it does not really matter, does it, Robert? I don't believe we can get any wetter or any muddier. What difference do a few more miles make?"

But he was in a deep depression. Although he had been the only one of his men to know about the Lines, to know that they were marching into safety, he had been quite unable to feel the elation he should have been feeling. He was wet and dirty and tired. Not that those conditions meant anything. He had long been accustomed to physical discomforts.

No, his mood had nothing to do with conditions. It had everything to do with arriving at last at Torres Vedras—a destination that the soldier in him had been longing for and the man in him had been dreading. Torres Vedras—it represented the end of heaven, the end of everything that he had come to live for.

He did not believe he would have the courage to say it until it was said. She was still smiling at him ruefully, but with her usual indomitable courage. "You will not be going any farther, Joana," he said quietly, taking her by the arm and leading her away from his company after nodding to Lieutenant Reid to take over for him for a while.

"What?" There was fear and understanding and denial in her glance. "I am coming with you to Arruda, Robert."

"No." He deliberately did not look at her, but at the street ahead of them, along which he was guiding her. "You have friends here. It is on the direct road to Lisbon. You must go, Joana. This is where our ways must part."

"No." She jerked her arm free of his and whirled to face him. "Not like this, Robert. I will come with you and spend a few more nights with you and see where it is you are going to be stationed for the winter. I want to be able to picture it in my mind. I will leave in my own time. Soon."

"The time is now," he said, taking her arm again and walking resolutely on with her.

"No. Stop this." She jerked at her arm again, but he kept his firm hold on it. She kicked at his shin so that he swore. "How can we say good-bye now, without any preparation, any privacy? Are you planning to say good-bye in the street?" She looked wildly about her, and he knew that she realized he was taking her to her friends' house.

"It will not be any easier at another time or in another place," he said. "It is better now, Joana. A clean break.

Go to your friends and forget about me. Go to Lisbon and marry your colonel."

"Imbecile. Barbarian. Bastard!" she hissed at him as he increased their pace along the street. She had to half-run to keep up with him. "Robert, don't do this. Oh, please don't do this. I am not ready." There was panic in her voice at last.

"Would you ever be?" he asked her. "If we had a night to spend together, knowing that the end would be tomorrow, would you be able to enjoy the night? Would you be ready to say good-bye tomorrow?"

"Not now," she said. "Not today. Oh, not today, Robert."

"Today and now," he said, and he could hear the harshness of his voice but could not soften it without giving in to his own panic. They had turned a corner and he could see the whitewashed wall that surrounded her friends' house at the end of the street. "It is better so, Joana."

"Let me go." Her voice was cold suddenly, and she had stopped struggling.

He released his hold on her arm and stopped walking when she stopped.

"Very well, then," she said, and her face was expressionless and her voice toneless. Her hair was plastered to her face and her dress to her body, but she lifted her chin and looked suddenly regal. "If I mean so little to you, Robert, you must not even trouble yourself by walking all the way with me. I shall be quite safe, thank you. I will say good-bye."

He had thought he had the length of the street left. He had thought that he would allow himself the indulgence of taking her once more into his arms at the door of her friends' house and of kissing her once more.

This was too sudden, too cruel.

"Good-bye, Joana," he said, and it was still the same harsh voice he heard.

She turned from him and walked away along the street without hurry and without a backward glance. He watched her until she disappeared into the courtyard beyond the white wall.

And then he continued to watch the empty street, some of the rain streaming down his face hot and salty.

It could not be over, he thought. Not so suddenly. Not without some definite and climactic ending. Not this way. It could not be over.

But it was.

29

JOANA did not leave Torres Vedras for Lisbon even when her friends, the owners of the house at which she stayed, did so for safety's sake. She stayed on in the house alone with the servants.

Not that being alone spelled loneliness. She was not lonely. She was the Marquesa das Minas again—Matilda had had the presence of mind to leave a trunkful of her clothes and other possessions at the house—and she was attending entertainments galore. Her court of admirers was as large as it had ever been, and she sparkled among them as brightly as she ever had.

And yet she was lonely for all that. For *he* had gone, and in all likelihood she would never see him again. Indeed, she hoped she would not, for there could be no future for them, and the pain of seeing him would be too great. And yet she pined for one glimpse of him, hoped against hope that he would be sent to Torres Vedras on some errand.

She had not forgiven him for their abrupt parting. She could understand why he had done it, could even admit that perhaps it had been a good idea. But she could not forgive him. For a relationship like theirs, since it had had to come to an end, needed a definite end, painful as it would have been. It would have been agony—he had pointed it out himself—spending a last night with him knowing that in the morning she was to leave, never to return. But it would have been a necessary agony. It was something she needed to remember. And yet it had never happened. The void was far more difficult to bear than the agony would have been.

But Joana would not mope, even for one moment. By the time she had reached her friends' house, dripping with rain and spattered with mud and indescribably tattered and shabby, she had already been cheerful and had greeted their shock with laughter.

She did not stop smiling and laughing for days afterward—in public. The terrible depression that touched on despair was given rein only in the privacy of her own rooms. But even there she would not allow tears. There were to be no telltale signs, like puffy or reddened eyes, that others might notice.

But oh, she missed him. God, she missed him.

And then Lord Wellington decided to host a grand dinner and ball and supper at Mafra in honor of Lord Beresford, who was being created a Knight of the Bath. Several officers of Joana's acquaintance from Torres Vedras were to attend, and several more were coming from Lisbon. It was altogether possible, she thought, that Colonel Lord Wyman would be one of them.

It would be good to see him again. It would be good to touch reality again and put dreams permanently behind her. And it was no unpleasant reality. She liked Duncan. Marriage to him, life with him, would be a good experience.

Joana accepted the invitation. And she smiled rather sadly at the thought of Robert, many miles away at Arruda. She thought of his aversion to glittering events such as the Mafra ball was likely to be. And she did not allow herself even a glimmering of hope.

At least, she did not do so with her mind. The heart cannot be ordered to do what the mind knows to be sensible.

"You're not going?" Lieutenant Reid looked at his superior officer with incredulity. "Isn't it more in the way of an order than an invitation, sir?"

"Not going?" Captain Rowlandson said. "You are the only damned officer in the whole regiment to be invited, Bob, except for the general himself, and you shrug casually and say you are not going?"

"I'll not be missed," Captain Blake said. "I don't think the Beau is going to personally notice my absence and be upset by it. I have been invited only because I was able to do him a little favor."

"That little favor being going to Salamanca and allowing yourself to be taken prisoner there so that you could lure the French into this trap with false information," Captain Rowlandson said. "Don't think the details have remained a secret, Bob. You're a bloody hero, man, but afraid to show your nose in public."

"Fear has nothing to do with it," Captain Blake said impatiently.

"Go," Captain Rowlandson said. "Give your men a break, Bob. You have been barking at them and overdrilling them ever since we got behind these damned Lines."

"That's not true." Captain Blake's head snapped up, but his friend merely nodded to him. He looked at Lieutenant Reid. "Is it, Peter?"

"The men don't mind," the lieutenant said, "because they know that you always look after them when there is danger. Besides, they all understand that you are missing the lady, if you don't mind my saying so, sir."

"I damned well do mind." Captain Blake was on his feet, his chair toppled behind him, his hands clenched into fists at his sides. "I'm a damned soldier, Lieutenant, not a bloody womanizer."

"Bob," Captain Rowlandson said firmly, "go to the ball. And come back and break our hearts with the details. Life is going to be dull if we are staying here for the winter. You would think at least Massena would try to make an attack, wouldn't you, for sheer pride's sake? But apart from that one rush on Sobral there has been nothing. Absolutely nothing. Go to the ball, man."

Captain Blake sighed. "Sorry, Peter," he said. "I don't know what has got into me lately. This damned rain, I think. All right, then, I'll brush my coat and wash a shirt and polish my boots and cut my hair and dazzle the elite with my splendor. And I'll even dance, goddamit. Are you satisfied now, the two of you?"

His two friends exchanged grins. "A happy devil when he is invited to a party, ain't he?" Captain Rowlandson said. "Can't contain his excitement."

Captain Blake swore and his friends laughed outright.

A ball and supper. It was all he needed. Such entertainments could send his spirits plummeting even when they were not in his boots to start with. He thought about the last two balls he had attended—one at Lisbon and one at Viseu. And he tried to shutter his mind.

No, he would not remember. And yet how could he not do so? Joana, glitteringly beautiful in pure white. Joana—the same woman who had trudged through the hills with him and endured all of the hardships of the journey without complaint and with unfailing good humor and high spirits. Joana—the woman who had been his lover. No, he would not remember.

He wondered if she was still in Lisbon or if Wyman had sent her off to England already. Were they betrothed? Had they even married hastily, perhaps before her departure? He would not think of it.

He would go to the ball at Mafra. Maybe it would be the best thing for him. And he would dance too. Doubtless there would be some Portuguese beauties there. He would dance and perhaps flirt. And he would find some woman in Mafra to sleep with. Perhaps some of his devils would be banished if he could just get his life back to normal again, to the way he had lived it for the eleven years of his service in the army.

He had told Joana that he would love her all his life, and he believed that he had spoken the simple truth. But he was not going to pine for her. He was not going to ruin his life—and make the life of the men under his command hell—for an impossible love. She was in his past, however agonizing that realization was. But in the meanwhile he had a present to live through, and perhaps something of a future too.

It was a wonderful, glittering occasion. Almost everyone who was anyone was at Lord Wellington's dinner and ball. All the officers wore their most splendid dress uniforms, making the Portuguese noblemen who were not in the army look quite drab in contrast. The ladies had all worn their brightest colors and their most sparkling jewels in order not to be outshone by the officers. Only Joana wore pure white.

She looked about her when she entered the ballroom after dinner to see what other guests had come, invited only for the ball and the supper. She was determinedly enjoying herself. It was difficult to believe that she was the same person as the one who had retreated through the hills of Portugal as Joana Ribeiro. She was quite irrevocably the Marquesa das Minas again.

"You will have to wait your turn, Jack," she said, tapping Major Hanbridge on the arm with her fan. "Duncan has claimed the first dance. And no, I will not promise the next. You know that I never promise dances in advance."

"And so, Joana," the major said with a sigh, "I must engage in a footrace when this set is done, and will doubtless be outstripped by some young lieutenant still wet behind the ears."

Joana smiled dazzlingly at him. And she noticed that the very shy Captain Levens was gazing at her worshipfully as if afraid to open his mouth in case she should laugh at whatever words should issue from it.

"Colin," she said, smiling sweetly at him, "would you be so good as to have some lemonade waiting for me at the end of this set? It is so warm in the ballroom already."

The young captain's eyes lit up as he made her a courtly bow.

"Come, Joana," Colonel Lord Wyman said, extending his arm for her hand, "the sets are forming."

She smiled at him. He had arrived in Mafra earlier that afternoon and had called upon her. He was going to offer for her again during the evening. She knew it as surely as she knew anything in her life. And she was going to accept him. Then her future would be assured and her present would be full and the past would be crowded out of her consciousness.

She was going to go to England and be an English lady. It was what she had always wanted.

"Arthur is not going to dance?" she said. Their host had come into the ballroom with a large following of senior officers, both British and Portuguese, and some important Portuguese civilians. They were all standing in a large group at one end of the room but showing no sign of joining the sets forming on the floor.

"Joana," Lord Wyman said, "when I asked you this afternoon, you were very secretive about what you have been doing since I last saw you in Lisbon. But I have been hearing strange things since visiting you. Are any of them true?"

She shrugged and smiled at him. "How would I know if I do not know what you have been hearing?" she said. "But I daresay most of them are not. One hears strange things in these times."

"Were you ever in danger?" he asked with a frown. "Lord Wellington or someone in authority should have insisted on having you escorted back to Lisbon as soon as the French began to invade. I should have come myself to fetch you. I blame myself for not doing so."

"That is the trouble with men," she said. "They always think to protect women and shield them from all the fun that is to be had."

"War is not fun, Joana," he said. "It is a life-and-death business. You should not even be as near to it as this."

She smiled at him. "But I have you to protect me, Duncan," she said. "I know that if a company of desperate Frenchmen were to break into this ballroom tonight, you would protect me with your own life. Is that not so?"

"Of course," he said. "But even so, it may not be enough, Joana."

"Then I should steal one of their guns or swords or daggers and defend myself," she said.

"Joana," he said, his eyes intense on hers, "you need protection. I cannot bear the thought of your being in any danger. I want you out of it. Permanently. I want you in England, in my own home, with my mother and my sisters. I want to know that you are safe there. You know what I am saying, do you not?"

The music was beginning. "How can I?" she said, moving into the steps of the dance. "You must put into words what you mean, Duncan, or perhaps I will misunderstand."

It was not the sort of dance for such a conversation, since the steps separated them frequently. But Joana was not annoyed. Quite the contrary. The declaration would surely come, and in the meantime she could savor the certainty that all she had dreamed of was about to come

about. And if seeing Duncan again had not brought quite
the surge of joy that she had hoped for, and if the prospect of living in England at his home with his family
brought no great uplifting of the spirits, then she would
have patience with herself. Life could not always be as
wildly exciting as it had been just a short while before.
She must have patience.

Lord Wellington was still with his cluster of dignitaries
and officers at one side of the ballroom, she saw, looking
about her as she danced, though they had turned to
watch the dancing. And in doing so they had revealed
the figure of the man with whom they had apparently
been talking.

A tall muscular officer dressed in a carefully brushed
though plain and somewhat shabby green uniform coat,
his face bronzed, his blond hair close-cropped—he had
had it cut again. The stiff and unsmiling figure of a man
who looked uncomfortable—perhaps at the whole setting
of the ball, perhaps only at the attention his presence
had attracted. He was standing where he usually stood
at public entertainments—in the most shadowed corner.
But he had not escaped notice. Far from it.

Joana lost a step in the dance and looked about her,
bewildered for the moment and unsure even what dance
she was performing. But she recovered herself instantly.
His eyes had found her. She knew it even though she
was no longer looking at him. He had seen her and she
would not give him the satisfaction of seeing that his
presence had discomposed her. Never.

Captain Blake had just been thinking that he had never
felt more uncomfortable in his life. All day he had been
regretting his decision to come to Mafra to attend the
ball. And when he had arrived, he had acted from instinct and taken himself off to the part of the room where
he was least likely to be noticed. He had scowled about
him at all the other splendidly clad guests, hoping by
such an expression to hide his discomfort.

But it had been worse than he expected. A thousand
times worse. For no sooner had Lord Wellington entered
the ballroom, than he, along with his large following of
the elite of the elite, sought him out to meet "the hero
of Salamanca."

Robert had bowed and answered questions and bowed and answered questions and felt his stomach tie itself into knots. He had longed for a battlefield and a sword in his hand and a rifle over his shoulder and the whole French army before him. He would have felt a great deal more comfortable.

Finally, blessedly, the music began, and his interrogators turned away to watch the dancing. He hoped that soon they would also wander away and he would be free to melt into oblivion for what remained of the evening. He had changed his mind about dancing. Besides, there were far more men than ladies present. There would be no one to dance with.

And then his eyes were drawn as by a magnet to one particular spot on the dance floor—to one splash of white amidst the myriad colors. And there she was. It was like a flash back in time. She looked as beautiful and as expensive and as remote as she had looked that first time in Lisbon. She was the Marquesa das Minas again, not Joana at all. And he found himself hating her again even as his stomach somersaulted with the shock of seeing her when he had imagined that she was in England already.

He hated her because she was the marquesa and he was merely Captain Robert Blake, a soldier who had raised himself through the ranks to become an officer, though he would never be able to make himself into a gentleman. For as long as he lived he would be a bastard, the son of a marquess but not of a marchioness. He hated her because he wanted her as he had wanted her in Lisbon and because she was as unattainable as she had been there. And he hated her for having returned from Lisbon instead of staying where he could never see her again.

He hated her because she smiled and looked happy and because her partner was Colonel Lord Wyman. And because she had seen him but her eyes had been sweeping away again even as his own caught them.

He clasped his hands tightly at his back and clenched his teeth and knew that he did not have the willpower merely to turn and leave the ballroom and the building. He knew that he would stay and watch her and torture himself.

And he knew that his misery had passed into a new

phase, that now he was gazing into the terror of despair. For she could not look so beautiful, so exquisite, and so happy, and love him. The idea was absurd. He had fallen prey to her charms after all and had forgotten that Joana lived to conquer male hearts. He had believed that she loved him—right up until a few moments before. But it could not be. How could she love him?

Despair became a tightening and a pain in his chest.

Duncan had asked her. He had taken her to stroll in the long hallway beyond the ballroom and he had made her a formal offer.

"It is what I have always longed for," she told him. "Marriage to an English gentleman and a home in England. England is where I grew up, you know."

He squeezed her hand as it lay on his arm. "The answer is yes, then?" he said. "You are going to make me the happiest of men, Joana?"

She looked up into his face and frowned. "Am I?" she said. "I would make myself happy if I married you, Duncan—at least I think I would. But would I make you happy? It is important in marriage, is it not—that we each make the other happy?"

"Joana," he said, "just your consent will make me ecstatic."

"Oh, no, Duncan," she said. "There is a great deal more to marriage than that. Years and years of being together with all the glamour and novelty gone. I don't know that I can make you happy." She drew a deep breath and said what she had not planned or expected to say. "There has been someone else, you know."

"Your husband," he said, patting her hand. "I understand, Joana."

"Luis?" She frowned. "I hated Luis. No, someone else, Duncan. Someone more recent."

He stiffened only a little. "You have many admirers, Joana," he said. "I can understand that sometimes flirtation leads to something a little more serious. But I shall not worry about it. You have a good heart."

"You mean you would not worry about it when we were married?" she asked. "You should, Duncan. I should certainly not tolerate even a little flirtation in you—toward another lady." She licked her lips. "I loved him."

"Did you?" She could tell that for some reason he did not want to discuss the matter.

"No," she said. "I used the wrong tense, Duncan. I love him. But I cannot marry him. I thought to marry you and live in the sort of contentment I have always wanted. But I find that I cannot marry you unless you know."

"You will marry me, then," he asked, "now that you have told me? The past will be the past, Joana. I am not interested in it."

She sighed. "I wish I were not," she said. "How long are you going to be here, Duncan?"

"A few days at the least," he said. "And when I return to Lisbon, I hope you will do me the honor of allowing me to escort you there."

"Ah," she said. "Give me those few days, then, Duncan. I shall give you my answer before we leave."

"I have waited so long," he said with a smile. "A few days longer will not kill me, I suppose."

"The answer may not be yes," she surprised herself by saying.

"But it may be," he said. "I shall live on hope."

She did not know why she had delayed, why she felt suddenly so reluctant to accept him. But of course she knew. How foolish to pretend that she did not. There was a dream she could not let go of.

"Let us walk about the ballroom," she said. "There are uniforms I have not yet admired and gowns I have not yet had a chance to envy. Take me on a promenade, Duncan." She smiled gaily at him and chattered brightly as he complied with her wish. They would be three-quarters the way around the room before they passed him, she thought. He still stood in the same place, though not in obscurity. Several people had gone there to talk with him.

She deliberately made their promenade a slow one. She stopped to talk with everyone she knew even remotely and to flirt a little with every officer who tried to attract her attention. She would give him every opportunity to move out of her way if he wished. Part of her hoped that he would leave before she had a chance to talk with him. Part of her felt panic at the very thought. But she would leave it to him. She would not maneuver him into anything that he really did not wish for.

"Ah, Robert," she said when they drew level with him. His very blue eyes looked directly back at her. He was not smiling—but then, she knew him well enough not to expect that he would. "You are not dancing?" It was a foolish question, since the dancing was between sets.

"No," he said after a slight pause.

"Do you remember Duncan?" she asked. "But yes, of course, he traveled with us out of Lisbon. Robert has become even more of a hero than he was, Duncan. Have you heard?"

"Rumors, yes," the colonel said. "About a daring visit to Salamanca and an even more daring escape. Congratulations, Captain."

"Thank you, sir," Captain Blake said.

"Ah," Joana said, turning and tapping her foot. "A waltz. Come, Robert, you may have the pleasure of dancing it with me." She laughed lightly. "You were about to ask, were you not? I want you to tell me about all those daring deeds."

She thought he was going to refuse, and wondered if she would laugh, blush with mortification, or beat him about the head. Fortunately, perhaps, he did not put her to the test.

"It would be my pleasure, ma'am," he said, bowing awkwardly and taking the hand she stretched out to him.

Ah, a dearly familiar hand, she thought, and wished that he had not come. Or that she had not come. She should have gone to Lisbon and stayed there. She felt an ache in the back of her throat as she smiled first at Duncan and then at him.

"You do dance, I remember," she said as he led her onto the dance floor. "Your mother taught you."

"Yes," he said, and one strong hand came about her to rest behind her waist and the other hand was held out for hers. She placed her own in it and set the other on his broad, muscled shoulder. And she breathed in the scent of some men's cologne. But she preferred the raw masculine smell of him, she thought.

Oh, Robert. The ache in her throat had become a lump.

"I have still not forgiven you, you know," she said as they began to move to the music, tipping her head back and smiling up at him. "I never will, Robert. You will go to your grave unforgiven."

"I should have taken you to Lisbon," he said without smiling, "and taken you on board the first ship bound for England, and tied you to the mainmast. I should have done that, Joana. I should have known how mad it was to leave you in Torres Vedras with your friends and expect you to act like any normal sensible woman. Did you even go to Lisbon?"

"No," she said. "I do not like to be told what to do, Robert. And I should have escaped from that mast, you know, even if I had had to pull it down and wreck the ship in the attempt. I would rather die trying to swim to land from the middle of the ocean than live under a man's well-meaning care."

"Yes," he said. "Oh, yes, I know that, Joana. It was foolish of me even to have thought of what I should have done, wasn't it?"

"Yes," she said, and she smiled slowly at him. He looked so much grimmer and more formidable than he had when they parted, though that had happened very recently. Perhaps it was the haircut. He had been looking almost like her gentle, poetic Robert again with it longer. Oh, not quite, perhaps, but almost. At least she had been able to see that they were one and the same person. Now he looked every inch the tough, seasoned soldier that he was—someone with such a different life from her own that they might as well inhabit different planets. "This is a foolish dance, is it not, Robert? Take me walking in the hallway outside and I shall explain to you why I cannot forgive you and you will persuade me to do so anyway."

"I think we should continue dancing, Joana," he said.

"You are a coward," she said. "You are afraid to be alone, or almost alone, with me again."

"Yes," he said. "Mortally afraid, Joana. It was why I

arranged that particular parting. Don't force me to say good-bye to you."

"I don't like stories without endings," she said. "In fact, they make me furious. Ours must have its ending, Robert. It must. Oh, do you not see why I could not leave Torres Vedras and why I had to put Duncan off earlier when he asked me yet again to marry him? There must be an ending for us."

"There must be pain?" he asked.

"Were you without pain before coming here tonight?" she asked. "Did it help, the way we parted?"

He danced on with her for several moments, looking into her eyes, his expression still grim. When they neared the door, he stopped and took her arm through his.

"Very well, then," he said. "Let us have an ending to this story, Joana. You must always have your way, it seems, even to the end. So be it, then."

She felt no triumph as she allowed him to lead her from the ballroom.

30

ALL he could feel was anger. He had thought it was all over. He had thought that the rawness of the pain would ease with time. And a little time had passed already. He had settled into his new quarters and into his new duties and he had waited patiently for the first, most painful phase of his loss to pass into the second—whatever that would be. All he knew was that it could not possibly be worse. It could only be slightly better, and so on and so on until he would be able to remember with nothing worse than sadness—until he would be able to get on with his life again.

He did not want this to be happening. He had not wanted to see her again. If he had known, or even suspected, that she might be at the ball, then he would have stayed away. He would not even have been tempted to go for one more glimpse of her. He had not wanted one more glimpse. He certainly did not want this—this talking with her and dancing with her and now being alone with her.

Yet he had to admit to himself that he had been selfish. He had not been able to bear the thought of a long, drawn-out good-bye and so had thought of a way of cutting it short. He had assumed that she too would be relieved once it was over. And yet it seemed that she needed a more definite end to their relationship.

And so he was angry partly at himself. He should have given her her ending when they were still together. He should have allowed her to go to Arruda with him and leave after a night of private good-byes. He should have put himself through that agony in order to satisfy her that their affair had reached its term. It would all have been over now, and he could hardly have suffered more than he had anyway.

But now it was all to go through again. And he was angry, partly with her, partly with himself.

"You look as grim as you looked on the morning of the Battle of Bussaco," she said, smiling up at him.

"Do I?" He looked straight ahead. "Strange. I feel grimmer."

"Oh, dear," she said, "this does not bode well. We had better get out of this hallway, Robert. It is too public."

"Is it?" he said. "The ballroom was too public, so we must move here. Now this is too public. What next, Joana? Do you have a cozy bedchamber handy? Is that the sort of good-bye you want?"

"Let us find a private room first," she said, "and then I shall tell you what kind of good-bye I want." She tried a door in the hallway, but it was locked.

The third door was not locked. It opened onto a darkened room that looked like a workroom. There was a large desk in the middle of it, and several upright chairs. He picked up a branch of candles from a table outside the door and set it on the mantelpiece while Joana closed the door. He turned to face her.

"Well?" he said.

She leaned back against the door and smiled. "It could not be like that, Robert," she said. "There was so much I needed to tell you, so much I wanted to hear. I needed your arms about me so that I would have the courage to leave."

And I wanted it over with, he wanted to tell her. *I could not bear to prolong the agony.* But he did not say the words aloud. Really both of them would have been meaning the same thing. They just had different ways of coping with pain. And yet, though he understood and even sympathized, he could not get rid of his anger.

"Say it, then," he said curtly. "And I shall tell you that I love you and that leaving you hurts like hell. And then I shall hug you and kiss you and it can be over with at last. Come on, Joana, speak your piece and then come here."

She continued to lean back against the door as she

looked at him. "I have been selfish, haven't I?" she said. "You do not want this at all. But I gave you time in the ballroom, Robert. I took forever promenading about the room with Duncan. I wanted you to have plenty of time to escape if you wished. But you stayed. You must have seen me coming."

He watched her silently. And it was true. He could have left. He had wanted to leave, had been on the verge of doing so. But his legs had not been willing to obey his will.

"Yes," he said, "I saw you coming."

"And stayed," she said.

"Yes."

"Robert," she said, and she paused for so long that he thought she had changed her mind about continuing. "I am a widow and you are unmarried."

"No, Joana," he said.

She smiled.

"I always knew there were certain things beyond my grasp," he said. "At least I knew soon after my mother's death. There are certain things, certain people, a certain way of life that the bastard son of a marquess cannot aspire to. And I accepted that. I have built my adult life around the knowledge. And I have been happy."

"But you are not happy now," she said.

"Because for a while I forgot," he said, "or at least ignored the knowledge. And you, Joana. There is a certain life that you have been born to and raised to, a certain life that you married into and have lived since being widowed."

"Except when I escape into the hills as Duarte's sister," she said.

"But those days are over," he said. "You have no further reason to be Joana Ribeiro."

She smiled at him again. "Except perhaps for a little fun," she said.

"There is no bridge long enough to connect our lives, Joana," he said. "Not permanently. Neither of us would be happy in the other's world once the first gloss had worn off our passion for each other."

She was looking at the floor in front of her, apparently deep in thought.

"Am I not right?" he asked after a lengthy silence.

She looked up at him and there was an imp of a smile lurking at the back of her serious expression. "You must be," she said. "You are a man. Men are always right."

"Well, then," he said.

"Well, then." She took a few steps toward him and stopped again. "I suppose there is nothing left, Robert, except that hug and kiss. It is rather a shame that this is not a bedchamber, isn't it? But I don't think I would fancy making love on the top of that desk, and there has always seemed something a little sordid about making love on the floor, though why that should be, I don't know, when we have made love many times on the ground outdoors. We have had some good times."

"Yes." He had expected her to be in tears. But when she came toward him and set her hands flat against his chest and raised her face for his kiss, it was glowing. She had the look in her eyes that experience had taught him to be wary of, the look that spelled trouble—for him. But it was merely her way of protecting herself from an emotional scene.

"This is good-bye, then," she said.

"Yes." He framed her face with his hands and moved his thumbs gently over her cheeks and lips. His anger had evaporated, leaving in its place a tightness in his chest, an ache in his throat and up behind his nose. "This is good-bye. I love you." And her face blurred before his vision.

"Oh, Robert." She threw her arms up about his neck and drew his cheek down to rest against hers. "You idiot and imbecile and fool. Men are such foolish creatures. Don't cry. I am not worth tears, am I? I have been nothing but trouble to you. You will live a far more peaceful existence without me."

"Yes," he said.

"Well, then." Her fingers were ruffling his short hair. "You will be well rid of me."

"Yes."

"You don't have to agree with everything I say, you know," she said. "Kiss me, Robert. Let us do this thing right."

"Yes." He did not realize how much he was trembling

until he tried to find her mouth with his. His eyes were tightly closed, the hot tears finding their way past the lids anyway.

She held his head and kissed him and he groaned and wrapped her in his arms and folded her against him, tried to fold her into himself. It was a desperate kiss, one that brought no joy at all.

"Christ!" he said long moments later. "Let this be enough. Leave, Joana, or let me leave." He swallowed convulsively. "Just tell me once more."

"That I love you?" she said. "I love you, and will until I am eighty and you are eighty-two. No, amend that. I plan to live a long time and you seem to have a gift for dodging bullets. Make it ninety and ninety-two. A hundred and a hundred and two."

"Go!" he said harshly. "Goddammit, woman, get out of here. I can't leave looking like this. Get out of here."

She touched his face with soft fingertips. "Men are so foolish," she said. "And I love this most foolish man of all more than I can find words to express. I love you, Robert."

And she was gone.

He had always found the notion of a broken heart rather amusing. But he was not amused as he crossed the distance to the desk and leaned both hands on it, bending forward with closed eyes. Not the slightest bit amused.

There were several things to be done, an irksome fact for someone who liked to act on impulse. But this was not an impulsive move, though the realization and its consequences had come upon her like a flash of lightning. And because it was not impulsive, then everything had to be done just so.

There were letters to write, several of them, in particular one to Matilda with an amount of money enclosed equivalent to two years' salary. And there were clothes to obtain. Her Portuguese marquesa's garments were totally unsuitable, but she was not displeased, she thought, looking at them—a row of unrelieved white—in the wardrobe, to have to abandon them forever. And Joana Ribeiro's dress would no longer do. It was past looking even shabby.

Indeed the housekeeper had looked dubious when offered it to use for cleaning rags. Besides, there was only one of it. A woman needed more than one dress.

The problem was not a particularly difficult one to solve. The friend at whose house she was living was only slightly larger than she was, and Sophia always wore pretty, serviceable clothes. Joana chose a number of them and began to take in seams and shorten hems. She had not been handy with a needle for a number of years, and soon enlisted the aid of a skilled servant. In the meanwhile, she wrote to Sophia and enclosed what seemed generous payment for the clothes.

And there was Duncan to talk with. She summoned him the day after the ball and told him of her decision almost before he had got himself quite through the door. She did not wish to raise any false hopes in him.

"I am sorry, Duncan," she told him. "I cannot marry you. I would not be able to make you happy because I would not be happy with the sort of life I would be living."

"But, Joana," he said, "I thought you said that you had always dreamed of an English husband and a home in England."

"Yes," she said, "I did, and I have had those dreams— for as long as I can remember. Sometimes we can be very blind, can't we? I would not be happy with such a life, or at least not with just that."

And it was true. Of course it was true. She had known it in a flash at the ball when Robert had uttered his foolish words. Except that to him they were not foolish and to her they would not have seemed so if there had not been that flash of insight.

Neither of us would be happy in the other's world once the first gloss had worn off our passion for each other.

She could hear the words as clearly as when he had been speaking them. Words that at first she had taken for granted were true. Certainly he would never be happy in her world. He was uncomfortable to the point of misery when he merely had to attend some social function. And she would never be happy in his. She was the daughter of a French count and the widow of a Portuguese marquess. She had always lived a life of wealth and privilege. She was a lady.

And then had come the flash of insight. Was she happy? Had she ever been happy? She found her normal day-to-day life tedious in the extreme, and useless and meaningless. There was nothing to add challenge and excitement to her life beyond flirting. And she did not really enjoy that. Life on a quiet English country estate? With Duncan's mother and sisters until he came home? She would go insane!

Had she never been happy, then? Oh, yes, she had. She had known happiness. It had come whenever she had put off the Marquesa das Minas and lived with Duarte and his band of Ordenanza for a while. And it had come and lasted during those weeks with Robert between Salamanca and Bussaco. Incredible, total happiness—not only because she had been with him but also because she had been free of the trappings of her own world, free to meet the dangers and the challenges and the wonders of life in another world.

And was she to give up that life in order to live the one she had been born into? Was she to give up Robert for Duncan? The idea was absurd. Totally mad.

She had realized it as soon as he had spoken. And she had almost told him her thoughts right there. She was almost always impulsive. It was not in her way to think first before acting. But she had done it on that occasion nonetheless. It was too big a decision in her life to be made impulsively. What if she had found afterward, on more careful consideration, that it was just her reluctance to say good-bye to him that had prompted her thoughts? She had known that she had to give herself time to know beyond any doubt that only one kind of life could bring her happiness.

And now she really was about to do it. She had not been mistaken. The man she loved lived in the only world that could challenge her and ultimately make her happy. There was only one sensible thing to do.

So for once in her life, Joana thought with a smile, she was going to do the sensible thing.

He had been billeted in a small house in Arruda, one that he had shared with Captain Davies for a short while until that gentleman had had to leave for Lisbon to have a festering wound sustained at Bussaco attended to. Now he was there alone—very much alone since the house had been abandoned by its tenants, who did not quite believe that the French army would be held back.

But it did not bother him to be alone. In fact he welcomed the opportunity of a place to which he could retire and be away from everyone. It was a luxury not often attained in the army. And he needed to be alone for certain stretches of time, until he had learned to cope with his emotions and not take out his own unhappiness on men who were at the mercy of his moods.

One of the women from the train of the army, the widow of a private soldier killed earlier in the year who had not yet remarried, came in the evenings to cook for him. She had indicated a few times, without the medium of words, that she would be willing to stay to offer other services too, but he had always sent her away as soon as he sat down to his meal. She was a good cook but he did not need her in any other capacity.

He was tired. Sometimes drilling his men and watching them as they did their part to keep careful guard over the Lines was as taxing on the time and energy as moving into battle was. It had been a long day, and there had seemed to be no time at all for relaxation. It was good to be home. And yet his nose wrinkled in some distaste as he lowered his head to pass through the low doorway into the house. Mrs. Reilly had burned his dinner?

He walked through the small living room to stand in the archway that led through to the kitchen. And he came to a stop there, feet apart, hands clenched into fists at his sides.

"What the hell are you doing here?" he asked quietly.

"Burning your food," she said, throwing him a glance over her shoulder to reveal a flushed, bright face. Her hair was tied back loosely at the neck. She was wearing a neat and serviceable green dress. "I put only one more stick of wood on the stove, but now it is burning like a furnace in hell. And what sort of a welcome home was that?"

He strode across to the stove, lifted the pot with its offensive mess of burned stew, and set it down away from the heat. He took her by the upper arm and swung her to face him.

"What the hell are you doing here, Joana?" he asked again. He was feeling furious enough to commit murder.

"Apart from burning your dinner?" she asked, raising her hands to play with one button on his coat. "I came here to marry you, Robert."

"I don't remember asking you," he said roughly. "I shall find someone to escort you to Lisbon. And then you will stay the hell out of my life."

"How lovely," she said, smiling. "I love you too, Robert. That is why I have come to marry you. Though if you do not wish to marry me, it does not matter. I shall just live in sin with you as I did before."

"Joana," he said, "we have talked about this before. You know it is madness."

"And you know that I am mad," she said. "If you will not allow me either to marry you or to live in sin with you, then I shall attach myself to the camp followers and become a cook or a laundrywoman. And when you find out how poorly I cook—have you already guessed it?—and how poorly I wash clothes, you will put me in your bed, where I can do less harm." She smiled up at him from beneath her lashes.

"When did you get this mad idea?" he asked. Despite himself he could feel his fury ebbing away and a desperate longing taking its place. And a certain suspicion that he was wasting his time arguing with her.

"At Lord Wellington's ball," she said. "You said that neither of us could be happy in the other's world, and of course it was the sensible thing to say and ought to be true. But it was not true, for all that, and I realized it there. But I wanted to be quite sure. I did not want to rationalize merely because I did not want to part from you. I have never been happy in the world I am supposed to be happy in, Robert. You cannot know how tedious my life has been, how empty and meaningless. How stupid. And what a dreadful waste of my life it would be to spend the rest of it in that world."

"And yet you have everything you could possibly want," he said.

"Oh, no," she said. "Only material things and a stupid

title, Robert. Of what value are they? I want freedom
and challenge and excitement—and even a little danger
now and then. Those things I can never find in my own
world, where I might as well be wrapped tightly and
safely in cotton wool. Sometimes I think I should have
been a man, but not always, for I like being a woman.
I would hate to be a man and not be able to love you
without creating the most dreadful scandal. But there
must be something to make life meaningful for women
too, otherwise life is even more unfair than I have always
thought it. I can find meaning with you in the world I
have lived in with you."

"Joana," he said. "You have no idea . . ."

"Don't I?" She leaned forward until her breasts
touched his coat, and looked up into his face. "Don't I,
Robert? I think I do. I have never been more happy than
I was after we left Salamanca—until we reached Torres
Vedras. I was so very happy being with you, not just
because we were lovers, but because . . . oh, because at
last life was alive."

"And lived on the verge of death," he said. "Either
one of us could have died at any time, Joana. Did you
not realize what danger we were in? And how could I
let you stay with me now and share my life? I am a
soldier. A soldier's business is to fight—with real weapons. I could be killed at any moment."

"And I," she said. "The ceiling might fall upon my
head." She looked up, and his eyes followed hers despite
himself. "Death will come, Robert, whether in the next
moment or sixty years from now. In the meantime, there
is life to be lived—and love to be loved."

He closed his eyes and lowered his head until his forehead touched hers. "Joana," he said, "this is madness.
There must be arguments I can use. There must be thousands of them. I have nothing to offer you."

"Stupid words," she said. "Oh, imbecile. You have
love to offer and yourself to offer. You once told me
that you would give the woman you loved a cluster of
stars and the sunrise. Give me those stars, then, and give
me that sunrise and I will be more happy than I have
words to express. Give me the sunrises, Robert, all of
them, every day of our lives, until there is only a sunset

left. And then we will remember that we did not waste a single moment of the single life that we each have—or of the two lives we shared."

"Joana," he said, and there was longing in his voice, and agony.

"I know you are trying to find the words to send me away," she said. "But you cannot do that, Robert. You do not have the authority. I have made my decision, and I have told you what it is. There is only your own decision to make. In what capacity do you want me? That is all you have to decide. I am not going away."

He inhaled deeply and drew her into his arms. He held her head against his chest and turned his cheek to rest against it. "Very well, then," he said, and he drew a deep breath before continuing. "We'll marry. I'll sell out. I am not as penniless as you may think me, you know. My father died recently and he left me property and a considerable fortune. You can live the life of an English lady, even though I will never be quite an English gentleman. You can have your dream and me both, Joana, if you are sure that is what you want."

She jerked back her head and glared up at him. "Dolt!" she said. "Fool! I will not accept you on such terms. How stupid you are. I want you as you are, as I fell in love with you. Do you think I would be happy if you gave up everything that makes you who you are and everything that gives your life meaning and happiness?"

"*You* make me happy," he said.

"Oh, yes," she said scornfully. "And being with me can make up for everything that you would give up? How foolish you are, Robert. For we are very different in that one way, you know. You would have to give up a great deal, while I give up nothing except that ridiculous title and all those tedious white gowns and all the other things that mean nothing to me." She smiled brightly at him suddenly. "But how I love you for being willing to do such a foolish thing. Is there a preacher to marry us, then, or is it to be a life of sin?"

"God," he said, "I love you. How you tempt me, Joana."

"My mother should have named me Eve," she said. "*Is* there a preacher?"

"Yes," he said.

"Can we afford a servant?" she asked him. "I am afraid I will starve you if we can't, Robert."

"Wives of officers are not expected to do for themselves," he said. "Of course we will afford a servant."

"Oh, good," she said, smiling. "It is all settled, then?"

He gazed at her for a long moment. "Am I being given a choice?" he asked.

"Only if you can tell me that you really do not want me and really do not love me," she said. "But you cannot do either, can you?"

"No," he said.

"Then you have no choice," she said. "Are you going to take me to bed? Since I have no dinner to offer you, I had better offer myself instead. Is it a good-enough meal to compensate you for a lost dinner?"

"Hush, Joana." He lowered his head to hers and kissed her lingeringly. "My mind is befuddled. There must still be nine hundred and ninety-nine arguments, but I cannot think of a single one of them. I suppose you are manipulating me as you have always done?"

"Yes." She smiled up at him. "But you are without a doubt the most difficult man to manipulate I have ever known, Robert. Take me to bed and let me love you witless. Otherwise, you are going to think of some of those stupid arguments, and I shall have to think of new wiles to convince you. I don't want to use wiles. I want to love you."

He sighed, then looked down into her eager face and somewhat anxious dark eyes and smiled slowly. "I suppose we will always fight, won't we?" he said. "Every day of our lives? Because I will always insist on being the man, Joana. I give you fair warning."

She lowered her lashes and peeped up at him from beneath them. "Good," she said, "because I will always insist on being the woman. I give you fair warning."

"This, for example," he said. "This is my job, not yours. Joana, will you do me the honor of marrying me?"

She gazed up into his eyes and her own grew luminous as she circled his neck with her arms. She bit her lower lip and surprised both him and herself when her eyes filled with sudden tears.

"Yes," she whispered. "Oh, yes, please, Robert."

He cupped her face in his hands and brushed two tears away with his thumbs. "Tomorrow," he said, "I will find someone to marry us. Tomorrow. In the meantime, there is no dinner, is there?"

She shook her head.

"*What* did you offer as an alternative?" he asked, lowering his head to touch his lips lightly to hers.

She laughed, her laughter all mixed up with a sob. "I'll make you forget that you are hungry," she said. "I will, Robert. All night long. I promise."

"And you," he said, touching his forehead to hers again. "Are you hungry?"

"Ravenous," she said. "You are going to have to feed me, Robert."

"All night long?" he asked.

"All night long."

"And then at the end of it," he said, "I have something to give you."

"What?" she asked as he stooped down to lift her into his arms.

"The sunrise," he said. "And everything that is beyond it."

"Oh." She hid her face against his neck as he carried her through to his—their—bedchamber. "Robert, I do love you so. I do. I wish there were words to say it. Oh, I wish there were."

He set her down on the bed and leaned over her, smiling fully and warmly down at her. "But then," he said, "who needs words?"

She smiled back and reached up her arms for him.

Historical Note

I have tried to keep as closely as possible to history in my description of the events leading up to and including the French advance into Portugal in the summer of 1810—the fall of Ciudad Rodrigo and Almeida, the Battle of Bussaco, and the allied retreat behind the Lines of Torres Vedras.

The existence of the Lines really was one of the best-kept secrets in military history. Very few even of Wellington's senior officers knew of their existence before the army arrived at Torres Vedras and found itself suddenly and unexpectedly safe from French pursuit. There is no historical evidence that the French had any idea at all of the existence of the Lines. That is my invention.

I have taken two other deliberate liberties with history, neither very serious, I hope. First, the Convent of Bussaco was in reality lived in by monks, not by nuns, as in my story. Second, the French paused for several days before the Battle of Bussaco at Mortagoa, not at Viseu. It was more convenient for my plot to make the change.

Any other errors of historical fact are unintentional.